SOMETIMES YOU LOSE

ALSO BY DALLAS GORHAM

The Carlos McCrary PI Mystery Thriller Series

Six Murders Too Many

Double Fake, Double Murder

Quarterback Trap

Dangerous Friends

Day of the Tiger

McCrary's Justice

Yesterday's Trouble

Four Years Gone

Debt of Honor

Sometimes You Lose

SOMETIMES YOU LOSE

CARLOS MCCRARY, PI
BOOK 10

DALLAS GORHAM

Released: July 2024
ISBN: 9781644572306

ePublishing Works!
644 Shrewsbury Commons Ave
Ste 249
Shrewsbury PA 17361
United States of America

www.epublishingworks.com
Phone: 866-846-5123

ACKNOWLEDGMENTS

My thanks to my editor Marsha Butler. Ms. Butler has edited all my fiction works. I keep hiring her because she makes me a better writer. Her email is swmpwriter@gmail.com.

My thanks also to Royce D. Wilson, former Assistant Professor of Criminal Justice at the University of North Georgia for his helpful comments on my manuscript. Professor Wilson (now retired) is a former Director of Forensic Services with the Hillsborough County Sheriff's Office in Tampa, Florida, and a former Crime Scene Investigator with the Tampa Police Department. He was also a licensed private investigator in Florida. Professor Wilson spent more than 35 years in law enforcement forensics. He is an expert in forensics, fingerprints, and crime scene investigations. Any mistakes in the story are solely my responsibility.

Sometimes you get and sometimes you get got.

Anonymous

PROLOGUE

The yellow light winked ominously. *Dammit.* She felt like she'd been driving for hours but it could only have been twenty-five minutes or so. The yellow *low fuel* light on her Mazda dashboard had begun to flash just as she'd punched the throttle bolting from her apartment parking lot.

A light-colored commercial van with green letters on the side had charged into her apartment lot and she had swerved and jumped the curb to avoid hitting it. Did that jolt cause the warning light to activate?

The van's driver leaned on the horn as she swerved around it and stomped the accelerator into the street. She was moving too fast to turn around and see where the van went. Did it turn around in the parking lot? Was it following her?

Her eyes darted back and forth from the road in front to the rearview mirrors. What if Tommy Valley or some other cartel thug was following her? What would they do to her if they caught her? Surely, they wouldn't kill her, would they?

Crap, crap, crap. She had been watching the gas gauge for the last three days, telling herself to buy gas. *Just fill the tank and be done with it, Angie.* She'd pretended she was too busy with some fascinating distraction in her giddy life. The truth was that money was so tight that she invented excuses to procrastinate.

Now the flashing yellow light meant her car needed fuel urgently; she could postpone the inevitable no longer.

Everyone knows there are still a few gallons of fuel left in the tank when those low fuel lights go on. Right? I must be okay for another thirty or forty miles, right?

The damned light was practically shouting at her now. Or was that her imagination? Her heart pounded in her chest. She squeezed the steering wheel tighter as if she could wring more mileage from the Mazda. *Why, why, why didn't I listen to my own advice yesterday?*

The last thing she needed was to run out of gas in the middle of the night on the side of a Texas highway miles from help. The battery in one of her cellphones had been dead all day and, in her haste to get out of town, she'd left the charger for her other phone in her bedroom. She beat on the steering wheel in frustration. *Great planning, Angelina Christina McCrary Garza.* Angie often called herself by her full name when her conscience reprimanded her for her many faults and failings.

A ruthless, fiery-tempered Mexican drug czar from the *Tres Equis* cartel was after her and she wasn't even sure why. Sure, she had shot a video on her phone of the partygoers the other night and the drug lord was one of them, but so what? She didn't know he was a big shot with the cartel, and she sure as hell didn't know her boyfriend Tommy worked for him. Apparently, *El Jefe* had learned about the video, freaked out, and sent Tommy to retrieve it.

In public Tommy was a charming, witty rock musician who played lead guitar for a Mexican American rock band trying to get noticed in the Houston area. Houston's metro area had over seven million people. Sometimes it seemed to Angelina that a million of them belonged to rock bands trying to get noticed. So far Tommy was just treading water in the music business, barely keeping himself from drowning.

She told herself that if Tommy's musical career ever took off, he wouldn't sell drugs to make ends meet. Then maybe they could have a more normal relationship.

Tommy the Rocker loved a good time as much as Angelina did. And he could be sexy too. So sexy that she sometimes did things with Tommy that made her blush when she woke up sober the next day and remembered them. Then a few days later, he would flash that smile that sent shivers up her spine. He would offer her a line or two of cocaine or a couple of pills from his personal stash, and they'd be off to the races again.

But sometimes Tommy raised a curtain and revealed the dodgy drug dealer hidden beneath his cool rocker surface. That part of Tommy sold an array of dangerous drugs to a collection of affluent yuppies who used them to spice up their weekends with a new sensation.

The drug dealer side of Tommy frightened the hell out of Angelina. Thank goodness Tommy was an easy-going rocker ninety percent of the time.

But after last night's party, Mr. Bad Guy had taken over. Or was the party the night before last? Was today still Saturday? Or was it Sunday now? Was it after midnight? *Hell, Angelina Christina McCrary Garza, it doesn't matter anyway; you're in the deepest do-do of your whole life.* Tommy had morphed into a monster again and exposed the *Tres Eques* cartel thug that he really was. He jumped when *El Jefe* pulled his strings.

The party had begun innocently enough. Angelina amused herself by shooting video of friends and strangers having fun. Some wilder than others, but nothing unusual. She loved to take party videos; did it at all the parties she went to. Depending on who was there and how raucous they got, she would post them online. She had to edit out the raunchiest events—mainly sexual antics—to get the video past the website's censors, but the clicks she received from viewers earned her a few badly-needed dollars from the website's advertisers.

This party had been different. She had played the video for Tommy's roommate, Lola, the next day and Lola even made a copy to give Tommy because they thought it was such fun.

Tommy had watched the party video and called Angie late that night to tell her that a higher-up in the *Tres Eques* cartel had been at the party and she had recorded him as he discussed business with some other cartel members in a corner of the backyard around the fire pit. Tommy's face on her iPhone screen was clenched like a fist, his countenance red and his eyes bloodshot. He'd obviously been on a bender—drugs or alcohol or both, she couldn't tell.

Angelina's throat had tightened when she saw him on her screen.

11

He had almost shouted at her. "Saco is deep-shit pissed about that video."

"Geez, Tommy, relax, I don't even know who Saco is. Why would he be on my party video?"

"Don't play dumb with me, Angie. It doesn't matter if you know him or not. You always video anything that breathes at these parties and then you plaster them all over the internet."

"I didn't video him on purpose."

Tommy had waved his hand, dismissing her lame excuse. "Answer me, bitch! Did you post it yet?"

"No. I haven't had time to edit it," she lied.

"Well, don't. Saco is *never* photographed and *never, ever* videoed, for God's sake." Tommy's voice got louder, his anger apparent. But what else had she heard in it? Fear? For himself? For her?

"Saco don't know about your side hustle of posting party videos on the internet. If he learns about that—and if his face shows up on the internet, you're dead, Angie. Dead! He wants that video back. And you better hope to God he never finds out about your side hustle."

Angelina had struggled to catch her breath. She hadn't known that one of the party people was the head of a Mexican drug cartel. How many clicks could she get with that? If it went viral, she could earn thousands of dollars, even tens of thousands. Some social media influencers earned six-figure incomes from images and videos they posted on the internet. Angelina kept hoping that one of her party videos would finally catch fire and end her money troubles.

But was a potentially viral video worth risking her life?

"If I give you the SIM card, you can give it to Saco," she'd offered. "Will that satisfy him?"

Tommy shrugged. "*Quién sabe?*" Who knows? "Most people who know Saco say he's half-crazy. That's when he's not high. When he's high, he gets vicious. Just bring me your phone and I'll take it from there." Tommy had flashed her a fake smile. "It's not like you have a choice, Angie."

"Okay, Tommy, okay. I'll bring it to you. Where are you?"

"On second thought, I'll come get it. I'm tied up with something just now. I'll be home in an hour or two. You park your ass in your apartment and don't leave. And don't you dare post that video."

"DUH! What do you think I am, stupid?"

"No, you just do stupid things sometimes."

After she disconnected, Angelina scurried around her apartment in a daze wondering what to do. She had told Tommy the truth—well, mostly. She didn't know who Saco was. Surely, Saco couldn't blame her for that. And it was true that she hadn't posted the video online...yet. But she had just finished editing it for the website censors.

What if I do post it? My God, there's no telling what this thing might be worth. A Mexican drug lord? This could be the party video post that goes viral—the ticket out of this dump and my seedy way of life.

Then her inner Angie took over. *Angelina Christina McCrary Garza, are you that stupid? Girl, Tommy says that Saco's half-crazy at best. And he's a kingpin in a Mexican drug cartel, for God's sake.* He would kill her for sure. Maybe she should just give the video chip to Tommy and let that be the end of it.

She answered herself out loud. "But I don't want to give it to him; I want to post it," she whined out loud.

Angie sat down at the dining table and turned on her laptop. Tommy was right; she wasn't stupid, but she often did stupid things. What was one more? This one could change her life. If it changed for the better, she might have enough money to live a life of self-respect, where she didn't scrounge for any job she could get to survive.

She sat at the table, envisioning what her new life would be like. The car she would drive—no, *cars* plural, where she would live, the clothes she would buy, what kind of different men she might attract now that her husband Teo had skipped town.

Who was she kidding? Only a self-destructive fool would post that video. She logged out of the website and shut down her laptop, feeling like she had just dodged a bullet.

The roar of a motorcycle brought her back to the present. Was it Tommy? Home early? Tommy and Lola lived next door to her. She had to get out of there before he came back.

It took a few minutes to copy the original party video. Then she hid the copy in a safe place in her apartment in case Tommy caught up with her and she had to surrender the original. Finally, she ran for her Mazda.

As she drove, she peered into the darkness hoping she wouldn't run out of gas before she found a service station open in the middle of the night.

A distant billboard grew in her headlights. A twenty-four-hour truck-stop at the next exit. She told herself that her luck was finally changing.

Checking her mirrors, she saw only two sets of headlights too far back to worry about. She flicked the turn signal and edged to the exit lane.

Unsure of how much gas she could buy with whatever was left on her credit card, she pondered where she could go. She had to choose somewhere safe and not too far away. Certainly not back to her Houston apartment. It sure wasn't safe, especially now. Did she have enough credit left on her card to drive somewhere safe?

As she pulled into the truckstop, it dawned on her. Home. That's where she should go. Not to her home in Houston, but to her real home.

She remembered the words of Robert Frost from her high school English class. "Home is that place where when you go there, they have to take you in."

The last time Angelina had seen her mother, they had had a terrible fight. But she was her mother, right? She would take her in. If she could just get to her childhood home in Adams Creek, she would be safe. Tommy didn't know her parents or where they lived. She would be safe there until she figured out what to do.

When she stopped at the gasoline pump, she would call her brother Carlos, who was a private investigator. He would know what to do. He would help her. Even as a child, her brother had always had her back when things got scary.

Yes, I'll call Carlos. Then I'll go home.

———

Behind her, one set of headlights eased into the exit lane. Driving in the shadowed edge of the huge driveway, the light-colored van followed her around to the back of the truckstop.

ONE

Carlos McCrary

Ruby Voight and I climbed to the top deck of the *Atlantic Dolphin* as it glided toward its anchorage a half-mile offshore of the downtown docks of George Town, the capital of the Cayman Islands. The sun peeked over the eastern horizon and cast long shadows from the low-rise buildings in the downtown business hub.

I took a deep breath. "That tropic air smells great."

"Salt spray and suntan lotion mixed with diesel fumes and burning trash," Ruby said with a grin.

"If you want to be picky, sure, but I detect a breath of coconuts and flowers hiding among the scents of civilization."

"That's what I like about you, Chuck. You always look on the bright side."

"It's a vacation. Everything is supposed to be roses and lollipops. It says so on the Atlantic Worldwide Cruise Lines website. If it says it on the internet, it must be true."

"Oh, look." Ruby pointed. A line of pelicans skimmed low across the water, wings barely moving. "Where do you suppose those eight beauties are going?"

"If we were in Port City, I'd say they were heading to the docks to mooch scraps from the fishing boats. Probably the same thing here."

I was as happy as I had ever been. My first cruise and my first getaway with Ruby. A whole week in the Caribbean to focus on each other and become closer. I glanced at my silent phone and considered leaving it turned off. Wasn't I entitled to a week without outside distractions?

Unbidden, the answer wedged itself into my mind: *No, you're not entitled.* A lot of people depend on me. I couldn't drop off the face of the earth for an entire week. If something bad happened that I could have prevented, I would never forgive myself.

I sighed and turned on my phone. "Time to reconnect with the real world." For me, the real world is mostly Carlos McCrary Investigations, LLC, my private investigations company in Port City, Florida.

"It was nice turning off our cellphones when we sailed over the horizon and lost our signal." Ruby spread her arms wide and twirled a 360 turn. "It felt... *liberating* to be out of touch."

"Well, it's Monday now and time to see what's happened back home that may need our attention."

My screen came to life. The local cellular carrier welcomed me to George Town and told me it was 72 degrees at 6:24 a.m. on Monday, May 5. A few seconds later civilization caught up with me when the phone signaled that I had twenty-one missed calls and nineteen new messages.

The first message was from a buddy with the Port City Robbery-Homicide Division working the weekend shift. He wanted to know if I was free for lunch. I hadn't told my friends about my planned cruise with Ruby. I didn't want to hear the jokes and snide remarks. I was hoping Ruby was The One, but our relationship was too new for that kind of stress. I sent my friend a text that I was out of town for a few days and was sorry I missed him.

The next message was from a law firm that wanted Carlos McCrary Investigations to help them defend a woman being sued for divorce. I called the law firm back. I left a voicemail accepting the assignment and told them I would be back in one week.

After a dozen other routine messages, the next one was from my sister Angelina in Houston that she had recorded at 2:30 a.m. Sunday after our ship left the Port of Miami. Angie called me every year to wish me happy birthday. Other than that, she only called when she was in some kind of jam and needed my help. Or my money.

Last time Angie called I loaned her a thousand dollars that she would never repay. Her modeling career was not going well. She couldn't or wouldn't explain exactly why, but from long experience, I knew she had done something stupid that was probably her fault. I loved my sister dearly and would do anything I could to help, but today I was hundreds of miles away and stranded on a cruise ship in Grand Cayman.

Calling at 1:30 a.m. Central Time meant something must be seriously wrong. What could be so urgent that it couldn't wait until daylight?

The reality of my challenging life threatened my daydream of a week in a tropical paradise with Ruby.

"Carlitos, it's Angie. I'm in terrible trouble." Her voice cracked.

My parents called me *Carlitos* from the time I was born until I entered high school. My first day at Theodore Roosevelt High School in Adams Creek, Texas, I came home and announced that I was too big to be called *Carlitos* anymore. My family and friends should call me Carlos or Chuck from then on.

Everyone in the family but Angelina agreed to call me Chuck. Angelina—God love her—she insisted on calling me *Carlitos*. Her nickname for me was a lifetime link between us.

My stomach stiffened when she said she was in trouble. Angelina was a drama queen, but even so, she sounded genuinely frightened. I leaned against the teak rail and pressed the phone to my ear as if that would bring her closer. I pushed my emotions aside and listened to the rest of the message.

"I have something they want. These people are dangerous." A stifled sob. "I'm so scared..." She sniffed. "I don't know what to do. Please help me. I can't call the cops about this, and I have nowhere else to turn. Call me. I know it's the middle of the night but call me no matter what time you get this message. *Call me, please, Carlitos.*"

One message from the real world had turned my daydream into a nightmare.

A computerized female voice recited my options. "To replay this message, press one. To delete, press seven. To return the message center call, press eight."

I pressed eight. The call went to voicemail. "Hi, this is Angie. I'm not available, but I'll call you as soon as I can. Please leave a message. *Ciao*."

Angie's *Ciao* greeting always sounded too cute by half, but she always tried too hard to be hip and fashionable. Maybe it went with being a fashion model.

A dull ache throbbed behind my eye.

"Angie, it's Chuck. I got your message, and of course I'll help. Unfortunately, I'm on a cruise with my girlfriend, Ruby. We've been at sea since Saturday afternoon. It's 6:30 Monday morning and we're in Grand Cayman until 4:00 p.m. They don't observe Daylight Saving Time, so that's 4:00 p.m. in Houston too. Call me. Whatever is wrong, Sis, we'll figure out what to do. Hang in there. I love you."

The sun was rising behind the low skyline of George Town, but I didn't see the buildings and no longer noticed the sunrise. The tropical breezes probably caressed my hair and rippled the fabric of my Hawaiian shirt, but I couldn't feel them. My mind was far away. In Houston.

I listened to the rest of the messages, hoping to hear a follow-up message from Angelina. Something like, "Never mind. I was worried for nothing. Everything is fine now." But there wasn't one.

I punched my voicemail number again. "You have one saved message. Saved message…" Angelina's message played again. What was that in the background? A truck shifting gears? Or a piece of large machinery? Whatever it was, it was close, and it was loud. Wherever Angie was at that godawful hour of the night or morning, she hadn't called from her apartment. Maybe a truckstop?

"To replay this message, press one. To delete, press seven. To return the message center call, press eight. To save, press nine. To listen to your next message, press three."

It was hard to concentrate on the other messages. I had left a message for Angie. There was nothing else I could do until she called again. I tried to focus on the other messages. After all, I had a business to run, even from hundreds of miles away.

Ruby stood a couple of feet away checking her own messages as the

Atlantic Dolphin dropped anchor and launched tenders to transport passengers to the dock.

Ruby finished the call she was on. "That was my realtor. The seller accepted my offer on the condo. Now I need to get a mortgage." She saw the look on my face. "What's the matter, Chuck?"

"It's my sister, Angelina. She's in some sort of trouble, but she's not answering her phone. I left a voicemail."

"Is she the model who lives in Houston?"

"Yeah. She sounded really upset. Frightened even."

"What sort of trouble?"

"She didn't say. She can tell me when she returns my call."

Ruby glanced at the fishing boats that spread across the clear blue bay. From our perch on deck 15, she could see the rising sun sparkling on North Sound in the distance. "What should we do about our snorkeling trip to Stingray City?"

"Let's take the trip. Until I hear from Angie, there's nothing I can do anyway. No sense hanging around the ship. What time does our tour leave?"

"Nine o'clock. The tenders start running at 7:00 a.m. Let's have breakfast before we go ashore."

———

Ruby and I found seats on the open-air shuttle bus that would take us to the boat dock on North Sound for our excursion.

I called Angelina again. When it went to voicemail, I disconnected and glanced at Ruby.

She raised an eyebrow.

I shook my head. "Straight to voicemail."

"Did you try her husband?"

"Geez, I completely forgot Teodoro." I found the number in my contacts and placed the call.

The shuttle lurched into motion. The guide tested the microphone and launched a humorous spiel about Grand Cayman and Stingray City.

I disconnected. "Something's wrong. Teodoro's number is not in service."

"When was the last time you talked to him?"

The couple seated in the row in front of us both turned around. The woman shushed us.

"Sorry," I mouthed.

I lowered my voice and leaned close to Ruby's ear. "I don't remember the last time I called him. To tell you the truth, I don't like Teodoro; I never thought he was right for Angie. That's why I always call Angie instead of him. I wonder if Teodoro's disconnected phone has anything to do with her trouble."

Ruby leaned against my ear. "Call your parents. You can't help Angie, but they're only a hundred miles from Houston. They can handle an emergency like this. Be sure to give them my best."

I made my way to the back of the shuttle where there was an empty row of seats. I faced the rear so I wouldn't disturb the guide's patter and made a call.

"Mom, it's Chuck. I'm in Grand Cayman on a cruise with Ruby. She sends her best wishes. Yes, I'll tell her." I listened for a moment. "We just got here, and we're on our way to go swimming with stingrays and dolphins. No, it's perfectly safe. Even little kids do it. Listen, Mom, I didn't call to talk about our cruise. I just got the strangest voicemail from Angie."

I related the message. "She sounded really scared and she was crying. Do you know anything about this? How long since you've talked with her? Why so long? What did you two argue about? Drugs? Angie? No, I never knew a thing. I'm so sorry to hear that. That doesn't sound like Angie. Yes, people can change, but—yes, ma'am. Another strange thing—I tried to call Teodoro and his number was not in service. You know anything about that?"

I listened for a while. "Okay, Mom, I will. I promise. I love you too. Let me know if Angie calls you. Just call my regular cellphone. It will find me here in Grand Cayman."

Ruby moved to the back of the shuttle and pulled me into a seat beside her. She gave me suspicious eyes. "What did you promise Andrea?"

I hoped my face hadn't reddened. "I promised I would pray for Angie and Teodoro. Mom said she's praying for them and asked me to also."

"You're a good son, Chuck."

I hoped that this cruise would help convince Ruby that I would be a good husband and father too.

"Sometimes, maybe."

"What else did Andrea say?"

"She hasn't talked to Angie in two months. The last time she visited them in Houston, Angie and Teodoro were both strung-out on drugs. She and Angie had a big fight. Angie told Mom—our *mother*—to go to hell."

I shook my head. "I just hope Angie hasn't gotten in over her head. I might have to fly to Houston."

"This is our first trip together, Chuck. Your sister is a grown woman. Let her solve her own problems for once. You don't have to answer every time a family member calls for help. She can call your parents or your grandparents or another sibling. Why is it always you?"

Ruby had a point, but I always put family first. "No, Ruby, it's possible she can't really call anyone else. I'm the only family member with my unique skills, so occasionally I am called on to untangle certain types of problems." I spread my hands. "That's just the way things are."

Ruby *harrumphed*. "Your family takes advantage of you, you know. It's not fair to you, and it's not fair to me."

What could I say? Ruby was right.

The atmosphere was prickly on our snorkeling trip.

———

When we were in line to board the tenders back to the ship, I called my father. "Dad, did Mom tell you about me calling from Grand Cayman this morning? Have you or Mom heard from Angie? How about Teodoro? That's too bad. How can a guy lose a job as a salesman when he gets paid on full commission? He doesn't cost his boss any salary. Oh, I see. He did, huh? That's bad all right. When was he fired? You know his phone's been disconnected, right? That sounds serious. Should I cut my cruise short and fly to Houston? See if I can get to the bottom of this?"

Ruby heard the last part of my conversation. "You're not planning to fly from here to Houston, are you? We've just started our cruise."

"Let me play her message for you." I called my voicemail and handed Ruby the phone. "Punch one to play the message."

Ruby listened to the message, then played it again. "I think she called from a truckstop."

"That's what I was thinking. Of course, if I fly to Houston, I can get the cops to ping her phone and find out for sure."

"She said she couldn't go to the cops. You know what that means."

I nodded. "She's into something illegal. Mom said she and Teodoro were into drugs."

"So maybe your parents shouldn't call the cops about this either."

"This sounds like it's serious. I should fly to Houston."

"You're seriously considering blowing off our entire cruise because of one voicemail message?"

"Angie said she was involved with dangerous people."

"Then she should call the cops like any normal person. Why call you? She's a grownup, for goodness sakes. Hell, she's your older sister. If anything, she should be the one looking after you. Not the other way around."

I shrugged. "She's family. Family always comes first."

"Then what the hell am I supposed to do? Finish the damned cruise by myself? Whoopee."

I took her hand. "I would hate like hell to do this to you, Ruby. This is the first cruise for both of us, and we've planned this together for weeks. But Angie is my sister."

Ruby pulled her hand loose. "I really shouldn't be surprised. We met when you came to Austin to look for your cousin Emily. You risked your life more than once to find her, and she's only a cousin. For you, it's all about family. I get that; really I do." She sighed. "It's just a shame this had to come right now, is all, just as you and I are getting to know each other better."

"Yeah. On the not-so-dark side, I may not be able to get a flight out of here this late in the day."

I called the Grand Cayman airport. The last flight to the States had already left. "I'll catch a flight tomorrow at our next port."

Ruby barely spoke at dinner that night.

———

Ruby and I sipped coffee at a table in the Lido Deck cafeteria as the *Atlantic Dolphin* approached Roatán Island in Honduras. Outside the window wall, the low, wooded mountains of the island grew larger, more distinct. I could just make out the small town where the cruise ships docked. A smaller cruise ship was moored.

A small private plane flew in front of the buildings. I tracked it with my eyes. "That must be the airport, right next to downtown. I don't see any other planes in the air though."

"Small island, small airport," Ruby said. "You may have trouble finding a flight."

A server came by and quietly removed the dirty dishes. "Would you like more coffee?"

Ruby shook her head.

I gave the server a smile. "Thanks, but we're good."

I checked my phone for the umpteenth time to see if it had a signal.

Ruby glanced at her own phone. "It's a well-known fact that watching the screen on your phone will make it find a signal faster."

I smiled. "Sort of like watching the water in a pot makes it boil quicker."

Finally, the phone welcomed me to Honduras, and said it was 28° Celsius at 11:43 a.m. on Tuesday, May 6. A few seconds later the phone signaled that I had sixteen missed calls and thirteen new messages.

I searched the missed calls list for Angie's number. No luck. I called Angie's cellphone again and left another message.

"This time her phone went straight to voicemail."

"That can't be good." Ruby's phone found a signal and welcomed her. "You'd better call your parents again in case she's been in touch with them. While you do that, I'll check my messages."

My parents had not heard from Angie.

"Roatán Island is a tiny airport," I said, "and we're due on Coconut Caye tomorrow. It's a private island that belongs to the cruise line. I'm not even sure it has cellphone service. If I wait until Cozumel, at least we'll get two more cruise days to enjoy together."

"That's a mixed blessing. With your sister in trouble, neither one of us will have exactly a carefree attitude."

"It's out of our hands anyway. We may as well enjoy ourselves if I can't get a flight today."

———

After breakfast, I worked my way to the head of the queue at the ship's office. "A family emergency has come up. I gotta fly to Houston. Can I get a flight from here?"

"May I see your cruise card, please?"

I handed over the blue magnetic card that served as both door key and credit card on the ship.

The concierge punched up my file on her computer. "Scheduled air service is pretty skimpy, Mr. McCrary. The island has a population of only 60,000. Most places like Miami, Atlanta, or Dallas only have one flight a week except in the busy season, which was over in early April. This time of year, the only flights are on weekends. I'll check, but I doubt you can get a flight out until Saturday at the earliest. If you'll give me a moment, I'll call the airlines."

"Thanks."

The other passengers in the atrium lobby were dressed in vacation clothes. Some talked at the tour desk. Others arrived or departed on the glass elevators that rose over ten decks to the top. The worst menace we faced was if our desired shore excursion had sold out. What menace did Angelina face?

I felt sick to my stomach.

Ruby had returned to our cabin. How did she feel about being abandoned by her boyfriend in the Western Caribbean so he could jump on his white charger and gallop off to rescue yet another damsel in distress. Probably she was plenty pissed. Nothing I could do about that. Family is family.

The concierge hung up her phone. "No flights or connections to anywhere in the USA until Saturday. You're better off waiting until Thursday when we get to Cozumel. There are lots of flights to Dallas and Houston every day from Cozumel.

At least Ruby and I could try to enjoy the next two days of our vacation as we had planned.

The specter of Angie's predicament would cast a pall over our tropical holiday. I dreaded two more sleepless nights worrying about Angie and feeling impotent. Well, not *impotent* surely. At least not literally. But I did feel frustrated that I couldn't do anything for Angie but wait.

———

The *Atlantic Dolphin* slowed as it approached the dock in Puerta Maya, Cozumel.

The concierge had reserved me a seat on the one daily nonstop flight from Cozumel to Houston that left at 1:00 p.m. If I missed that flight, the next one was at 4:04 p.m. It changed planes in Dallas and didn't arrive in Houston until after 10:00 p.m.

While I waited for the ship to dock, I called Angie one more time. The recording said her voicemail box was full. Pressure throbbed at the base of my skull. I worked my head from side to side to loosen my neck. It didn't work.

"I'd better grab my bag and head down to the concierge desk. She arranged for me to disembark through the crew gangplank so I can maybe make it to the airport in time for the 1:00 p.m. flight."

Ruby placed a hand on my forearm. "I've decided to fly to Austin and visit my family. I'll ride to the airport with you. I already packed too."

My heart skipped a beat. Ruby's parents didn't approve of her relationship with me. I didn't want them to have a few days to try to convince her to break up with me.

"What about the dive trip we signed up for? You can still go. You don't have to go home."

"I've visited Cozumel a couple of times before, when I lived in Austin. It's a nice place, but it's no fun diving by myself with a bunch of strangers. Then there's just a sea day tomorrow before the ship gets back to Miami. I'd rather spend a couple of days with my folks. I haven't seen them since I moved to Port City and I'm a little homesick."

Ruby's parents had been against our relationship since day one. Her parents wanted Ruby to marry a black man. I suspected they would take every opportunity to bad-mouth me while she was with them.

———

I opened the rear passenger door for Ruby, then watched the taxi driver stick our bags in the trunk.

I tipped him as I got in the other rear seat.

"*Aeropuerto, por favor.*"

"*¿De qué manera, señor?*"

"What did he say?" Ruby asked as she buckled her seat belt.

"He wants to know which way to drive. The concierge says there's a scenic seaside street, but it might take a little longer. I'll tell him to take the fastest route."

I turned to the driver. "*La forma más rápida, por favor.*"

Twenty-five minutes later, we scurried through the terminal, dragging our bags to the ticket counter. The monitors on the wall announced in Spanish and English that the flight to Houston was boarding.

There were two other passengers in the queue ahead of us. We each had two carry-ons and a backpack. My heart rate increased as the minutes passed. The *boarding* notice on the monitor began to flash red as we made it to the ticket clerk. "My friend has a connection to Austin and I'm getting off in Houston. Can we still make the flight?"

The ticket clerk handed us boarding passes. "It will be close, *señor*. You and your friend must hurry. I will telephone the gate."

Keep calm, I thought. *You will make it or you won't.* I had a backup reservation on the 4:04 flight. That was as good as it was going to set, so no point in getting my shorts in a knot.

As we worked our way through the security line, the minutes seemed to move faster. Ten minutes before flight time, we had reached the x-ray machine. The x-ray made a loud sizzle and stopped working. By the time we switched to another security line, the nonstop flight to Houston had left.

I watched the airplane take off through the window. I turned to Ruby. "On the bright side we have time for a leisurely lunch before our flight at four o'clock.

We finished clearing security, changed our boarding passes at a passenger service desk, and found a table at the restaurant on the security side of the terminal.

After we ordered lunch, I excused myself from the table and found a quiet spot to call my grandfather, Magnus McCrary.

"Grandpa, this is Chuck. Did Mom or Dad talk to you about Angie's message to me?"

"Both of them have been calling me almost hourly, wondering if I've heard from Angie or Teodoro. Unfortunately, the answer is always no. It's like the earth swallowed them up. Teodoro's phone is disconnected, and Angie's voicemail box is full. Your grandma and I are so worried that we're chewing our fingernails right up to the elbows. Are you going to Houston?"

"Ruby and I are at the airport in Cozumel. I'm on a four o'clock flight to Dallas, connecting to a flight to Houston. I get into George Bush airport after ten tonight."

"What about Ruby?"

"She's going to skip the rest of the cruise and fly to Austin to visit her parents."

"Uh-oh," said Grandpa. "You know what that means."

"It can't be helped. Either Ruby will stand up for me with them, or she won't. She's close to her parents."

"Your relationship has had its up and downs, hasn't it?"

"Grandpa, every relationship has its ups and downs. We'll get through this—I hope."

"Son, I like Ruby, but I know how hard it is to resist relentless pressure from your own parents. Remember none of us ever liked Teodoro either, and you know how that turned out. I'll keep you both in my prayers."

"Thanks, Grandpa. That couldn't hurt." It probably wouldn't help either, but I didn't say that.

"Are you going to start working tonight, or wait till tomorrow to start the search?"

"You know me, Grandpa. There's no time like the present. I'll rent a car and drive to Angie's place tonight. It can't hurt to at least knock on her door. Maybe I'll get lucky."

Grandpa scoffed. "It's too late for luck, son. You call me when you get to her apartment, no matter how late it is."

I protested at first, but finally agreed.

Ruby and I barely talked during lunch. When I walked with her to her gate, our goodbye was decidedly frosty. As I moved to my own departure gate, I had a bad feeling about our relationship.

This would not be the first time I lost a girlfriend because I put my family first.

TWO

My flight landed at George Bush International Airport at 10:15 p.m. on Thursday, May 7. After spending all day traveling from Cozumel with a plane change in Dallas, I was not in the best of moods. Still, I didn't want to leave things with Ruby as tense as they were when we'd said goodbye at the Cozumel airport.

I called when the plane landed. "Did you get to your folks' house okay?"

"Dad met me at the airport. Mom fixed us a pitcher of Margaritas and I'm showing them my cruise pictures. Speaking of our cruise... my folks are pissed at you for running out on me."

"I don't blame them. I'm pissed at me too."

"They say you're unreliable."

That was expected. Her folks had been opposed to our romance from the get-go even though they had never met me. Nevertheless, I didn't know how best to respond to the charge, so I didn't answer.

"Chuck, are you there?"

"I'm still here. Your parents are not wrong. Sometimes life interferes with my plans, and I change course without prior notice. So, yes, sometimes I am unreliable."

"Well, just remember: You don't have to be unreliable. You don't have

29

to change your plans every time a family member calls for help. There are other people your sister could call."

Our thorny vacation had ended when we boarded separate planes that morning. I was back in the real world. A world that revolves around Carlos McCrary Investigations, LLC., my private investigation company in Port City, Florida. Client demands often dominate my personal life, but family loyalty trumps everything else, including my personal relationships.

Ruby sighed. "Where are you?"

"At George Bush airport in Houston waiting for the rental car shuttle."

"You plan to rent a hotel room, or do you start the search tonight?"

"Anything I do tonight, I won't need to do tomorrow."

"Workaholic, that's what you are. On the other hand, the sooner you find your sister, the sooner you come home to Port City."

"Right. The glass is half full. How about you? What are your plans?"

"I'll spend this weekend with Mom and Dad and fly back to Port City Sunday evening. When will I see you again?"

There it was again—the question I could never answer.

My stomach twisted. Ruby wouldn't appreciate my reply. "I can't predict that. I'm unreliable, remember?"

Why the hell did I say that?

With relationships, I am my own worst enemy. "My Grandpa Magnus always asks, 'How long is a piece of string?'"

"What does that mean, smart guy?"

"The search for Angie will take as long as it takes. I can't predict how long that could be."

"This will be like your search for your cousin Emily, won't it? The search for the Holy Grail. It might take forever."

"Not forever. That I guarantee. I quit the search for Emily the first time after a month, once the trail hit a dead end."

"But worst case, you don't have a clue how long the search for Angie will last."

"Not yet, but my track record's pretty good. I usually win."

"And sometimes you lose, hot shot. Like the first time you searched for Emily."

"Hopefully not this time, Ruby."

There was a long silence on the line.

"Chuck, I'm deliberating whether our relationship is working for me."

"Your folks still carping about me?"

Ruby is black, and I'm Mexican-American, which to her parents means I'm white. Or at least *white adjacent*. Their preferred plan for their only daughter was for Ruby to marry a black man and raise black grandchildren for them. I was a perceived threat to that plan.

I never understood their objection. I have a Caucasian cousin who married a black man, and they have two gorgeous interracial children. Both smart as can be.

Ruby sighed again. "Never mind my parents. I am close to them, but it's not just that. We can still be friends. Let's meet for dinner once you get back to Port City."

I'd heard that song many times. *Let's be friends* might be my theme song.

"Goodbye, Ruby. I'll keep in touch."

"But you'll call me once you get home, right?"

"Sure." Maybe. Sometimes life happens.

———

I parked in a visitor's space at Angie's apartment complex. The dashboard clock on my rented Jeep read 11:30.

I had agreed to call Grandpa when I arrived at Angie's apartment, no matter how late the hour. But this late on a Thursday night, calling seemed like a bad idea. Grandpa Magnus was an old man; he needed his sleep. He and Grandma usually went to bed at 9:30. Besides, he lived a hundred miles away in Adams Creek. I decided not to call and wake him.

No light shone from the windows of Angie's apartment or the apartments on either side. My phone rang and Grandpa's face lit up the screen. "Hello, Grandpa. I was just about to call you."

"Don't bullshit an old bullshitter, boy. You weren't gonna call me, were you?"

"Busted, Grandpa. Sorry, but there's nothing you can do from Adams Creek, and, besides, it's late."

"Look over your left shoulder, son."

Grandpa was standing beside his old Honda Odyssey parked in Angie's assigned parking spot. He strode over to me, arms extended for a bear hug.

"I brought my key to their apartment, so you won't need to pick the lock." He tossed a key ring in the air and caught it. "See? I'm already a big help."

I laughed as we slapped each other's backs. "Okay, Grandpa, but let's knock on the door first."

We walked to the foot of the stairs.

"You'd think that Angie and Teodoro could at least rent an apartment with an elevator. Didn't they consider that Grandma and I would visit?"

"They didn't ask my opinion before they signed the lease, Grandpa. Why don't you give me the key and wait in your car?"

"I drove a hundred miles to help you and Angie, son. I can manage one flight of stairs. Heck, Grandma and I climb these steps every time we visit." Grandpa held the railing with one hand and trudged up the steps to the second floor. "But I swear they get steeper every time I climb them." He pressed the doorbell, then knocked on the door. No response. He handed the key ring to me. "You take the lead, son. This is your department."

I shined my phone's flashlight on the doorknob and dead bolt.

"What are you doing, son?"

"Looking for signs of forced entry, Grandpa. See? There are no gouges or scrapes on the hardware or door jamb. That's a good sign."

As I opened the door, I inhaled through my nose before switching on the lights. If Angie or her husband Teodoro had been dead inside for more than a few hours, I would smell it. Then I could warn Grandpa about it before he saw the bodies.

The air was musty, but I didn't smell blood or decayed bodies.

I flipped on the lights, then pulled my Glock.

The apartment had been tossed. Cushions were pulled from the couch and chairs. Drawers from the credenza lay on the floor. Pictures had been pulled from the walls and tossed aside.

Grandpa stopped just outside the door. "Jesus and Mary. Somebody's ransacked the place."

I raised my hand. "Wait here, Grandpa. I'll be right back."

I did a cursory walk-through to confirm that my missing relatives weren't newly dead or unconscious inside and that whoever had searched the place was gone.

I returned to Grandpa, who waited just outside the front door. "It's better if you don't come inside. I need to search for clues or evidence, and you don't want to contaminate the crime scene by accident."

"Yeah, I see that on the television cop shows. You gonna call the cops?"

"No. Angie's voicemail said she couldn't go to the cops. So whatever she's involved in is probably illegal. We can't afford to involve the cops yet. I'll try to sort this out by myself first."

Despite the generally trashed condition of the apartment I had seen on my first walk-through, I could tell the place had been a mess before the searchers had rifled it. Dirty dishes covered the kitchen counter and towels lay on the bathroom floor.

Grandpa made a sour face. "Last time Connie and I visited, we knew something was wrong. Before that, Angie and Teodoro kept things neat as a pin. Drunks and drug addicts don't care enough to be tidy." He scanned the living room and sniffed. "Or clean."

"It's too late for you to drive back to Adams Creek, Grandpa. Why don't you stay with Aunt Catherine for the night?"

"Great minds think alike. I called Catherine before I left Adams Creek. She said she has room for you too. She would love to see you, even just to say good night."

"*Nah*. She lives in Spring. That's at least a two-hour drive there and back. I'll rent a hotel after I finish tonight's search. Thanks for the key, Grandpa."

He opened the door. "God go with you, son."

I laid a hand on Grandpa's shoulder. "Yeah. Give Aunt Catherine a hug and kiss for me."

———

I searched Angie's closet in the master suite first.

The invaders had left her clothes heaped randomly on the floor of the closet and the bedroom. Even in the closet's disarray, the scent of her perfume transported me back. I inhaled and recalled happier days.

I searched her clothes as I hung them back on the closet rods. Hanging them kept track of what I had searched. No idea what I was looking for, but I would recognize a clue if I found one.

Eight fabric-covered storage baskets that had probably been on the top shelf were heaped in a corner. Hats, gloves, scarves, and other accessories sprawled across the carpet. A Smith & Wesson revolver in a leather holster lay on the shelf. Why hadn't the housebreaker taken it? I sniffed the muzzle. It hadn't been fired since the last time it was cleaned. I opened the cylinder; all five chambers were loaded. Perhaps Angie had stored the gun there and forgotten it.

The contents of the nightstand nearest Angie's closet had been dumped. An empty holster for a larger handgun lay near the overturned nightstand. Where was the gun that belonged with the holster? Nail-polish remover and other contents near the nightstand indicated Angie slept on that side of the bed. Had she taken the missing weapon with her? Or had the burglar taken it and left the holster?

A three-piece set of pink luggage lay open on the floor. My parents had given it to her one Christmas. All three pieces were there. Wherever she had gone, she didn't take time to pack. That was uncharacteristic of my fashion-model sister. She had brought all three suitcases plus a carry-on for a two-day visit to Adams Creek for Easter the previous year.

This couldn't be good.

The other nightstand was still upright with its top drawer half open and the two lower drawers dumped nearby. The condoms in the top drawer hinted that Teodoro slept on this side of the bed. There was another empty holster, a twin to the one near Angie's nightstand. "His" and "her" hand-guns? Why not? After all, this was Texas.

I returned to Angie's closet and finished sorting through the contents. Nothing told me where she'd gone.

I collected six purses from around the room and lined them up on the bed. I felt each purse's sides, bottom, and top for hidden compartments or objects sewn into the lining. Three purses held condoms in zipper compartments that had been unzipped, possibly by the intruder. They were a different brand than the ones in Teodoro's nightstand.

Teodoro kept condoms in his nightstand. So why did Angie carry condoms in her purses? I didn't care for the obvious answer to that question. My heart sagged in my chest when I considered that her marriage was probably in trouble.

Another purse held a coke spoon fashioned from a crucifix. The top of the cross was a tiny loop that a gold chain slipped through. A crucifix made into a spoon to snort cocaine. The savior and the sinner represented in one little implement.

At the bottom of the purse was a cellphone charger with an LG logo on it.

A dozen pairs of shoes hung on metal racks. Nothing was concealed in her shoes.

Teodoro's closet lay in a similar state of disarray. It yielded a shoebox on the floor holding small spoons, empty baggies, a glass pipe, and syringes. Drug paraphernalia. Was Angie involved in drugs? So far, I'd found no drugs in the apartment. Possibly the previous searcher had found drugs. If so, he had taken them with him. Or her.

One or both of them was into cocaine and heroin. That was no surprise since Grandma had told me that when I'd called her from Grand Cayman. Still, the drug paraphernalia in Teodoro's closet worsened the chance for a happy ending to my search for Angie.

Matted marks pressed into the carpet under Teodoro's side of the bed showed that he had also had a three-piece luggage set. The two smaller suitcases were tossed toward a corner. The largest suitcase was missing.

The master bath contained the typical items a woman uses: birth control pills, deodorant, toothbrush, toothpaste, headache medicine, tampons, etc. All had been dumped in the lavatory.

Angie was on the pill, yet both she and Teodoro carried condoms. Odds were, she was sleeping with someone other than Teodoro, or vice versa, or she was afraid her own husband would give her an STD. Neither explanation boded well for their marriage.

There was no second toothbrush, razor, or aftershave. Teodoro had packed for his trip. He could be anywhere from Seattle to Sarasota.

A kitchen drawer dropped on the floor still held legal papers: an apartment lease, insurance policies, warranty papers for two LG cellphones, two laptops, one iPad, and a television. There were no cellphones, laptops, or iPads in the apartment.

A collection of paper cellphone bills was fastened with a rubber band. This was a scene from the last century, but Angie had been that way since forever. Another drawer contained a dozen monthly credit card bills and last year's and this year's bank statements. I stuffed the bills in one jacket pocket and the bank statements in another.

Two handguns were gone. Angie or Teodoro might have them, or the thief who rummaged the apartment stole them. Since I found no evidence of a break-in, the intruder used a key or picked the lock.

If the intruder had a key, it probably was someone Angie knew.

I found no address books or appointment calendars, but my generation uses smartphone calendars.

I spent two hours rummaging through the kitchen, bathrooms, closets, and furniture. Exhausted and depressed, I asked my phone to direct me to a nearby hotel.

It was 3:30 a.m. by the time I rented a room and tumbled into bed. Before I closed my eyes, I wondered where Angie was sleeping.

As exhausted as I was, you'd have thought I would fall asleep immediately, but I didn't. My sister was missing, and I tossed and turned while I planned the steps I could take tomorrow. Images from our childhood flew through my mind. Her senior prom when our mother said she looked like a fashion model in her prom dress. Angie cheering from the sidelines in her cheerleader's uniform when I caught my first touchdown pass as a tight end on the Theodore Roosevelt High School Roughriders.

Where was she now? Did she even have a place to sleep? Assuming she was still alive.

I lay on my back and stared at dark nothingness. Tears spilled and ran across my temples toward my ears. My eyes stung. Was I ever going to find her or was she already dead?

I wiped the tears on the pillowcase. Enough melancholy for one night.

THREE

I reached for my phone and silenced the alarm. Nine-thirty is mighty early when you don't fall asleep until 5:00 a.m. I considered rolling over for another hour of sleep. Then I contemplated Angie. Where was my sister? What was she feeling? Did she have a bed to sleep in?

I sighed and stepped into the shower.

At eleven o'clock, I let myself into Angie's apartment again. Natural light from the windows made things appear different than the artificial light at night. I recalled a case when I was a rookie detective with the Port City Police Robbery-Homicide Division. The sunlight through a bedroom window had revealed a spot on a hardwood floor where someone had cleaned it with bleach to remove a bloodstain. My mentor and partner, Raymond "Snoop" Snopolski pointed out the extra clean area. The clue helped prove the death was murder and not suicide.

The previous night I was tired from travel. I re-examined the two empty holsters from the nightstands. In the sunlight I noticed faint grooves in the leather of the holster from Teodoro's side of the bed. It had been used a great deal. Angie's holster was brand-new. I filed the information in a corner of my mind.

Making a final survey of the apartment, I locked the door and pocketed the key.

———

I pressed the doorbell of the apartment next door, then backed away so I wouldn't appear threatening. After a minute, I rang the bell again.

I didn't know whether the neighbor was a couple, a man, or a woman. I slipped my hands into my pants pockets and leaned against the railing opposite the door. Just a friendly neighbor knocking on the door. A strange man at the door makes anyone nervous. That is not conducive to a productive conversation.

A female voice carried from inside. "I'm coming. Keep your shirt on."

The deadbolt clicked open. The door cracked a few inches until a security chain stopped it.

A brown eye with smeared mascara squinted through the gap. "Yeah?"

"Good morning. My name is Carlos McCrary. I am looking for my sister Angelina Garza or her husband Teodoro. Have you seen either of them lately?"

The woman blinked and forced her eyes wider. "Just a minute." She closed the door, slid the chain off, and opened it. "Helloooo, Carlos. Yes, I seen your picture on Angie's phone. You're better looking in person. Come in." She stepped back, clutching her white satin robe to her. She wobbled into the living room and nearly tripped on her own bare feet.

"I'm sorry, ma'am. Did I wake you?"

"*No problemo*, Chuck. Can I call you Chuck? Angie says everybody calls you Chuck, and I'm part of everybody. Sorry, I'm rattling on. I partied late last night. Still high. *Whoopee!* Have a seat." She waved her hand at a chair, and her white satin robe fell open.

Satin is shiny and slippery. Pretty, but not practical for a robe. The sash slipped loose, revealing ornate tattoos that curled like clinging vines around her breasts and down to her abdomen.

She posed long enough to give me a good look, then clutched her robe closed.

"Lola Salazar. Angie and I are friends. How do you like your coffee?" She giggled. "I need it to finish sobering up. It gets my heart pumping."

"Thanks, I'd love coffee."

"Give me a minute." Clutching her robe together, Lola left the room. In the hallway she stopped and glanced back over her shoulder. She winked.

"I won't be long. Don't you go away."

I gave her my hundred-watt smile. "I wouldn't dream of it. I'll be right here."

The living room was the twin of Angelina's and Teodoro's. When I visited Angie and Teo the previous summer, I hadn't realized they lived in a furnished apartment. Same couch; same upholstered chairs; same bookcase. Only Lola's had not been ransacked.

Lola rustled about the other room making coffee. She hollered from the kitchen. "It's brewing. I'll throw on some clothes. Give me a second."

I raised my voice. "No problem, Ms. Salazar. I'll wait here."

"Call me Lola, Chucky," she hollered as she walked to the bedroom.

I glanced up as she crossed the hall. Lola opened her robe and flashed me. She grinned and winked before she disappeared.

I do not understand women.

Lola's bookcase held CDs and DVDs in Spanish and English. The plastic cases were dumped on the shelves. Some lay on the floor. Angie's bookcase displayed family pictures. Did nobody in either apartment own a book?

Lola reappeared in cutoffs and a concert tee-shirt from a band I didn't recognize. She had applied fresh makeup which hid her red nose, and her hair was combed. The writing on the tee-shirt was in Spanish. "Let's sit at the kitchen table." She shuffled to the kitchen, poured coffee into two chipped mugs, and opened the refrigerator.

I sniffed toothpaste and mouthwash on her breath. I spotted a half gallon of non-fat milk. "A splash of milk will do nicely."

Lola poured a dollop of milk into both mugs.

The milk curdled as it hit the hot coffee. Probably expired. Oh well, it wouldn't kill me.

She lifted her coffee in a mock toast. "*Salud, amor y pesetas.*"

I recognized the old Spanish toast: To health, love, and money. I finished it. "*Y tiempo para gozarlos.*" And the time in which to enjoy them.

"Oh, you speak Spanish," she said. "Angie's Spanish is better than mine."

I already knew Lola's Spanish was weak when she had said *no problemo*. *Problema* is one of those masculine gender Spanish words that ends in *a*, like *dia* for the English *day*. Most Americans say it wrong because that's the way Arnold Schwarzenegger said it in *Terminator*.

"You can't be born in Texas and not speak a little Spanish."

My mother was born and raised in Mexico, and Angie and I were raised bilingual thanks to summers spent with our Mexican grandparents. But some sixth sense told me to keep personal information to myself. There was no way to know what else Angie had told Lola about me.

We clinked coffee mugs. Lola tasted hers. She didn't seem to find the taste off-putting.

"My father was Mexican, but my Spanish is only fair. Mainly I speak Spanglish. Ya know? I use that toast because I enjoy a good time." She eyed me and winked. "Do you enjoy parties, Chucky?"

She had called me Chucky again. I wasn't a character from the old *Child's Play* slasher film movie franchise. But it was good that she treated me like an old friend. I could extract better information from her.

"Who doesn't?" I replied. "Now, getting back to Angie... When did you last see her?"

I sipped my coffee. Yep, curdled. I'd drunk worse.

"I haven't seen Angie in a week. I ran into her at a party somewhere."

"What day was that?"

Lola's forehead wrinkled. "Was it a Friday? I remember the guy who threw the party hung a T-G-I-F banner on the wall. What's today?"

"Friday."

"Okay, it was last Friday, seven days ago."

"Where was the party?"

A vertical line creased between Lola's eyes. "Stefan's house? At least, I think his name was Stefan. Or was it Esteban?" She smiled dreamily. "There was an S and a T in there, and it ended with *AN*. Me and Angie met him at this bar. He bought us a drink and invited us to a party at his house."

"You said you ran into Angie at the party."

"I forgot. We was out at the neighborhood bar."

"Which bar?"

"Third Base. It's a couple blocks up the street." She waved vaguely.

"Don't tell me. Their sign says, 'Stop here before you go home.' Right?"

Lola thumped my bicep playfully. "How did you know that?"

"I've seen it in other towns. Was it just you and Angie at Third Base? You weren't with dates?"

Lola giggled and patted my forearm. "Not at first. Third Base is a great place to meet new people. We met this Stefan guy there. He gave us a ride to a party at his house, and I didn't see much of Angie once we got there."

"Was she with anyone else at the party?"

"That's hard to say. Must have been over a hundred people there. In the front yard, the backyard, the pool, the hot tub. Everybody was with some-body if they wanted to be, ya know? But not necessarily the same guy the whole night. Angie could have hooked up with someone, but I was pretty high. I didn't pay no attention."

"How high was Angie?"

"Stefan gave us each a line of coke in his car on the way to his house. I don't know how much she snorted later."

"Was Teodoro there?"

"Teodoro?"

"Teodoro Garza. Angie's husband."

"Oh. Teodoro… Yeah, that's right… Angie used to hang out with a guy named Teodoro. You say they was married? They didn't act married. They had a big fight and he moved out a couple of months ago." She snickered. "I don't remember so good. I suffer from CRS disease."

"CRS?"

"Yeah. You know: Can't Remember Shit." She snickered.

It wasn't that funny the first dozen times I had heard that so-called joke, but I laughed with her. "That's a good one. CRS."

I gave Lola my hundred-watt smile again. "You say Angie and Teodoro had a fight?"

"Yeah. I would overhear them through the wall, shouting day and night sometimes." She gestured with her coffee and sloshed some on the table. "*Oops.*" She snatched a napkin. She gave the spatter a feeble swipe but missed most of the spill.

"What did they fight about?"

"Beats the hell outta me. They was fighting over something. They coulda had money troubles, but I'm not sure. I talked to him once or twice. He and Angie seemed more roommates than lovers. Didn't have much in common."

A toilet flushed in the rear of the apartment.

Lola noticed my puzzlement. "That's Tommy. He's awake."

A tall, rail-thin man with greasy shoulder-length hair streaked with purple and green walked in. He wore tattered blue jeans with no shoes and no shirt. A steel loop with three short spikes hung from one earlobe. A black stud with a stylized skull hung from the other.

A cartoon heart was tattooed over Tommy's real heart and a guitar tattoo balanced it on the right side of his chest. He hadn't shaved in a week, but you couldn't call it a beard; Tommy hadn't shaved his neck either. Maybe he was disguised as a homeless person.

Tommy acted like a guy who wouldn't want to shake hands, but I could be wrong so I slid my chair back and stood, thinking I might learn Tommy's last name. Since he lived next door to Angie, he might know something about her disappearance.

Tommy ignored me and stopped inches from Lola. "Who the hell is he?" he sneered, taking a sip from her coffee mug. He spit the coffee onto the floor. "Curdled milk. Damn it, Lola, how many times do I gotta tell you to check the expiration date before you buy the freakin' milk?"

"This is Carlos. He's Angie's brother."

Tommy glanced at me and back at Lola. "Hasn't that crazy bitch caused enough trouble?" He stalked from the room with the coffee mug.

I wondered what kind of trouble this Neanderthal thought my sister had caused.

Even though Tommy No-Last-Name knew something useful, his attitude told me he wouldn't volunteer to enlighten me. It's hard to believe, but sometimes people resist my charm.

I sat. "Do you recall where the party was? The one where you last saw Angie?"

"It was at this guy Esteban's house. Three or four miles from here. Or was it Stefan? Stefano? I met him a couple times, but I never remember his name."

First, she said she met the man at Third Base, and he drove her and Angie to his house. Then she said she had met him a couple of times. Which version was true?

"Could you locate the house again?"

"I was pretty wasted by the time we left the bar, and the blow on the way in his car didn't help my CRS. Oh, wait. I forgot. Remember my CRS disease." She giggled. "Whatever this guy's name was, he gave me his business card when he hit on me. I kept it somewhere. I'll be right back." She stood, then clutched the back of her chair. "Ooh, still high." As she left the room she peeked back over her shoulder and winked again as she wiggled her derriere.

A door slammed at the rear of the apartment. Tommy raised his voice. "You didn't need to invite him in. A perfect stranger. You could talk to him outside. I've had too much grief from Angie. Get rid of him."

Lola responded. I couldn't make out the words, but she sounded angry.

I risked another sip of curdled coffee and decided I wasn't that desperate for caffeine.

Lola reappeared. Her cheeks flushed. She glanced at a silver business card in her hand. "His name is Esteban Espinoza. He's a movie producer. He asked Angie and me to audition for one of his films." She handed the card to me.

Las Peliculas Fantasia. The best in Spanish-language adult films.

"The guy makes porno movies?"

Lola's cheeks colored again. "They call them adult films. He says they're done in good taste." She cleared her throat. "Anyhow, me and Angie enjoyed the party. We didn't make no auditions. I like sex, but I don't want strangers to watch me do it." She snickered. "At least, not on a big screen."

"Was the party at the address on this card?"

"Yeah. His film studio is behind his house. Keep the card. I have more."

I slipped the card in my pocket. She met the guy the one time, but she kept several of his cards. What else was she lying about?

"Tommy said Angie had caused trouble. What kind of trouble?"

Lola's gaze drifted to one side. "I don't know what he was talking about. Tommy don't own me, though he acts like it. I'm my own woman. In fact, we're throwing a party tonight and I can invite anybody I want. Things start to hop after ten or ten-thirty." She ran her fingers across my forearm. "I promise I'll make you feel welcome, Chucky."

"Sure. I love parties."

"In case I remember something about Angie," Lola said, "you and I should exchange phone numbers."

She handed me her phone. "You do the honors."

I called my cellphone with Lola's phone and labeled her number "Lola Salazar."

Lola said, "Label your number on my phone as Chucky Lucky."

I grinned. "Chucky Lucky? Where did you come up with that, Lola?"

She trailed her fingers across my biceps. "It means you might get lucky at my party."

Back in my Jeep, I maxed the air conditioning and considered my next move. At Lola's party I might find other friends of Angie who might shed light on her whereabouts.

Rule Twelve-A: *In vino, veritas.* In wine, truth. Catching someone drunk or high increases the odds that useful information slips from uncontrolled lips. The party would provide access to lots of uncontrolled lips.

Lola lied when she claimed she didn't know what Tommy No-name meant about Angie causing trouble. Perhaps I would uncover what sort of trouble Angie caused Tommy.

I drove to the apartment complex's office. A one-story building that matched the style of the two-story apartment buildings. I found a visitor's parking spot and opened the office door.

A thirtyish woman rose from her chair behind a wooden desk.

"How may I help you?" She wore a white silk blouse with a string of pearls. Small gold hoops in her ears. Glen plaid pants.

"My name is Carlos McCrary. My sister is Angelina McCrary Garza. She and her husband Teodoro live in apartment 287."

"Oh, yes. The Garzas, Teodoro and Angie. I'm Geneva Howell. How can I help?"

"They are both missing. Their neighbor, Lola Salazar, said she hadn't seen Teodoro in a long time and Angelina has been gone for a week. Do you know where they are?"

"May I see some identification, Mr. McCrary?"

I presented my Florida driver's license. No point flashing my PI license. That was not germane to this conversation.

"Angie gave me a key to their apartment. I checked inside to make sure they hadn't been murdered or something, but they've vanished." I didn't tell Howell that the apartment had been searched. She might want to make a police report and I didn't want that. At least, not yet.

"Do you have any idea where Angie and Teo went?"

"I don't keep tabs on the tenants. Do you think we should call the police? File a missing person report or something?"

"Not yet. Can we check their mailbox to see if they've collected their mail?"

"Sure. I keep keys to the tenants' mailboxes in case of emergency." Howell opened a desk drawer and withdrew a green metal box.

She stopped with the box in her hands. "How do I know you're Ms. Garza's brother?"

"Do you list an emergency contact for Angelina in your file?"

The manager read a card in the box. "Yes, they are Michael McCrary and Andrea McCrary."

"Those are my parents. Her parents too. Why don't you call them and ask them to describe their son Carlos?"

"Oh, wait. There's a third contact in the file. She added it two months ago. Carlos McCrary."

Angie had added my name to her emergency contacts list. Why? What had happened two months ago? "Why don't you call the number?"

She did and my cellphone rang.

I responded. "Hello, Ms. Howell."

Howell smiled and disconnected. "Okay. I'm sorry I doubted you, Mr. McCrary."

I smiled back. "It's good that you take security seriously."

She opened the metal box and selected a key. "Let's check their mailbox."

The apartment mailboxes were next to the office. The manager opened one and the mail spilled out. "It's overfilled."

A recycle bin sat next to the mailboxes.

I scanned the fallen envelopes, advertisements, and magazines from the box, pitching most of them in the recycle bin. "Judging from the postmarks, it hasn't been picked up in a week." I stuffed the remaining mail in my pocket. "I'll leave the mail on their kitchen table. Can I ask you something else?"

"Sure."

"Are they current on their rent?"

"Let me check." She led me back into the office and consulted a file. "They haven't paid the May rent, and they were ten days late in April. We are scheduled to serve them a Three-Day Notice to Pay or Quit on Monday."

"How much do they owe?"

The manager told me.

"Can I pay their rent?"

"Of course."

I hoped Angie would have a chance to repay me. It wasn't for the money; it would mean I had found her. Alive.

As I returned to the Jeep, my stomach reminded me it was past lunchtime. Shoving the rental in gear, I steered toward a barbecue joint I passed the previous night.

On the way, I telephoned my mother and brought her up to speed. "Angie added my name to her emergency contact list with the apartment manager. She did that two months ago, roughly the time when Teodoro disappeared. The timing might mean something."

"You always tell me Rule Seven: *There is no such thing as a coincidence.*"

"I know, Mom."

I decided not to tell my parents about the party Angie attended at the porn house.

"I'll call or email when I uncover anything significant, but don't expect me to report in every day. I'm at a barbecue joint and I haven't eaten lunch. I love you. Give my love to everyone."

I ordered a brisket plate with coleslaw and baked beans.

As I waited for my lunch, I pondered my next move. There were lots of options, far too many rabbits to chase them all: Angie's cellphone, Teodoro's cellphone, Teodoro's former employer, Angie's modeling agency. And I hadn't even read the mail. Which choices were better left for Monday, when businesses would be open?

My food arrived. I thanked the server and began to eat. We have good barbecue in Florida, but there's just something about barbecue that tastes better in Texas. Perhaps it's because I was born and raised there.

If I were in Port City, I could ask one of my police contacts to ping Angie's and Teodoro's phones and trace them for the last six weeks. And they would do it on the downlow.

But I was in Houston, not Port City. On the other hand, so what? Technically, a Port City cop could survey a Houston cellphone. Or one in East Mountain Goat, Montana, for that matter.

I finished lunch, returned to my Jeep, and called Port City Police Captain Jorge Castellano's personal cellphone.

The phone shifted to voicemail. "Jorge, this is Chuck McCrary. My sister Angelina went missing earlier this week and I'm in Houston to find her. I need your cop skills. Call me please."

Jorge and I had been friends since my first year as a Port City cop—over ten years ago. Jorge caught a gangbanger's bullet meant for me. Later, I saved his life by solving a homicide the killer tried to hang around Jorge's neck. Jorge always said he could never repay me. I told him the same thing. As you can imagine, we were pretty close.

Nothing to do but wait for Jorge to call back. I studied Esteban Espinoza's card. The pornographer's house and studio might be the last place anybody saw Angie alive before she disappeared.

That was one lead I could pursue right now.

———

I chose an indirect route to Espinoza's house to get a feel for the side streets of the blue-collar neighborhood where the real people lived. Single-family houses shared blocks with apartments, Mom-and-Pop stores, and small businesses run from converted homes.

I stopped at the curb. A professionally painted sign hung on a pair of stainless-steel chain links from a shiny metal frame in the front yard. *Las Peliculas Fantasia* was painted in glittery silver paint on a shiny black enamel background decorated with stylistic stars of various sizes and colors.

The house was single-storied, midcentury modern style. If it were a person, it would've been old enough for Medicare. The composition roof would need to be replaced soon, but the stuccoed concrete block walls were recently painted. Triangular windows atop the decorative brick front wall showed the cathedral ceilings inside the house. The St. Augustine front lawn needed mowing, but not badly. The low maintenance generic shrubs growing close to the house needed a trim. Three palm trees grew in the front yard between worn spots that showed where visitors' cars parked on the lawn. Two late-model vehicles, a sedan and an SUV, were parked on the lawn. There was no driveway. I referred to my phone's satellite view. A paved alley behind the house served to access rear-entry garages for the entire block. This house featured a two-story detached garage between the free-form swimming pool and the alley. Perhaps the garage had been converted to the film studio. Or the studio was on the second floor of the garage.

I buzzed the windows open. The Jeep's dashboard told me it was 84 degrees. A nice breeze from the south wafted through the windows.

Two boys and a girl pedaled past on colorful bicycles. I wondered why they weren't at school before I realized it was after school hours. Or the children were homeschooled. A lot of homeschooling in Texas. Also in Florida.

The palm trees rustled in the breeze.

A few minutes later, the front door opened.

I snapped several photos of the woman and man who exited. The woman appeared underage to me, but I haven't dated teenagers in the last decade. The man was fortyish. I photographed the two vehicles' license plates. Rule Six: *You never know what you'll need to know.*

The couple paid me no mind. They climbed into the sedan and drove away. Next, a classic antique convertible arrived and parked on the lawn.

I photographed the man who drove it and the convertible's license plate. The man paused on his way to the front door and peered in my direction.

I waved at him. The wave told him, "Nothing suspicious here, only a guy with nothing to hide."

The man's body language said, "Should I recognize this guy?" He waved back tentatively and continued to the front door. It was unlocked. He glanced back one last time and stood in the door. He shrugged and went inside without knocking.

I logged and photographed the comings and goings at the porn house for an hour and a half. Always at least one vehicle was parked in front and never more than four.

The Jeep's Bluetooth picked up Jorge Castellano's call. "Hey, Jorge. Thanks for calling."

"Your sister Angelina, is she the one who's the fashion model?"

"Yes, and she's also missing."

"Sorry I was so long getting back to you, amigo. I was fishing offshore and just got in cellphone range."

"You on your boat?"

"Yeah. I'm a half-hour from the launch ramp."

"I need you to trace three cellphones for the last two months."

"Whose are they?"

"Angelina McCrary Garza, her husband Teodoro Garza, and their next-door neighbor, Lola Salazar. Lola is the last person I've uncovered who saw Angie before she disappeared."

"Text me the numbers and I'll do it at the precinct."

"And Jorge…" I paused.

"Yeah, yeah. Keep it off the books."

"*Gracias*, amigo."

I returned to my stakeout.

The sun dipped behind the house next door. Shadows lengthened. The day was nearly over. Two men walked out the front door. The previous men who entered or left the house were youngish, slender, and attractive. These men were fortyish, muscular, and decidedly not attractive. Despite the heat, they wore jackets that bulged over their holstered guns.

Look up *thug* in the dictionary and you'll see their pictures. Someone inside the house had noticed my presence and taken exception to me being there. Perhaps they had something to hide other than the obvious.

I didn't carry weapons on the cruise, and I flew straight to Houston from the cruise ship. I didn't even have a knife to take to a gunfight. Not good odds and nothing to gain.

Time for a strategic retreat. That was okay; I was hungry again. I cranked the Jeep and slipped it in gear. In the rearview mirror I could see the two heavies staring at my Jeep. One raised his phone to snap a picture. I wasn't the only one who recorded license plates.

As I traveled from the porn house to Angie's apartment, the neighborhood grew progressively worse: dilapidated fences, cracked sidewalks or none at all, buildings in need of paint, and abandoned vehicles sprouting from the weeds in overgrown yards. In the last block of the trip, conditions improved immediately near Angie's apartment. It was a blue-collar island in a low-class sea.

Copious opportunities in the neighborhood for Angie to get in trouble.

I queried my phone for Mexican restaurants nearby and selected one with good ratings. I wouldn't consume any food or drink at the party but didn't want to be hungry in case something unexpected happened.

After dinner, I returned to my hotel for a nap and set my alarm for ten p.m. Being well-rested is nearly as important as being well-armed. I debated a trip to a gun store but decided to wait. I didn't plan to do anything rash at the party. Mainly talk with, and listen to, people with their guard lowered.

It turned out my crystal ball was cloudy.

FOUR

The visitor parking at Lola Salazar's apartment complex was full. Vehicles spilled out onto the street.

People crowded the second-floor walkway in front of Lola's apartment. Some danced to music I couldn't hear through the Jeep's closed windows. Two women sat a few steps up the stairway. They schmoozed with three men who stood at the bottom. A dozen in the driveway chattered, smoked, and drank. Some smoked cigarettes; others joints. No one seemed concerned about being arrested.

I idled along the driveway, dodging the party guests, until I reached Angelina's assigned parking spaces. A late-model Mercedes occupied one. Three Harley-Davidson motorcycles filled the other. One Harley featured a license plate from the Mexican state of Coahuila.

Across the lot another parking spot held four motorcycles, all with Texas plates.

I parked half a block down the street and walked back to Lola's apartment. I wended my way through the people at the bottom of the stairs, dodged the two women on the steps, and wedged my way through the crowd at Lola's door.

The music was louder inside, but manageable. The scents of perfume, beer, and body odor overlaid the cigarettes and marijuana smoke that clouded the rooms. I tried not to breathe deeply.

Scanning the congested living room, I dodged my way toward the hallway. I sidestepped through the throng until Lola's roommate blocked my way.

Tommy No-name still wore no shirt; instead, he wore a denim vest with a Harley-Davidson logo and a Mexican flag patch. His left earlobe featured another tiny Mexican flag. His right carried a gold hangman's noose. His Harley-Davidson motorcycle boots hadn't been shined since the Obama administration. Shabby chic.

A dark leather belt with a stainless-steel wallet chain held up Tommy's black denim pants. The wallet chain disappeared into a pocket, a classic biker cliché. There were a couple other biker types in the room.

Tommy wore a silver necklace holding a coke spoon made from a crucifix. A twin to the one I found in Angie's closet. A variety of odors from Tommy's breath and body assaulted my nose. I instinctively moved a half-step back.

"What are you doing here, asshole?" Tommy must not have wanted to make a new friend.

"It's nice to see you too, Tommy." I gave him a crocodile smile. "Lola invited me. What are you doing here?"

Tommy's face reddened. "I live here, smart ass, and me and Lola, we had enough trouble from Angie. Do yourself a favor. Stay the hell away from Lola, okay? Otherwise, you could get hurt. Lola don't need to get involved with whatever crap you're planning."

"My plan is to locate my sister. Do you know where she is?"

"Screw you, asshole. Stay away or you'll regret interfering." He pushed past me and melted into the crowd.

Tougher men than Tommy No-name have warned me off. I surveyed the room. The other men dressed like bikers had disappeared down the hall. I stepped into the hallway. The bikers were not in sight.

Lola leaned against a bedroom wall chatting with a woman with purple hair. Both women pulsated, bobbing to the music blasting from the living room.

They were already high. Good thing I hadn't waited until later to arrive. Lola might have been crashed in a corner somewhere.

Lola spotted me over Purple Hair's shoulder. She grinned, squeezed past the woman, and tottered toward me. She clasped the front of my shirt. Lola wore a low-cut shirt that displayed the top of the elaborate tattoos on her breasts. A cocaine spoon on a gold necklace hung in her cleavage. It was made from a crucifix. "I'm glad you made it, Chucky."

I placed my hands over Lola's and rubbed them. "I love a good time."

She tugged me closer. "You're in the right place, hot stuff." She stood on tiptoes and kissed my neck, too short to reach my lips. I smiled but kept my mouth out of reach. No telling where her mouth had been.

She staggered a bit, and I grasped her arm to steady her.

"We should talk, Lola my lovely. Someplace more private."

"I know just the place." She gripped my hand and led me to a closed door. Then yanked me behind her and knocked on the door twice. "Come out, come out, whoever you are," she sang. "It's our turn." She leaned backwards against me and ground her hips against my pelvis. No doubt what she was after. She stretched up and back with her other hand and stroked my hair.

The door opened and two men and a woman wobbled out.

Lola dragged me into the bedroom and locked the door. She wrapped her arms around my neck and nuzzled me. "Let's party."

She giggled, reaching into a pocket and extracting a baggie of white powder. With practiced fingers, she opened the baggie and dipped the coke spoon in, scooping the powder and sealing the baggie with one hand. She pressed a finger to close one nostril. Holding the coke spoon to her other nostril, she sniffed the powder up her nose. *Poof*, it vanished.

She drew a deep breath and smiled. "Want a hit, Chucky Lucky? This snow is the real McCoy for a real McCrary. Get it?"

"Do you do cocaine with Angie?"

"Sure. I like Angie, and she likes me. We do lots of things together. We're besties."

I lifted Lola's coke spoon with a finger. "What a curious spoon. Tommy wears a similar one as a necklace and I found one in Angie's closet."

Lola squinted at the spoon. She struggled to focus her eyes. "Oh, yeah. That's right. He gave one of them to Angie."

"Who gave it to her? Tommy?"

She opened her mouth to speak, then stopped. "Tommy? That cheap-skate never gave nobody nothing but grief."

"Then who gave Angie her spoon?"

Lola's eyes started to close, and she jerked them open.

I was afraid she would pass out before she replied. I let the spoon hang between her breasts and wrapped my arms around her to prop her up. I gripped her buttocks with both hands. "I want some of that 'real McCoy'. I can't buy good quality blow in Adams Creek. Small town, and the cops know everybody. Where'd you get it?"

She leaned against me and nuzzled my neck. "Russell. Angie hooked me up with him. Russell's been selling us high-quality blow since Thanks-giving. He gave me and Angie the spoons for a present."

"When was that?"

"Last New Year's Eve. He called it a late Christmas present. That's the joke, see?" She fondled the coke spoon. "Christmas is when Jesus was born, and the crucifix is when he died."

She dropped the spoon and licked my neck. "Speaking of Christmas, I have a present for you. You're gonna *love* it." She tried to guide me toward the bed.

I didn't move. "Is Russell his first name or his last?"

Lola leaned back and tried to focus on my face. "What difference does it make? He don't take checks. He's just 'Russell.' You want his number?"

"Sure."

Lola licked her lips. "I'll give it to you when you take me to that bed." She winked. "Let's party, Chucky; it's time to get lucky." She fumbled for my belt buckle. "Lucky Chucky."

No way would I be intimate with Lola Salazar. I wasn't averse to sexual performance in the line of duty. I had consorted with a prostitute during a case where I flew to a Caribbean banana republic. I went under-cover as a gangster from Mexico City. No, it was that I wouldn't risk unprotected sex or a wet kiss with a woman who indicated she was both promiscuous and irresponsible.

I clasped Lola's hands and stopped her from unfastening my belt. "Give me Russell's number first."

"What the hell...find it yourself." She handed me her phone. "It's in my contacts."

She fell back on the bed, eyes closed, and began to snore softly.

I scrolled through Lola's contacts. Most entries were first names or nicknames. Few included surnames. I forwarded Russell's info to my phone. I forwarded Tommy's info also. His entry showed no surname either. I would add Lola's contacts to the ping list I sent Jorge Castellano.

I read her recent messages. There was a group of messages with Russell last weekend regarding "exchanging presents." Another referred to "meeting U and A." Could the A mean Angie?

I glanced at Lola lying on the bed. I searched her pockets, extracted the baggie of cocaine, and slipped it in my pocket. I left the room to locate Tommy.

Tommy stood on the porch with a woman. They lounged against the rail and passed a joint between them, conversing in Spanish. I didn't recognize Tommy's accent. Maybe he was the biker from Coahuila. The woman's accent was Puerto Rican. The joint was down to a nub.

I paused eight feet away and waited for Tommy to move away from the woman. I didn't care to make him madder by interrupting.

Tommy inhaled one last hit on the joint and dropped it to the walkway. He pushed off the rail and stumbled to the stairway. He wobbled to a Harley parked in Angie's assigned spot with me behind him. It was the Coahuila bike I had cruised past earlier.

If that was Tommy's bike, did he park in Angie's assigned spot because he knew she wasn't coming back?

Two other men dressed in motorcycle attire sat on the other bikes. They wore Harley-Davidson boots, but different styles than Tommy's. They nodded to him.

Stopping six feet from Tommy, I cleared my throat.

Tommy peered at me, then at the other bikers. He returned his focus to me. "Why are you following me, asshole?"

The other men dismounted and stepped closer.

One man was pudgy, with a long, bushy beard and hair. He reminded me of Grizzly Adams, but without the smile. Grizzly was drinking a Mexican beer. The other biker was so lean his shaved head resembled a skull. Skinhead was smoking a joint.

The two bikers stepped around their bikes to stand on either side of Tommy. Skinhead tossed his joint, pulled a switchblade, and snicked it open. Grizzly crushed his beer can, slid his belt off, and wrapped it around his fist. The sharp-edged buckle swung like a mace at the end of the leather strap.

I regretted not making that trip to the gun shop. Defense-wise, I was practically naked. Except for my fists, elbows, and feet. And my head.

Note to self: Next time make it a priority to be armed.

My dad says, "Son, you're so good at fighting that there's a tendency to use your fists instead of your head. But fighting should never be your first choice. Try to solve controversy with discussion before using fisticuffs. Easier on the cuts and bruises to boot."

Good advice, so I tried to deescalate the situation. "I came to apologize for any trouble my sister Angie caused."

"The damage is done, asshole. Saco heard what she did. Your meddling makes it worse."

"Tommy, I don't give a rat's ass if you are dealing drugs. I'm no threat to you unless you interfere with me finding my sister. I'm only here for Angelina."

"Too late, asshole. You don't want to come to the attention of certain people—people you don't mess with. Now we..." He glanced at the men on either side. "...we will make sure you don't interfere no more. Ever."

"You should rethink that, Tommy. I don't intend to permanently damage you or your buddies, but if three of you attack, I'll smash, crash, and trash all of you. You could find yourself in the hospital. Or worse. Don't push me."

My hand-to-hand combat instructor's voice spoke in my memory: "Where an enemy has you outnumbered, you should consider it a target-rich environment."

My trainers in the Special Forces taught me moves, countermoves, weak points in the human body, and how to exploit them. But the first thing they taught me was *mindset*. In combat, there is one rule: *Survive*. Ideas of fairness from the boxing world or the wrestling ring become disadvantages when you fight for your life.

Rules make you hesitate. Hesitation gets you killed.

Tommy tensed.

"This is your chance to walk away," I said. "Don't do something you and your friends will regret."

Tommy telegraphed his attack by sliding his right foot back. He aimed a right-handed punch.

I sidestepped and seized his wrist. I used his momentum to fling him toward the Mercedes parked in the next spot. His head slammed into the rear door, and its car alarm shrieked.

I caught Skinhead's wrist above the switchblade, swung his arm high, rotated under the uplifted arm, and pitched him over my shoulder in Tommy's direction. As he flew over my shoulder, I clutched his knife-holding wrist with my other hand and twisted the forearm the opposite direction. His elbow bent the wrong way and the joint snapped.

Pivoting to Grizzly with his swinging belt buckle, I caught the belt above the buckle and jerked the biker forward. Stiffening my fingers like a shovel blade, I thrust my hand like a battering ram, past the fat and into Grizzly's solar plexus. It's better to punch soft tissue with your hand than a jawbone or the side of the head. Less likely to break a finger or knuckle.

The biker doubled over. Experience told me Grizzly would barf within a few seconds. I booted him in the testicles and stepped back.

The fat man fell, vomiting on the way to the pavement.

I booted Grizzly in the ear. Then I kicked him in the kidney. They had been warned.

Skinhead tried to stand. I booted him in the ribs hard enough to put him in the hospital, but not hard enough to puncture a lung. Then I kicked him in the stomach, but soft enough not to rupture an internal organ.

I scanned the pavement until I spotted the switchblade. I stepped on the blade and lifted the handle, breaking the knife.

I yelled over the car alarm. "You didn't need to fight me, Tommy. I want to talk. Let's step away from this noise." I tried to help him off the pavement.

He jerked his arm away. His nose was bloody where he'd slammed into the car. "Leave me alone, asshole."

"You said 'Saco heard what she did.' Who is Saco and what did Angie do?"

"You don't want to know who Saco is, asshole."

"I do if he had anything to do with my sister's disappearance."

Tommy tried to sit up and fell back, bumping his head on the pavement. His head lolled to one side, and he stopped moving.

I felt his pulse. It was strong, I straightened his neck and limbs to make him comfortable. I needed him alive so I could get more information.

Even the world's greatest PI can't question an unconscious person. Fortunately, there were other ways to obtain information.

I tugged the stainless-steel chain that secured Tommy's wallet to his belt. Opening the wallet, I photographed his driver's license. Thomas Valley was the name, and his license was from Texas even though his motorcycle was from Coahuila.

Searching further, I discovered a Mexican driver's license with a Coahuila address which I photographed. The name was Tomás Valenzuela. The wallet held several hundred-dollar bills and some smaller bills. I removed the hundreds and ignored the smaller bills. Spoils of the war that Valley started.

Frisking Valley, I discovered two cellphones, a Samsung and an iPhone. The iPhone was locked. I pressed Valley's thumb to the screen; the phone unlocked. The Samsung was already unlocked. I could keep the batteries charged, and the phones should stay unlocked indefinitely. I slipped the phones into my pocket. Rummaging in Valley's bike storage compartment, I found a three-headed phone charger. I stuffed it in my pocket too.

I searched Grizzly and Skinhead, photographed their Texas driver's licenses, and discovered two more cellphones which I kept. I removed the hundreds from their wallets also. All's fair in love and war. The name on Grizzly's license was Alejandro Fajardo; the name on Skinhead's was Ronald Trojanik.

I photographed the three bikers, including their tattoos, clothes, and boots. I photographed the other motorcycles in the area. Rule Six: *You never know what you'll need to know.*

Time to check whether Jorge Castellano had sent the cellphone information I requested and return to my motel.

FIVE

Tommy Valley

Tommy Valley shivered and rolled his neck to one side then the other. What was wrong with the damned pillow? It didn't feel right. He tried to roll over and the rough pavement grated his palms and elbows. That wasn't right either. He smelled vomit and gasoline and blood and marijuana and tire rubber. He opened his eyes and winced at the bright streetlight above him in the black sky.

What the hell?

He tried to stand, kicking off a splitting headache worse than any he could recall ever. He waved his hand, and it slapped his motorcycle wheel.

Now he remembered. He was in a fight. Who with? Ah, Angelina Garza's brother. What the hell was the asshole's name? Carlos something-or-other. He tried to sit up again and couldn't.

He touched his nose. It hurt and it was sticky. He peered at his fingers. Blood, semi-dried. He rubbed his cheek with his other hand and checked his fingers. More blood. Oh, yeah. He glanced at the Mercedes beside him. A red smear marked the rear door a foot from the pavement.

He recollected now. Not even a fight. More of an annihilation. He hadn't landed a single punch. He'd swung his fist and found himself flying toward the Mercedes. That's all he recalled.

Valley shoved himself to a seated position. He rolled over to his hands and knees, his muscles protesting. Every sinew in his body ached but he couldn't stay there. The pavement dug into his kneecaps through his jeans as he struggled to his feet.

He reached for what he considered his American cellphone. Gone. How did he lose it? He cast his eyes around the lot. Did he drop it? No. He had used the phone in his apartment, then he'd stuck it in his pocket. Did Angie Garza's brother steal it? The phone stored his customers' contact information. Okay, everything was backed up online and he could buy another phone and download the info from the Cloud, but that was lots of trouble.

He patted his other pocket for his Mexican cellphone. Also missing. That was worse than losing the American phone. The Mexican phone held his supplier contacts.

What the hell was Angie's brother going to do with his cellphones?

He didn't dare tell Saco. If Saco learned that Valley lost his phone to this Carlos, and that Carlos had Saco's cellphone number, he would kill Valley for sure. Maybe even send him to the chipper to make an example of him. He shuddered at the thought.

If the Mexican phone fell into the hands of the American police, Saco would go on the warpath. Actually, if either phone did, Saco would explode with anger. First, Valley couldn't find Angelina Garza's phone, and now he had lost his own phones.

And the big score was less than two weeks away.

The solution was inescapable: Saco must never find out, even after the big score was over. Saco would still kill him.

On the other hand, after the score, Valley would be where Saco would never find him. All Valley had to do was not do anything stupid.

Valley could buy new phones identical to the ones he lost and restore his files. Saco would never find out.

Valley was so intent on his missing phones that he hadn't noticed Fajardo and Trojanik sprawled on the pavement. Fajardo's belt lay limp in his right hand. Trojanik groaned and held his ribs on the left side. Blood trailed in a long red streak from his bald scalp toward the small puddle of blood where his head rested on the pavement.

My God, Carlos had hammered the three of them. Was Carlos that good, or were he and his buddies that bad?

Valley needed to hide while he healed, replaced the phones, and restored the files. He knew a place. He touched his back pockets. His wallet was backwards to the way he normally carried it. Carlos had opened his wallet. Why did he do that? He thumbed through the bills. All of his hundreds were missing. Assuming Carlos stole the money, why didn't he steal the smaller bills? And who stole his phones? Carlos said he wasn't interested in Valley's drug business. Could a stranger have happened by, found him unconscious, and taken advantage of the situation? He might never learn the answer, but it didn't matter.

Valley threw his leg over the bike saddle. Jabbing the keys in the ignition, he growled the Harley to life and thundered off.

Neither Carlos nor Saco would find him, by God.

SIX

Carlos McCrary

S aturday morning, I slept until ten o'clock—unbelievably late for me.
My sister had been missing almost a week. The odds of finding her alive had shrunk with every day she was gone. I was almost to the point of hoping just to recover her body.

Facing that ghastly prospect, I emailed my parents that Angie was into cocaine and that I knew her dealer's name. I told them a higher-up drug dealer with a bad reputation was angry with Angie. If I never found her, that foreshadowing might soften the blow if Angie never came back.

I checked my email. Jorge had sent me the track maps of the three cell-phones for the last 60 days with the addresses or GPS coordinates for every stop each phone made. Also a text:

Haven't tackled Russell's and Tommy's phone numbers yet. Kinda busy with unimportant things like CRIME in Port City. In case you forgot, the Port City taxpayers pay me more than you do.

He ended the text with a winking happy face icon.

Teodoro's phone had the shortest track. I cross-referenced the final map coordinates: Flathead Pipe Supply. An internet search revealed the company was an oil casing, drill pipe, and tubing company in an industrial neighborhood east of town near the San Jacinto River. Teodoro's phone dropped off the network on March 15 at 10:53 p.m. The Ides of March, when Julius Caesar was assassinated according to Shakespear.

Angelina's and Lola Salazar's phones had rambled over half the city in the last two months.

Angelina's phone stopped moving at 2:32 a.m. on Monday, May fourth, at GPS coordinates that identified a spot a mile from the nearest entrance or exit on the Sam Houston Parkway, a toll road that looped around Houston. That was an hour after she had called my phone. When she left her voicemail, her phone was at a truckstop beside the Sam Houston Parkway. After stopping on the Parkway, the phone sat there until Tuesday morning at 11:16 a.m. when its battery played out. What happened in the hour between the voicemail message and the phone stopping on the Parkway? Where was she going? Was Tommy chasing her? Was she even driving her own car at that point?

Lola Salazar's and Angie's tracks needed a detailed analysis, but first, I needed to gear up. Rule Nine: *You can never carry too much firepower.*

I drove to a large gun store named The Armory.

An eager young man stood behind a counter in a black polo shirt and khaki pants. *The Armory* was printed across the shirt in gold letters.

"Can I help you, sir?"

"If you work on commission, I will make your day. Better fetch a sheet of paper and a pen."

"Yes, sir." The clerk reached under the counter for an order form. "What do you need, sir?"

I showed him my Florida driver's license and Concealed Weapon Permit. "You can use these in lieu of a background check. I want a Glock 17 with three extra magazines, a clip-on holster, 400 rounds of ammunition, a magazine speed loader, a Browning .380 with an ankle holster and 200 rounds, a concealable ceramic knife with a forearm scabbard, and a floating armored vest."

"Do you need a speed loader for the Browning magazine, sir?"

"No. Both pistols are the same caliber."

"Oops. I should know that."

"*Nah.* You can't remember everything, my friend. I'm familiar with those two pistols."

Thirty minutes later, I clipped a Glock 17 to my belt. I also strapped on a Browning .380 in an ankle holster, a ceramic knife to my left forearm, and a Ka-Bar knife strapped to my left calf.

"Geez, mister, you're a walking arsenal."

"I suffer from an inferiority complex."

The clerk grinned. "I doubt that, but thanks for the business. Anything else we can do for you?"

"I need a bug detector. Do you sell those?"

"No, but I know an electronics store nearby where you can buy spy equipment." He wrote down the name and address.

————

After buying the bug detector and a box of GPS trackers, I found a bookstore and bought the largest paper map they carried of Houston and Harris County, Texas, and markers in different colors.

I returned to the car rental office and swapped the blue Jeep for a silver Toyota 4Runner.

"Was there anything wrong with the Jeep, Mr. McCrary?" the clerk asked.

The real reason was the two goons at the porn palace had photographed the Jeep. "No. It was a fine vehicle, but a friend told me he loved his 4Runner, so I decided to try one."

"Okay. Have a nice day, Mr. McCrary."

I needed to discover who Saco was. He was upset with Angie: That much I knew even if I didn't know why. I could ask Lola when she was high. Rule Twelve-A: *In vino, veritas.* Perhaps that also applied when someone was high on drugs.

Until then, I needed someone with local knowledge who wasn't afraid to talk to me about Saco.

Fortunately, I had a friend with local knowledge. In fact, I had known her since middle school.

———

Bettina Simpson

After a breakfast of raisin bran and coffee with skim milk and sugar substitute, Bettina Simpson admitted it was time to dress, though she dreaded the prospect. She had lived alone since she divorced Barry the Bastard five months ago. She shouldn't spend another weekend binge-watching rom-com movies in her pajamas. People would suspect she was a recluse. Especially her parents.

She trudged to her bedroom suite. Bettina used the larger closet for everyday clothes. She used the smaller one for items she seldom or never wore: three bridesmaid's dresses she had worn at the three weddings she had been in—other than her own ill-fated one—ski clothes and the fur-lined parka she had bought for a ski trip fourteen years ago and never worn since.

She kept the dirty clothes hamper in the smaller closet.

Bettina stepped into her closet, hung her sleep shorts and tee-shirt, and considered the almost bare shelves and numerous empty clothes hangers.

Laundry was far down her list of favorite things to do, ranking right above changing a flat tire and dancing the polka with her Uncle Orville. That's why her closet was bare of clean clothes; she had procrastinated for three weeks. She was down to her last pair of clean panties and out of her nicer pants and blouses. She dreaded the prospect of going commando and wearing outer clothes she should donate to the poor.

She felt strangely vulnerable walking naked to the other closet where she confronted her overflowing dirty clothes hamper. "Am I strong enough to lift you?" she asked aloud. Her own voice startled her. She lightened the task by sorting the whites and colors on the floor and carrying the hamper full of whites first. She staggered to the utility space wedged behind double doors beside her kitchen.

She didn't recall ever walking through her condo and doing laundry naked before. It felt uncomfortable but strangely liberating to do it consciously.

The air-conditioning switched on. The cool air raised goosebumps on her skin—she felt exposed. She told herself she was silly. There was no one else there. No one to see her but God. Somehow, that didn't comfort her.

The cellphone rang on her nightstand, and she hurried to the bedroom. The ringtone told her it was a voice call. Thank goodness it wasn't her parents. They usually made video calls each weekend. They would say, "We like to see our lovely daughter's pretty face." Then, "You should go out more, Bettina. Losing Barry wasn't the end of your life. Somewhere out there is the man for you, but you're not going to meet him moping around your apartment."

She had met Barry and done the expected thing. Her parents reminded her that her biological clock was ticking. Her mother told her she was supposed to want children. Barry had been available and acceptable to her family. And he seemed to want children.

She snatched the phone and touched the speaker button.

"This is Bettina."

"Bettina, it's Chuck McCrary. Remember me?"

She glanced at the phone. Chuck's picture she'd snapped five years earlier showed on the screen. In a flash she recalled the last night he spent in her guestroom at her old apartment. Remembered the way she'd ached for him even though he was in a relationship with a woman in Port City. What was her name?... Terry something-or-other. Five years was a long time for a relationship to last. Perhaps the Terry relationship was over. Perhaps this time...

She glanced in the mirror, surprised. She was blushing like a pink rose from head to foot. Parts of her body stirred that had lain dormant since her divorce. Chuck had affected her like that even in high school—heck, even in *middle* school for goodness' sake. Why was Chuck McCrary calling her after five years? Was it the booty call she'd dreamed of since high school? She chuckled. One way to find out...

She held the phone to her ear.

"Will wonders never cease? It's the long-lost Carlos McCrary, man of mystery. The man who entered my life following an absence of ten years, camped a few days in my guestroom, and shamelessly used my police contacts. Then he disappeared without a trace. I should be mad at you, buster. You've been a ghost for five years."

The instant she said that, she regretted it. *Don't run him off, you idiot.*

"Didn't you receive the flowers I sent to your desk at the police station every Valentine's Day?"

"Yes, but you never called." Bettina regretted the whiney complaint the instant she said it. Why did she say the wrong things? She would have welcomed Chuck into her life on any terms, even for a short time. *Don't blow it, stupid.*

"To tell the truth, Chuck. I didn't call you either. Are you in town?"

"Yeah. I flew in Thursday night. I'm in Houston for a while."

Her cheeks felt hot. Since the divorce, she hadn't felt like dating. Chuck reappearing was a sign from above. That is, assuming he was single. If he wasn't, she could offer him her guestroom for another platonic visit. He was an old classmate from high school. That was worth something, wasn't it? And friendships sometimes developed into romantic relationships. Sometimes…

"Business trip or pleasure?"

"Hard to say. Call it personal business. You remember my sister Angelina?"

"Sure. She was about two years ahead of us, wasn't she?"

"Yes. I'm here because Angie is missing. So is her husband, Teodoro Garza."

"I didn't know her very well. Angie was the Homecoming Queen and Head Cheerleader type, and I was the captain of the volleyball team. Angie was the one to ask for tips on makeup and hair styles. I was more interested in improving my volleyball smash. So, you came to Houston to search for them?"

"Mainly I'm searching for Angie. Teodoro and I don't get along."

"Where are you staying?"

He told her.

"Never heard of it. Where is it located?"

Chuck gave her the address.

"That's not a good neighborhood. Why there?"

"It was 3:00 a.m. by the time I finished searching Angie's apartment, and it was the closest motel. It's a Château El Cheapo. I'll rent a better motel this afternoon, but the last two days I've been too busy."

"You're not staying one more night at a motel. Not when I have a guestroom. You'll stay with me for the duration, no matter how long it is. And you will make no objections. Are we clear on that?"

"Okay. You won't get an argument from me."

"Come for lunch and we can discuss your sister, and I can yell at you for ignoring me for five years. Deal?"

"But aren't you mad at me?"

"You still don't understand squat about women, do you, Chuck?"

"Guilty as charged."

"Where are you?"

"I'm in my rented Toyota 4Runner in front of the apartments where Angie and her husband live." He gave her the address.

"I know the neighborhood. You eaten lunch?"

"Not yet."

"I'll make enchiladas."

"You remember me well."

"Good. Since I saw you last, I bought a condo."

She debated telling Chuck she had married and divorced. No, better to avoid any unnecessary complication. He had agreed to lunch. Take the win. Don't give him an excuse to change his mind.

"I'll text you my address. I'm off this weekend. In fact, I'm standing here stark naked doing laundry. I need an hour to get decent and cook lunch." Let Chuck ponder that mental image for the next hour.

Couldn't hurt, even if he was in a relationship. She chuckled. *Especially* if he was in a relationship, she amended. Chuck McCrary checked all her boxes except he didn't live in Houston. But he was born and raised in Adams Creek like her. Maybe he missed Texas. You never know… The world was survival of the fittest—every woman for herself.

She had missed out on Chuck in high school when Liz Johannes got her hooks into him. She missed again when he came to Houston five years earlier to work on the Simonetti case.

They always say *Third time's the charm*.

Bettina's doorbell rang at one o'clock. She glanced at the door camera view on her cellphone and smiled. Chuck carried flowers. He had done the same thing five years before when he first arrived at her old apartment.

She opened the door, and he handed her the bouquet, still wrapped in cellophane from the supermarket. "I hope you enjoy these."

Bettina grinned. "Like last time."

She accepted the flowers in one hand and touched the back of his neck with the other. She drew his head down to kiss his cheek. *Anything more might be excessive after five years. Hell, he might even be married. He probably expects to stay in the guestroom again.*

She glanced at his left hand. No ring, but he could be in a relationship in Port City. Another relationship kept Chuck away from her the last time. She swung the door wider. "It's great to see you. You look great. Haven't changed a bit."

"You look great too. I seem to remember that you had darker hair five years ago."

Bettina fluffed her hair with one had. "A few months ago, I decided to test whether blondes have more fun." She had lightened her hair after divorcing Barry the Bastard. Turning over a new leaf.

Chuck laughed. "Well, are you having more fun now?"

"Well, you're here. That's certainly more fun than I was having before you came to Houston." She turned aside. "Let's go put these in water."

Chuck trailed her to the kitchen. "Didn't you plan to yell at me because I haven't called you the last five years?"

She waved a hand. "Oh, my complaint was *pro forma*. Ours was an alliance to solve a crime while we worked on your case. You and I never had a romance. I was surprised you sent the card and flowers each Valentine's Day. I never gave you another thought except when the flowers arrived." Well, that was almost true.

She opened a kitchen cabinet. "Hand me the vase on the top shelf."

Chuck lifted a ceramic vase shaped like a tall wicker basket off the shelf. "Is this the same one?"

"Yep. That's the one I put your flowers in five years ago. You have a good memory."

"After all, I *am* the world's greatest PI."

She pointed. "Scissors are in that drawer. Cut one inch off each stem and arrange them in the vase. I'll add the water and the preservative."

Chuck carried the flowers to the dining room table.

"Where's your luggage?"

"In the 4Runner. Are you sure you want me to stay? I don't want to intrude."

"Don't be silly. You said last time: 'What are friends for if you can't use and abuse them occasionally?' I put an enchilada casserole in the oven. It'll be ready in twenty minutes."

She opened a cabinet and handed him a bottle of wine. "Open this and we'll take a couple of glasses to the living room."

Five minutes later, they were in the living room. Bettina sat on the couch. She wished Chuck would sit next to her, but he sat on the upholstered chair.

Oh God, was he involved with someone? If so, she would give him the guestroom instead of sharing her bedroom. It would be nice to have a man in the house regardless, and Chuck was a friend and fun to be with even though she hadn't talked to him for five years.

"What shall we toast, Chuck?"

"To renewing old friendships."

"Good one. Let's renew an old friendship." They clinked glasses.

Bettina plunged ahead. "Chuck, since you were last here, have you gotten married?"

"No. I would've told you instead of sending you Valentine flowers."

"That makes sense. Are you seeing anyone else? Like a steady girlfriend?"

"Three days ago, the answer would have been yes. But now... I'm not sure."

Her breath caught in her lungs. Not sure? "Did something happen three days ago?"

"For the last six months I've been dating a woman named Ruby Voight. In fact, Ruby and I were on a Caribbean cruise earlier this week when I learned Angelina was missing. We cut the cruise short in Cozumel on Thursday. I flew to Houston, and she flew to Austin to visit her parents. She was pretty pissed off. I'll try to mend fences once I locate Angelina and return home."

"If I were a polite person, I'd wish you good luck with that, but since I've had a crush on you since high school, I will wish you good luck in finding your sister."

There, she'd said it. She'd risked rejection and put her feelings right in front of him. No guts, no blue chips.

Now the ball was in his court.

———

Over a plate of enchiladas, they summarized events from the last five years, except Bettina still didn't mention her failed marriage.

"I didn't tell you, Chuck, but I'm a detective sergeant in the Burglary and Theft Division."

"Congratulations. Last time we talked, you were a patrol cop. What made you decide to become a detective?"

"You did. Working with you on that crooked lawyer case was more interesting than patrolling the streets in a black-and-white. I made detective three years ago." She laid a hand on Chuck's forearm. "Now I have direct access to police resources, and I don't need to ask a detective friend for a favor. I can do the work for you myself."

"You mean you'll help me find my sister?"

"We're friends, aren't we? Help goes with the territory." She lifted her wine glass in a toast motion. "To friendship."

"To friendship," he responded.

"After you left five years ago, I followed the Simonetti murder case on the internet. Renate Crowell wrote a long article on the murder, and I figured you were the 'person knowledgeable about the case' she quoted. Since then, I Google you occasionally. When that crooked cop tried to frame you for murder, then tried to kill you, I downloaded all the newspaper accounts."

"It's marvelous how much you learn on the internet." He grinned. "Some of it is even true."

"And your buddy Bob Martinez won the Super Bowl. I figured you were connected with the rumors surrounding his fiancée."

"My buddy Snoop Snopolski and I did rescue her from kidnappers. That's a matter of public record. I neither confirm nor deny anything you heard or imagined *vis-à-vis* the Super Bowl."

Bettina shrugged. "Doesn't matter. I read about the New Jersey gangsters who killed each other in a gunfight on Mango Island the night before the Super Bowl. The cops concluded the dead mobsters killed each other." She peered at him and raised one eyebrow. "I won't bother to ask whether you were involved."

Chuck ate another bite. "These enchiladas are delicious."

"Then there was the gunfight in the old phosphate mine in the Everglades where you and your buddy Ray Snopolski killed four Chicago assassins."

"Yeah, that was a real butt-pucker situation. For future reference, nobody calls him Ray. His nickname is *Snoop*. He was a homicide cop for thirty years. He taught me most of what I've learned about being an investigator. I hope you'll meet him someday."

"In the event I visit Port City, I'd like that. Later you and Tank Tyler rescued the woman kidnapped by that loan shark and those Asian women who were smuggled into the country and forced into the sex trade."

"Am I blushing with embarrassment?"

"The point is, Chuck, that I've followed your career despite not talking to you for years."

Chuck lowered his fork. "I notice you didn't mention Miyoki Takashi, my fiancée, who was kidnapped and seriously wounded."

Bettina laid her fingers on the back of his hand. "I cannot imagine how hard that was."

McCrary's eyes filled. "Excuse me please." He left the table. A few minutes later he returned.

"Sorry."

Bettina waved it off. "I shouldn't prattle on about your past. I apologize. Let's change the subject."

They continued to play *catch up*, but she could not bring herself to reveal her failed marriage. Perhaps later. Or not.

————

Carlos McCrary

I rinsed the lunch dishes and loaded Bettina's dishwasher.

"You didn't need to do that, Chuck."

"My parents taught me to be the type of guest that people invite back. Point me to where the coffee fixings are, and I'll make the coffee. Then I'll brief you regarding the case. You might notice something I missed. Okay?"

"Sure." She opened a cabinet door and gestured. "Grinder, beans, filters. Go for it. I'll fetch the mugs."

Eight minutes later, we returned to the living room with Bettina carrying coffee service on a tray.

Bettina poured my coffee, then her own.

"Tell me what you've learned so far,"

I related my search of Angie's apartment and meeting Lola Salazar.

"Lola invited me to a party at her apartment last night." I told Bettina everything I had done and discovered. "There is a gangster named Saco who is angry with Angie. He scares everybody he deals with. I asked Tommy Valley who Saco was, and he clammed up. He regretted telling me Saco's name and told me to forget Saco for my own good. Does the name Saco mean anything to you?"

Bettina stroked her chin with a thumb and forefinger. "Scuttlebutt in the Houston PD is that Saco is an upper-level chief in the *Tres Equis* Mexican drug cartel. Maybe even the big chief. If he's in Houston, you should tell our Organized Crime Unit. They've tried to arrest him for years, but he seldom visits the States. OCU never seems to learn of his visits until they're over, and Saco is back in Coahuila. Could he be connected with whoever searched Angie's apartment?"

"I only know that the intruder probably had a key to Angie's apartment."

"No evidence of forced entry, huh?"

"Right. I don't know where Saco is, but it's good to know who and what he is in case I hear his name again."

"When did you last hear from Angie?"

"She left me a voicemail at 2:30 a.m., Eastern Time, on Monday, May fourth. I'll play it for you."

Bettina smiled. "Star Wars Day."

"Huh?"

"Star Wars Day. *May the fourth be with you.* Get it? It's a pun on the line from Star Wars, *May the Force be with you.*"

"Oh, yeah. I forgot about that."

I sampled my coffee. "I hope I didn't make it too strong."

"It's fine. Play me your sister's message."

"Sure." I called the voicemail system, switched my phone to speaker, and played Angie's message. I sipped coffee and watched Bettina.

She leaned closer to my phone—close enough to smell her perfume. It was delightful. Did she do that on purpose? I responded in ways I did not expect.

"Play it again."

I played the message.

"Again, please." She poured a package of sugar-free sweetener into her coffee while the message played.

I was impressed that Bettina dove so deeply into the message.

"I've heard enough for now," she said. "She's been missing a week. You know the odds of locating someone who's been gone that long."

"Not good, but she may be alive. Until I find her body, I'm not giving up hope."

"Hope is an illusion that prevents us from accepting reality."

"That sounds like a quotation."

She smiled. "It's from an episode of *Downton Abbey*. The Dowager Countess said it."

"I won't give up hope. My cousin Emily was missing for four years, for crissakes. And I found her alive. Now, let's hold on to hope, because it costs us nothing to assume she's alive."

Bettina inclined her head. "Of course. Optimism costs us nothing." She clapped her hands once. "Let's consider the first part of her message. 'I have something they want.' Could be something tangible. She wasn't merely in the wrong place at the wrong time. This is more than what she saw. She has something tangible that's dangerous to these dangerous people."

Bettina's eyes widened. "Yes. It isn't that she *knows* something they don't want her to know. Or she *saw* something she shouldn't have. Those problems are simple; they kill her." She jumped. "Oh, I'm sorry Chuck. I should not have said that."

"*No problema*, Bettina. When I work on a case, I set my emotions aside the best I can. And I agree. They would kill her, but she was alive long enough to figure out they wanted this… let's call it the Doohickey. Assume someone demanded she give them the Doohickey. They threatened her. And she ran. Angie has *something*. Something tangible is out there in the wind. Something to bite them in the ass. They need to locate Angie and steal the Doohickey back before they kill her. Therefore, it's possible she's alive."

"I'm not optimistic, but for the sake of discussion, let's pretend we both are. Angie said, 'these people are dangerous.'"

"'These people' implies a level of organization. Either a street gang or an organized criminal faction. In Houston, when it's not a street gang, it's more likely a Mexican drug cartel than the Mafia. Saco could be the gangster to whom she referred."

"*Whom*?"

"Yes, *whom*. I wasn't just a volleyball jock at Teddy Roosevelt High. I made an A in Mrs. Sandifer's English class."

"To Mrs. Sandifer." I lifted my glass.

"Mrs. Sandifer," Bettina echoed.

"That's why I called you first, Bettina. You're smart and you have local knowledge. There was drug paraphernalia in Teodoro's closet. He is or was a user and Lola said he was a dealer. Lola said Angie uses cocaine."

"Yeah, I heard her sniff on the recording. The sniff could be a runny nose from crying, or…"

I finished the sentence. "From a cocaine habit. Or both."

"You noticed she wouldn't call the cops. Whatever she's ensnared in, it's illegal."

"That's why filing a missing person report might reveal enough garbage to subject Angie to a prison term. I prefer to keep this case close to my chest for now. Is that a problem for you?"

"No. I'll help you as a friend, not a police detective. I'll warn you if I consider making the case official. Another thing, your parents and mine live in the same neighborhood in Adams Creek. They're a hundred miles away. A simple two-hour trip. Why did Angie say she had nowhere else to turn? Did she call your parents?"

"No. They fought a couple of months ago about her drug use. My mother Andrea—you remember her?"

"Sure. She and your dad attended all your home football games and most of the away ones."

"Mom said Angie and Teodoro were high the last time they visited them. Angie and our parents argued over her drug use, and she told Mom to go to hell."

Bettina shook her head. "If you were the last person she could call for help, what happened to her old friends? Does she still have friends in Adams Creek?"

"Probably not. As far as I know, she never attended a high school reunion."

She squeezed my hand. "High school reunions are a great way to stay in touch with old classmates."

"It worked for you and me at least." I squeezed her hand back. "Anyhow, Lola Salazar is Angie's friend, but she's a druggie. Perhaps all Angie's Houston friends are junkies."

"Or her friends are part of the illegal activity. Even though your sister fought with your parents, she could still call them. Sounds like she was on the run when she called you, and maybe she had no way to get to Adams Creek."

"If so, she's been hiding for the last week. That's doubtful."

Bettina held both my hands. "Can I speak frankly to you?"

"Sure. My skin is thick as an alligator's."

"I plan to tell you something you need to hear."

"I'm listening."

"It may make you angry enough that you'll not want to stay here."

"I doubt that."

"You've popped into my life for at least a few days. Best case, you won't stay in Houston long, and I would hate to run you off the first hour you're here. However, I wouldn't be a true friend unless I told you this."

"My God, woman, now you've made me a little terrified. What is it?"

"When I observe you, I maintain an exterior viewpoint. In other words, I see you better than you see yourself."

I smiled. "If not *better*, at least *differently*. That's why you can give me advice."

She cleared her throat and sat straighter. "You may wonder why I'm holding your hands. It's to keep you from running once you hear what I say."

"Okay, I understand: You intend to hold me while you say whatever this is."

"Right. I may be smiling but this is a nervous smile. I'm dead serious. Okay, here goes… You said Teodoro is on drugs."

"Right."

"And Lola Salazar told you he disappeared two months ago. He's probably dead or blew town and is gone for good."

"Okay, that's a reasonable assumption, but that's not what you were hesitant to tell me. Go on."

"Your sister benefited from a solid family upbringing, the same way you and I did. But somehow, she got into drugs."

The direction Bettina was taking made me uncomfortable. I tried gently to free my hands.

She wouldn't let go. "Angie chose, for whatever reason, to use drugs. Maybe it was Teodoro's bad influence. We may never learn why. But whatever the circumstances were, she could have said 'no.' Right?"

I said nothing. There was nothing to say; she spoke the truth.

I swallowed hard. "Everyone in the McCrary family said Teodoro was wrong for Angie from the moment we met him."

"But Angie married him despite the family's opposition. Love is a powerful motivation."

"In this case, the motivation was lust, not love. Teodoro got Angie pregnant. Our parents dropped their opposition to the marriage. Three months later, Angie miscarried, but by then they had tied the knot, and the McCrary family frowns on divorce."

Bettina squeezed my hands harder and waited until I met her eyes. "And you have put your life on hold, and your career in Port City, and your relationship with Ruby, for God knows how long. You're diving into a cesspool of drugs and criminals, and risking your life, all to rescue her."

"She's family."

"Yes, and that leads to my first point. You say 'she's family' as if family is a get-out-of-jail-free card. It overrules all other considerations."

"What's wrong with that?"

"That's my second point, Chuck: It *shouldn't*. Family should be *one* factor in your decision to drop everything to rescue Angie from her own mess. Even an *important* factor, but not the *only* factor."

I stared at my hands. Bettina gripped them. I gave her hands a squeeze and lifted my gaze to her eyes. "Can I drink my coffee now?"

"You won't run out?"

"No. And I will consider carefully what you said."

"Do want me to mind my own business?"

"No. Your advice is good. It just may not be good for me."

"Your family… the rest of them are fine people, but I harbor doubts regarding Angie and her husband."

"Doubts?" I said. "What do you mean?"

"There's an old adage: You choose your friends, but you can't choose your family."

"Of course. That goes without saying."

"But the problem is that we *should* say it more often to remind ourselves that it's true. You did not *choose* your sister; she was there when you were born. Imagine Angelina was not your sister; with your present knowledge, would you choose her for a friend?"

I was stunned. I'd never considered my family in that sense. Of course, you didn't choose your family; they just *were*. They were an article of faith, like *Remember the Alamo* or *Salute the Flag*. Not to be questioned.

I mulled over my family and my in-laws in a new light. They nearly all passed muster. Given the choice, I would choose nearly all of them, even Crazy Aunt Carrie. Carrie's heart is in the right place. *Nearly* all... but what about Angelina? Was her heart in the right place? And Teodoro... he had never acted like part of the family.

I noticed that Bettina had fallen silent, waiting for my response. Would I choose Angelina for a friend?

I studied the backs of my hands. "I can't answer that, Bettina, but you've given me something to ponder."

"Angelina doesn't deserve a brother like you."

"Okay, Bettina. I take your point: Family shouldn't receive an automatic pass simply because they're family."

I lifted my coffee cup and held it.

"Chuck, you are the most complicated man I know."

"How so?"

"In middle school back in Adams Creek, you challenged the bullies on behalf of weaker students. You're a paladin—a champion for people who can't protect themselves."

"I know what a paladin is. Mrs. Sandifer's English class. I took it too."

Bettina smiled and continued. "I believe that's the real reason you joined the army. It wasn't a broken heart over Liz Johannes. Sure, Liz dumping you didn't help, but you would've joined the army eventually. And Special Forces was the way you chose to protect people."

"In grade school my dad told me I should have been born a thousand years earlier. I would have been a knight errant."

"It could be you *were* born a thousand years earlier. Perhaps you *were* a knight errant. You and Sir Lancelot. Except instead of a white charger, the twenty-first century paladin rides an SUV. Another thing is your attitude toward justice: You use the legal system to get the bad guy when possible. But if not, you put on your vigilante hat and dispense frontier justice."

She raised her hand. "Don't bother to deny it, Chuck. I can read between the lines of a police report. Most of it's on the internet. We haven't talked for the last five years, but I monitor you on the internet. I'm a cop too. In fact, I've been a cop longer than you have."

"Bettina, have you ever fired your weapon on the job?"

"Not yet. I've drawn my weapon a few times, but I never shot at anyone, and no one has shot at me. God willing, I hope they never do."

"Two-thirds of all cops have never fired their weapon in the line of duty. The figure is higher for female cops—nearly 90 percent have never fired them except in training."

"Forgive me for being blunt, but so what?"

"You believe I'm a vigilante, but the truth is: When I was a cop in Port City, I was a member of that two-thirds of male cops who never fired their weapon on the job. But since I became a PI, you've read about some of the people who've tried to kill me. When a bad guy comes after me, he's often close enough that I have less than a second to defend myself. And I seldom wear an armored vest like I did when I was a cop."

"Why not? You've been shot at more times than 90 percent of most cops. You face more risks."

"If a client spots me wearing an armored vest, they might freak out."

"I can understand that. You were saying you have a fraction of a second to act…"

"Yeah. Sometimes I have no choice but to aim for center mass and stay focused enough not to jerk the trigger. The action is over before I catch my breath. If not, I miss my one shot and the next thing that happens is *I'm* dead instead of the bad guy. It's not vigilantism; it's self-defense."

"You ever killed anyone when it wasn't self-defense?"

"Bettina, the fact you asked that question proves you don't understand me despite reading dozens of articles posted on the internet. I've never killed anyone who wasn't trying to kill me. I admit I was tempted once or twice. But each time I've been in a gunfight, someone attacked me, or I defended an innocent person whose life was in danger."

I gripped Bettina's hands. "As cops, you and I trained to handle emergencies. So do the Green Berets. But until you stare down the barrel of a gun in a bad guy's hand or dodge a sniper's bullets, you can't grasp how it feels in your gut. I hope you never do."

As I spoke, I grasped that I had a penchant for frontier justice, even though I wouldn't admit it.

"And your concept of loyalty," she said. "I learned about your battles with the Chinese soldiers when they kidnapped your friend in Port City, and with the Russian Mafia when they tried to kidnap your other friend's fiancée.

"I told you I'd consider—"

She gave me a stop motion. "Don't interrupt, Chuck. I'm on a roll, standing here on my soapbox."

I smiled and waved her to continue.

"The concept of 'serve and protect' was high on your list of purposes in middle school. It still is, even though you're a PI instead of a cop."

"And I help old ladies cross the street."

She chuckled. "That being said, you may be complicated, but you are also the simplest man I know."

"Thanks a lot."

Bettina patted my cheek. "I mean that in a nice way. I mean you appreciate what you do, you do it superbly, and you don't want to do anything else."

"Almost true. I also want to have a family."

"You have a family already. That's part of your problem."

"I don't mean my extended family; I want my own family. One I don't share with anyone else."

"Families are always shared, Chuck."

For a moment, I thought Bettina had made the most profound statement I had heard in a long, long time. Then the moment passed. "I mean that I want sons and daughters, not nieces and nephews and someday grandsons and granddaughters, not just godchildren."

She smiled a sad smile. "Plenty of people want children, but for some of us, it won't ever happen. So good luck with that."

———

We took a break for coffee.

Once we returned to the living room, I drew a small notebook from my pocket and reviewed my comments. "I confiscated four cellphones from the three bikers who jumped me last night. I'd like to backtrack them once we get to your office on Monday. Also, Lola mentioned a guy named Russell—haven't identified whether it's his first or last name—who supplies her and Angie with cocaine. I got his phone number from Lola so we can check him out."

I showed Bettina the baggie I had taken from Lola. "Lola Salazar was snorting this last night. It hit her harder than she expected, and she passed out. I suspect it's pure enough that it's dangerous to use. Can you recommend a private lab to give me a confidential report?"

"Sure. First, we run to the precinct Monday and ping the phones and contacts you... uh, accumulated. Great way to develop a list of suspects."

"Thanks."

"Then we drop the baggie of cocaine at the lab." She glanced at her watch. "How long since you worked out?"

"Too long. Our cruise scheduled a sea day between Cozumel and Miami, and I planned to run ten miles looping the promenade deck, enjoy a sauna and a nap, and hit the ship's gym. Why? You want to work out?"

"Yeah. I was in spectacular shape when I played volleyball in high school and college. It's tough to stay in shape now. There's a neighborhood city park with a half-mile track. My condo association's gym has a sauna. I can't supply an ocean view, but you and I can get a thorough workout—including the shower—before dinner tonight."

Lunch had been late, so I treated Bettina to dinner at 8:30. We returned home a little after ten o'clock and watched the last of the local news.

Once the news was over, there was an awkward moment when we said goodnight. She placed her hands on my chest and gazed up at me. She swayed close enough to breathe on my neck.

And close enough for me to smell her perfume.

Even though I left my hands at my sides, a strand of sensuality threaded through the moment.

"Still planning to mend fences with Ruby in Port City?"

I couldn't catch my breath, so I cleared my throat before I replied. "I've invested six months in my relationship with Ruby. I can't abandon it without trying. Until then, I'm a one-woman man."

She kissed me on the cheek and stepped back. "I understand. I expected no less from you. Good night."

"See you in the morning."

Before bed, I texted Jorge.

Don't bother to trace the last two phones I sent you. I reestablished contact with a friend of mine who is a Houston police detective. I worked with her before, on the Simonetti case. Thanks for your help, amigo.

Jorge texted back.

This Houston detective, is she pretty?

I replied.

Hot as a new frying pan.

SEVEN

Tommy Valley

Tommy Valley rattled the door open. The cloudy sky paraded a hint of gold in the west. He glanced up the alley, deserted at 9:00 p.m. on a Saturday. Good. He had hunkered down all day as other customers came and went. He didn't want witnesses.

Valley rolled his motorcycle out the door and slid it closed behind him. Threading the padlock through the hasp, he jammed it closed and tugged to ensure it was secure.

He cranked his bike and coasted along the alley. No twisting the accelerator. No racking the pipes. No calling attention to himself. Not today.

Rolling at the speed limit in the twilight, Valley returned to the apartment he shared with Lola Salazar. All the partiers would have left by dawn this morning, and Lola might be out with friends on a Saturday night.

He unfastened his saddle bags and hung them over his shoulder. He started to climb the steps two at a time, then stopped, his knees and shoulder flamed with aches. Damn Carlos McCrary. He had banged Valley pretty bad when he threw him across the parking lot. Valley rolled his shoulders and flexed his knees before he climbed the remaining steps one at a time.

The apartment door was unlocked. No surprise there. Valley walked down the hall and through his bedroom door.

Staring in the bathroom mirror, he cleaned off the dried blood. Nothing he could do about the bruises. At least his face was not cut badly. His unshaven face helped conceal the cuts. He disconnected his laptop from the external monitor. Dropping to his knees to unplug the power cord under the desk, he groaned in pain as his knee hit the carpet. He yanked the cord from the wall, leaned against the desk to steady himself, and heaved his body upright.

He crammed the power cord and laptop into a saddlebag. Time to lie low. Passing Lola's open door, he glanced inside. She was sprawled on top of the bed, arms and legs at odd angles. Weren't those the clothes she'd worn last night at the party? Oh my God, did she OD? Stupid bitch. Never knew when to stop. He held his ear to her chest. Her pulse was steady. Sighing, he straightened her limbs and found a blanket in the closet. He spread the blanket across her and closed the bedroom door.

On his way out, Valley locked the apartment door behind him.

It was full dark as he parked his Harley at a discount store.

He replaced both his Samsung and iPhone and activated them.

Stopping at a McDonald's for dinner, he used their Wi-Fi to restore both phones' contact lists. Laboriously, he sent separate text messages to each of his contacts.

As you know, I change phone numbers periodically. This text is to give you my new number. The old number no longer works.

He finished the text messages near midnight. He visited a neighborhood all-night grocery store and bought enough food to fill his other saddlebag before returning to the safe house.

Time to disappear. He needed another week to heal. He couldn't be seen in public looking like he had lost a fight.

And in a few days, none of this would matter. He would have more money than he could spend for the rest of his life. And a new identity to go with it.

EIGHT

Bettina Simpson

S unday morning following breakfast, Bettina drove Chuck to her police substation. The parking lot was nearly empty.

Bettina booted her personal laptop on the desk. She downloaded Tommy Valley aka Tomás Valenzuela's call history, contacts, and texts from Valley's Samsung phone.

Chuck studied the process. "I knew you could download from a cellphone, but I've never had occasion to do it on a case."

"It's easy. You need a USB cable and the right app." In seconds she saved two text files on her computer. "I'll import the text files into spreadsheets so we can sort them."

She revolved her laptop to face Chuck. "You do the iPhone the same way."

She printed the texts from both phones.

They did the same for the phones Chuck seized from Valley's biker friends.

"Did you notice most of the contacts and calls on Tommy's Samsung phone were in Texas?" Chuck asked.

"Yes. He uses the iPhone to call Mexico. Security is better on an iPhone. If you hadn't unlocked it with his thumbprint, we'd never crack it."

"The texts on the iPhone are in Spanish and the Samsung texts are in English," Chuck said. "You read the English texts and I'll translate the ones on the iPhone."

Bettina glanced over Chuck's shoulder. "Another detective is coming over, and he's an officious prick. Follow my lead."

A man in a wrinkled suit stopped at Bettina's desk. "Hey, Bettina. Isn't today your day off?"

She waved in Chuck's direction. "Art Devlin, Carlos McCrary."

Chuck stood to shake hands.

"Chuck is an old friend from Adams Creek. He was a robbery-homicide detective in Port City," Bettina said. "We worked a case together in Houston five years ago. I brought him here to brag on our new gee-whiz tech on cellphone tracking."

"Nice to meet you, Chuck," Devlin said. "What brings you to Houston?"

"Visiting old friends like Bettina and some family in Houston and Adams Creek."

Devlin glanced at the four cellphones sitting on Bettina's desk. "What are those?"

"What do they look like?" Bettina retorted.

"Are you working a personal case, Bettina? On your day off?"

"I told you I'm showing Chuck our technology. Didn't you hear me?"

"Demonstrating our equipment is not an acceptable use of department resources."

"Art, you're in Organized Crime; I'm in the Burglary division. Your cases are your responsibility, and I wouldn't dream of telling you how to investigate your cases. I expect the same professional courtesy and respect from you." She gave Devlin a hard expression. "Don't you have cases to work? Or is this your day off too?"

Devlin's face reddened.

"Have a nice day, Art." Bettina pivoted back to her desk, turning her back on Devlin.

Devlin grunted wordlessly and walked away without a reply.

Ten minutes later, Bettina positioned the pages of printed texts on her desk. "The English texts prove Tommy is a drug dealer. He sells heroin and cocaine retail in small amounts. Primarily to individuals for personal consumption. What did you learn from the Spanish texts?"

"Tommy buys bulk heroin every month or so from a contact in Coahuila state," Chuck said, referring to his printout.

"That's the *Tres Equis* cartel. That's the one Saco is involved with. According to Organized Crime, they have the Houston market sewed up."

"Should we tell Art Devlin?" Chuck asked. "He's in OCU."

"Between you and me, Chuck, I don't quite trust Devlin. He gives me weird vibes."

"Do you mean he would rat you out for using the police resources on a personal case? Or do you mean he's playing for the bad guys' team?"

"Maybe Devlin is only a world-class jerk and not a crooked cop. For now, let's not bring him in. It's common knowledge that the *Tres Equis* cartel moves a bunch more than one kilo a month. Tommy Valley is one cog in a big machine. He probably services one small territory."

"Like a franchise," Chuck said. "*Drugs R Us. We deliver the goods.* Some of the texts indicate Tommy uses a location somewhere in Houston to cut the heroin and cocaine for retail distribution."

"Did you read anything to tell you where Angelina is?"

"No, but I haven't compared Tommy's and Lola's contacts with people whom Angie contacted."

Chuck raised an eyebrow. "*Whom* again?"

"Mrs. Sandiford's English class again."

"How can you locate Angie's contacts?" Bettina asked. "You told me her phone is missing."

"Angie kept her phone bills for the last year in a drawer in her kitchen." Chuck showed her the envelopes from his jacket pocket. "They list all calls she made or received."

Bettina stared at the stack of envelopes. "Paper bills? Who gets paper bills anymore? Is your sister a dinosaur?"

"Angie has been suspicious since she was a little girl. It started as a kid, way before the internet. She believed the phone company or the electric company or the credit card company were overcharging her. She gets paper bills and scrutinizes them each month. I have her credit card bills and bank statements too."

She stacked the spreadsheets, stapled them, and handed one to Chuck. "You analyze half of Tommy's phone bills and I'll do the other half. We'll compare your sister's phone calls to Tommy's."

Chuck considered the sheets of printed calls and texts. "Let's do the last two months' phone bills first. The recent ones will more likely yield actionable information."

"Actionable information? You been reading those heavy books again?"

———

Carlos McCrary

Two cups of coffee later, I had a list of twelve phone numbers appearing both on Angie's bills and Valley's texts, phone calls, and contacts.

We ran Angie's phone calls against the other two bikers' calls; there were no matches.

I handed the list to Bettina. "Nice work. Can you identify to whom these numbers belong?"

"Of course. You're not the only superhero in the room, big boy. Stand back while I flex my superpowers."

Ten minutes later, Bettina printed out the list of contact information on the twelve numbers. "This will keep you busy tomorrow while I work. Promise me you won't get into any gunfights tomorrow."

"Gunfights are not on the schedule until Wednesday at the earliest. In the meantime, please ping the four phones of the three bikers who attacked me and Russell, the guy who supplies Lola's cocaine. I want to know where they've traveled since the first of May."

"Can do. You want me to ping Angie, Lola, and Teodoro?"

"My buddy, Jorge Castellano, with the Port City PD did that for me. Thanks anyway."

"Sure. Anything else you want since I'm in a cooperative mood?"

I smiled. "Later. Once we get back to your condo."

———

Bettina Simpson

Bettina drove Chuck back to her condo. On the way back, she considered what Chuck meant about wanting something once they got back to her condo. He had politely declined her advance the previous night, so what did he mean?

She parked in her assigned space.

"Bettina, I noticed you had raisin bran and coffee with skim milk and sugar substitute for breakfast this morning."

"Yes. A light breakfast helps control my weight."

"Could I buy breakfast foods for me and general groceries to contribute to the larder?"

"Of course. I'm sorry; I should have thought of that."

"No problem." He opened the passenger door. "I'll drive my SUV."

"There's an H-E-B a mile and a half away. Ask your GPS. Sloppy Joes and tomato soup okay for lunch?"

"Sure. Thanks."

"I don't recall; you take your tea sweet or regular?"

"Unsweetened. Sometimes I squeeze a touch of lemon or lime juice in it, but I can drink it plain."

"Buy a half dozen lemons at H-E-B. I'll make lemon chicken."

———

Carlos McCrary

I parked in the H-E-B lot and called Ruby.

She answered on the second ring. "Hey, Chuck. How goes the search for your sister?"

"We developed some leads. Nothing important yet."

"You said 'we.' Who is 'we'?"

"Bettina Simpson. She's a Houston police detective, a friend of mine from high school days. She worked with me on the Simonetti case five years ago. You may have heard me mention her."

"No, I don't recall. She's helping you search for your sister?"

"Yeah. When she's off duty."

"Off duty? Does that mean you didn't file a missing person report?"

"Not yet, but I didn't call to discuss the case, Ruby. I called to talk about us. Are you still in Austin?"

"Yes, but Mom is driving me to the airport right now. My flight to Port City departs in three hours. We'll allow extra time for TSA screening. At least I'll sleep in my own bed tonight."

"Glad to hear it. Have you given any more consideration to our relationship?"

The longer the silence stretched across the phone, the lower my hopes sank.

Ruby sighed. "No, I haven't. Look, I didn't intend to hurt you; I really didn't. But I tried to make it clear that our relationship isn't working. I do want to remain friends— maybe even friends with benefits... just not lovers anymore."

My situation with Ruby reminded me of Liz Johannes, the first girl I ever loved and the first girl who dumped me. Liz broke my heart in high school, and my next serious relationship wasn't until years later with Terry Kovacs, a Port City Police Detective. Terry abandoned me when I was arrested for murder. Then my fiancée Miyoki Takashi was kidnapped and almost murdered because of me. After she got out of the hospital, I never heard from her again. Later Terry reconciled with me but dumped me a second time when I left for Austin to search for my cousin Emily. And now Ruby had done the same thing.

Well, that made my day.

―――――

After lunch I researched the phone numbers Angie had called that were not on Valley's contact list. Seven were burner phones. The rest were mundane: the apartment office, a beauty salon, a spa, and a fitness gym.

I opened Angelina's professional website. Her image from a magazine ad for cosmetics filled the screen. My sister was indeed beautiful. On the menu bar, I clicked "Contact Angelina" and noted her agent's company name and phone number. I punched in the number.

"Texas Reps Agency, Miranda speaking. How may I direct your call?"

"Lavinia Evans, please. Carlos McCrary calling."

"Will she know what this is in regard to?"

"I am Angelina Garza's brother. Tell her Angelina is missing."

"She's on another call. Please hold."

Four minutes later… "This is Lavinia Evans, Chuck. Long time, no see. What's this I hear about Angie Garza being missing?"

"No one has heard from her for over a week. I'm in Houston searching for her. Any idea where she is?"

"Chuck, I haven't talked to Angie since before Christmas, and we haven't received any requests for her since last year. I sent her to a photo-shoot in December, and she arrived higher than the national debt. The client told me he wouldn't use her anymore. I told Angie to get her act together or she was finished in the modeling business, including for mature photo spreads."

"She was on drugs last December?"

"Unfortunately, yes. Hell, we've seen it before—rock musicians, movie stars, athletes, you name it—they get a taste of the so-called 'good life' and lose everything by sniffing it up their nose or shooting it into their arm. Angie is thirty-eight and hasn't taken care of her body. Sorry it happened to Angie, but that's life, Chuck—sometimes you lose."

"If she contacts you, will you tell me?"

"Sure thing, Chuck, but don't count on it; she's closer to you than she is to me. Hell, she's your sister. It's been so long since I heard from her, I'm not sure I'm still her agent."

"Your company name and phone number are still on her website, so she thinks you're still representing her."

"Or else, she hasn't updated her website in a long time. Anyway, if I hear from her, I'll let you know."

"Thanks, Lavinia. Take care."

I disconnected and looked at Bettina.

"Angie hasn't worked as a model since last year."

"What's she been doing for money?"

"I'm almost afraid to find out."

"When was the last time you Googled Angie?" Bettina asked.

"Never."

"Why not? Weren't you ever curious?"

"Hell, she's my sister and I've known her all my life. Why would I need the internet to find out anything about her?"

"Why indeed?" Bettina said.

We returned to Bettina's precinct station, and she ran printouts of every location each phone of interest had visited since April first. The number for Teodoro's phone was last used on March 15. Teodoro had packed a bag; he was long gone. "Those maps and lists will keep you plenty busy tomorrow, Chuck."

Back at Bettina's apartment, I unfolded the Harris County map on the dining room table. Using the colored markers, I marked the locations Angie, Lola Salazar, and Tommy Valley and his two biker friends visited since the first of April.

"Look at this, Bettina. That's the location of the adult film producer that Lola described. Lola said she and Angie went to a party there once, and that was last weekend, but these phone tracks say Lola was there four times in the last two months, and Angie was there three times."

Bettina read the list. "To the rest of your family, Angie's life looks like a walk in the park. But underneath... she's into some risky activities. Certainly drugs, and possibly making porn. How does a fashion model wind up in porn movies?"

"Lola calls them 'adult films' and says they're 'in good taste.'" I made air quotes.

"To me they're still dirty movies."

"Yeah. Me too. So, assuming that's true, how can I tell our parents?"

"You'll find a way, Chuck. You believe Lola and Angie were making porn?"

"Angie made money some way."

I booted my computer and searched for *Las Peliculas Fantasia*.

"The company has a website."

I clicked on the link. "It's in Spanish."

Bettina changed chairs to sit beside me. "Use the search bar. Search for films featuring an actor named Lola."

I did the search. "Nothing under Lola. I'll search for Angelina... Nothing."

"Search for Lolita."

I typed the name. "Bingo." I pivoted the laptop screen toward Bettina. "I recognize the tattoos on her chest."

Bettina gave me dubious eyes. "When did you see her tattoos before?"

"First time I interviewed Lola, she had been asleep."

"She sleeps nude?"

"I don't know. When I knocked on her door, it woke her up. She threw on a satin robe before she came to the door. You know how satin is. Real slippery. Her robe slid open. She gave me a real good look before she refastened it. Then later she flashed me."

"She came on to you?"

"Twice. And at her party that night, I practically had to fight her off me. Fortunately, she passed out before things got too heavy."

"She's pretty."

"In real life, she ain't that pretty," I said. "The professional makeup and lighting accentuate her better features."

Bettina chuckled. "No one will notice her face anyway. Not with *that* staring at them. Do you recognize the male actor?"

I peered closer. "Yeah. The guy with the guitar and the heart tattoos is Tommy. He shares an apartment with Lola."

"Are they sharing an apartment, or are they boyfriend and girlfriend?"

I pointed at the screen. "From what they're doing together, I'd say they were boyfriend and girlfriend. On the other hand, they have separate bedrooms in Lola's apartment."

"The sex is not definitive, nor is the separate bedrooms. They might have a professional relationship. Or one of them snores."

"Good point," I said. "They didn't seem to get along when I first met them. Although at her party, Tommy was defensive about Lola and warned me against bothering her."

"Possibly Tommy was defensive to keep your attention off himself, not Lola. He could frame his opposition around Lola to hide his own concerns."

"See? That's why I wanted you involved in the case."

"Flattery can get you all kinds of places." She smirked. "Search for Angie or Angelina."

I pecked the keyboard. "Nope. I'll try Angel... They list over a dozen actors named 'Angel,' of both genders. I'll try Angelica... and bingo."

My heart plummeted when I recognized my sister. I had to tell my parents.

I leaned back in my chair and pointed. "Bettina, I'd like you to meet my sister Angelina aka Angelica the porn star. That's her in the flesh, literally. Certainly, it's more of her flesh than I've seen since we were small children."

Bettina gazed from the screen to me. "I'm so sorry, Chuck."

"Well now we know how she's making money."

"What would cause a fashion model to make porn?"

"Her agent thinks the drugs ruined her fashion career. On the other hand, Angie's pushing forty. She's too old for the magazines."

"You must not read the same magazines I do. Nowadays, advertisers use models of a variety of ages, races, and body types. They don't need to be beautiful—just have a pleasant face."

"That's good to hear. I'll mention that once I find her. Speaking of finding her, I'll visit Esteban Espinoza and ask about Angie."

"You think he'll tell you?"

I smiled. "People usually talk to me when I ask nicely."

I pulled up Tommy Valley's cellphone track and showed it to Bettina. "This address is familiar."

"Punch it into a map website."

I did. "It's Flathead Pipe Supply."

I flipped back in my notes. "Teodoro Garza's phone was last at Flathead Pipe Supply, where it disappeared from the network on March 15." I referred to a calendar. "That was a Sunday. Tommy Valley's phone was at Flathead early morning on May fourth, the day Angie disappeared."

"That's unlikely to be a coincidence."

"Time for me to take a road trip," I said. "Rule Two: *When in doubt, follow somebody*. I can't follow Tommy Valley or Teodoro Garza, but I can sure as hell follow their cellphones."

"You want me to ride shotgun?"

"It might be dangerous."

"So am I, Chuck. So am I. I'm an armed police officer, even off duty."

"This whole… situation with Angelina is my responsibility, not yours. I've asked you for a few favors, but I don't expect you to risk your life. You don't have a dog in this fight."

"To protect and serve." Bettina said it like she meant it. "Angie is a citizen of Houston, and you are a visitor to Houston. My duty is to protect the citizens and visitors to Houston. A good cop is never 'off duty.' I'll ride with you. Having backup could be useful, and let's hope you don't need it."

"Rule Eighteen: *Always have a backup*. I'd love to take you, assuming it's no trouble."

Bettina smiled. "Sunday afternoon. It's not like I made other plans."

"Then by all means, ride shotgun."

I couldn't predict at the time how true the *riding shotgun* would be.

———

I clicked on Google Earth and zoomed in on Flathead Pipe Supply. The monitor showed an industrial area in rural Harris County east of Sam Houston Parkway.

Bettina peered over my shoulder. "That area south of Highway 90 is filled with dozens of oil exploration and production supply companies. I see them every time I drive east on Highway 90. Zoom out and you can view the whole property."

I zoomed the satellite image out. "What are those things?" I pointed at the screen.

"Those are row upon row of stacks of drill pipe and well casing." She tapped the monitor. "Those grid lines are a network of two-lane roads flanked by drainage ditches. The terrain is flat as a pool table. Needs lots of drainage."

I pushed back from Bettina's dining room table. "How could an oil and gas production and exploration support facility be connected with drugs?"

"Isn't that why we're taking this road trip? To learn stuff?"

"Right you are. As the Lone Ranger said to Tonto: Let's mount up."

Closing the app, I slipped my laptop in a briefcase and lugged it to the 4Runner.

An hour later, we exited Highway 90 on southbound State Highway 13, a two-lane street that ran straight south. I bumped across a railroad spur, then pushed east on Old Powerline Road, a two-lane road that led toward the San Jacinto River.

A mile down Old Powerline Road, the road passed a pine tree farm and curled 90 degrees to the north. A mile further on, the street crossed the railroad spur again.

"Your destination is ahead on the right," the GPS said.

"That's wrong," Bettina said. "The land on the right looks like virgin forest. It's never been developed."

"The factory on the left matches what Google Earth shows."

Two hundred yards later, a weathered sign at the entrance said *Flathead Pipe Supply.*

Bettina snapped a picture. "Ta-da."

The second line of the sign read *Drill Pipe and Well Casing.* The third line said *NO TRESPASSING!!!*

Just past the sign, a culvert had been laid in the drainage ditch and covered with gravel to allow vehicles to drive onto the site.

The Flathead site was several acres of flat, graveled land without trees or a blade of grass. A gust of breeze stirred a whisp of dust from the surface.

A one-story white metal building stood twenty yards back from the drainage ditch beside the entrance. The setback allowed a truck to pull off the street before stopping at the gate. *Building 1* was painted above the door.

I glanced at the rearview mirror. Old Powerline Road was empty. "The place looks deserted." I wheeled the 4Runner across the graveled ditch and stopped at the open gate.

"Why leave the gate open?" I asked. "The other plants we passed had their gates locked."

"Yeah, but they were fenced all around. This site is as wide open as a public beach. The gate is useless. Perhaps it's a symbol to say 'Stop here and check in.'"

I turned to Bettina. "What do you think? The sign says no trespassing. You think they mean it?"

"They built a gate beside Building 1, but there's no fence. Then they leave the gate wide open. Anyone could bypass the gate and Building 1 without stopping. I say let's go for it."

"I agree. No guts, no blue chips." I pressed the accelerator.

Bettina snapped pictures. "A security camera mounted under the eave covers the entrance. See the funnel-shaped thingy? That's a siren to go with their burglar alarm."

"Then they may have installed alarms on all the buildings."

"I would if it were my factory. It's all empty on nights and weekends out here in the country."

Beside Building 1, the gravel entrance road ran straight west. "That must be the main street that accesses the back of the property," Bettina said.

The road bisected the property into a northern and southern half, reaching a vanishing point at the western boundary. On the north side, stacks of drill pipe and well casing stretched hundreds of yards to another pine tree farm on the north. Gravel roads traced straight lines between the stacks.

South of Main Street lay the manufacturing area. The structure on the south had *Building 3* painted on both sides that we could see. The western structure had *Building 2* painted on the long side. A dozen beige panel vans were parked beside Building 2.

Two pickup trucks were parked at Building 3. A Peterbilt tractor with an empty flat-bed trailer was parked by a truck door. The truck door was closed and not a soul was visible on the grounds. Not surprising; it was late on a sleepy Sunday afternoon. Anyone who was working there earlier should have gone home.

"The open gate seems like an invitation despite the no trespassing sign."

"At least we're not breaking and entering," Bettina said. "Just entering."

"We're still trespassing," I said as we coasted through the open gate toward Building 2.

The Watcher

Twenty miles away in a high-rise building in downtown Houston, the image of McCrary's 4Runner inched across a monitor. The watcher had been reading a romance novel while seated at the monitors. She noticed the motion in her peripheral vision. She bookmarked the novel and inspected the screen. She clicked a screengrab, zoomed the image, and copied the vehicle's license plate. Within a few seconds she identified the rental car company owner, accessed the company's rental records, and determined the name of the renter, his driver's license number, and his contact information. *His driver's license picture is handsome. Nice smile. Six-foot-two and an organ donor.* She entered his name into her computer: *Carlos Andres McCrary*

She consulted another file. McCrary was not a regular visitor. He lived in Florida. Why was he at the plant? She kicked back in her swivel chair, admired the Nordic dreamboat on the romance novel's cover one more time, and continued reading, but she kept one eye on the monitor.

Carlos McCrary

I aimed the 4Runner toward the parked pickups. "There's a coat of dust on the trucks," Bettina said.

"The whole neighborhood is full of dirt roads," I responded. "They might have parked the trucks a few hours ago or a few days. Hard to tell."

I curved right, circumnavigating Building 2.

Bettina snapped photos of each side. Security cameras mounted under the eaves covered both entrances on the north and south walls. Truck doors gave access on each side, with a personnel door beside each truck door. The windows were at the top of the twenty-plus-foot walls.

"The windows provide natural light inside," I said. "They must not have offices in this building."

"Did you notice the panel vans?" Bettina said.

"Yeah. So?"

"They could have been parked there for weeks."

"Building 2 may not be occupied."

Bettina showed me her palms. "Duh. That's what I meant."

"You think the building is not in use?"

"Building 3 has personal vehicles parked by it. Building 2 has those trucks, and they may be parked there permanently. The oil drilling business is in bad shape, what with the emphasis on renewable energy sources. Perhaps the company cut back to a one-building operation. They parked the trucks out of the way at Building 2 because no one needs them until business improves."

"Assuming it ever does," I said.

Building 3 had a row of windows near the ground on the side nearest the street.

"Must be where the offices are," Bettina said.

Cameras covered all four sides of Building 3. A rail spur ended behind the building.

I bumped the 4Runner across the rail spur and continued until we cruised around both buildings and Bettina had photographed all sides of both, along with the license plates of the trucks and the empty trailers. Behind the manufacturing area, the stacks of drill pipes continued. Everything indicated an industrial district that should be deserted on a weekend.

"What now, Chuck?"

I steered the 4Runner toward the ditch bordering Old Powerline Road. "Let's not do the job halfway."

I pushed north between the pipe stacks and the ditch and traced the perimeter of the property to the corner, hung a left and paralleled the north ditch a few hundred yards. At that corner of the property, I turned south.

———

The Watcher

In the high-rise, she tipped her chair upright. This McCrary, whoever he was, had circled both main buildings. That was unusual on a Sunday, but not cause for further action if he were just a curiosity seeker. But instead of leaving with his curiosity satisfied, McCrary continued to explore the property. What was he searching for?

McCrary's visit was a surprise. Surprises were not welcome. Things would come to a head in two weeks. There was little margin for error and would be less as D-Day approached.

Somebody better check out this McCrary guy.

She punched a number on her encrypted cellphone and reported the gatecrasher to her boss.

"Good work. I'll send somebody to check on it. Run a background search on McCrary."

———

Carlos McCrary

Following the rear ditch, we approached a smaller gray metal building not visible from the street with walls approximately fifteen feet high—one story, but a high-ceilinged one-story.

"That building wasn't on the satellite image," I said.

Bettina snapped pictures. "Google Earth images are often several years old. This is a newer building. Circle it. I'll snap more pictures."

"Logically, they should paint *Building 4* on it, but they didn't," I said. "Wonder why?"

The building measured approximately thirty by sixty feet. Truck doors were installed in the shorter end walls with personnel doors beside each one.

"I would expect to spot more security cameras covering the entrances," Bettina said, "but there aren't any."

"This building is gray, and the other buildings are white. A different design from the others also. Stands out like a penguin in an aquarium."

I stopped at one corner of the building. "Snap a close-up of the manufacturer's plaque on the corner. It has a serial number. Rule Six: *You never know what you'll need to know.*"

Bettina examined the photo. "There are security cameras on the other buildings. Why not on this one?"

"One of life's little mysteries." I paused the 4Runner in the middle of Main Street. Our own dust cloud blew away and there was no sign of anyone else on the property.

Switching my cellphone to a mobile hotspot, I rolled the satellite images back in time. "Most of the industrial areas south of Highway 90 were developed in the late twentieth century," I said, pointing to the laptop screen.

I advanced the timeline. "The Flathead property was developed in 2003. The current satellite image is four years old."

"So what?"

"This small building at the rear of the property was built within the last four years. It's too short to manufacture drill pipe or well casing. You live here, Bettina. Any idea what its purpose is?"

"Not a clue, but once we return home, we can research old building permits online if you like."

"The site is deserted," I said, "and I don't see an alarm system on this building. Since we're here and the place is deserted, we may as well search inside the building."

Opening the driver's door, I stood in the opening to command a higher viewpoint and scanned a 360-degree view.

"Oh, crap." I jumped back in the vehicle. "There's a big vehicle, an SUV or pickup truck, driving toward us through the entrance gate."

The approaching vehicle trailed gravel dust in its wake, moving fast.

"Who are those guys?" I asked. "Curiosity seekers? Flathead employees? Spies like us?"

"Somebody must monitor the security cameras in real time," Bettina said, "unless we triggered a motion detector when we arrived. Could be bad guys, maybe even security personnel. Don't take chances until we learn their intentions. Perhaps they were serious about the 'no trespassing' sign."

Slipping the 4Runner into gear, I idled straight on Main Street toward the entrance and the approaching vehicle. "We act like we belong here." I kept my speed slower than ten miles per hour. "Snap a picture of their license plate. Better yet, video the vehicle."

The other vehicle expanded as it approached. It was a black SUV. I raised a hand from the wheel and gave a two-finger wave. "Sometimes a wave will fool people. Hell, it worked at the porn house."

The SUV driver automatically responded with his own wave, but the passenger's body tensed, and he yelled something at the driver.

The driver spun the wheel, swerving the SUV across the gravel road and stopping with its bumper three feet from a stack of drill pipe, blocking our way. The passenger lowered his window and pointed a handgun in our direction. Another handgun peeped out the rear window.

Bettina slid her phone into her purse. "They didn't buy your neighborly wave. I stopped the video after I recorded a good shot of them pointing a gun at us."

"Oh crap. They must be serious about not trespassing. Let's get the hell out."

I jammed the front wheels to the right and slammed the brakes, then accelerated. The 4Runner drifted into a right turn.

A gunshot rang out.

I sped south between the piles of drill pipe. Punching the brakes, I jerked a left and sped toward the entrance on a gravel path parallel to Main Street, kicking up all the dust and dirt the four-wheel drive could muster.

A hundred yards ahead, the path we were racing along ended at the western wall of Building 3.

"You can't go straight," Bettina said, "but a left turn leads us to the street with the SUV. Those guys have at least two shooters, could be more. Run for the railroad gate."

"All right. Here we go."

The rail spur lay on the south property line. The spur had a gate that allowed access to trains. If a train could get in, our 4Runner could get out. Worst case, I would crash through the railroad gate. Better than being shot for trespassing.

I held the accelerator on the floor toward Building 2. When we were twenty yards from the wall, I twisted the wheel and veered off the street. Flooring the gas, I spun all four wheels and sped past Building 2. I arrowed toward the back side of Building 3 where several trucks were parked near the spur.

Glancing at the rearview, I spotted our own dust trail. I pushed harder and the 4Runner rushed toward the exit behind Building 3.

Seconds later, the SUV burst through the dust cloud behind us, guns blazing from the open windows on both sides.

We had a hundred-yard head start. Handguns aren't accurate beyond forty or fifty yards for even a gifted shooter with a stable shooting platform. In a speeding vehicle, firing through an open window, odds were a hundred-to-one that any one bullet would hit either of us. Unfortunately, the 4Runner was a much bigger target.

"We're mechanical ducks in a carnival shooting gallery."

Bettina drew her handgun. "Even at a hundred yards, Chuck, it's only a matter of time until a wild shot hits something important—like me."

"Even if they keep missing us, they'll catch us soon. We have to slow at the exit to bump across the rail spur and drive along the railroad right-of-way. Let's slow those guys down; discourage them from pursuing us. The best defense is a good offense."

Keeping my eyes on the mirrors, I said, "Yesterday, you said you'd never fired your weapon in the line of duty. It's time to fire your weapon for real."

I told Bettina what I had in mind.

We unbuckled our seat belts. Seconds later, I slammed to a stop, jumped out, and remained motionless in front of the open driver's door. Bettina mirrored my stance in front of the passenger door.

The SUV's driver instinctively stomped the brakes when Bettina and I jumped from the 4Runner. The SUV dipped a few degrees then leveled itself when the driver punched the accelerator again.

I assumed a two-handed Weaver firing stance, left hand supporting the shooting hand. That took less than one second, during which the SUV closed to 85 yards.

I aimed at the base of SUV's windshield in the center. *Imagine a firing range. Easy squeezy, nice and easy.*

The SUV was closing from eighty yards away... seventy...

I stopped breathing and squeezed the trigger precisely and methodically. *Bang... Bang... Bang... Bang...*

Bettina raised her pistol. *Bang... Bang... Bang... Bang...*

Three bullet holes bloomed in the SUV's grill and one spider-webbed the windshield. The SUV slammed the brakes and skidded sideways as the driver spun the steering wheel.

I drew another breath.

Bang... Bang... Bang...

Bettina fired again and again.

Steam and liquid sprayed from underneath the hood. The SUV completed its sliding 180-degree turn and sped back the way it had come.

I drew another long breath.

Bang... Bang... Bang...

The rear window of the SUV shattered, punctured by a bullet. The SUV veered sideways and crashed into a stack of drill pipe before its own drifting dust cloud obscured it.

"Cease firing." I stepped up in the 4Runner's open door and rotated 360 degrees. "No one else is visible. The security cameras at Building 2 recorded the attack and our response. Nothing to do about it. Replace your used magazine with a full one."

"Already did."

We jumped into the 4Runner. Bettina grinned and extended her palm toward me. We slapped a high five, laughing.

With the pursuing SUV disabled, I steered toward the main entrance. "So, Bettina, how do you feel after your first gunfight?"

"It was… strangely *exhilarating* with bullets whizzing past as we were fighting for our lives. It felt like the fifth set of a close volleyball game. In fact, now that it's over, I feel…" She lapsed into silence.

I glanced in her direction. Her eyes were wide and her face was flushed.

"What were you about to say?" I figured she intended to say, "turned on." Sometimes a brush with death activates a survival instinct that includes the desire to procreate. I was turned on myself, but neither Bettina nor I would dare admit it.

"Nothing," she said. "But I feel my heart beating in my chest. Is that normal?"

"It's the adrenaline. You're just scared. It passes."

"Weren't you scared back there?"

"Sure."

"Oh, yeah? This is you, being scared?"

"Yes."

"Why didn't you *look* scared?"

I smiled at her question. "I practice hiding it. Besides, being scared doesn't change anything. You still gotta defend yourself."

Bettina shivered. "I can't stop shaking."

"That's the aftereffect of the adrenaline. The shakes don't last long."

"You saved my life back there."

"I could also say that *you* saved *my* life. God knows what would have happened if you hadn't backed me up. It would have been three shooters against one instead of three against two. It was my fault you were in harm's way to begin with. This road trip thing was my mission, not yours."

"Okay, we owe each other big time. Let's call it square."

"Deal."

Bettina fastened her seat belt. "What now?"

"Did you notice how soon the SUV showed once we arrived?"

"Yeah. The person monitoring the cameras had someone waiting within a fifteen-minute drive."

"You read my mind. They caught us snooping and dispatched the SUV to investigate. We must assume they know our vehicle's license plate and have learned it's a rental."

"And if whoever monitored us is well connected," Bettina said, "they know by now that you rented it."

"Which means they can shadow this vehicle's built-in GPS."

"And our cellphones? Can this mystery person monitor our phones?"

"Let's play it safe and remove the batteries." I handed Bettina my phone. "I'll buy us burner phones."

"You'd better return this vehicle," Bettina said, "and rent another from a different rental company."

"You're reading my mind. We can use a rent-a-wreck type car rental company with an older non-GPS-equipped fleet."

"Okay. Drive me to my car and I'll trail you to return this 4Runner. Then I'll chauffer you to another rental company."

"But on the way to your condo, we need to buy burner phones. Rule Fourteen: *When you think someone is out to get you, they probably are.*"

The Watcher

She monitored the one-sided gunfight from her post in the downtown high-rise. What kind of trigger-happy morons did the boss send to check out the visitor? Damn. A police report on the gunfight would draw unwanted attention to Flathead Pipe Supply. She would ask her boss to prevent the Flathead contacts from reporting the incident.

The watcher admitted that McCrary had more balls than a pool table. And who was the blonde? She zoomed the picture, searching for a good shot of the blonde's face. Too far away. When the 4Runner turned, the watcher switched to the cameras on Building 1. Bull's-eye. As they passed, she captured a fair picture of the blonde's face, but her head was angled, talking to McCrary. The watcher scrolled back to the instant they entered the main gate. Yes, that was a better picture of the woman. She cropped the photo, enhanced it, and sent it to a facial recognition app.

The watcher made another phone call. "The morons you sent started a gunfight with McCrary. He and a blonde woman with him sent them running with their tails between their legs. The way she handles a gun, she's either a cop or another government agent. I'll send you a video. You'd better keep an eye on both of them before they screw up everything."

"Who is the woman?"

"Don't know yet, but I will soon."

NINE

The watcher tapped the vehicle tracking system of the 4Runner's rental company to shadow McCrary and the blonde to a condo building.

She hacked into the cameras that covered the building's parking lot, but none were aimed the right way. No problem. She would stay on him until she caught a break. It was just a matter of time…

The 4Runner left the condo property. The watcher stalked McCrary. The vehicle was returning to the rental company. Smart guy. More than a pretty face. McCrary figured out they could track him, and he planned to return the 4Runner.

The watcher tapped into the security cameras at the car rental company. She would note which new car McCrary rented so she could monitor it. She recorded the camera images of the rental counter as McCrary returned the 4Runner.

Whoa. McCrary didn't rent another vehicle. He walked out the front door and squeezed into the passenger seat of a black Honda Accord in the parking lot. The watcher switched from camera to camera, seeking a view of the driver.

There wasn't one. The watcher located a view of the Honda's license plate as it accelerated away and made another screengrab.

In seconds, the Honda's ownership record painted the screen. With a few keyboard clicks, the watcher downloaded everything on the internet concerning Bettina Simpson, including a portrait of her in her Houston police uniform with an American flag and Texas flag in the background.

She was a Houston cop. Even worse, a Detective Sergeant. Not good.

Her hair was chestnut in her official portrait. The watcher thought Simpson looked better as a brunette.

The condo where Simpson and McCrary finally stopped was the registered address on Simpson's car title.

The watcher started a new file: *Simpson, Bettina.*

The watcher switched to the vehicle tracking system in Simpson's car and shadowed it from satellites. It carried McCrary to a rent-a-wreck company specializing in older vehicles.

Damn, McCrary rented a car too old to have a GPS. At least the watcher copied the license plate of the old Tahoe. Might be useful. She reached for her secure cellphone.

––––––

Carlos McCrary

I rented a fifteen-year-old metallic gray Chevy Tahoe with over 200,000 miles on it. The rental company assured me it was in tip-top shape and the company earned good online reviews and a good rating from the Better Business Bureau.

Bettina was going to buy takeout Indian food on her way to her condo. I arrived a few minutes later in my Tahoe.

"Thanks for the taxi service."

"*No problemo.* There's Indian food on the table. You hungry?"

"Always."

Bettina spooned a dollop of *Murgh Makhani* onto her plate and mixed it with the basmati rice. "I feel strange when I recall the gunfight. I get short of breath and my heart starts thumping." She forked a bite of the *Murgh Makhani* into her mouth.

"An aftereffect of the gunfight." My hand shivered as I held it over the table. "See? Adrenaline affects me too. We'll both return to normal soon."

I nibbled a bite of *naan* and sipped my iced tea. "Changing the subject, I talked to Ruby this morning when I went shopping at H-E-B."

Bettina stopped chewing. Motionless, she waited for me to continue.

My gut tightened. What was I supposed to say next? Bettina had the right to know I was finished with Ruby. Or rather, Ruby was finished with me. How best to say that?

Bettina set down her fork. "You can't just announce that you talked to Ruby and then stop, buster. That's a signal that you want to talk about her. I'm a good listener and you surely figured out I'm a dedicated dispenser of unsolicited advice. So spit it out."

"I agree with you, but I'm no good with, uh, romantic relationships and touchy-feely stuff. Or at least no good discussing it. I wouldn't know where to start."

"Start with how you and Ruby met."

"Last fall I returned to Austin to renew the search for my cousin Emily, who had disappeared four years earlier. I found evidence in Emily's abandoned car that the detectives missed in their first investigation. I gave the evidence to the detective in charge of her missing person case. Guy named Rodrigo Ortega. I asked him to reopen the case."

"How did Ortega feel about that?"

"I was as welcome as a case of Covid. Ortega got defensive because his guys missed the evidence. I went with him to the crime lab to ensure he gave them the new evidence. Ruby was the fingerprint technician with the Austin crime lab who got first shot at classifying fingerprints before passing the evidence on to a forensics technician. I gave her a business card."

Bettina smiled. "See how easy that was? I presume you were working with Detective Ortega. Why did you give Ruby your card?"

"With Ortega's lousy attitude, I figured I could use all the friends at the police department I could find. Ruby seemed pissed at Ortega's attitude. I figured she was a potential ally."

"And that's what started your relationship?"

"No. A couple days later she called to invite me to lunch. Much later I discovered her therapist told her to be more assertive with men. Her therapist said it would help her heal."

"Heal? From what?"

"Three years before, Ruby was raped. I'm not telling her secrets. She's quite open on the subject. She even testified at the trial where the sorry SOB was convicted. Ruby was, and is, in therapy, and she is putting her life back together, including her relationships with men."

"I cannot imagine how being raped affects the way she views men. I've never been raped or even threatened."

"I didn't learn about the rape or her therapy until later. Ruby invited me to lunch, but I assumed she was attracted by my movie star looks and effervescent personality."

"Effervescent? Do you even comprehend what that means, genius?"

"Vivacious and enthusiastic. But don't ask me to spell the long words."

"Yeah. Don't want to give you a headache."

"Anyway, Ruby's therapist told her to be *pro*-active rather than *re*-active with men. It turns out that the therapist assigned me as a project to help Ruby restore control of her life and her... romantic relationships."

"You gotta be kidding. Her therapist made you a guinea pig? An experiment in female assertiveness?"

"Yeah, but I didn't know that until later. Another woman friend of mine in Port City, an attorney named Vicky Ramirez, tells me I view my relationships like a Norman Rockwell painting."

"My grandparents have Norman Rockwell prints hanging in their kitchen. Happy married couples with 2.3 children, church on Sunday, good neighbors, salt of the earth types. But I never thought of you as one of his magazine covers. You're more like a comic book hero."

"Batman, right?"

"No... A military hero."

"Captain America, I bet."

"Try Dudley Do-Right. But in your case, it's Studly Do-Right." She gave my shoulder a friendly shove.

I felt my face flush. I hate it when that happens.

Time to change the subject. "I'm great at trashing relationships. I believe there's something wrong with me. You recall Liz Johannes?"

"I remember Liz. She was your high school sweetheart whom I couldn't compete with."

"In fairness to you, Bettina, once Liz Johannes hooked me and reeled me in, I never paid attention to another girl. I was so in love that I was certain Liz and I would live happily ever after in Adams Creek—a Norman Rockwell painting in real life. But she dumped me the minute we graduated, and it had nothing to do with my profession or calling or whatever you call it. I guess I simply wasn't enough for her."

"Chuck, that's nonsense. We were seventeen or eighteen years old—overgrown children without a thimble full of life experience to give us perspective and context. Hell, we were full of hormones and barely mature enough to practice safe sex. Nobody in high school is ready for a lifetime commitment."

"Remember Terry Kovacs," I said. "My profession caused that breakup."

"What about her?"

"After I closed the Simonetti murder case, Terry and I became exclusive."

"What happened with her?"

"Later, I was arrested for murder, and she bailed on me. Said she couldn't deal with the stress. That was the fault of my chosen profession. A couple of years later, after I was forced to kill the weirdo who was stalking Cleo Hennessey, the country singer, Terry and I reunited."

"But the relationship failed again, or you wouldn't have been dating Ruby Voight."

"Right. Terry bailed on me when I went to Texas last year to search for Emily. Again, my chosen profession was the cause."

"Maybe it wasn't your profession so much as your priorities."

"What do you mean?"

"Your decision to fly to Austin to search for Emily wasn't part of your profession. Nobody hired you to look for your cousin. You went because she was family. So don't blame your profession. If anything, blame your Dudley Do-Right personal code."

"Maybe you're right. I'll stew on that for a while."

"What happened with Ruby?"

"I called her today, and she said she didn't want to hurt my feelings, and she wanted to remain friends, but not lovers. She said our relationship wasn't working for her."

"Does that mean you're single?"

"I guess so. Yes."

"How does being single make you feel?"

There was that subject *feelings*. "Bettina, I'm lousy at feelings. I don't know how I *should* feel. For example, Ruby tried to break it to me gently when we talked three days ago. I didn't recognize her subtle message hidden between the lines. She needed to slap me in the face with a wet mop for me to understand we were finished. I'm not good at relationships. I can't read subtle clues that other men see."

Bettina guffawed. "What? You believe other men read 'subtle clues'?" She made air quotes. "Hell, lots of women can't read subtle clues from men. Subtle clues cause everyone a problem, buster, no matter what gender."

"Really?"

"You're not the Lone Ranger, Kemo Sabe. Chuck, there's something I haven't told you. I was married and divorced since you were here five years ago. I divorced Barry the Bastard six months ago. A month later I bought this condo. I couldn't handle the memories of him in my old apartment. And I became a blonde to give myself a new start."

"I sympathize. Everywhere you turn something reminds you of someone you'd rather forget. I've been there several times, although my losses never involved a broken marriage. Just a broken engagement. When did you divorce?"

"The twenty-second of December, last year. We signed the papers right before Christmas."

"Ooh. Not a merry Christmas."

It was good that she told me. My heart had been broken a few times also.

"For the last five months," Bettina said, "I haven't dated anyone. Other than my work, I've been a recluse. Now my parents are on my case, telling me it's time to reenter the real world and reinvent my social life."

"Any way I can help, Bettina, I will. Grandpa Magnus says everybody has a story to tell and sometimes the best thing a friend can do is listen to their story. So, anything you feel like telling me, I'll listen. I have a few stories of my own."

"I don't need to discuss your feelings, Chuck."

"Then we can talk about yours. How did you feel after your divorce?"

Bettina paused.

Oops. I'd said the wrong thing. "I'm sorry, Bettina. That's none of my business. Forgive me for asking."

"No, no. It's okay. To tell the truth, I felt devastated. Like a total failure. My parents convinced me that I'm supposed to have children to feel complete. They told me that after age thirty-five, my biological clock starts ticking and I should start a family ASAP. I bought into the idea and married the first man who said he wanted children and also wanted to marry me. After I lived with Barry for a few months, I realized that I didn't want children—at least not with him."

"How do you feel about having children with a different husband?"

Bettina waffled a hand. "I've thought about it a lot. I'm not as starry-eyed about motherhood as I was when I married Barry. I've been a hermit the last five months except when I'm working."

"If you haven't dated, are you on birth control?"

"Of course. When the divorce was final, I started on the pill again. Be prepared, in case I got lucky."

I grinned. "So, you're single now?"

Bettina smiled back. "Why else would I have made a pass at you last night?"

"To tell the truth, since I called yesterday and you told me you were doing laundry stark naked, I haven't been able to erase the image from my memory. Although to tell the whole truth, I haven't tried very hard."

"What image? You've never seen me naked. At least not yet."

"I am blessed with a vivid imagination."

Bettina rose from the couch.

"Since I work on your sister's case on my time off, you owe me big time."

"What do I owe you? A draft choice named later?"

She walked over to my chair and sat on my lap. "A *favor* named later. Live in fear, big boy; live in fear."

I grinned. "I'm used to the feeling."

She kissed me slowly, deeply, and with conviction.

"I waited five years for that kiss," she said, rising to her feet.

"Happy to oblige." I stood and cradled her in my arms.

As I carried her to the bedroom, she said, "I won't keep you in suspense over that favor. How skilled are you at giving back rubs?"

"I'm the world's greatest amateur masseur. I'll start at your feet and work my way *slowly* up to the back of your neck. I make up in enthusiasm what I lack in skill, but I'm better at giving *front* rubs."

She dimpled. "I can hardly wait."

————

Later, in the shower, Bettina stroked the scar on my left thigh. "What's this?"

"A souvenir from Fallujah."

"What happened?"

"A suicide bomber nearly killed me and two of my fellow Green Berets."

Her fingers traced another scar on my shoulder. "And this one?"

"That was from an Iraqi terrorist I thought was dead. As we advanced past him, he shot me in the back. That scar is where the bullet exited. Peek at my back and you'll find the entry wound." I leaned to my right.

"It's a small circle, resembles a cigarette burn."

"Yeah. The exit wound was worse."

She explored the rest of my body with her fingers. "My God, how many times have you been shot?"

"You keep touching my body, and we'll never finish showering."

She smiled at me. "You say it like that's a bad thing."

————

Later in bed, she rolled up on one elbow. "You never answered my question."

"Which question?"

"How many times have you been shot?"

"Shot? Or do you mean 'wounded'?"

"What's the difference?"

"The first scars you noticed on my thigh were from an explosion of a guy in a suicide vest and burns from diesel fuel. Then there were the knife fights."

"Okay, let's include only gunshot wounds."

I paused. "I lost count once it reached double digits."

Bettina laid her head on my chest. "Try not to get shot in Houston—or anywhere ever again."

"Not even a flesh wound?"

"No, not even that."

"You trying to take the fun out of my life?"

TEN

Monday morning at 5:00 a.m. I slipped out of bed without waking Bettina. I grabbed my clothes and shaving kit and eased the bedroom door shut so she could sleep while I poked around the kitchen. I put the coffee on to brew, then used the guest bath to shower, shave, and dress.

I carried my coffee to the dining room and booted my laptop.

Our hostile reception at Flathead Pipe Supply told me that Angie and Teodoro were in deeper trouble than I had imagined. Angie had been hanging with Tommy Valley and Valley was linked to Flathead Pipe Supply. And Teodoro's phone was last heard from at Flathead.

Rule Seven: *There is no such thing as a coincidence—except when there is.*

People that open fire at strangers without cause or warning are not good people to hang around with. Yet Angie was—if not connected directly to Flathead—at least connected to Tommy Valley.

Maybe porn was not the only dodgy thing Angie was into.

Yesterday I didn't have a clue that Angelina was making porn. It would have been the furthest thing from my mind. What other side hustle was my sister snarled in?

I punched her name into Google and then Bing…

I found my sister's side hustle after a twenty-minute search. Angie was reinventing herself as an internet influencer. She had been posting party videos on her own MyVideoTube channel under the title *Wow! What a party!* for the last two months. The first video was posted three days after Teo's phone went dark.

Angelina signed herself *Angie, the Party Girl*, and had uploaded eleven party videos so far. That's a lot of partying in just two months. Especially for a woman who can't pay her rent.

I subscribed to her channel and watched her first video, *Woodlands Watery Wonderland*. The program revolved around a swimming pool party at a mansion in The Woodlands, an upscale master-planned community on the north side of Houston that slops over into adjoining Montgomery County. It included a professionally done virtual tour of the mansion that would have made Robin Leach jealous.

Other videos covered a celebrity-studded fundraiser for a Houston art museum that featured overdone ball gowns and tuxedo-clad waiters, a barbeque tailgate party before a game where the Houston Texans hosted the Dallas Cowboys, a picnic at a nude beach on South Padre Island on the Gulf Coast, a premier of a movie filmed in Austin, and a chili-cookoff on Galveston Island. You get the idea.

A video of a party at an adult-movie studio might make a dynamite episode on Angie's *Wow! What a party!* channel.

When I heard Bettina stirring in the bedroom, I started breakfast. A few minutes later, I added milk to her raisin bran, plated my western omelet, and took both dishes to the dining room.

Bettina came out dressed for work. "How nice. You already have my cereal, juice, and coffee. That is so sweet. Thank you."

"You're welcome. Can we make this a working breakfast?"

Bettina glanced at my open laptop. "Sure. What do you have?"

"While we eat, we should watch some videos Angie made. I found them on the internet." I turned my laptop toward her and played Angie's party videos for her while we ate.

Angie pushed her empty cereal bowl to one side.

"Did you know Angie had that kind of talent, Chuck? I'm no expert, but to me the videos look very professional. Of course, as a fashion model, she would know about staging and cameras and lighting. Do you think her video of that last party was what Saco was looking for? Could that be the doohickey?"

"Angie never mentioned her internet channel to me. Of course, I haven't seen her much the last couple of years. Mainly at Christmas or Easter and she didn't come to Adams Creek this Easter. I'll find the last party video and watch it, but it's a good bet that could be the doohickey."

Bettina finished her coffee and gathered her dirty dishes. "What surprises me is that she already has 14,000 followers."

I picked up my dishes and followed her to the kitchen.

"I just hope one of those followers isn't Saco."

———

As Bettina left for work, she paused in the doorway. "I'll cook tonight. Any requests?"

"Surprise me."

"Remember, Chuck, you're not scheduled for more gunfights until Wednesday."

I drove to the chemical lab she recommended. I left them a sample of Lola's cocaine and slid the baggie with the rest of the white powder in my pocket.

Next, I returned to Angie and Teodoro's apartment. I had already searched it once, but since my discussion with Bettina concerning the doohickey, I planned to thoroughly search the place again, specifically with a phone's memory chip in mind. Whatever the doohickey was, locating it might help find my sister.

If it was a memory chip the size of a thumbnail, it wouldn't be easy.

I worked my way from the front door to the kitchen in an hour. This time, I opened the cabinet doors underneath the sink where I found a plastic trash can, window cleaner, dishwasher soap, spot cleaner, and a dozen other chemicals, some toxic.

I removed everything and set the collection on the kitchen floor. I used my cellphone's flashlight app and searched behind the pipes. Nothing. Sticking my head in the cabinet, I shined the light up on the space behind the sink, alert for a fingernail-sized microchip taped to the underside of the kitchen counter or sink. Nothing.

One by one, I replaced the various chemical bottles and cans. I was left with the trash can, half full of gamey refuse. I removed the trash can liner, glanced inside for anything I should investigate, and tied the top. A small envelope lay in the bottom of the empty trash can. I held it to the light. Something was inside. Opening the flap, I dumped out a 32 Gigabyte SDHC card, the kind cellphones and digital cameras use for memory.

Bingo!... Maybe.

I slid the memory card back in the envelope and the envelope into my pocket.

Was this the doohickey? Had Angie hidden a crucial piece of evidence before she ran away?

———

I figured Lola would be awake and sober by the middle of the afternoon. The party had been Friday night and today was Monday. Three o'clock in the afternoon was late enough for me to wake her without making her too angry to talk to me. I hoped.

I stopped at Dunkin' Donuts for a dozen mixed. The donuts would make a peace offering along with two large cups of coffee. Then I bought two more cups. If Lola was in a conversational mood, I intended to stay for a long time.

Before climbing the stairs to her apartment, I scanned the parking area for Valley's Harley. It wasn't there. That didn't prove he wasn't home, but it was an indication.

I rapped on the door. A minute later, I rapped harder. I waited a decent interval then pounded the door with my fist—a cop knock. Nothing.

I picked the lock and stepped inside, closing the front door behind me. The odor of unwashed bodies and clothes and a hint of marijuana smoke and perfume emanated from the upholstery of the living room furniture.

Listening to the stillness, my eyes adapted to the gloom of the darkened apartment. A faint snore emanated from the hallway, but no other sound.

"Hello. Anybody home?" I called. "Lola, are you awake?"

I set the sack of donuts and the coffee carrier on the kitchen table. Moving along the hallway, I paused at the door to the bedroom where Lola had passed out Friday night. I opened it.

Lola lay alone on the bed, partially under a blanket. She wore the same clothes she'd worn at the party two days ago. The cocaine spoon made from the crucifix—her indispensable fashion accessory—hung from her neck.

Did Angie spend her nights at parties like that before she disappeared? Whatever the chain of events, it was pointless to speculate.

I prowled through the rest of the apartment. I didn't want Valley or his biker buddies to surprise me. Empty.

In the second bedroom, men's clothes hung in a closet. The closet exuded a faint odor of Tommy Valley. A simple wooden box sat on the shelf above the closet rod. It was a jewelry box, but simple enough for a man's sense of masculinity. I own a similar box that I keep on my closet shelf for cufflinks I haven't worn in years. Valley's box held over a dozen different earrings and a few finger rings. I returned it to its position.

The bed was still made, but I saw butt prints from Friday night party goers. A variety of used glasses sat abandoned on every horizontal surface in the room.

A computer monitor sat on a cheap wooden desk shoved against a wall, but there was no laptop on the desk. The monitor's HDMI input cable draped across the back of the desk. A rubber mousepad and a cordless mouse sat under the monitor. Valley had swept them to one side. A cordless keyboard was jammed against the wall. Where was the computer?

I peeked under the desk on the off-chance Valley had a tower computer underneath. Nope. Just a thin spot in the carpet where Valley's feet had worn a thin spot while he worked on the missing computer.

The rest of the apartment was unoccupied.

I carried a kitchen chair to the bedroom and positioned it beside Lola's bed.

She had rolled onto her side but was still asleep.

I switched on the lamp on her nightstand and the glare fell across her face. She mumbled something unintelligible.

Moving to the other side of the bed, I switched on the other lamp.

Her eyelids flickered and she muttered.

"Good afternoon, Lola," I said. "Time to greet the new day."

Returning to the kitchen, I fetched a cup of black coffee which I set on her nightstand. I removed the lid and the aroma of brewed coffee filled the room.

"Rise and shine. There's Dunkin' coffee on your nightstand."

Lola opened her eyes and blinked. "What time is it?" She sat up and the blanket fell away.

Yep, she still wore her clothes from Friday night's party. Had she slept the clock around? Twice? Unlikely. She must have gotten up once or twice to visit the bathroom, but I was ignorant of how drug addiction affected people's sleep cycle.

I edged the coffee closer to her. "Time to rise and shine."

"How can you act this cheerful at this ungodly hour of the morning?"

"It's a gift. Anyway, it's afternoon."

"I was asleep. What time is it?"

"It's 3:00 in the afternoon, Lola. You don't plan to spend the day in bed. There's a lovely world that deserves the pleasure of your company."

Lola stared at me for a moment, then smiled. "I'm ticked off at you, Chucky Lucky. Coffee?"

"Thanks, Lola, but I brought coffee and donuts. They're in the kitchen."

Lola tossed the blanket off. "Gotta pee."

She stumbled to the bathroom, slammed the door behind her, and returned in ten minutes with combed hair and fresh lipstick.

The scent of toothpaste on her breath reached me. "There's coffee on your nightstand. We can talk here or in the kitchen."

She grabbed the coffee. "What makes you think I have anything to say?"

"Angie is your friend. I plan to ask a few questions that might help find her. Should we talk here or in the kitchen?"

Lola was silent while she processed that. "Okay. The kitchen." She left the room.

Carrying the chair, I trailed her into the kitchen and sat at the table. I laid out napkins from the sack. Opening the donut box, I nudged it toward her. "Help yourself, Lola the Lovely."

"I'm sure I don't look lovely at this time of the morning."

No need to remind her that it was afternoon. To Lola, whenever she woke was, by definition, morning.

She picked through the donuts and selected one with pink icing. "This smells good. Strawberry?"

"Whatever it is, I bet it's delicious."

I selected a chocolate-covered donut. "Why are you ticked off at me?"

Lola nibbled on her donut. "You didn't stick around last night. I missed giving you your present."

"I would have stayed, Lola, but you were a little higher from that blow than you expected. You passed out on the bed just when things got interesting."

I didn't tell her it was now Monday. She had blacked out Saturday and Sunday. No point in correcting her.

"To tell you the truth, Chucky, I don't recall much of last night." She bit off another small piece. "Yeah, it's strawberry. Want a taste?"

"Sure." I leaned toward the woman and let her feed me a bite of her donut. Good to let her feel closer to me. Carlos McCrary, the master people person.

I broke off a piece of my chocolate-covered. "Care to try a bite of mine?"

She waited for me to hold the donut sample in place. She grasped my wrist and licked my fingers before she took the donut. "That's a sample of the present I intend to give you."

I grinned. "Next time, for sure."

She rubbed my wrist and released it. "Did you see Tommy last night? He wasn't here this morning."

"The bedroom down the hall..." I gestured to the right. "That's Tommy's bedroom?"

"Yeah, so what?"

"That's where he keeps his computer?"

"Sure. Me and him bought computer desks at Ikea. Tommy helped assemble mine. Why do you ask?"

"His computer is missing. Where is it?"

"How the hell would I know? Tommy comes and goes whenever he fancies."

"Does he carry his computer with him?"

"Sometimes. He bought larger saddlebags to fit his latest laptop, but it barely fits in them, so he don't travel with it much."

"Thanks for telling me." I sipped my coffee. "Tell me about Teodoro Garza. Why did he disappear?"

Lola stared at me.

I let the silence extend.

She raised her coffee cup to her mouth and peered over the rim. "You don't know, do you, Chucky?"

"No, I don't."

"Teodoro worked part-time for Tommy and Russell. He was a dealer, but he used his own product too often. He shorted a supplier. That's why he was in money trouble."

"Who did he short? Who was mad at him? You said Russell and Tommy. Who was after Teodoro?"

"I said too much." Her mouth squeezed into a tight line.

"Teodoro was a drug dealer?"

Lola gave me a look. "How could you not be aware of this? She's your sister, for God's sake."

"I haven't talked to Angie since Christmas, and I was never close to Teodoro. To tell the truth, Lola, I don't like him. From the day I met him, I said he was wrong for Angelina. The whole family felt the same way, but Angie wouldn't listen to anyone."

"I hope something bad hasn't happened to Angie," Lola said. "I hope she ran away. Far, far away."

She rotated her coffee cup on the table. "Your sister was in way over her head. And she couldn't swim with sharks."

"What happened to Angie?"

"I wish I knew, Chucky. She was my friend."

She referred to Angie in the past tense. Was it a slip of the tongue, or did she know something she hadn't told me? "What do you *suspect* happened to her?"

"Some bad people were searching for Angie. People you don't want pissed at you."

"Does this have something to do with Esteban Espinoza's party?"

Lola squinted her eyes before she shook her head.

"Espinoza's party had something to do with it, didn't it?"

Lola's hand holding the coffee stopped halfway to her lips. "Who?"

I pulled Espinoza's business card from my pocket and positioned it on the table in front of her. "I visited Espinoza's website."

Her grip on the coffee cup tightened.

"I searched for 'Lola' and there was nothing." I paused, and she lifted her cup.

"Then I searched for 'Lolita.' I watched part of *Inside Lolita*. Your tattoos displayed beautifully. So did Tommy's."

An array of expressions flitted across her face. Again, I waited for her to respond.

Her eyes flitted randomly. "I didn't realize Esteban recorded Tommy and me."

"Lola, half the time, you smiled straight into the camera. In fact, you winked at the camera and blew a kiss." I waved a hand dismissively. "That's not the point. What you do with your life is not my business. Frankly, I was impressed with your flexibility. My one interest is locating Angelina. You and Angie are closer friends than you let on. There is something you haven't told me—something important."

Lola sipped her coffee, avoiding eye contact.

I waited.

Finally, her shoulders slumped. "Angie's modeling career is history. She told me she hadn't done a photo shoot in months. While Teodoro lived with her, he dealt drugs to pay the bills. With Teodoro vanished, she was broke. She considered dealing drugs but decided it was too risky, dealing with addicts for customers and drug gangs for suppliers. I told her a woman alone would be ripped off—either by a customer or a supplier."

"At least she avoided that mistake."

"Angie was desperate. Did you find her MyVideoTube party channel?"

"Yes. I watched all the party videos this morning."

"She's actually making a little money from them now. Not enough to live on, but it's gradually building a following. Until she scores a viral video, she needs money real bad. I've made a few adult films for Esteban. He pays damned well, and I introduced her to him. Angie made some films for him."

Films. She said films, plural. That meant more than one film.

"Did you find her films on Esteban's website?"

My gut knotted at the memory. "Not under Angelina. When I searched under 'Angelica' there she was, in the flesh, in a manner of speaking."

"Did you watch the one she made with me and Tommy? We were a smoking hot threesome. Me and Angie acted in the films rated NC-17. Esteban makes a few R-rated films, but the NC-17s are more fun to make."

I tried to hide it, but my stomach growled in protest, and it was hard to swallow the bile that rose in my throat. I was glad I stopped viewing the website before I found that particular video. There are certain things that, once seen, you cannot *un*see. Even the idea of Angelina doing that was hard to bear.

"No, I didn't finish the first video. Just enough to confirm it was Angie. Watching porn is not my thing, and she's my sister. What were you and Angie doing at Esteban's party on Saturday night nine days ago? That was the night she disappeared. What are you not telling me?"

Lola stood and paced the kitchen.

I hoped she was gathering courage to say something. I drank coffee and waited.

She stopped pacing. "Me and Angie didn't meet Esteban at Third Base the Friday before last. You figured out that we met him before, and we made films for his company. To tell the truth, Esteban invited us to his party a couple of days before that. We heard he threw great parties."

"Tell me about the party," I said.

"Where should I start?"

"Tell me everything Angie did."

She collapsed into a kitchen chair. "I was lit up pretty good. I'm not real sure. I mean, it was a *great* party."

How did Lola define "a great party"? Drugs? Food? Sex? Music? All the above? I clenched and unclenched my fists below the table where the Lola wouldn't see them. I drew a long breath and let it out. *Easy, fellow*, I told myself. *You catch more flies with honey than with vinegar.*

I remembered Rule Twelve-A: *In vino, veritas.* Time to try the lip loosener. If alcohol worked, why not cocaine?

I was undecided whether to return her baggie of cocaine. I disapprove of recreational drugs, but I believe the use and possession of drugs is a victimless crime. Consider marijuana: legal in some states, illegal in others. Who was right and who was wrong? The cocaine was illegal, but it was her property, and I am no thief.

I thought of Angelina and where she might be. Lola had avoided telling me something. Something that might tell me whether the memory chip was the doohickey. And this Saco drug dealer that Tommy Valley blabbed about. Was he behind Angie's disappearance? Weighing the pros and cons, I extracted the baggie of cocaine. "I forgot to give this back to you."

Lola jumped to her feet. "Where the hell did you get that?"

"You gave it to me Friday night and offered me a snort. You said it was Russell's best and insisted I try it. Then you passed out on the bed. I was afraid you had a heart attack or something. I stuck the baggie in my pocket and made sure you were okay. Then I forgot to give it back. It was outstanding blow. First quality."

Snatching the baggie, she opened it, jabbed the end of the crucifix/cocaine-spoon into it, and took a hit.

She sprawled across the chair. The drug coursed through her bloodstream. She smiled a dreamy smile. Her body language changed as the cocaine kicked in.

Lola giggled. "You want a taste, Chucky Lucky? Then we can screw our brains out, eh?"

"Maybe later. Right now, let's discuss Esteban's party. What did Angie do at the party?"

Her eyes opened a bit before half-closing. "Everyone was high, and Angie started making selfies with anybody who would pose for her. She'd laugh and shoot a selfie. Then sniff another hit and ask someone else to make a selfie with her. She made one with almost everyone at the party."

"Why did she do that?" I asked. "Did she know everybody at the party?"

"Hell, no. Most of them were strangers. People do stupid stuff when they're high. She figured it would be fun."

Lola took another snoot full of cocaine.

I tried to finish the interview before she passed out. "Okay, Angie made selfies with everyone. What else do you recall?"

"Me and Saco were in the background of a few shots, so I made faces while Angie shot the photos." She chuckled. "She took a lot of video too."

"Was that when Saco got mad at Angie? When she videoed him?"

"No. Saco never noticed her taking the video. It was later."

"What happened?"

"Before she left, Angie used her phone to video while she did a walka-bout in Esteban's house making videos of everybody and everything. She did the same thing at the pool."

"When did you learn Angie made the video?"

"Later that night. Angie played the video on the TV in my apartment."

"Why not play it in her own apartment?"

"My TV is bigger. We enjoyed the video so much I made a copy to give Tommy."

"Is that why Tommy was angry with you and Angie when I first met you?"

"Who the hell knows or cares what makes Tommy mad? The SOB is mad most of the time. When Angie made the video, me and another guy were doing it in one of the bedrooms. Tommy hasn't been paying enough attention to me except while we're on camera. I wanted to make him jeal-ous. Tommy watched the video and said there was things on it what shouldn't be there."

"What did he mean?"

Lola shrugged. "Who the hell cares? Tommy flies off the handle for any reason or none at all. Probably got pissed at somebody at the party. I haven't seen him since. That's the way Tommy is."

"Why was Saco mad at you?"

"Saco don't want to be photographed or videoed. The next day Tommy told Saco there was a video of the party. Saco sent Tommy to bring Angie's phone to him. He planned to personally erase the video."

Bingo. The video. It was the doohickey that put Angie in danger. But was the chip from Angie's trash can the video? Or was there something else in Angie's phone?

"What went wrong?"

Lola swung her head back and forth to loosen her neck. "Tommy went next door to Angie's apartment and didn't return until the next day. He told me that Angie hadn't been home, so he went to look for her. He searched all night, but he never found her." She spread her hands. "*Poof.* Her car was gone. I ain't seen her since."

"How did Tommy get in her apartment since she wasn't home?"

"Oh, hell, half of Houston has a key to Angie's apartment. Mine too."

"So, Saco was pissed at Tommy because he didn't find Angie's phone."

"Yeah. And Saco is the kind of guy you don't want mad at you. I erased the copy I made for Tommy. You mess with Saco, you can wind up dead."

There was another reference to Saco's deadly reputation. I knew the GPS coordinates where Angie's phone stopped and later dropped off the network, but I didn't know why it stopped so far from an exit. Or Angie might have had more than one phone, and I was tracking the wrong one. Valley could have lied to Lola about not finding Angie. He might have recovered Angie's phone chip and tossed the phone away. Or he discovered the chip was missing and threw the phone away. Following that, Valley might have taken Angie to Saco. That final possibility chilled me to the bone.

Or Angie pitched her phone out the window to keep it from being captured. Perhaps she intended to return later, but she was kidnapped first.

But how did the chip end up hidden in her trash? When did she hide it?

My stomach knotted. For the first time, I accepted that Angie was likely dead. Then I took courage from knowing that my cousin Emily had disappeared for four years, but I rescued her from the psycho who'd held her captive. Her captivity damaged Emily psychologically, but thank goodness, she was physically unharmed. With therapy, love, and a change of scenery, Emily was moving forward with her life. I chose to be optimistic.

The first task was to find Angie's phone. Then I would learn what was on the micro-chip.

ELEVEN

I switched on the hazard lights and stopped on the shoulder of Loop 8 aka Sam Houston Parkway. This section of the highway was elevated. Further south the tollway sloped back to ground level. The access road paralleled the highway twenty feet below. The space between the tollway and the access road was filled with trees and wild grasses.

I glanced west. A couple of hours left before sunset.

Pine forests lined both sides of the Sam Houston Parkway so thick I couldn't see five yards into the underbrush. I slowed the Tahoe to walking speed and observed the GPS on the dashboard. I reached the coordinates where Angelina's phone had stopped pinging. I idled another fifty yards further along the shoulder. I edged close to the concrete safety barricade and parked.

Exiting the vehicle, I scanned the surroundings.

Twenty meters. Sixty-five feet of accuracy in the GPS coordinates. Angie passed this point at approximately 2:00 a.m. on Monday, May fourth. Assuming she chucked her phone out the window of a speeding car, where would it land? The traffic lanes were twelve feet wide. Three lanes are thirty-six feet wide. The left shoulder was eight or ten feet wide; the right shoulder was twelve feet. The coordinates positioned her anywhere from the left shoulder to the right. No way to tell which lane she drove in.

It was even possible Angie no longer had her phone. Perhaps her kidnappers had been carrying it.

An eighteen-wheeler stormed past me; the wake of displaced air nearly knocked me over. It kicked up a cloud of dust and dirt that pelted my face and hands with a thousand tiny pinpricks. I shifted closer to the concrete barricade and walked northbound, against the traffic.

Angie's phone had been moving southbound. Driving in the left lane, she would tend to toss the phone out the driver's window onto the shoulder. Or she might have tried to pitch it over the divider onto the northbound side where it fell on the left shoulder. But suppose she used the right lane? What would she have done?

That was unknowable. Rule Eight: *Sometimes there is no substitute for shoe leather*. Most oncoming vehicles swerved to the center lane to avoid me. That made the dirt tornados easier to survive. Scrutinizing the shoulder, I walked one hundred yards. No phones. In fact, there was a notable absence of trash and debris. The highway department must send street sweepers along the shoulders periodically. If the phone landed on the shoulder, the street sweeper had collected it, and it was forever lost.

I scrutinized the area across the concrete barricade and returned to the rental. Thick grass and scattered trees made it impossible to spot a phone hidden in the shadowed undergrowth below.

I rethought my conclusions. Suppose Angie stopped on the shoulder and lobbed the phone into the thicket below? Good thing I brought a metal detector.

I took the next exit and looped under the tollway, making two U-turns to the southbound access road. I analyzed the GPS images and moved closer to the target spot. I bumped over the curb on the left lane and parked on the grass. Flicking on the hazard lights, I popped the rear hatch and put together the metal detector.

Twenty-five minutes later the metal detector beeped at a cellphone nestled in the grass against a pine tree.

Bingo.

I opened the phone and looked in the chip slot. It was empty.

———

Back at Bettina's condo, I set the phone on the dining room table.

Bettina walked in from the kitchen. "I ran the plate on the SUV that shot at us yesterday. It belongs to a shell company, Escondido Sendero LLC. The address is a post office box in El Paso."

"*Escondido sendero* means hidden trail in Spanish. Drug connection perhaps?"

"Lots of things in Houston are drug-connected. I assumed you'd be glad to hear that I followed up."

"Yeah. Good job."

She scooted out a dining room chair. "When you called, I put the meat-loaf in the oven. It'll be done in a half hour. Is that Angie's phone?"

"Yeah. I rented a metal detector and found it between the access road and the main highway where the GPS coordinates said it last was."

I told Bettina what I'd learned from Lola. "Angie's party video must be the doohickey—the thing Angie owned that the gangsters want. Saco is on the video Angie made. Saco doesn't want to be photographed or videoed."

"The doohickey is a phone memory chip, like a micro-SD card?"

"Yeah. And this morning I found an SD card hidden in Angie's apart-ment." I handed the envelope to her.

She dumped the chip onto the table. "Did you view the chip?"

"No. I've been busy with other things first. Let's watch it now."

I inserted the chip into Angie's phone and tried to switch it on. The screen flashed and went dark.

"It needs charging," Bettina said. She studied the charging port. "I may have one that fits."

She carried the phone to the kitchen and opened a drawer filled with assorted junk. "Found it," she said, after fumbling in the clutter for a few minutes.

She plugged in the phone. A *charging* symbol lit the screen. She laid the phone on the counter. "It takes a while to charge. Why don't we pour a glass of wine before dinner?"

"Sounds like a plan."

"Bring the Pinot Grigio from the fridge. I'll get the glasses."

Returning to the living room, Bettina lifted her glass. "What should we toast?"

"You choose."

She winked as she lifted her glass. "To friends with benefits."

"Friends with benefits. Am I blushing?"

Bettina clinked my glass. "Not yet, but I have hopes."

She set her goblet on the table. "Where was the memory chip hidden?"

"In an envelope under her kitchen sink. It was underneath the plastic liner in a trash can."

"She removed the chip from her phone before she ran away?"

"That's the likely scenario, but she tossed her phone from her car. Probably to prevent someone from finding the phone and learning the chip was missing. Of course, there could be more than one chip. You can buy the things for practically nothing."

"But this chip wasn't in the phone. Giving the chip to Saco might have satisfied him. Why hide it and run?"

"Panic? Angie has been out of her depth for months. According to Lola, Angie's a doper, and dopers make bad decisions." The moment I said it, I twinged at the thought that my own sister was reaping what she had sown. I was conflicted; I felt guilty for even considering that Angie did not deserve my help. I suppressed the thought.

I sipped my Pinot Grigio. "Lola said Saco sent Tommy to get Angie's phone. Tommy told Lola he couldn't find Angie, but he didn't get home until the next day. Possibly he found Angie, but he didn't find her phone."

Bettina twirled her wine glass by the stem. "Or Tommy caught Angie and she still had the phone. He opened her phone, noticed the memory slot was empty, and threw the phone away in frustration."

"That's possible."

Bettina glanced at the clock. "Ten more minutes for the meatloaf."

She laid a hand on my forearm. "You're not ready to believe Angie is dead yet, but filing a missing person report lets me help you as a Houston police detective. Any persons of interest you pursue are more likely to cooperate when I flash my badge. If not, we bring search warrants."

"Not yet, Bettina. Angie may be dead, but I want to check out one more thing before I file the missing person report."

"What thing?"

"You should put out a BOLO on Angie's car. Locate it, and we may locate evidence of foul play."

"What reason should I use for the BOLO?"

"I'll report it stolen. I'm next of kin."

"Let's eat. Then we watch Angie's video."

———

Angie's phone was charged. I opened the *Gallery* app and selected *Videos*. There were dozens of thumbnails of various videos. I played the most recent one.

The video showed Angie from the chest up. She wore a red sleeveless shell with deep cleavage. The cocaine spoon made from a crucifix dangled between her breasts. She bounced to music. "I'm at the coolest party ever," she bellowed above the roar.

The image blurred, then switched from selfie mode to the camera on the phone's back side. It showed a view across a living room with colored lights strung across the walls and hanging from the mantel of an artificial fireplace. A TGIF banner hung on one wall. The room was jammed with people laughing, drinking, and enjoying themselves.

One gorgeous brunette with a nose ring and a row of piercings on one ear lobe noticed the camera. She handed her drink to a salt-and-pepper gray-haired man in a Hawaiian shirt standing with his arm around her. She lifted her bedazzled T-shirt and flashed her breasts at the camera. There were no tan lines across her chest. The brunette laughed and retrieved her drink. She winked her thanks to the man. "*Diviértete*, Angie," she shouted and blew a kiss.

Bettina touched my arm. "What does that mean?"

"It means 'Have fun.'"

Hawaiian Shirt lifted his glass in greeting and waved.

The image swung past a bar standing in the archway between the living room and dining room. The dining room held no other furniture. Instead, it was filled with people.

Angie wedged her way down the hall and passed the kitchen where three people in chef's toques prepared *hors d'oeuvres* trays. One chef waved and smiled at the camera. The view shifted into the kitchen where the chefs were preparing the food. "Tell me what you're preparing here? It smells delicious," Angie asked.

The chef gave a short explanation of the various dishes they were preparing.

Angie's bare arm moved into the frame and snatched an *hors d'oeuvre*. Her voice carried from off-camera. *"Delicioso."*

As the image continued down the hall, the music grew quieter. Angie entered a bedroom through an open door and scanned the people inside. One couple was making out on the bed. The camera zoomed in, held the kiss for a moment, then zoomed out. Others sat on the bed ignoring the amorous pair.

I stopped the video. "The woman on the bed is Lola Salazar. The man with her is not Tommy."

"Yeah," Bettina said. "This guy has different tattoos."

I continued playing the video. A half dozen people sprinkled across the room, chattering in English and Spanish over the music. One woman mouthed "¡*Hola!*, Angie," and made a kissing motion.

The image continued along the hall and through an enclosed lanai arranged with wicker furniture and occupied by more standing and seated partiers. Several noticed the camera and lifted their drinks in greeting. I read one man's lips when he called Angie's name. Interesting. Several people at the party recognized Angie.

The videoed image passed through the open glass sliders into an expansive backyard. The pool lights showed three women and a man skinny dipping. The picture paused for a few seconds on a disordered pile of bathrobes sprawled on the pool deck, then panned to the hot tub which held four women and three men, most of whom lifted their tropical drinks and waved at the camera.

In one corner of the yard, three men sat beside a fire pit built into a stone patio. One man leaned away, struck a Zippo lighter, and lit a joint. The men leaned close to one another and conversed privately. The picture blurred. The phone's camera automatically adjusted the picture for the difference in distance and lighting. The picture snapped into high definition.

I froze the video. "Do you recognize any of those men?"

Handling the phone, Bettina used her fingers to zoom the image. "This guy looks familiar." She pointed to the man on the left. "Could be a local drug dealer. I'll check our mug shot files at the precinct. I don't recognize the other two." She handed the phone back. "Is one of them Saco?"

"Somebody on this video is." I started the video again.

One man in the hot tub climbed out and shrugged into a bathrobe. He noticed the camera and grinned at Angie. He unwrapped the front of the robe and flashed the camera. "*¿Quieres algo de esto, Angie?*"

Angie's voice sounded faintly from off camera. "*En tus sueños, diminuto.*" The image jiggled from Angie laughing.

Bettina reached over and paused the video. "What did they say?"

"The man said, 'You want some of this, Angie?' and my sister said, 'In your dreams, tiny.'"

As Bettina started the video again, I pondered how my sister became involved in a culture of drugs and promiscuous sex. It was alien to everything in Adams Creek where we were raised. Of course, Angie had left Adams Creek after high school and spent the last two decades in Houston.

The image bobbled from Angie strolling near the pool, blurred, and then the camera panned across the three men on the patio. The man smoking the joint was clicking his Zippo lighter open and closed, a nervous habit one of my fellow cops had when I was on the job. My cop buddy wasn't even aware he was clicking the Zippo; he did it at a subconscious level. It annoyed the hell out of the rest of us.

Angie paused to let the camera refocus.

I stopped the video. "This is a different view of the three men. Do you recognize anyone from this angle?"

"No, but that gives us another chance to ID them through facial recognition. Two viewpoints are better than one."

The video panned back across the backyard, through the lanai, then the hallway. Angie edged over to let a chef pass with an *hors d'oeuvres* tray.

Angie stepped back into a bedroom where Lola was having sex with the man on the bed. Several bystanders observed, laughing, and applauding. Lola grinned at the camera and waved. "Save a horse; ride a cowboy," she said.

The camera went in for a close-up, then zoomed back out.

The image proceeded back to the living room and ended.

I closed the phone's Gallery app. "Was that video anything worth killing my sister for?"

"That depends on who the men are. If they are top dogs in the *Tres Equis* cartel, then the answer is 'yes.'"

"Whoever they are, they were there for a business meeting, not a party."

Before bed, I emailed my parents covering most new developments. The hardest part was to tell them Angie made porno films. As I typed the email relating Angie's fallen status, it was all I could do to keep from crying when I thought about our family's reaction. I called them *adult films* to downplay it the best I could, but there wasn't much I could do to soften the blow.

But the bad news was just getting started.

———

I input the truckstop's address where Angie recorded the fateful voicemail.

The truckstop was a combination service station, convenience store, and fast-food restaurant. I followed the perimeter of the site. Security cameras covered every square foot except the very back of the lot.

Parking my rental near the C-store entrance, I asked the cashier where the office was. I went to interview the truckstop manager.

I gave the manager a business card. "I'm trying to locate a missing woman who made a cellphone call from your truckstop on May fourth of this year. She was last seen here. Would you help me access your security footage to figure out what happened to her?"

"What time did she make the call?"

"At 1:30 a.m. on Monday, May fourth. Her cellphone records show she was at this truckstop."

The manager rubbed under his chin with a finger. "I'm no expert in our security system. Our national HQ handles stuff like that. I never think about it until the cops come to investigate a stolen car. I believe we can access the video from that far back. You know how to work these systems?"

"Yes, thanks."

The manager led me to an adjoining room with a no-frills desk and office chair, a tower computer on the floor under the desk, and an array of six computer monitors, each divided into four camera views. "Here you go. Help yourself. I hope you find her."

"Thanks."

The manager pulled the door closed behind him and the background noise of the convenience store and truckstop was cut off like throwing a switch. All I could hear was the whisper of the fan and an occasional faint tick from the tower computer as it recorded the dozens of security cameras.

Sitting at the keyboard, I scrolled through the control panel on one screen until I figured out how the app worked. Next, I solved how to select the date and time. I sorted through thirty-seven different camera views. Ah, the glamor and excitement of detective work.

The thirteenth view showed a blue Mazda driving onto the property from the access road. It tracked close enough to read the license plate. Freezing the image for a few seconds, I zoomed in. Yes, it was Angie's car. The car coasted out of the frame. I inserted a flash drive in a USB port on the computer and copied the video segment.

I searched three more camera views before I found the Mazda stopping at an available pump. A woman exited the vehicle and tapped a credit card against the pump panel. The image was not sharp enough to recognize her except I recognized her car. She tapped the card again, then slipped it into her purse and glanced over her shoulder. Probably concerned that someone might notice her card was declined. Typical Angie, concerned with appearances.

She staggered from the Mazda, bracing herself on the fender and hood, and exited the frame, tottering toward the main building.

Was her clumsy gait caused by stress or drugs? Maybe a little of both. The funny ache in the back of my throat told me that my eyes were tearing up.

Suppressing my emotions, I copied the segment to the flash drive.

Shifting the camera view to one covering the cash register, I watched

Angelina enter the frame and stop at the counter. The picture was sharp enough to identify her. Our mother gave Angie the dangly garnet birthstone earrings for her thirtieth birthday eight years before.

She fumbled in her purse for a bill which she slid across the counter. The cashier collected the twenty and handed Angelina a receipt. She pocketed the receipt and disappeared from the frame. I copied that segment also.

Restroom next? I tried the camera that covered the restroom entrances. Yep. There she was.

Four minutes later, Angelina exited the restroom, and I switched cameras to monitor her return to the Mazda. She walked with her eyes down, shoulders slumped as though carrying a great weight. I could feel my own shoulders droop in sympathy.

She inserted the nozzle and latched the pump in the open position. She leaned against the rear door and fumbled with her cellphone.

The time index on the screen read *01:28*.

I sat straighter. This was her call to my voicemail. My chest tightened. Angie was in obvious distress, and I couldn't reach back through time to help. I was watching a train wreck happen and was powerless to stop it.

She tapped her phone screen and raised it to her ear. Once Angelina recognized my recorded voice, she straightened her posture and began to speak. Her lips stopped moving as the recorded voice gave instructions to record a voicemail. Her shoulders slumped again while she waited for the beep.

Even with no sound from the surveillance system, and the camera twenty or thirty yards away, I imagined I was reading her lips in my mind. "Carlitos, it's Angie. I'm in terrible trouble. I have something they want. These people are dangerous." Angie's shoulders shook with the sob I had heard more times than I could count. "I'm so scared... I don't know what to do. Please help me." She gazed off camera when she heard the loud noise of a truck shifting gears. Her gaze shadowed the unseen truck. "I can't call the cops and I have nowhere else to turn. Call me. I know it's the middle of the night but call me no matter what time you get this message. *Call me, please, Carlitos.*" The picture was not sharp enough to make out the tears I knew marked her cheeks.

Tears trickled down my own cheeks. I wiped them away with the back of my hand.

She returned the phone to her purse and hung the nozzle on the pump. Opening the driver's door, she tossed her purse in the passenger's seat and sat behind the wheel. The door closed. Brake lights flashed. The chassis torqued from the engine starting. The brake lights went out and the car rolled off the screen.

As Angelina's Mazda coasted out of the frame, a beige van entered the picture and followed. Large green letters on the side read *Flathead Pipe Supply*.

My breath caught in my throat until the beige van had vanished from the screen.

I added that video segment to the flash drive copies.

I scanned the additional cameras until I located one with Angelina's Mazda rolling away. The brake lights flashed, and the car jerked to a halt at the exit, a hundred yards away. The Mazda changed direction and moved toward the rear of the property where it stopped.

Why did she stop? Why did she drive to the rear of the site?

The panel van parked behind the Mazda, blocking it from view. The van's nearer rear door opened.

I zoomed the image. From my viewpoint, I saw the window in the van door and the space between the bottom of the door and the pavement. A man's head leaned into view behind the window. His face was a dark blob. He jumped to the ground. Freezing the image and zooming it to maximum, I made out a pair of boots. Was I imagining it, or did I make out a Harley-Davidson logo shining on them? Were those the same boots I photographed at Lola's party? There were at least six bikers at the party.

I replayed the video, and another pair of boots jumped from the van, perhaps Harley-Davidsons, but a model with a strap and shiny thing that was an ornamental buckle. The two men walked to the van's other side. A minute later, two pair of boot-shod feet reappeared dragging a woman between them.

I zoomed the picture on the woman's shoes. At that magnification, the image pixelated. The shoes must be Angie's, but the scene was too distant to capture detail.

One man scrambled into the van and the other man shoved the woman in after him. The outside man slammed the door, and I froze the image. Too far to identify him. He wore black pants, a black hoody, and a baseball hat. The man slapped the door twice. The van accelerated away, revealing Angelina's Mazda. The man walked to the Mazda.

I froze and expanded the image. Even in the high-def picture, the hoody and baseball hat obscured his face. The kidnapping was too far and too dark to make positive ID. The kidnapper got in the Mazda. Did he rack the seat back? The Mazda trailed the van from the truckstop.

What did I know? Two men jumped from the van, and two men dragged Angie to the van. They were not necessarily the same two men. There might have been a third man in the van. Tommy Valley could have driven the truck until it stopped behind the Mazda. He helped force Angie into the van and a second man replaced him in the panel truck.

I selected the three bikers' photos and studied the pictures of their boots. The styles were not inconsistent with the boots in the truckstop video. For example, they were the same color—black. Big deal—every motorcycle boot I ever noticed was black. Not definitive evidence, but it didn't prove they *weren't* Valley and his cohorts. But Valley could be friendly with the other bikers at the party.

I reversed the video until I spotted the van's license plate, which I noted. I searched the security cameras until I documented the van's entire path through the truckstop, which I copied onto the flash drive. The van stalked Angie's Mazda from a distance as she arrived. It lurked fifty yards away when she stopped by the gas pump. I let the video run.

While Angie entered the building, a person in black pants, a black hoody, and a baseball hat trotted to the Mazda carrying a dark blanket. He opened the back door and lay on the floor behind the front seats. He pulled the dark blanket over himself before he closed the rear door. With the tinted passenger windows, Angie never noticed him hidden in the back.

Angie rolls away, and the hidden man sits up and holds a knife to her neck. He tells her to drive to the rear of the property and park. Another man exits the van and joins the hidden man at the Mazda, and they drag her to the panel van. Yep, that's one way it could have happened.

I scanned every view for an angle where I could see inside the Flathead van's cabin, but the interior was dark and the truckstop's lights reflecting on the windows made it impossible to see inside. Too bad; I wanted photos to show the cops.

I rechecked my notes and the segments saved on the flash drive. I had copied all videos showing the panel van, the Mazda, and Angie. And an unknown person that might be Tommy Valley. No proof yet. My gut said it was Valley, but my gut wouldn't stand up in court. Hell, a gut feeling wasn't good enough for a search warrant; more's the pity.

An ominous theory that had been lurking in the corner of my mind clicked into sharp focus: The kidnapping occurred over a week before and there had been no ransom demand. Odds were that Angelina McCrary Garza was dead. And had been for several days.

I pushed my emotions for my lost sister aside so I could keep working the case. Grieving was a luxury I could save for later.

———

Returning to Bettina's condo, I edited the videos into three timeline sequences. First, Angelina's movements from the time she arrived at the truckstop to the time she was forced into the panel van. Second, the panel van's actions from its arrival at the truckstop to its departure. Third, the complete track of Angie's Mazda, including while she paid the cashier.

And the three timelines intersected at Angelina's kidnapping.

As I finished editing the videos and made two copies, I wiped the tears from my eyes. I was glad Bettina was not there to see me cry.

I had proof Angie was kidnapped. Next task was to place the proof in the hands of the Houston Police Department. Then they would grant Angie's case the respect it deserved.

TWELVE

I met two detectives from the Organized Crime Unit at the West Freeway police station. I shook hands with Lieutenant Royce Wilson and Sergeant Art Devlin.

"Didn't I meet you on Sunday?" Devlin asked. "You're Bettina Simpson's friend, right?"

"Right. I received a voicemail you need to hear." I played Angie's message and briefed the OCU detectives on the case and what I'd discovered so far. I did not mention my incursion with Bettina into Flathead Pipe and Supply.

"I found a video of the actual kidnapping and another video my sister made at a party that was attended by three possible organized crime members, maybe members of the *Tres Equis* cartel."

"Okay," said Wilson, "let's see them."

"This is a compilation of security videos from various cameras at the truckstop where Angie made the call." I played the edited video for the detectives.

Wilson said, "That says 'kidnapping' to me. How did you get the videos?"

I told the detectives how I obtained the videos. "I was a cop, and this ain't my first rodeo. I made photos and IDs of three men I suspect were in the Flathead van. You want them?"

I showed Wilson and Devlin my photos of the bikers. "I believe the guy driving my sister's Mazda is Tommy Valley aka Tomás Valenzuela, but I can't prove it. The other guys in the kidnap video, you see only their boots, and you never see more than two people at a time. You might differentiate the boots by enhancing the video. But all three men who attacked me in Angie's parking lot wore biker boots in different styles. Plus, there were other bikers at the party. There were at least six bikes in the lot." I zoomed the photos on my laptop. "The Harley logos and the different buckles, harnesses, and so forth on the boots are consistent with the ones in the truckstop video."

Devlin studied the photos. "Are these men unconscious?"

I considered how to answer. Finally settled on the truth. "They are."

"It's none of my business, but how did that happen?"

"Tommy Valley aka Tomás Valenzuela—that's this one—he insisted I stop searching for my sister. The other two bikers interrupted our conversation to, uh… argue on Valley's behalf."

Wilson chuckled. "And they finished unconscious?"

"We engaged in a spirited debate. They were drunk and/or on drugs."

"And they passed out? All of them?"

I smiled. "Not from the drinking. They suffered from over-confidence."

I lifted four plastic sandwich bags from my briefcase. "I acquired these phones from Valley, Fajardo, and Trojanik. Valley carried two phones. The iPhone is full of Mexican contacts—presumably his suppliers. The Samsung has U.S. contacts—likely his customers. Backtrack their phones and you'll discover all their phones pinged at the truckstop at the time Angie was kidnapped. That's why I believe they're the kidnappers. Then all four phones traveled to Flathead Pipe Supply's factory. You should get a warrant and search for Angie there. Or her body."

Devlin sneered. "You solved the case, McCrary. What the hell do you need us for?"

I ignored his sarcasm. "I'm glad to help. I plan to find my sister and bring her kidnappers to justice. If she's dead, I plan to bring the murderers to justice. That's why I need you two detectives."

Wilson made calming motions with his hands. "Guys, we're on the same team, right?"

"No," I said. "We're on the same *side*, but we're not on the same *team*. One more thing, Royce: My brother-in-law Teodoro Garza's phone was last pinged at Flathead Pipe Supply also. It's possible he was murdered there."

"Thanks, Chuck. You mentioned a video Angie made at a party?"

I played Angie's party video.

When the video finished, I told the OCU detectives what I had discovered in Angelina's apartment.

Devlin frowned. "Was this the personal case I caught Detective Simpson working on with you in the precinct last Sunday?"

My shoulders straightened and my eyes narrowed. "No, Devlin, it is *not*. You didn't *catch* Bettina doing anything. Catching her implies she was doing something wrong. Last Sunday we had not ascertained that Angelina had been kidnapped. I discovered the party video on Monday, and I tracked down the security videos this morning."

Devlin's jaw tightened. His right hand clamped into a fist.

I spoke to Wilson. "I suggest we direct our attention to solving actual *crimes*. Did either of you recognize any people in the party video?"

Wilson cut his eyes to Devlin. "Art, why don't you copy the video and run the three guys through facial recognition?"

Wilson handed a flash drive to me. "Can you make us a copy?"

I copied the file and passed it to Devlin, who left the room.

Wilson said, "You found drug paraphernalia in your sister's apartment?"

"In her husband's closet, yes."

"But no actual drugs?"

"That's right. Whoever entered their apartment and stole their computers and the guns may have stolen any drugs that were there. I bet you'll find Tommy Valley's fingerprints there."

"Possibly," said Wilson. "You found no proof the apartment was broken into. Your grandfather has a key. Who else has keys? Some people hand out keys like candy to their friends, and Valley was her next-door neighbor."

"Lola Salazar told me Tommy Valley has a key to Angie's apartment. Lola has one too."

Wlson spread his hands. "There you are. No break-in. This might not be a drug cartel thing. It might be gang related. The three kidnappers may belong to the same biker gang. That's organized crime, but a different crime level than a drug cartel. We need to send our own CSI unit to process the apartment. Too late to send the unit out today. The woman's been missing nine days. Won't hurt to process the apartment tomorrow."

"Every day's delay lets the trail grow colder," I said. "You should send the CSI unit out today and get search and arrest warrants for the three kidnappers immediately."

Wilson frowned. "This is my case and I make the schedule, Mr. McCrary. We will do it tomorrow. I won't spend overtime in my department budget to chase someone involved in a dispute with a local biker gang. And if this is a drug cartel disappearance, which we found no evidence for, we may never locate her body. This thing could be a time waster where we won't obtain a scintilla of evidence admissible in court. I've worked these drug things before. These guys don't leave loose ends."

I couldn't believe Wilson was saying these things. I put my life on the line to search for Angie, and this cop didn't treat her disappearance seriously. What the hell was I cooperating with the cops for?

"Your department doesn't intend to do anything on her kidnapping and possible murder until tomorrow?"

"No, we'll do something, I assure you. Art Devlin is running facial recognition on the possible cartel members. We'll put BOLOs out on Angelina's and Teodoro's cars and the three motorcycles for the bikers who attacked you. We'll get arrest warrants on the three bikers for suspicion of kidnapping. We'll get a search warrant for the Flathead panel van and try to get a warrant to search the entire Flathead factory site. We can do those things from the office—with no overtime."

Wilson stood. "Please wait here and I'll check with Art on how the facial recognition is coming. I won't be long." He left the room.

Waiting in silence, my muscles tensed. I hated this part of a case. I had advanced the investigation to the point where I must rely on others to work the case. Others to search for Valley, Fajardo, and Trojanik. Others to search for Angie's and Teodoro's automobiles. Others to identify the cartel members in the party video. Being passive doesn't sit well with me.

I rose and stretched the tension from my back and shoulders. At least I tried to.

Detectives Wilson and Devlin returned.

"Good news," said Wilson. "We identified two of the three men in the party video." He tossed two photos on the table with reports stapled behind them. "These are your copies. The men are Jesus Ramon Santos aka Ray, and Valentino Dias Torres aka Val. This is a report on Santiago Ruiz Iglesias aka Saco, but we have no photo." Wilson plunked another sheaf of stapled paper on the table.

I set the two pictures side by side. "Who is the third guy? Is he Saco?"

Wilson shrugged. "Not certain yet."

"According to Lola Salazar and Tommy Valley, Saco was at the party and his face was captured on Angie's phone. Hell, he might be the guy having sex with Lola Salazar."

"Or someone in the crowd," said Wilson. "Keep the copies." Lieutenant Wilson stood, signaling the meeting was over. Devlin did the same. "We're on this, Chuck. I assure you. Let us do our job. This isn't our first rodeo either."

"When do you intend to search for Tommy Valley, Alejandro Fajardo, and Ronald Trojanik?"

"Let us do our job, Mr. McCrary. Thanks for coming in. We have your contact information. We'll call you when we learn something or have further questions."

As I left the conference room, I thought, *Yeah, fat chance. They'll call me on July 35th.*

THIRTEEN

I fired up my rented Tahoe and cranked the air conditioner to *Arctic*. I studied Esteban Espinoza's business card. Espinoza knew which one was Saco. If I identified Saco for the OCU, it would prove the drug cartel connection and help the search for Angie. Or her body.

It was close to the end of Bettina's shift. I texted her:

I met with Detectives Wilson and Devlin. I am not confident they will advance the case. Are you nearly finished with your shift?

Bettina called my cellphone. "Where are you?"

"In your police station's parking lot."

"I'm on my way there. After I check in with the desk sergeant, I'm off duty. Can you wait there?"

"Sure."

A few minutes later, Bettina's black Honda parked beside me. She gave me a "one minute" gesture and walked into the station. When she returned, she dropped into the Tahoe's passenger seat. She winked. "I'm all yours."

I opened my laptop and laid it on Bettina's lap. "This morning I found the truckstop where Angie called me. They have a good security system, which they let me access. I spent three hours, but I was able to copy videos of Angie being kidnapped."

I pointed at an icon on the desktop. "As the TV news anchors say, 'This video may be disturbing.' Click on that."

Bettina played the video.

"You were right; that's disturbing. At least she's no longer a missing person. We can prove she was kidnapped. I couldn't tell whether there were two kidnappers or three. Could they be Tommy Valley and his two stooges?"

"Yes, but the video isn't clear proof because of the hoodies and hats. I hope the OCU guys can enhance the pictures of their boots. They could compare them to those of Valley and his flunkies."

"Did you compare the van's license plates with the ones we photographed on Sunday?"

"Yeah. It wasn't parked there on Sunday."

"It could have been in the unmarked building at the west end of the Flathead property."

"That's what I figured. And, since Teodoro was last on the cellphone network at Flathead, his car and Angie's might be in the building."

"What do Royce Wilson and Art Devlin think about this video?"

"They said they would ask the judge for search warrants. They'll have the warrants tomorrow. Or not. They don't seem in a hurry."

Bettina nodded. "If Valley or other bad guys get wind of our investigation of Flathead Pipe Supply, they could destroy any evidence in the building."

"You ever look into who the guys were that shot at us?"

"Yeah. I checked whether anyone at the company reported the shooting at their factory on Sunday. They didn't file a police report."

"It's possible whoever monitored the Flathead cameras identified us. I presume they are well-connected, and they already tapped my phone and played back Angie's voicemail."

Bettina glanced at the cameras on the police building. "Let's go. We're under surveillance, and not only by the HPD."

"Here's a better idea. You go home, change clothes, do whatever you normally do."

"And what will you do?"

"Espinoza may know which man in the party video is Saco. It was his party. I'll talk to him before I call it a day." I held Espinoza's card where she could read it.

Bettina steadied my hand with hers and read the card aloud. "*Las Peliculas Fantasia*. The best in Spanish-language adult films.' It's ironic that a producer of Spanish-language porn prints his business cards in English."

I retrieved the card. "Maybe I'll ask about that."

Bettina smiled. "Maybe not."

———

I parked near the porn house where I parked the previous Friday. Cars still parked in front, three this time. The front lawn was shaggy before. Today it was neatly mowed. Was Espinoza planning another party? The sun dipped below the trees on the west side and a cool breeze ruffled my hair. I locked the Tahoe and walked to the front door.

Two gunmen had chased me away the first time I visited. Neither were in Angie's party video. Either they weren't at the party, or they remained out of sight of the guests and Angie's camera.

Deciding to play it straight, I rang the doorbell rather than walk in unannounced. I backed to the edge of the porch, five feet from the door, where I wouldn't invade anyone's space who opened the door, especially a woman. The sign out front must attract weirdos or pranksters.

I smiled at the video doorbell.

"May I help you?" The male voice originated from a speaker built into the doorbell. The voice might belong to one of the gunmen I'd spotted the first time I was there.

"I'm here to speak to Esteban Espinoza. May I come in?"

"Is he expecting you?"

"I am searching for my sister, Angelina Garza. She attended a party here on Friday, May first. May I come in?"

"Let me check with Mr. Espinoza's assistant. Please wait."

The doorbell speaker was silent for three minutes. Then the speaker clicked. A female voice said, "I'm Desiree, Mr. Espinoza's assistant. You're Angie Garza's brother?"

"Yes."

"Is Angie missing?"

"She disappeared right after your party."

"That's awful. Everybody loves Angie."

"That's good to hear. Your party was the last place she was seen." That was fudging the truth. I told myself it was for a good cause. "I'm here to interview Esteban Espinoza regarding the party."

"Esteban is filming a scene for the next hour. Could you come back later?"

"Thank you. Please tell him I'll be back in an hour."

At least Espinoza's assistant didn't tell me to pound sand or deny he was there. That was progress, wasn't it? Of course, Desiree wasn't Espinoza. Who would open the door when I returned in an hour? Might be one of the gunmen.

Back in the Tahoe, I called Bettina. "I'm at the porn palace. Espinoza is filming a scene and his assistant named Desiree said to come back in an hour. Can you make time for a quick dinner, or would you rather wait until I finish interviewing Espinoza? That could take a couple hours."

"I just got home. There is a great deli near you. I'll meet you there for a sandwich. You shouldn't keep the porn king waiting."

We met at the deli. My nose inhaled the savory mix of aromas that transported me back to a trip to New York a few years before. New York City has the best delis in the world, but this one smelled great.

Bettina ordered a corned beef sandwich, and I chose a pastrami. We carried our orders to an outside table. "Didn't you tell me that two gun-toting thugs accosted you last time you were there?"

"Yes, but in their defense, I staked out the house and photographed everyone who entered or exited for an hour and a half. I admit it—I acted suspiciously. I don't blame them for investigating."

Bettina blotted a smidge of mustard off her mouth. "Couldn't they recognize you from the doorbell camera? They could set you up for an ambush when you return."

"Are you angling for an invitation to ride shotgun again?"

"I came in handy at Flathead Pipe Supply, didn't I?"

"You saved my neck, is all. Are you sure you aren't curious what a porn movie studio looks like?"

Bettina snickered. "That idea crossed my mind. But at least two gunmen lurk around the film studio. Don't forget Rule Eighteen: *Always have a backup.*"

"I could tell Espinoza you came along to audition for a starring role."

Bettina smirked. "And I'll tell Espinoza you're hoping for pointers to improve your bedroom skills."

———

It was twilight as I parked at *Las Peliculas Fantasia* studios. Bettina stopped behind me. This time five vehicles were crammed into the front yard.

"When I was here before, they had three cars. They must do more filming at night."

Bettina laughed. "That way it doesn't interfere with the actors' day jobs."

I rang the bell and stepped back.

A male voice replied. "Yes?"

"Carlos McCrary and Detective Bettina Simpson to see Esteban Espinoza. He's expecting us."

"Wait one minute, please."

Three minutes later, the voice returned. "Mr. Espinoza is not available."

"An hour ago, Desiree told me to return in an hour and he would be available. It's been an hour, and here we are. We want to meet with Mr. Espinoza."

"Wait one minute, please."

Two minutes passed before the voice returned. "Mr. Espinoza changed his mind. He does not choose to talk to you."

"When would be a convenient time?" I asked.

"Wait one minute, please."

I winked at Bettina. "This is getting old. It's never easy, is it?"

She grinned. "That's why we make the big bucks."

The male voice returned. "Mr. Espinoza does not choose to talk to you. Period. Unless you have a warrant."

Bettina elbowed me aside and held her badge for the camera. "I am

Detective Sergeant Bettina Simpson with the Houston Police Department. If I return with a search warrant, our CSIs will seize your computers, your digital media such as DVDs, CDs, and your inventory of programs you've already produced. We will remove your paper files also. We will haul the evidence to our crime lab for forensic analysis. A *thorough* analysis, which could take over a week. Ask Mr. Espinoza how that would affect his business. And yes, we will 'Wait one minute, please' while you talk to him. But if this door does not open within four minutes, the next time you see me, I will bring a warrant and a panel van to load your entire office and haul it away."

She showed her phone to the camera and set the timer to *4:00*. "I'll give you four minutes. Tell your boss I'm tired of playing games."

Seconds later, the door opened, thrust forward by an attractive woman in a blood-red T-shirt with strategically placed cutouts and fashionably shredded jeans. She wore a gold ring in her right nostril and a row of gold rings decorated her left ear lobe. Bettina and I gazed at each other. It was the woman who'd flashed Angie's camera on her video. "I'm Desiree, Esteban's assistant. I'm sorry Angie is missing. Me and her and Lola made a few movies together. We became close friends. I hope you find her. Please come in." She closed the door behind us.

I handed her a business card. "Thanks, Desiree. I appreciate your concern. You call me anytime twenty-four/seven if you remember anything."

Desiree studied the card for a moment, then stuck it in a pants pocket. "I'll be sure to call you." She smiled. "Twenty-four/seven."

She glanced at Bettina. "If y'all will follow me..." Desiree gripped my hand and led us into the house.

The living room furniture that was against the walls in the party video was arranged normally. The dining room held a table, chairs, and a server. We passed the kitchen. A man and woman were fixing sandwiches. The bedroom doors were closed.

Desiree led us down the hall. "Anytime there's anything I can do to help Angie, call me." She squeezed my hand.

A fortyish man in a Hawaiian shirt, cargo shorts, and flip-flops sat in the lanai that overlooked the swimming pool. He was the man hugging Desiree in Angie's video.

In the pool, two women and one man cavorted while a camera operator videoed the *Ménage à trois*. In the back corners of the garden, the two gunmen sat in lawn chairs and stared at the lanai.

Hawaiian Shirt stood when the three of us arrived and closed the sliding glass doors. "If the scene they're filming makes you uncomfortable, I can close the drapes."

"It doesn't make me uncomfortable," said Bettina, "it's just a distraction." She glanced at me; I shrugged. "Perhaps it would make our conversation more private with the drapes closed."

He complied with my request and sat down. "I'm Esteban Espinoza. Do I need an attorney?"

Bettina gave him a cop stare. "I don't know. Do you need an attorney?"

"I've done nothing wrong. We have nothing to hide here."

"That's good to know." Bettina handed business cards to Espinoza and Desiree. "I'm Sergeant Bettina Simpson. This is Carlos McCrary, Angelina McCrary Garza's brother."

I handed a business card to Espinoza.

He read the card. "A private investigator? Angie's brother is a freaking private eye? Jesus, what the hell is this?"

"Mr. McCrary is assisting our investigation in an unofficial capacity," Bettina said. "Mr. McCrary and I are here at your invitation, and you are cooperating in the investigation of Angelina's disappearance. Is that correct?"

Espinoza waved a hand dismissively. "Whatever. Have a seat. Either of you want something to drink?"

"Coffee is nice," I said. "A little creamer, no sugar."

"I'm good," Bettina said.

"Desiree," Espinoza said, "please bring Mr. McCrary a coffee, and bring Sergeant Simpson a bottle of water in case she changes her mind."

Desiree smiled at me for a second longer than necessary, then left.

"Carlos found a video Angelina made the night she disappeared," Bettina said. "We want you to watch it." To me: "Carlos?"

I cued the video and stood. Stepping closer to Espinoza, I handed the phone to him. "Press play." I shifted to one side where I observed the video and Espinoza simultaneously.

He viewed the video without expression until the image progressed to the back yard. The camera focused on the men at the firepit, and his brow wrinkled. The camera found them the second time and he squinted. When the scene showed Lola Salazar and the man on the bed having sex, he frowned.

Desiree returned with a paper cup with a lid on it and a bottle of water. She set the drinks on a coffee table. Slipping across the room, she peered over Espinoza's shoulder at the phone screen.

The video ended and Espinoza handed the phone back. "So, Angie made a video. Plenty of people make videos. Nothing on that video was illegal. Everyone was of legal age. Consenting adults. Only thing the couple on the bed was guilty of was poor taste."

I fast-forwarded the video to the three men sitting at the firepit. I paused it and handed the phone to Espinoza. "Who are the three men and what were they doing at your party?"

Desiree's eyes widened. She flicked her gaze at me, then at the phone.

Was that an unspoken message?

Espinoza huffed indignantly. "There were a hundred people at that party. Some were invited by my associates, others by my performers. I didn't recognize half the people there."

"But you recognize these three, don't you?" I leaned closer to Espinoza. "Who are they? Why were they here?"

Espinoza tossed the phone on the coffee table and leaned back.

I leaned with him. "Who are they, Espinoza? Who the hell are they?"

Espinoza's face colored. "I don't have to talk to you, McCrary. I don't have to talk to nobody. Leave me the hell alone." He crossed his arms. His lips pressed into a thin line.

Bettina yanked me back into my chair. She was playing Good Cop now. She turned to the other woman. "How about you, Desiree? Who are these men and why were they here?"

Espinoza pivoted to Desiree and raised his palms in her direction. "She don't know neither. Nobody knows nothing. You're wasting your time and ours. I'm asking you to leave."

He tried to smile at me. "Carlos, buddy, I'm real sorry Angie's missing. She's a nice girl—naïve, but nice. I hope you find her. But we don't know nothing concerning her disappearance."

Desiree handed my phone to me. She held eye contact an extra second while I took the phone.

I palmed the piece of paper she placed in my hand and slipped the phone into my pocket. I tilted my chin at Bettina. "We're finished. We can find our way out."

"Hey, sergeant," Espinoza said, "you're not gonna get a search warrant, are you? Believe me, there's nothing in our files to help you find Angelina."

Bettina marched toward the door. "Perhaps we will see you later, Mr. Espinoza. If we do, we will bring a warrant."

As the front door closed behind us, she held my arm closer to her. "We'll let the uncooperative bastard stew over the threat of a search warrant. Next time he'll have second thoughts before he claims ignorance."

I walked Bettina to her car and opened the driver's door for her. "Desiree slipped me a note when she handed me my phone." I showed it to her.

"I noticed." She read the note. "'Meet me at my condo in one hour.' That must be her home address. And she gave you her phone number."

"Desiree reacted to those three men's faces on your phone. She knows who they are, and she did say she wanted to help Angie."

Bettina handed the note back and slipped behind the steering wheel. She buzzed her window down. "Or she only wants to lure you to her place like a spider lures a fly. I say she wants to use you for sex and then carve another notch on her spider web."

"You're mixing metaphors. Only one way to find out which of us is right."

"It would be awful for a six-foot-two, 225-pound man like you to be accosted by a sexy, 110-pound woman who planned to have her way with him. Perhaps I should go with you to protect your virtue."

"I would feel guilty for hogging your off-duty time."

"You can laugh, Chuck, but I guarantee Desiree wants to jump your bones."

"Don't be silly. She wants to talk privately so Espinoza doesn't find out. That way, she avoids trouble with him."

"Trust me, Desiree may want to help Angie, but she intends to tack your scalp—or your private parts—to her bedpost."

"You're serious? You think she's crushing on me?"

"Chuck, I have experience crushing on you; I've done it ever since high school. And since I have a personal interest in your private parts, I'll come along."

"You're the expert, Bettina. Thanks for the help."

"Lead on, Sir Carlos, and I, your trusty Squire Bettina, will travel along."

"I'm Batman and you're Catwoman."

"No, you're Batman and I'm Robin. I'm on the side of truth, justice, and the American way."

"Truth, justice, and the American way is Superman," I said.

"Whatever."

"Okay, Robin it is. BTW, I didn't get to drink Espinoza's coffee before we left. Let's stop at a drive-thru and buy a coffee on the way."

"Let's get a snack too. Desiree won't be home for an hour."

"You know me; I was born hungry."

———

Bettina and I arrived at Desiree's condo at 9:30. Her reserved parking spot was empty, but I knocked on her door to make sure she was not home yet.

While Bettina and I waited in our car, I sent another email update to my parents, telling them about the videos of Angie's kidnapping.

Less than a minute later, Dad called.

"I read your email about the kidnapping, son. Has there been a ransom demand?"

"I haven't received one, Dad. Angie recorded her voicemail on May the fourth, and it's now May twelfth. They haven't asked for a ransom. Bettina and I suspect that a Mexican drug cartel was searching for Angie.

She had evidence that could hurt them. Could be the video she made at the party."

Dad sighed. "That's what Mom and I were afraid of. Do you think they found her and killed her?"

I waited a few seconds before I responded. The pause was part of my answer. Let the truth settle on him gradually. "I'm not certain, but we haven't heard from her for eight days... The odds aren't good."

———

Desiree rolled into her reserved parking spot at 10:00 p.m.

We walked to her door with me slightly in the lead.

Desiree smiled when I reached her front porch. Then Bettina stepped out of the shadows, and Desiree's brow furrowed. Her gaze rested on Bettina a second longer than it should have.

"Sorry I'm late, y'all." She unlocked the deadbolt. "Esteban had a couple more tasks for me. Thanks for waiting." She swung the door open and flipped on the light. "Make yourselves comfortable. What can I fix you to drink?"

"I just finished a coffee, Desiree, but thanks."

"I'm good," said Bettina.

"You sure? I have a well-stocked bar. Something to make you relax from a long, hard day?"

"No, we're good."

"Care for a sniff? I have some boss blow."

"No, thanks, Desiree," Bettina said. "We're not into drugs."

"Oh, that's right. It's Sergeant Simpson, isn't it? I forgot. Am I in trouble?"

"You are in the privacy of your own home, and I'm off duty. You're not in trouble with me, Desiree. Especially if you give us information to help locate Chuck's sister."

Desiree stared at me. "Chuck? Your card says your name is Carlos."

"Carlos is Spanish for Charles. In English, Chuck is a nickname for Charles. People call me Chuck or Carlos. I answer to both."

Desiree tapped her temple with her fingertips. "Duh... I should have

161

figured that out. My real name is Felicia Moreno." She grinned. "Desiree is my professional name. Like I said, I act in some of our adult films. That's how I met Angie. When I'm in the real world, like now, people call me Felicia."

"Okay. Felicia Moreno it is, since we're in the real world."

Bettina and I had decided she would handle the interview. Desiree, now Felicia Moreno, might be more forthcoming with another woman. "What can you tell us about Angie?"

"If anything I tell you gets back to Esteban, I stand to lose a cushy job. He told me not to tell nobody nothing."

"He'll never learn anything from us," Bettina said.

"I know the three men in the video. Will telling you their names help Angie?"

"It could. One or more of those men could be involved in Angie's disappearance. We're gathering all available information, and we'll sort through it later. Some information helps; some doesn't. What can you tell us about them?"

"Show me the video again?"

"Sure. Chuck?"

I cued the video and handed the phone to Felicia. "Push the play button."

She played the video until it reached the scene with the three men. She paused it and showed me the phone. "This guy is called Saco. He says he's the big boss, and I don't believe he's bragging. Everybody is terrified of him. I don't know his real name, but one time when he came here, he wore a shirt monogrammed with *SRI*."

"Here?" Bettina asked. "He's visited your home?"

"Saco gets the hots for me sometimes, so he calls to make sure I'm home, then he comes over. He's not the kind of guy you say 'no' to. But at least he's a big tipper." Felicia stopped talking and an uncertain expression crossed her face. "That don't make me a whore, does it? I don't feel like no whore. Me and him don't discuss money, but it's not like I have a choice. Actually, we don't discuss anything except what he wants me to do and how he wants me to act. Then he leaves money on the coffee table. He tells me to buy something nice for myself. He acts like that makes everything okay."

"But it doesn't, does it?" Bettina asked.

"Sometimes he's a little rough. Like I said, he's not a guy you say 'no' to."

Bettina frowned. "I'm sorry to hear that." She paused a beat. "Anything else you want to say about Saco?"

"Nah. Let's just get this over with." She held the phone where we could see it. "This guy beside him is Val Torres. I don't know the rest of his name. And this guy is Ray Santos. His real name could be Ramón, but I'm not sure."

Felicia handed the phone back. "Does any of this help?"

"Yes, it does," said Bettina. "The man you called Saco is uber-dangerous. You were right—he is the big boss. It's crucial he does not discover that you talked to us. We believe he would kill you without hesitation."

Felicia's face flushed. "Kill me? He might kill me? What have I gotten into? You're a cop. You gotta protect me."

Bettina reached for her hand and squeezed it. "Don't worry, Felicia. Should it become necessary, the Houston Police Department will protect you. I doubt it will be necessary so long as you don't tell anyone you talked to us. Continue to be Desiree. Act like nothing happened."

"And as Bettina said," I added, "we won't say anything."

"The other two men are local drug dealers," Bettina said. "Saco is head of a Mexican drug cartel that supplies them with narcotics. Why were they at the party?"

"Saco invests in Esteban's films," Felicia said. "He enjoys fringe benefits of sex with the girls, but I'm his favorite."

Felicia frowned. "Is he using Esteban's films to launder drug money?"

"Probably. That makes this a potential federal case."

"If I had to testify against Saco, he'd kill me in a heartbeat."

"I doubt you know anything the prosecutor could use at trial," Bettina said.

"That's a relief. Anything else you want to know?"

"You have any idea where Angie is?"

"I haven't heard from her since the party."

Bettina grabbed her purse. "Okay, we have what we came for. We appreciate your cooperation, Felicia." She stood and I mirrored her.

As the three of us reached Felicia's door, she opened it and touched my arm. "Bettina, may I have a private word with Chuck?"

"Or course. I'll wait in the car, Chuck."

Felicia closed the door behind Bettina. "I didn't dare say anything in front of Bettina, but I hoped you'd come alone. I wanted to ask you something personal."

Uh-oh, perhaps Bettina was right. "It doesn't hurt to ask. I can take the fifth." I smiled to soften my response.

"Okay. That's fair. Most men I meet treat me like Desiree and interact with me like the porn star. But that's a small piece of who I am. Outside of work, I'm Felicia Moreno, not Desiree. Now, in the real world here with you, I'm Felicia. You see the difference?"

"Yes, I do. Right now, you're Felicia."

"I hope I'm not too aggressive, Chuck, but I don't find many chances to meet a nice guy like you in the real world. You know I have lots of sex in my professional career, but's that's physical. It's not real. I have sex as Desiree, but there is no actual affection. The emotion is fake. I don't have much social life when I'm Felicia Moreno."

"I follow you. Desiree gets plenty of action, but not enough affection. As Felicia, you crave real affection."

"Right. What I planned to ask was: Are you and Bettina, uh... together... romantically? If you and Bettina have something going, I'll bow out. But if not, I'd enjoy meeting you socially. You could come over and I'll cook dinner. I'm an exceptional cook. Despite being Mexican American, I specialize in French cuisine."

"You're a woman of many talents," I said.

"Are you free Saturday night?"

"Felicia, I'm flattered by your... invitation."

"Oh crap, don't say you're flattered."

"Why not?"

"That's what nice guys say when they plan to say no."

"But it's true; I am flattered. You are a lovely young woman and I love French cuisine, but Bettina and I are seeing each other socially."

"I sensed a vibe between you two, but I had to ask. You know what they say: If you don't ask, you don't get." She tugged my arm toward her, stood on tiptoes, and kissed me on the cheek. "Good luck to you both."

She opened the door and shook my hand. "Call me anytime if I can help with Angie..." She winked. "Or anything else. You saved my phone number?"

"Yes. I kept your note."

"If things don't work out between you and Bettina, give me a call. I really am a good cook."

Bettina buzzed the window open as I walked to the driver's side of her car.

"You called it; Felicia propositioned me. Said if you and I don't work out, I should call her. She even offered to cook dinner for me."

"If she cooks dinner for you, you know what she'll serve for dessert. Don't be surprised if she contacts you again. Just saying."

"I have no control over that. Changing the subject, I have another errand tonight. Don't wait up."

"You plan to search the small building at Flathead, don't you?"

"Yeah. Tommy and the other bikers carried Angie to Flathead. That building is begging to be searched. The cops are slow-walking the investigation, so it's up to me. And sooner rather than later, before somebody leaks our interest to the bad guys."

"You want me to back you up?"

"Not this time. You have your own job responsibilities, and you work tomorrow. I can sleep late, and no one will complain. However, I could use a kiss for luck."

I leaned through the window, and she kissed me goodbye. "Chuck, did you forget to shave this morning?"

"I didn't forget. I didn't shave yesterday either."

"You decided to grow a beard?"

"We face a sophisticated enemy, so I am changing my appearance. Growing a beard is pretty effective after a week. So far, Tommy Valley is the one bad guy who saw me close enough to recognize me."

"What about Lola?"

"Good point," I said. "However, I believe she's a victim, not a perpetrator."

"The five-o'clock shadow looks sexy."

"Last time I grew a beard was in the Middle East. It itched for a month before I got used to it. I'm afraid it will be scratchy in a few days when it gets longer. It might irritate you when you kiss me or when I rub my cheek against… let's say, a sensitive spot."

"Don't worry, Master of Disguise, I've dated men with beards before. It's more ticklish than scratchy, especially on the sensitive spots. I'm looking forward to your beard."

FOURTEEN

I idled with the headlights off, rolling at walking speed for the last half mile. Wee hours in an industrial neighborhood, there was not a light in sight. No buildings and no streetlights. Thin scattered clouds reflected the lights of Houston and supplied enough ambient light to stay on the two-lane road. I monitored the GPS and rolled east. A barbwire fence on the north side stopped at a steel gate across a dirt road that led north into a pine tree farm.

Stopping at the gate, I opened the door and the dome light switched on. *Oops!* I'd forgotten to switch it off. I did that now.

The pine trees smelled like nature's perfume in the humid night. The steel gate had a heavy chain wrapped around the gate and the fence post. The padlock was fastened in a single link and draped across the entrance to appear locked. I unwrapped the chain, swung the gate inward, and bumped across the plowed firebreak. Stopping twenty yards away on the other side, I parked the Tahoe at the edge of the trees. Jogging back to the gate, I wrapped the chain the way I found it.

The sound of a vehicle on the street grew louder. I dove into the long grass growing under the fence and plastered myself to the ground. The vehicle grew closer. The sound faded as it passed.

Breathing a sigh of relief, I listened to the silence. Nothing but the breeze in the pine needles and an owl's call. I stood and rotated a slow 360, alert for signs of life. Nothing.

Starting the Tahoe, I coasted at idle speed along the dirt road, bumping my way closer to Flathead Pipe Supply to the north. In the faint light the opening at the end of the track grew larger. I had reached the border of the tree farm. Continuing to the cleared firebreak beside the railroad tracks, I made a K-turn and parked ten yards into the pines, facing south in case I needed a quick getaway.

Showtime.

Slinging my backpack across my shoulders, I crossed the railroad tracks and hopped the ditch that marked the Flathead property's southern boundary. I hiked toward the unmarked building Bettina had photographed the previous Sunday, the one we had called *Building 4*, even though there was nothing to mark its exterior other than its size.

My boots crunched softly across the stones.

Stepping quietly, pausing to listen, I soon reached Building 4.

I circled the building. No vehicles outside and no sounds from inside, but I did detect a funky stink that overpowered the scent from the pine tree farm.

I eyeballed the road where the unexpected shooters had appeared. What had they been trying to protect? The mysterious building sat silent, ominous. The rotten odor made my skin crawl.

Removing a stethoscope from my pack, I listened at the south personnel door for sounds of occupation. Nothing. The funky scent grew stronger near the door, then became a stink I recognized only too well.

I crept to the north personnel door again and listened. Still nothing but the odor I remembered as the stench of death.

My heart rate increased. No point waiting; time to breach the mysterious building.

Donning nitrile gloves, I picked the lock and opened the personnel door. A sharp odor of decay issued from the pitch dark inside the building.

Odors trigger vivid memories, and the stench transported me instantly to Afghanistan. My Special Forces unit, Operational Detachment Alpha 777, better known as the Triple Seven, had cleared a village by expelling the Taliban. My Green Beret team kicked in a locked door and stumbled upon the remains of a long-dead family brutally murdered by the Taliban. In an instant, I absorbed the sight and scent of a grotesque display of the vilest evil to which people can descend. I ran into the street and vomited until I had the dry heaves. So young. So naïve. So long ago.

In the present moment, ghostly memories threatened to overcome me. I slammed the personnel door, rushed a few yards away, and puked. I drew slow breaths until I regained control. Opening a water bottle, I rinsed the sour taste from my mouth, rinsed it again, and finished the bottle.

That's why I don't watch horror movies. I've experienced enough real-life horror for several lifetimes.

That was fifteen years ago and thousands of miles away, I told myself. I was in Texas now, not Afghanistan.

Satisfied I had centered my attention on the present time and the present circumstances, I returned to the door.

Slipping inside, I closed the door behind me. The odor was nearly over-powering in the enclosed space. Total darkness. No windows. No night-lights. No red or amber indicator lights on idle electronics. Darker than the inside of a black cat's stomach.

The odor was so powerful it seemed I would see the visible fumes if I flipped on a light. I had read somewhere that all odors are particulate. My God, I was inhaling molecules from a dead body. Or bodies.

Stepping back outside, I staggered a few yards upwind until I drew an untainted breath. A hazmat mask would control the godawful stench, but that was not in my typical field equipment. Drawing an N-95 Covid-19 mask from the pack, I slipped it on, returned to the door, and stepped inside.

Okay, tough guy, it's only a smell. You did your preliminary recon. There was no one inside to attack you. No one alive, at least, and you don't believe in ghosts.

The death scent was there. Satisfied no light could get in or out, I braced myself for the horror-movie scene I expected to confront. Holding my breath, I flicked on my headlamp.

An industrial towable woodchipper squatted directly before me. The massive throat opening was 12 inches by 24 inches. Large enough to shove a body in. The skin on my arms prickled like insects were crawling on it.

The intake hopper's yellow paint was stained brown—the remains of dried blood. The discharge chute was aimed to direct the chips into a trash can positioned under it.

I studied the ground where I stood. The gray gravel floor became brownish the closer it came to the center of the building. Was I standing on a body disposal site? I fought the urge to gag.

Sweeping my gaze clockwise, I spotted Teodoro Garza's Jeep parked by the wall in the southeast corner. To the right of his Jeep was the south personnel door, then the south truck door.

Next was a beige panel van marked *Flathead Pipe Supply* in green letters. I relived Angie's kidnapping in my mind. This had to be the van the bastards heaved my sister into. Yes, the license plate matched. It was parked next to the wall in the southwest corner. Angie's blue Mazda was parked behind it. I pictured the panel van rolling through the north truck door and curving toward the corner of the space, its tires crunching across the rocks, trailed by the Mazda. In my mind, the man in the Mazda got out and opened the rear doors to the van. Inside the van, two other men shoved Angie out the door. Did she fall when she landed? Did she skin her hands on the grisly gravel?

I willed my imagination to stop at that point. I could not confront the rest of this imaginary scene.

Forcing myself to continue my scan, my gaze fell on a metal workbench in the northwest corner. An assortment of tools hung on a pegboard wall above the workbench.

Switching on the interior lights, I videoed a 360-degree panorama. A similar group of light switches beside the other personnel door allowed the lights to be controlled from either entrance.

Dreading what I would discover, I crept closer to the chipper and peered into the trash can. The headlamp revealed it was empty and clean. Belatedly, I noticed a hose bib on the wall behind the chipper, along with a garden hose with a spray nozzle coiled on a rack beside it.

A shovel leaned against the wall. My breath caught in my throat. A ghastly sequence of events swept uncontrolled through my imagination, a flood from a broken dam.

I swallowed hard and closed my eyes, waited a few seconds before I opened them, pausing for the universe to stop spinning.

Regaining my composure, I collected a few rust-colored rocks from various points scattered across the floor and dumped them in evidence bags. The forensics lab could use the DNA to identify what I feared were multiple victims.

I videoed the trash can interior, the hose and sprayer nozzle, and the shovel against the wall.

I photographed the van's license plate.

Wait. Did my headlamp spark a red flash from the gravel?

A garnet earring lay on the rocky floor. I recognized the gold wire mounting. Did Angie drop her earring like Hansel and Gretel's gingerbread? *Yes, Chuck, it's me, Angie. Come rescue me!*

I opened the van's rear doors and peered inside. A few cut plastic cable ties curled on the floor. The kidnappers had used them to secure Angie in the back.

The unavoidable conclusion enveloped my mind: My sister was dead. And we would never recover her body for a proper burial because of the disgusting woodchipper.

I prayed they'd killed her before disposing of her body.

How could I tell our parents? How could I tell them I was sure she was dead, but, no, we cannot—we will not—ever recover her body. They would need to hear the reason the family could not give Angelina a proper burial.

I thrust the question into the background. *Do your job now and deal with your parents—and your emotions—later.*

I slipped the earring into an evidence bag. I hoped one of the kidnappers had touched it. A long shot, but stranger things have happened.

Climbing into the van's cab, I rummaged through the glove box. More cable ties, the vehicle registration, an insurance card. I photographed the registration and insurance card. Nothing under the van's seats.

I ransacked Teodoro's Jeep. The usual junk, plus his large suitcase that was missing from his and Angie's apartment was in the back seat.

My search of Angie's Mazda yielded no usable information. Her purse had been emptied on the back seat and discarded.

When I reached the opposite personnel door from where I entered, I videoed another full circle panorama. Rule Six: *You never know what you'll need to know.* The different camera angles could reveal something useful upon later analysis.

Thankful I was finished with the mission's toughest part, I dowsed the lights and exited through the south personnel door. My stomach squirmed and complained all the way back to the Tahoe.

I paused as I reached my vehicle in the woods, jogged a dozen steps into the trees, and hurled again.

I cranked the Tahoe and punched the air conditioning to *max.* I opened another water bottle, rinsed my mouth, and drank the rest of the water.

God, I hoped I never visited a crime scene like that one again.

How was I going to tell Mom and Dad?

FIFTEEN

Bettina was asleep by the time I arrived at her apartment. I waited until morning to tell her what I found.

"That must have been terrible. You're sure Angelina was murdered in Building 4?"

"That explanation fits the evidence."

"Did you tell your family?"

"Not yet."

"Why not? You've been emailing them whenever you uncover something."

"I don't know what to say. No, that's not right; I don't know *how* to say it. My first goal was to find Angelina. I guess you could say I found her, but what I found out is too horrible to spring on my folks."

"You're procrastinating."

"I'll call them later."

I met Royse Wilson and Art Devlin at the Organized Crime Unit. I identified the third man at the firepit: Saco. I told the OCU detectives that he was investing in Espinoza's films.

"Good way to launder drug money," Wilson said. "Report the drug profits as income from selling adult films. The IRS is satisfied, and the money is legal for Saco to invest in legitimate businesses."

"I have something else to help justify your search warrant for the Flathead plant." I laid an envelope on the table.

Wilson poked the envelope with a letter opener so the detectives could read the message. "What's this?"

Devlin read the note printed in anonymous handwriting. *"Evidence from inside the unmarked building at Flathead Pipe Supply."* I had printed it with my left hand.

He glanced at me. "What the hell?"

I nodded at the envelope. "It was under my SUV's windshield wiper this morning." That was true; after sealing the envelope, I had placed it there myself before retrieving it. "Whoever left this wanted me to give it to you. My fingerprints are on the envelope. I removed it from the windshield wiper before I learned what it was."

Wilson gloved up and held the envelope to the light. "It's lumpy and heavy. X-ray it before we open it, Art."

Ten minutes later, Art Devlin returned with the envelope. "No explosives. X-ray shows a flash drive and a few evidence bags inside."

Wilson sliced the envelope open with a letter opener and peeked inside. "Give this to the fingerprint gurus before we handle it further. We won't find usable prints, but we gotta follow procedure."

Devlin made a phone call. A minute later a uniformed woman entered and left with the envelope.

"Have you located Tommy Valley?" I asked.

Wilson frowned. "Don't worry, Chuck. He'll show."

"What did you find when you backtracked his cellphones? Any places he frequented?"

Wilson waved to Devlin. "Art, that was your department. You have anything?"

"Nothing yet, Royce."

"Have you backtracked his cellphones, Art?"

"For your information, McCrary, I don't answer to you. You told us what you discovered, and we thank you for that. Now's the time for you to cool off and let us do our job."

That meant Devlin had not tried to trace Valley's movements. Why not? Was there something the OCU detectives had not told me? Was Devlin lazy, crooked, or incompetent?

"And the search warrants for the Flathead factory site?"

"They're in process, regardless of the evidence in the envelope. Either way, we will have the warrant tomorrow."

"By tomorrow, the kidnappers could destroy the evidence and transfer Angie to a new location, assuming she's still alive."

"Our CSIs are processing Angelina's apartment. We'll execute the search warrant on Flathead after we receive the CSI's report on your sister's apartment."

"One thing has nothing to do with the other." I fought back tears of frustration, irritation, and exasperation. "You do both at the same time, detectives. Damn it, delay could be fatal for Angie."

Devlin scowled at me. "Back off, mister. We're doing our job. You are a civilian. Don't make me arrest you for interfering with our investigation. You would be obstructing justice. So back off."

I didn't answer. Protesting was a waste of breath. This whole case was on my shoulders.

I looked from Devlin to Wilson. "Have a nice day, gentlemen."

I walked out.

———

Back at Bettina's condo, I examined Tommy Valley's cellphone tracking list again. Where was the next likely spot Valley would hide?

I sorted his prior locations by frequency. Any place he visited three times or more since April 1. The shorter list included four addresses.

Valley visited *Las Peliculas Fantasia* six times. That made sense. He was a porn actor, but he wouldn't hide there. Too many people not connected with his illegal activities would learn where he was.

Valley visited the *Spoke and Sprocket Pub*, a biker bar, six times, four times on a weekend. I checked the tracks on Alejandro Fajardo's and Ronald Trojanik's phones. The other bikers visited the bar four times. Might be a biker favorite, but not suitable to hide out, unless there was a back room. I would check it out unless someplace else on the list seemed more promising.

Next on the list was a street address with no description. Valley traveled there four times. I entered the address on Google Street View. It was a storage facility called *Your Grandparents' Attic*.

Your Grandparents' Attic had a two-story bungalow with a neatly trimmed lawn and colorful flower beds in front. The office occupied one end of the bungalow and had a separate entrance and parking spaces outside of the fenced area. An eight-foot chain-link fence with three barb-wire strands on top surrounded the storage area.

I searched the name online to figure out whether it was part of a chain. A chain store would have cameras covering every nook and cranny. An independent one might not. Can you spell *privacy*?

I scoured the property ownership online. Roberto and Geraldine Hernandez bought the site seven years earlier. They built the storage facility on the vacant land. There was no mortgage on the multi-million-dollar property. Where did they get the money?

Roberto and Geraldine Hernandez's residential address was the storage facility. They must live onsite and probably managed the property.

Roberto was a retired airline baggage handler. He had been a person of interest in a ring of baggage handlers involved in smuggling drugs into Houston on flights from foreign airports. No charges were ever filed, and he testified as a material witness at the ringleader's trial.

Geraldine was a retired secretary at the Harris County Appraisal District office. Eight years before, the district was targeted by newspaper articles questioning the low tax appraisals on properties owned by persons connected with a member of the District's Board of Directors. Nothing was ever proved, but the director involved resigned and Geraldine, his secretary, retired at the same time.

That was right before Geraldine and Roberto bought the vacant land for cash and built the storage facility for cash.

Hmm.

I jumped in the Tahoe and told the GPS to navigate me to the storage facility's street address.

I parked at a strip center across the street in front of a furniture store and studied the site for an hour through binoculars. Security cameras covered the entrance and exit gates. No other cameras were visible inside the fence.

Unit renters entered a four-digit code in an access box at the entrance gate by the bungalow. The third time someone entered the code, I calculated it was 6701. The entrance gate stayed open ten seconds before closing—long enough for a second vehicle to enter. The piggyback happened twice more as a second vehicle entered without punching a code into the box.

To exit, anyone inside approached the separate exit gate on the bungalow's left side, and a motion sensor slid the gate open.

The Hernandez couple's background indicated they would ask no questions if Tommy Valley rented a storage unit for criminal activity.

I drove to the entrance gate. I entered 6107. I waited ten seconds and entered 6107 again. After the third time, I parked at the office and walked inside.

A stocky, gray-haired woman sat behind the desk. Her name tag read *Geraldine*.

I spoke to her in Spanish. "Excuse me, ma'am, but I am Carlos Calderon, Tomás Valenzuela's friend from Saltillo."

I paused to establish whether the woman understood me and whether she reacted to Valenzuela's name. Her Hispanic surname, Hernandez, was her husband's, and while the Hernandez family might have lived in Texas since it was part of Mexico, it didn't mean she spoke Spanish. Regardless, her speaking Spanish might be a link to gain her trust.

The woman's eyes narrowed but she said nothing.

I switched to English. "You might know him as Tommy Valley. I'm supposed to meet him here, but the access code he gave me does not work." I handed her a piece of paper on which I had scribbled the code.

Hernandez accepted the paper and studied it. She responded in Spanish. "Whoever wrote this mixed the Mexican way to make a seven and the gringo way. He left the crossbar off the seven so it looks like a one, and he wrote the one so sloppy that you mistook it for a seven. The code is 6701."

"Muchas gracias, señora."

I stopped at the access box, entered the code, and steered into the secured area. At idle speed, I explored every driveway, alert for Valley's motorcycle or any clue as to his location. True, Hernandez's reaction didn't indicate whether Valley was a tenant, but she didn't say she'd never heard of him either.

Before stopping at the office on the way out, I activated my phone's audio recording app. I dictated the date and time though the phone imprinted it automatically.

I walked into the office. "I searched every street and didn't find Tomás's Harley, and he's not answering his phone," I said in English. "Could you give him a message if you see him? May I borrow a piece of paper?"

"Which unit did you check? He rents three units."

"Tomás didn't give me his unit number. He said to drive in, and I would see him. I figured his unit was at the front. He said I'd recognize his bike."

"That was *estupido*. His units are at the back. But you covered every street, you say?"

"Yes, ma'am. No Harley. Could be I remembered the time wrong. Can I leave a message with you?"

"He seldom stops at the office, but you're welcome to write a note." Hernandez handed me a notepad with the storage center's logo on it.

I wrote in Spanish. "Carlos. Call me." I wrote one of my cellphone numbers down, tore off the sheet, and handed it to the woman. "Thanks."

"I'll stuff the note in his box. He might read it; he might not. No guarantees."

Bingo. Hernandez confirmed Valley rents three units in *Your Grandparents' Attic*.

Unfortunately, the customer boxes faced the other way, and I couldn't see Valley's box number.

Returning to the Tahoe, I called Royce Wilson. "I have proof Tommy Valley rents three storage units at a self-storage business near Northwest

Freeway. I suspect he's gone to ground in one of them. I'm coming over with the proof. Will you be there?"

"What's the proof?"

"Where are you? I'll show you when I see you. Are you at the station?"

"Art and I will be back at the station at 5:00 p.m. Does that work for you?"

"See you there."

———

I was waiting in the OCU conference room when Royce Wilson and Art Devlin arrived.

Wilson sat across from me. "Whatcha got, Chuck?"

"An audio recording of a conversation I had with the owner/manager of *Your Grandparents' Attic* storage facility. She offered to take a message for Tomás Valenzuela aka Tommy Valley." I played the recording I'd made on my cellphone.

"She didn't tell which units were his, though."

"Hey, Royce, I can't do all the work for you. Show Geraldine Hernandez your badge and she'll tell you. You know how it works."

Wilson cut his eyes to Devlin. "Call for backup. Assign a couple of uniforms and we'll arrest him. We can pop his units with an arrest warrant. If he's not there, we post the uniforms on his units while we obtain a search warrant."

"He occupies three units," I said. "They may not be together. If they're not, you should send three uniforms to secure them until you get the warrant."

"Good point," Wilson said. "We'll take two black-and-whites with us." He stood. "Nice work, Chuck. We'll call you later. Tell you how it worked out."

"Great. I'm taking the rest of the day off."

While I caught up on my sleep, somebody worked behind the scenes to turn all my work finding Angie's killers to ashes. Literally.

SIXTEEN

T hursday morning, I arrived at the Harris County Sheriff's Office and
     Detention Center at 9:00 a.m.

"I'm here to visit Tomás Valenzuela aka Tommy Valley. Detectives
Wilson and Devlin arrested him last night."

The desk sergeant glanced at her computer monitor. "Are you his
attorney?"

"No. A friend."

"Spell the last name please."

I did.

"Ah, yes. Processed in last night at 11:32 p.m. Supposed to be
arraigned this afternoon."

I slid my Florida driver's license through the slot under the bulletproof
window.

The sergeant shoved the license back. "Unless you're his attorney, visi-
tation is 1:00 to 5:00 p.m. and 7:30 to 10:00 p.m. Last visit starts at 9:30
p.m. Come back then. Your friend's not going anywhere."

I kicked myself for not knowing the visiting hours.

Four hours to kill. I still hadn't told my parents Angie was dead. I
couldn't find the words for the message that would bring their world
crashing to the ground. A message to tell them I failed to save Angelina.

No, not failed; I had succeeded to the extent I learned her fat couldn't find the words to tell my family.

Returning to Bettina's condo, I changed into running clotl pounded out five miles at the city park. Then I worked out in the the condos. On a weekday morning, I was the only one there. I retu The Armory where I'd bought my weapons. I hadn't practiced s since before the cruise. I fired one magazine with each hand wi weapon. My hands ached afterward, but it felt good to whet the edge skills.

But I hadn't contacted my parents.

A quick lunch at a Korean restaurant and I was back at the County Detention Center at 12:59 p.m.

A different desk sergeant was on duty. Shifts change at 11:00 a.m.

"I'm here to interview an inmate named Tomás Valenzue spelled it.

The sergeant clicked his keyboard. "Tomás Valenzuela... Ah, he is." He studied the monitor for a moment, frowned, and tapped the He made a phone call. The conversation lasted several minutes.

The sergeant disconnected and frowned. "He was transferred to fe custody at ten o'clock this morning."

"What do you mean?"

"I mean two federal agents came in with a judicial order to take Va zuela into their custody."

For a moment, the earth shifted beneath my feet. Federal agents? V called the FBI?

"Where is Valenzuela?"

The sergeant showed his palms. "Ask the feds."

"What were the agents' names and badge numbers?"

The sergeant studied the monitor and maneuvered the mouse. "Does say."

"Shouldn't there be signed paperwork involved in transferri custody?"

The sergeant's forehead wrinkled. "Yeah. There should be." H jiggered his keyboard. "That's crazy. There's nothing here. The compute is supposed to have a copy of the paperwork and the signatures, but it'

not there." He looked at me, wide-eyed. "I can't explain it, sir. It's not there."

My world rocked off-kilter. I laid both hands on the counter to steady myself. What the hell was happening?

"Thank you for your efforts, Sergeant." I left and called Royce Wilson.

"Hey, Chuck, I assume you read my text last night that we arrested Tommy Valley. We booked him into a holding cell at 1200 Baker last night. He'll be arraigned this afternoon at 3:00."

"Things have changed, Royce. I went to 1200 Baker Street to visit Tommy, and the desk sergeant says two feds came in and took him into federal custody at ten o'clock this morning. Did you know about that?"

"What do you mean 'took him into federal custody'?"

"The desk sergeant said they carried a judicial order."

"That's news to me. You mean our suspect isn't in our jail anymore?"

"Nope," I said. "You should start shaking the bushes. He's out there."

"Count on it," Wilson said. "Something fishy is going on."

"Did you get your search warrant for Flathead Pipe Supply?"

"Yeah. I have a crew executing it as we speak."

"I'd like to go to Flathead and look in on the search. Can you call your guy in charge and arrange for me to observe?"

"That's against protocol, Chuck."

"Royce, it's my sister who's missing. Will you clear it with your guy?"

There was a long silence on the line. I waited. I had made my case.

"Yeah. I'll call her," Wilson said. "She's Sergeant Gabby Dillon."

"Thanks, Royce. I owe you one."

"No, you don't, Chuck. You unearthed *Your Grandparents' Attic,* and you brought us the envelope supposedly containing evidence from the building at Flathead. If that checks out, I owe *you* one."

———

I arrived at Flathead Pipe Supply mid-afternoon. The area near Building 3 showed a beehive of activity with cars and trucks both moving and parked. An eighteen-wheeler rumbled across the culvert and rolled in my direction on Powerline Road. Its flatbed trailer was stacked high with metal pipe.

The main entrance gate was still open, but a black-and-white was parked at the entrance; two uniformed cops sat inside it.

I stopped next to the driver's open window and lowered my window. "Carlos McCrary to see Sergeant Gabby Dillon. She's expecting me." I flashed my driver's license. No point telling them I was a PI.

"You know how to get there?"

"It's the small building at the back, right?"

"Right." The cop waved me through.

A morning shower had soaked the gravel roads, and I didn't kick up a dust cloud moving at a brisk pace. I parked the Tahoe beside the CSI van.

I jerked to a stop as I reached the unmarked building, the one I had designated as Building 4. The roof was curled and blackened from a fire. The outside paint was cracked and charred. The building was a burnt, gutted wreck. The opposite end was a pile of twisted metal, probably from the gasoline tanks of the three vehicles inside exploding.

The rollup truck door from the building's north end lay nearby. The heat had warped the door or its rails to the point that it couldn't be opened. The CSI unit had attached a chain to the door bottom and dragged it away behind the CSI van.

A woman with salt-and-pepper hair waited inside the doorway. She wore khaki slacks, black sneakers, and a Houston Police Department black and silver golf shirt with a CSI badge printed on it.

She glanced my way and walked through the opening. "You Carlos McCrary?"

I handed her a business card. "I have a new number. Let me mark it on my card." I scratched through my "official" cellphone number and wrote in my burner number. "Royce Wilson sent me. Call me Chuck."

"I'm Gabby Dillon. I'd shake your hand but…" She showed her gloved hands. She studied my card before slipping it in a pocket. "You're a PI from Port City? What brings you to Houston?"

"Searching for my missing sister. She lives here. I mean, I *hope* she lives here. I mean, assuming she's still alive."

"Royce said you're the one who found this place."

"Not me. The Flathead plant was the subject of a package left on my SUV. For some reason, an anonymous benefactor picked me to deliver the evidence. I don't even know for sure if it's from this site. It's common knowledge to everyone I talked to that I'm searching for my sister. A person or persons unknown stuck an envelope with clues under my wind-shield wiper. It contained a video with a note from an unknown person. The note said the video was recorded 'inside the unmarked building' at this site. This is my first visit here." In my defense, I did have my fingers crossed behind my back.

Dillon turned toward the blackened equipment and vehicles inside. "Someone torched it before we got here, and they did a good job. We found the remnants of three vehicles that exploded inside. We'll haul everything to the lab, but it won't yield anything useful."

"I worked Robbery-Homicide with the Port City cops a million years ago. Fire destroys evidence."

"Sad but true." She handed me a pair of footies. "Here. Cover your feet and walk with me. I haven't played the video yet. Since you have, you could add context to what the arsonist left us."

I sat on the rear bumper of the CSI van and slipped on the shoe covers. "Yeah. The envelope contained sandwich bags with evidence. I played the video a couple times. Maybe I can help."

I led Dillon into the building's interior. Portable lights were in the two corners that did not explode, and three technicians worked in various places in the interior. "This blistered scrap metal pile was an industrial-sized woodchipper."

"Hang on a second, Chuck. Okay for me to video you while you give me the tour?"

I considered the pros and cons. I needed to be careful what I said so I didn't inadvertently reveal I had gathered the evidence. "Okay, sergeant."

"Call me Gabby." She tapped the video recorder app on her phone. "Okay, let's restart."

I pointed. "This is—or was—a woodchipper. In the video, you can see brown stains on the intake hopper. The stains looked like dried blood. It was large enough to chew up a body. In the video, the discharge chute was aimed at a large trash can. That shapeless, melted lump over there could be the trash can."

Gabby paused the video app. "Oh, God. This is so damned *creepy*. It's something you'd see in a horror movie." She shuddered, then restarted the video camera. "Let's continue, Chuck."

Stepping to the right, I gestured. "Notice the hose bib over there?"

"Yeah. Probably had a hose connected but it burned. The female coupling is on the faucet." Gabby moved closer and videoed the hose's remnants. "Was that thing a sprayer nozzle?"

"Yeah. In the video the hose had a dark-colored spray nozzle on the end." I stepped closer. "The nozzle must have been rubber or plastic because all that's left is the metal tip. The charred shovel on the ground was leaning against the wall beside the hose bib."

"And the vehicles?"

"That scrap pile is, or *was*, my brother-in-law Teodoro Garza's Jeep. I identified it from the license plate in the video. Your lab techs can recon-struct the license number and the VIN if you can find them in the wreckage."

"This is the first I heard of Teodoro Garza. Is he a victim too?"

"His cellphone went out of service at 10:53 p.m., March 15. The last spot it pinged was a cell tower a half mile away. He's been missing ever since. I assume this is where he was murdered, and that—," I pointed at the woodchipper, "—is how they disposed of his body."

"I've been to some awful crime scenes, Chuck, but this one… It's in a class of spooky all by itself."

"It's taking me awhile to be able to stomach it, and I've watched the video before. But in person…"

"Yeah. The reality is far worse than a video conveys."

"Let's continue," I said. "I want to finish this ASAP."

"Right. Please continue."

"That piece of metal was part of a beige panel van with *Flathead Pipe Supply* on the side in green letters. You can still make out a few of the letters. It's part of a fleet I saw as I drove in. I identified this one from a security video at the truckstop where Angie was kidnapped. This tangle of metal is the van they… they threw her in." My voice cracked and I waved for Gabby to pause the video. I needed a few seconds to regain my composure.

"You all right, Chuck?"

For a few seconds I couldn't speak without losing control. Shaking my head, I swallowed my gorge and stared into the distance until my emotions flattened.

Gabby, to her credit, looked away and waited patiently. "What a stupid question. Of course, you're not all right."

"Sorry. It's just…"

Gabby patted my shoulder. "Let's hit *pause* for a minute. This wreck of a crime scene isn't going anywhere."

After a few seconds, I continued.

"And that—," I pointed, "—was Angie's blue Mazda. I see a little blue paint remnant in the wheel well."

"Yeah. I'll copy the kidnapping video and the one the anonymous person sent, and I'll make sure my lab techs compare them."

I scuffed the gravel on the floor. "The envelope had six sandwich bags with rocks in them. At the time I couldn't figure out why they gave me rocks. Now that I see this gravel floor, I believe the rocks were collected from this building. They haven't been burned, and you might find DNA on them."

"Thanks for the info, Chuck. We'll do our best."

"When I can help you with anything or give you background or if you want a knowledgeable outsider for a sounding board, call me twenty-four/seven. You have my card. Angie was my sister, and I'll do anything to bring her killers to justice." I waited until the CSI looked in my eyes. "And I mean *anything*."

"We haven't located her body," Gabby said. "It's possible they moved her someplace else."

"Right, and garbage doesn't stink, and gophers don't dig." I sighed. "It's not practical, Gabby, but if you processed the gravel on this floor at the bottom where the flames didn't reach, I would bet a Cadillac against a cup of coffee that you'd detect my sister's and her husband's DNA. Since the fire, the six rocks from the envelope are our only DNA clues.

"The video was time-stamped early Thursday morning. Less than forty hours later, someone torches the building's contents. Who knew the cops were seeking a search warrant? Could there be a mole in the Houston PD?"

I thought about Devlin. *Maybe he's just a lazy, incompetent asshole, but somehow I don't trust him.*

"God, let's hope not." Gabby glanced at the phone she was still holding. "*Oops.* I forgot to stop the video recording." She closed the app and returned the phone to her pocket. "Here's my card in case you recall anything else."

I slipped her card in my pocket. "Thanks for letting me observe."

The good news from my visit to the crime scene was that I figured out how to tell my parents.

———

The Watcher

The watcher called her boss. "McCrary showed at Flathead again. He spoke to a uniform at the entrance. He drove to the back of the plant and gave the CSI sergeant a personal tour of the burnt building."

"How could you know that? We didn't put cameras back there."

The watcher figured she would impress her boss with both her initiative and her tech skill. "I tapped the CSI's phone, boss. She videoed McCrary's tour. He explained what each piece of burned equipment was for. I'll send you the video."

"Nice work."

"Thanks, boss. I had to get creative to copy the video from her phone, but it worked. One other thing McCrary says on the video: He suspects the Houston cops have a mole in the department."

The voice on the other end laughed. "A mole. If McCrary uncovered the truth, he'd crap his pants."

"This McCrary guy is already too close. He was at the county jail earlier today trying to interview some guy named Tommy Valley. He revealed that federal agents collected Valley this morning. Who is Tommy Valley?"

"He's nobody."

The watcher didn't believe this Valley guy was nobody, but the boss was the boss.

"Stick to your surveillance. This pest will endanger the operation unless we stop him. What's his weak point?"

"I've been researching McCrary. So far, I haven't unearthed a weakness. He's a poster boy for Captain America."

"Everyone has a weakness. It's a matter of locating it and pushing the right button."

"He's a Special Forces veteran with a long list of decorations and medals. Maybe we can appeal to his patriotism."

SEVENTEEN

Carlos McCrary

I drove to the West Freeway Police Station and squeezed into a visitor's spot.

I texted Bettina:

I'm meeting Royce Wilson and Art Devlin in OCU. You free for dinner later?

Seconds later Bettina smiled on the screen.

I accepted the video call. "That was fast."

"I figured why text when I can call and see you practically in person. I'm in River Oaks finishing a burglary report. I'll write this up at the station. Give me a couple hours. I know how hungry you get, but I estimate eight o'clock before we eat."

"That's fine. Tell you what—there's no telling how long I will be with OCU. I'll text you when I finish and wait at the condo. Otherwise, I'll wait for you here."

"Sounds like a plan." She blew me a kiss and disconnected.

Bettina had blown me a kiss. What did that mean? Sure, we were sleeping together, and I had massaged every inch of her body, but blowing a kiss? That seemed more intimate than sex.

The desk sergeant entered my name in the visitor's log. "You know the way, Chuck?"

"Sure. I was here yesterday."

I stopped at the snack machine and bought a package of peanut butter crackers. Then I bought another. Eight o'clock was a long time to wait for dinner. Pocketing the snack packs in my coat, I poured a coffee from the break room and carried it to the OCU bullpen.

Wilson and Devlin sat at adjacent desks, their chairs swiveled to talk to each other.

Wilson snagged a chair from an empty desk and scooted it over. "Have a seat, Chuck."

I opened the first snack pack. "I'm starving. Hope you don't mind me nibbling a couple of peanut-butter crackers." I removed two sandwiches from the package and held it toward the two detectives. "Help yourselves. I have another package in my pocket."

Wilson lifted a cracker sandwich. "Thanks."

Devlin waved them off. "I'm good."

I bit off half a cracker sandwich and chased it with coffee. "Did y'all locate the feds who stole your collar?"

Devlin and Wilson shared a glance.

I couldn't read the expression that passed between them, but whatever it meant, it was not good news.

Wilson swung his chair in my direction. "Tommy Valley is off-limits."

I swallowed the cracker bite. "What does *off-limits* mean?"

"It means should we accidentally trip over him, we do not arrest him. The feds are protecting him."

"Why does the FBI protect a man whom we are 95 percent certain kidnapped and killed my sister?" I poked the rest of the cracker sandwich in my mouth.

Wilson spread his hands. "Best guess? He's a CI."

I washed down the bite with more coffee. "I was a Port City detective, and we protected our confidential informants. We might not bust them for possession. Or I might fix a parking violation or a speeding ticket if no one was hurt. But we wouldn't protect a CI who committed kidnapping or murder. Who told you Valley was off-limits?"

Wilson glanced at Devlin before responding. "Our captain."

"Why would your captain get involved?"

"Here's what happened, Chuck," Wilson said. "I started by calling the local FBI office. They transferred me from one agent to another. Finally a flunky asked me to leave a message. Said someone would get back to me." He drew a deep breath and blew it out through his lips. "Forty-five minutes later, Captain Higgs—she's our boss—calls us into her office and tells us to stay away from Tommy Valley. She said the message trickled down from high on the chain of command."

"Somebody at the FBI went over your head?" I said.

Wilson spread his hands in a *that's life* signal. "They went straight to the Chief of Police. The Chief leaned on Cap'n Higgs."

"Where is Tommy Valley?"

Wilson spread his palms. He seemed embarrassed. "In the wind. According to Cap, the Feds released him."

I swallowed the rest of the cracker sandwich, chased it with a swig of coffee. "Say what? Did you say they released him."

Royce Wilson's face reddened. "I did say that: The goddam feds released our goddam suspect."

I removed the remaining two cracker sandwiches from the package and tossed the wrapper in the trash. I stuck a sandwich in my mouth whole and chewed it. Finishing the sandwich, I did the same thing to the last one.

Wilson and Devlin glanced at each other.

Devlin said, "Well? What will you do, McCrary?"

I remembered Grandpa Magnus's advice: *Sometimes silence is the best reply.*

I swallowed the remaining cracker crumbs and scooted the chair back where it belonged. "I wish you gentleman a good day."

Devlin jumped to his feet with clenched fists and blocked my way. "That's not what I meant, McCrary. What do you intend to do with Tommy Valley? Will we have trouble with you?"

I smiled, but the smile never reached my eyes. "Devlin, I will ask one time. Will you please let me pass?"

Devlin's face was red, and he clenched and unclenched his fists. He started to say something, but Royce Wilson stood and laid a hand on his shoulder. "Art, stand down."

Devlin lowered his hands and moved aside.

I moved for the door. "Good day to you both."

———

Returning to my SUV, I cranked the engine and maxed the air conditioning. I opened the second snack pack and considered this unexpected development in the case. I opened a water bottle from the pocket on the door. Yuck, the water was warm from sitting in the parked car all day. At least it washed down the peanut-butter cracker. I ate the crackers.

Something was not kosher; the feds protecting a suspected murderer. Confidential informants are subject to rules designed to protect the public. It seemed silly to mention, but a CI does not have a get-out-of-jail-free card. People cannot kidnap or murder someone with impunity. But the FBI was protecting a kidnapping and murder suspect in this case.

I finished the peanut-butter crackers and the water and crushed the empty bottle in the litter bag.

The Special Agent in Charge of the Port City FBI office was Eugene Lopez. I'd worked with him on several occasions in the past, including a kidnapping case that led me to uncover a human trafficking gang. He wasn't a friend, but he did give me his direct phone number. On rare occasions, when it served the interests of justice, he bent a rule for me. Damn, it was 7:30 in the evening in Port City. Lopez would not be in his office.

You don't ask; you don't get. Referring to my regular phone's contact list, I called Lopez from the burner phone.

Three rings later, he answered. "Gene Lopez."

"Gene, it's Chuck McCrary."

"I don't recognize your phone number, Chuck."

"I'm calling from a burner phone."

"I'm sure there's a good reason for that. What do you want this time?"

That was Lopez. Right to the point.

"There's something happening in the FBI's Houston office that's not kosher."

"Ahh, that explains your Houston area code."

"Yeah. I've been working a case in Houston."

"Can you tell me what case? Or is it confidential?"

"My sister Angelina McCrary Garza and her husband Teodoro Garza are missing. They live in Houston. I've been investigating for the last week, and I'm 90 percent certain they were both murdered."

"Geez. I'm sorry to hear that, Chuck."

"Thanks, Gene."

"And the FBI is involved in the murder because it's a suspected kidnapping?"

"No. The Houston cops never called in the FBI. The feds materialized out of the blue once the Houston Organized Crime Unit arrested a suspect, Tomás Valenzuela aka Tommy Valley. We believe he is involved in the disappearance and probable murder of Angelina's husband Teodoro and the confirmed kidnapping of my sister. The FBI involvement may be off the books."

I told Lopez two federal agents hauled Tommy Valley away and then released him. "The Houston detectives who arrested him called the FBI for information. They got stonewalled."

"You mean the FBI never called back with the info?"

"Worse, Gene. Rather than return the detectives' call, someone at the FBI went over their heads. Within forty-five minutes, the detectives' own captain called them. She received orders from high on the command chain that Tommy Valley was off-limits. I've never heard of any law enforcement agency—especially the FBI—letting a CI off on a kidnapping rap, let alone a murder. Can you check this out and tell me who the agents are? I'd like to talk to them and untangle this mess."

"You said the Houston OCU made the arrest. Were drugs involved?"

"Yeah. The suspect is a distributor for the *Tres Equis* cartel from Saltillo, Coahuila. The reason I'm using a burner phone is we believe someone is illegally surveilling me and a third Houston detective. When you call back, call the burner."

"Yeah, Chuck. This ain't my first rodeo. Speaking of surveillance, assuming a Mexican cartel is involved, the feds who nicked your suspect might be DHS, not FBI."

"I never considered Homeland Security. I've never dealt with them."

Lopez laughed. "Not that you *know* of. There are rumors the DHS has gee-whiz spy tech from the National Security Agency to use on their cases. DHS could surveil your phone, your car, your bank account, and your credit cards and you would never be aware of it."

"Isn't that a comforting thought? The reason I bought the burner phones is we suspect we're being surveilled."

"We?"

"Yeah. I'm collaborating with an old friend who is a Houston Burglary-Theft detective. She's dipping her oar in the water when she's not on duty."

"Make sure she uses a burner. Whether the DHS is involved... well, let's wait until I make inquiries. I'll call you back on this number." He disconnected.

Department of Homeland Snooping? I had not considered that angle. But the *Tres Equis* cartel smuggling drugs into the U.S.? The DHS might want to be involved.

DHS surveillance would explain the SUV full of shooters attacking Bettina and me when we entered the Flathead site. The DHS hid its legally questionable activities under the Patriot Act's umbrella. But would DHS agents open fire on law-abiding private citizens? That didn't make sense.

Unless the two feds were crooked, using government assets illegally.

If the feds were protecting Tommy Valley, whether it was the FBI or DHS, he might feel secure enough to return to his apartment.

Glancing at my phone, I calculated I had an hour to kill.

I texted Bettina.

Change of plans. I found a lead to pursue until you are ready for dinner. Text me when you finish your paperwork.

Time to pay another visit to Lola Salazar and Tommy Valley's apartment. Couldn't hurt.

———

I idled through the parking area until I spotted Valley's motorcycle parked fifty yards past their apartment. Good. The drug dealer was home.

There was no good spot to hide a GPS tracker on Valley's bike. Under the rear fender toward the back was the best I could do. The tracker was matte black and blended into the shadows.

I parked where I could surveil the front door. The sun slumped behind the pine forest across the street and the pavement lay in deep shadow. Good spot not to be noticed. Rule Two: *When in doubt, follow somebody.*

I didn't expect Valley to lead me anywhere that night, but I had to pursue every opportunity.

Twenty-five minutes later, Bettina called. "Hey, Chuck, I'm logging off the system. Where do you stand on that lead? Do you need more time?"

"*Nah*. I'll tell you when I get to your condo. That will take twenty minutes."

"See you then." She disconnected.

I slipped the Tahoe in gear and idled toward the exit. My burner rang. It was Lopez. I stopped at the curb before answering.

"That was fast, Gene. I didn't expect to hear from you until morning or on Monday."

"I talked to the SAC in Houston."

My dashboard clock said it was 8:15. Was the Houston SAC working late on a Thursday night? Or did Lopez call him or her at home? Either way Lopez figured this shouldn't wait until Friday morning.

"Yes, and she investigated the release of Tommy Valley. It wasn't us. She dug deep because there was no footprint in the FBI records of your OCU detectives calling."

"Isn't that unusual?"

"Yeah, which she found disturbing, as did I. She kept digging until she discovered what had happened. The OCU call was transferred until it reached an FBI agent with a friend in DHS. Our agent called his buddy, and the DHS buddy asked him to delete the phone message. Said it was a national security matter and there should be no traces in the Houston FBI's records. Said it was a 'need to know' thing and nobody in the FBI needed to know."

"Did she give you the contact info on the DHS buddy?"

"No, and it was a tug of war to get answers. I tell you, Chuck, this thing is above my pay grade. The SAC told me she talked to her agent. Her agent said he couldn't give the DHS agent's name to her, his own boss, because—get this: She didn't have a 'need to know.'"

"Can you give me the name of the FBI agent in Houston you talked to?"

"Chuck, I expect you're tempted to not accept this 'national security' two-step. But she wouldn't tell *me* the FBI agent's name. Since she wouldn't tell a fellow SAC, you won't discover anything. I advise you to let this slide. Powerful people are behind this. Dangerous people."

Moving against dangerous people never bothered me. "Gene, Tommy Valley is a suspect in my sister's disappearance and probable murder. You expect me to say, 'That's life' and walk away?"

There was silence on the line. Finally Lopez replied. "My hands are tied, Chuck. If it were me..."

"But it's not," I finished the sentence.

"Watch your six, Chuck. Whoever these DHS guys are, their operation is big enough for them to strong-arm the Houston SAC and overlook a kidnapping and murder. There's no telling what else they're willing to do."

———

I slipped the Tahoe into gear. Lopez's last words echoed in my mind. "There's no telling what else they're willing to do."

I called Bettina. "I'm on my way. Got a call from an FBI contact. It delayed me five minutes."

"It's nine o'clock. Let's eat in. I already started cooking."

"I'll bring a bottle of wine."

I didn't tell her I was bringing a bug detector. And why.

———

I slotted into a visitor's spot at Bettina's condo and dug through my backpack for the bug detector. When I scanned the Tahoe, the red light blinked. Damn, how long had the tracker been stuck to my SUV? I moved to Bettina's car. No red light. Of course, DHS knew Bettina Simpson's identity by now. Her late-model car had GPS built into it. They could locate her anywhere by tapping into her GPS module. I had rented an older Tahoe for that reason. But they had tagged me.

Maybe they didn't have a mole in the HPD. Maybe the tracker was how they discovered I had been inside Building 4. They tagged my Tahoe and monitored the tracker to the pine tree farm where I parked.

This was not good. The conspirators were serious and competent, and they would know everywhere I went.

At best, Bettina and I had inadvertently spooked a DHS taskforce that had gone overboard. I violated the old maxim: Never poke a hornet's nest with a short stick. The outlaws ignored the Fourth Amendment to the U.S. Constitution and ran rough-shod over innocent civilians.

I couldn't let Bettina continue to work the case with me; the risk was unacceptable. Angie was my sister, not hers.

Best case, the law was on my side, and I could block the operation by collecting evidence and threatening to go public. I could bring Tommy Valley to justice for my sister's kidnapping and murder, along with anyone else involved. And I would have the law's blessing.

Worst case, Bettina and I had stumbled on a rogue group operating underground within the DHS. The group ran a black operation with no oversight and no accountability. Imagine *Enemy of the State* meets *The Fugitive*. But they could attack me with the law on their side. On the other hand, I would be "obstructing justice" with each move I made to derail them.

No way I could let Bettina face such risks.

Staying with Bettina had been nice while it lasted.

I tapped on her door before using my key to enter.

She was standing by the kitchen island. "You needn't knock. That's why I gave you a key." She continued chopping the salad ingredients.

"It seems polite to give you a heads-up that I'm here."

She squeezed my hand. "That's sweet. I'm making another meatloaf. Does that appeal to you?"

"I never met a meal I didn't like. And your meatloaf is special."

I opened the refrigerator and selected a beer. "Can I bring you anything?"

She gestured to a wine glass sitting on the counter. "I have a glass of wine over there."

I unscrewed the cap on the beer bottle and took a swig. "There are few things in life as perfect as the first taste of a cold beer at the end of a long day."

Bettina lifted her wine glass. "Hear, hear." She sipped and lowered the glass. "How was your day?"

I debated how to tell her I was pulling away. She had been helpful and willing from the moment I asked. She might prefer to stay involved despite the risks, but that option was no longer on the table. "My day was eventful."

"Sounds interesting."

"Did I tell you I bought a bug detector last Saturday after I armed myself at the gun store?"

"No, I don't believe you did, and you're telling me because…?"

"Someone tagged my car."

"Tagged?" She scraped the chopped parsley into the mixing bowl.

"With a GPS tracker. Someone tagged my Tahoe because it does *not* have a built-in GPS. Now they know my vehicle. I checked your car. They didn't tag it because they trail you with the internal GPS. And you can't switch it off on your car."

"Should I rent an older car like you did?"

"*Nah*, I haven't bothered to remove the bug on my Tahoe. I'm not dressed to crawl under a car, but it's gotta be a GPS tracker. I use them all the time."

"Don't you need a warrant to use one of those unless the car owner gives you permission?"

"Sure. Either the conspirators got a warrant, or they don't mind breaking the law. Or both." I drank another taste of my beer.

"No, I meant isn't it illegal for *you* to use a GPS tracker?"

"Me? I don't need no stinkin' warrant."

"Oh, I forgot. A twenty-first century knight in shining armor doesn't need a warrant because his heart is pure."

"And don't forget my dimples."

Bettina chuckled and touched one of my dimples with a fingertip.

"Cutie pie, you said the bad guys might have gotten a warrant. How could members of a drug cartel get a warrant to track your vehicle?"

"Because I learned other bad news from the SAC of the Port City FBI office. He called back while I was on my way here. The bad guys aren't the drug cartel; they're federal agents."

I briefed Bettina on my visit to the county jail, the OCU detectives, my two conversations with Eugene Lopez, and my tagging Tommy Valley's motorcycle.

"You've been busy today." She began to dice tomatoes.

"The operation we stumbled into may involve *Tres Equis* smuggling drugs or even terrorists into the U.S. That's why the DHS is involved and not the FBI or the DEA. Gene Lopez said if they have the balls to overlook a kidnapping and probable murder, the black operation reaches high in the DHS."

"That can't be good," Bettina said. "What can we do to stop it?"

"The last thing Gene said to me was to watch my six. Gene said if their operation has enough juice to strong-arm both the Houston police and the FBI to overlook a kidnapping and murder, there was no telling what else they were willing and able to do."

"We're in more danger than we figured."

"This is way hairier than the missing person case you volunteered for. You don't need that much trouble. Since the criminals are the DHS, I'll check into a motel."

"Let me sleep on it, Chuck."

I waved a hand noncommittally, but I couldn't let her stay involved in this case.

I planned to go more rogue than ever. On other cases, I've crossed swords legally with the Port City PD and the FBI. Even the Secret Service. So far, each time I emerged triumphant and unscathed, but the law was on my side.

But in this case, this deep, perverse operation could be stopped only with a force smarter and more ruthless than they were. I was forced to transform to full-on vigilante.

"I'll buy work clothes this evening so I can crawl under the Tahoe and remove the bug."

———

Following dinner, I laid my cards on the table.

"Bettina, I thank you for the help, the lodging, the food, and the company." I placed my hand on hers.

"Whoa, Kemo Sabe. You sound like the Lone Ranger planning to ride into the sunset, but without Tonto."

"You're not wrong. This case is far more than a missing person case. You've been an immense help and a good friend. Someday I hope to repay the many favors you've done for me the last few days. But now, every second I stay close to you puts you in danger. I'm checking into a motel tonight."

Bettina's forehead wrinkled. "Do I have the right to an opinion?"

"Of course, but this is my case and my decision. Whether you stayed involved or not, if anything bad happened to you… Whether my actions threatened your career or, God forbid, your *safety*… I could never have that on my conscience."

I collected the dirty dishes. "I'll do the dishes before I go." I toted the dishes to the sink.

Bettina gathered her dishes and trailed me as I rinsed the tableware. Placing her dishes next to the sink, she stepped behind me and wrapped her arms around my waist. She laid her cheek on my back. "Okay, Chuck. I can still help. Call me for anything, anytime. I'll keep the burner phone."

"I will."

———

I circled the parking lots at three motels before I located one fitting my requirements: A chain motel with utility and construction trucks with Louisiana license plates parked in the lot. Houston was growing fast. There was a perpetual labor shortage. Local companies often hired out-of-town crews to work.

I checked in, found an all-night discount store, and bought coveralls. Returning to the motel, I changed clothes and crawled under the Tahoe with a Maglite. Yep, there it was. I yanked off the tracker and stuck it under a Louisiana work truck. Even if the crew went home on weekends, the truck probably stayed in Houston.

That should confound the enemy.

I drove the Tahoe to a Mom-and-Pop café four miles away where I ordered pecan pie. Texans make the best pecan pie. It's a matter of pride; the pecan is their State Tree.

I ate my pie and emailed my parents that I had seen Building 4 after it was burned and exploded. I reported my conviction that Angelina and Teodoro were murdered there.

Again, Dad called within a minute.

"From the way you describe the crime scene, we'll never recover either Angie's body or Teodoro's."

"That's right."

Dad was silent a moment. "My great-grandfather went missing-in-action in World War II. They never located his body either. The family erected a cenotaph in the Adams Creek Cemetery to honor his life. My great-grandmother is buried right next to it."

"You said your great-grandfather was Irish."

"He was, but everyone has two grandfathers and four great-grandfathers. This was my mother's maternal grandfather. We can erect cenotaphs for Angelina and Teodoro."

"Teo wasn't much of a family member though, was he?"

"Don't speak ill of the dead, son. In death, we will honor him. He was a member of the family."

The server arrived with my pie. I waved my thanks and she left.

"Uh, Dad… I hate to appear stupid, but what's a cenotaph?"

"You're not *stupid*, son; you're *ignorant*. A cenotaph is a monument to honor someone whose remains are buried elsewhere."

"I didn't know that."

"Few people do. It was common in earlier generations with overseas wars. Are you closing the case?"

"No. I know who killed her, but I haven't proved it in a way that qualifies in court. Yet."

"It's silly to say it but be careful. The whole family worries every time you accept one of these cases."

I disconnected and ate my pie. I ruminated on this entire bloody mess.

My instructor at Special Forces taught me to prepare for the enemy's *capabilities*, not their *probabilities*. I wasn't certain the DHS was monitoring me, but it could be fatal if I guessed wrong.

The DHS knew the make, model, and license plate of my Tahoe, which I rented with a credit card. To lose the DHS tail, I must cut the trail.

I decided to buy a car rather than rent one.

I called Tank Tyler, my friend, CPA, and financial advisor.

"Hello."

"Tank, you still have the burner I gave you a while ago?"

"Of course."

"Is it handy?"

"No. It's in my desk downtown at the office. I'm hosting a dinner party here at home."

"I'm sorry to interrupt," I said. "This thing can wait until tomorrow morning. But do it before 10:00 a.m. your time, okay?"

"Don't worry, bro. We're into the brandy. Everyone's enjoying themselves and they won't notice if I leave the room."

"This is a confidential thing, bro. Avoid attention."

"There's Gregory's phone. He's discreet." Gregory was Tank's butler, not that Tank wanted a butler, but Tank has a soft heart. Gregory was the butler at Tank's mansion before Tank bought it. Gregory was far past retirement age with no family and no place else to live. Tank put him on the payroll. It's nice to be a billionaire.

"Good. How long before you have Gregory's phone?"

"He's serving the drinks."

"Make it ten minutes. Take Gregory's phone to your study. I'll call in ten minutes."

At the appointed time, I called and Tank responded.

"Hello. What did you step into this time, bro?"

"Can you send me $30,000 to an Amscot Money Store in Houston?" I read him the store's address.

"It's Thursday night after business hours, Chuck."

"That's okay. First thing in the morning is fine."

"You plan to tell me why you're in Houston and why you need $30,000 in cash?"

"Not over the phone. I'll tell you once I get home to Port City. In fact, I'll buy you dinner."

Tank sighed loudly. His way of saying I was a pest, but he would do it anyway. "You'll do more than that, bro. You'll spot me a stroke a hole next time we play golf. The money will be there at 9:00 a.m. your time. Don't spend it all in one place."

Next, I called my friend Clint Watkins in Gainesville, Florida. "Clint, I hope you didn't make any plans this weekend. I need your help." I explained what I wanted.

EIGHTEEN

Friday morning, I returned the Tahoe and walked around the corner until I was out of sight of the rental company's cameras. Even if the DHS hacked the security cameras at Rent-a-Wreck, they couldn't track me on foot.

After walking to a shopping mall a few blocks away, I booked a taxi to a random location on a residential street a block behind the Mom-and-Pop café where I had ordered the pecan pie the previous night. I paid the driver in cash.

I walked to the café for breakfast. While drinking a second cup of coffee, I consulted Craigslist.com on my phone and selected a cheap Honda Pilot too old to have a built-in GPS. I called the owner to make sure he had the title and made an appointment.

I took a taxi to the Amscot, had him wait while I retrieved the money Tank had sent me. Then I had him take me car shopping.

By noon, I held the title to a used Honda Pilot in my hand. I could wait a few days to file it so it would be a while before the DHS discovered I owned it.

I checked out of last night's motel and moved to a different one. With the DHS tracker on a Louisiana truck, the DHS might believe I was staying there.

I texted Gunner and Clint with their new destination.

Stopping in a Subway, I bought a foot-long and six bottles of water and settled in the far corner of Valley's parking area where I could observe the front door to Lola's and Valley's apartment. I picked a spot under a live oak tree and opened the Honda's windows.

Valley's bike sat where it had been the day before. Unless he hitched a ride with someone, he was at home, sleeping in.

Switching the radio to a low volume, I awaited developments.

I'd finished half my sandwich by the time Bettina video-called. "What are you holding?"

I pointed the camera at it. "A sandwich. I'm staking out Tommy Valley."

"I could have brought you a sandwich, Chuck."

"For your own safety, I'm physically avoiding you. Even if the feds aren't surveilling me, they're surveilling Valley. Since I'm near Valley, they should never see you with me. At least not until this, uh… situation is over."

Bettina frowned. "I appreciate your efforts, but that doesn't mean I like it. I've already gotten used to you sleeping beside me."

"That's the nicest thing I've heard in a long time. I miss you too. I appreciate your call," I said with a goodbye tone in my voice.

"Not so fast, master detective. I have information. I researched the ownership of Flathead Pipe Supply."

"Good job, Bettina. What did you learn?"

"Two years ago, the property was purchased from Amadeus Oil Support Trust by Escondido Sendero LLC, the outfit that owns the SUV that tried to kill us."

"Escondido Sendero LLC is the *Tres Equis* cover for their drug trade assets?"

"That's not all, Kemo Sabe. A week after they bought the Flathead property, they applied for the permit to build Building 4."

"That's good information. Thanks. I'll advise Gabby Dillon."

"Gabby Dillon? Her name is familiar. Who is she?"

"The CSI sergeant who processed what was left of Building 4."

"Oh yeah," she said. "Royce Wilson mentioned her yesterday. Should I call her?"

"No. No one in HPD should hear you're working with me. Keep this on the downlow. I'll call."

"Art Devlin knows I was running the cellphones you… uh, *obtained*."

"Devlin may have forgotten that. Let's let that dog continue sleeping."

"Okay, Chuck. If you need anything else, call or text me."

We said our goodbyes and I called Gabby Dillon. I left her a voicemail.

"Gabby, this is Chuck McCrary. You know by now that Escondido Sendero LLC owns Flathead Pipe Supply. Escondido Sendero is a shell company whose address is a post office box in El Paso. After they bought the Flathead property, they built the building you processed. I discovered other assets Escondido Sendero owns that make me suspect the *Tres Equis* cartel owns the company. You might search to find what other assets Escondido Sendero owns, like vehicles or other real estate. Call me if I can help."

I disconnected and returned to waiting for something to happen. The Honda Pilot didn't have satellite radio, but I discovered a good country station without too many commercials.

A spring thunderstorm passed over. I raised the windows and cranked the A/C. It poured for five minutes, then cleared. If you don't like Texas weather, wait five minutes.

Nothing happened the rest of the day. Tommy Valley was catching up on his rest.

There was always tomorrow.

———

At 4:40 Saturday, Valley descended the stairs and looked up. More scattered rain was forecast, but he fired up his Harley anyway. Then it occurred to me that he might not even own a car. Tailing him a hundred yards or more behind, I kept him in sight. Another shower—this time without lightning—soaked Valley. One of the disadvantages of a motor-cycle compared to my comfy SUV.

Valley rode to the Spoke and Sprocket Pub.

The parking area was practically empty. Small puddles dotted the pock-marked pavement. He parked next to two other motorcycles and entered the building.

The whole time I worked as a detective, I worked with two CIs, and both communicated with me by phone. Undercover cops, however, often meet with their CIs in person. Having no idea what arrangement Valley had with the DHS, I intended to trail him until I discovered who he met.

I paused at the three motorcycles and photographed the two new ones so I could compare the license plates to the ones from Lola Salazar's party.

Valley last saw me eight days before when he and his two friends attacked me in his parking lot. Since I stopped shaving four days earlier, I was scruffy but still recognizable. I had bought a faded Houston Texans baseball cap at a thrift store. Placing it on my head, I flipped up the collar on my denim jacket and entered the bar.

The good news was that the bar was semi-dark. The bad news was the absence of a Saturday night crowd to hide in. The place was practically empty. I picked a corner booth and sat with my back to the wall.

A server with a tattoo-covered right arm walked over. She wore cut-off jeans short enough to highlight her shapely *tuchas* and a Houston Astros tank top over a push-up bra that accented her curves. Good for tips. Her dreadlocks were tied into a ponytail. I speculated—as I always do when I see a nose ring—how the ring piercing her nostril affected her ability to blow her nose when she caught the sniffles. Better not ask.

"You want a menu?"

"Cheeseburger, no onions, French fries, and a *Dos Equis*, please."

"Got it." She pivoted and walked away, sashaying as she went.

Valley slumped at a table across the room with two other men in biker attire. I didn't recall them from Lola's party, but the light wasn't good. I pretended to look at my phone while I snapped a covert photo. I switched the flash off so the three men wouldn't notice I'd photographed them. The photo might not be usable, but I could enhance it.

The server brought my order; I focused on eating until I finished. I tossed a few bills on the table and left.

I waited in the Honda for Valley's colleagues to leave. I knew the truth about Valley; now I was interested in the two new guys.

Valley was the first to leave. As he approached his Harley, I caught a reflection from the earring hanging from his left ear. It was the mate to the one I carried in the evidence bag in my jacket pocket.

Angie's earring.

There was only one way Tommy Valley could have obtained Angie's earring: He stole it from my sister the night he kidnapped her. It didn't prove he killed her, but it proved he delivered her to her fate.

Valley wore the evidence of his guilt dangling from his ear.

I could feel my blood pressure rising.

The other two men came out as Valley roared away. They climbed on their bikes, and I snapped better pictures in the late afternoon sunlight.

If they were undercover cops, they would be alert for anyone tailing them. The fact they rode together made them easier to tail. They drove slowly to stay side-by-side. The wet streets and scattered showers also slowed them. I followed a hundred yards behind, missed a traffic light, and they were out of sight by the time the light turned green. Pushing the Honda Pilot, I powered ahead, hoping they hadn't turned off.

I caught them a half mile later. No harm done. Both men rode into a large, two-story apartment complex. I parked at the curb and waited. They disappeared around a corner. Ten minutes later, I spotted their bikes parked in a space reserved for apartment 1106. I photographed the bikes and the number on the door.

The next shower rolled across, and I hustled out and stuck GPS trackers on both bikes.

Mission accomplished.

———

I returned to my motel to learn my Dodge Grand Caravan had arrived.

I knocked on Gunner Knutson's door. Eric Gunnar Knutson was my teammate in the Triple Seven Special Forces unit in Iraq and Afghanistan. Naturally, we nicknamed him Gunner. With a good rifle, he could hit a poker chip at 1,000 yards, but I was better looking. On this mission I was more likely to need his sniper skills than I was to hold a beauty contest.

That is why I told Gunner to pack the Rock River Arms Varmint rifle,

5.56 mm with a suppressor. I bought it a few years ago for my friend Tank Tyler to cover me while I met with the head of a drug gang in Broward County back in Florida. A nice weapon, semi-automatic, with a thirty-shot magazine, accurate to 400 yards.

Clint Watkins opened the door. "Hey, Chuck. We arrived an hour ago. We're starving."

Gunner waved from the couch. "Nineteen hours on the road, Chuck. Clint and I stopped to eat, use the toilet, and fill the tank. Why the big hurry?"

"For security reasons, I couldn't talk to either of you on the phone while you were en route. I texted you both with my burner, and we may be safe on that one because the bad guys may not know to tap your phones yet. Let's eat dinner and I'll explain everything."

When we were seated at a booth in the rear of my new favorite Mom-and-Pop cafe, I ensured my friends that no one was close enough to eavesdrop. "We all go off the grid starting now. It's too late for Clint to fly back to Gainesville today and the hotel is full tonight. Gunner, I rented you a double room next to mine. Okay for Clint to share with you tonight? I reserved him on a flight tomorrow morning, and you'll have the room to yourself after he leaves."

Gunner grinned at the younger man. "He doesn't snore, does he?"

I ignored him, too focused on our security for light banter. "No credit cards for either of you until you're back in Florida, and we use burner phones." I handed Gunner a cellphone and an envelope. "Here's $2,000 for incidentals. I'll give you more when necessary."

Gunner pocketed the envelope without counting it. "What's the big secrecy thing for?"

I explained my search for my sister. "I uncovered the guy responsible for the kidnapping, and I spoon-fed him to the local cops. They arrested him Wednesday night. I went to interview him in the Harris County jail on Thursday. That's when I learned he had been released to two federal agents. I called Gene Lopez to ask if he could find out anything about what was happening in Houston."

I glanced at Clint. "Gene Lopez is the SAC of the FBI's Port City Office."

"You worked with him on the Chicago mobster thing, didn't you?"

"Officially, Clint, the Chicago mobster thing never happened. Okay?"

Clint gave me a zipped-lips signal and smiled.

I said to Gunner, "Thursday night, Lopez called back. The federal agents who walked out with our suspect were not FBI. They are agents with the Department of Homeland Security—still federal agents for sure, but *rogue* agents. They can access DHS resources that include NSA spy tech. Assume the feds will tap every credit card transaction, every email, every phone call. That's why the big secrecy."

"Chuck, my spring semester classes are finished. I'll stay and help find Angie," Clint offered.

"I appreciate the offer, Clint. However, this project is dangerous at a sophistication level that requires more experience than you have. Gunner and I will operate at the bleeding edge of legality, and we'll obstruct a federal agency's operation. Your involvement could result in you being charged with interfering in a federal investigation or some other infraction we might not discover until too late. It could taint your future after you graduate, whether you plan to join the U.S. Armed Forces or a police department or even need a U.S. security clearance."

I clapped Clint on the shoulder. "No, you do your summer internship. Gunner and I are on this like a tick on a hound dog."

"Okay, boss, what's our mission?"

"To uncover the DHS agents' identity and prove whether they are running a legit undercover operation. Or are they rogue agents running a crooked operation off the books so they can collect drug money."

Gunner eyed me. "By the way you talk, boss, you already decided they're rogues."

"That's right, but I need to prove it."

"Did the Harris County jail's cameras record an image of the two agents?"

"Good idea. I can't access the recording, but I know a friend who can."

I called Bettina.

"Hello, Chuck. How is the case progressing?"

"I caught a break today and located a couple of leads to the bad guys' identities. But that's not why I called. Can you access the cameras at 1200 Baker Street and copy a picture of the feds who pinched Tommy Valley?"

"That's not my bailiwick, but I'll try. I'll go tonight at 10:00 p.m. The deputies will be processing the Saturday night fights. I'll sneak in and out without anyone noticing I was there. Where are you staying?"

"It's better I don't tell you. Email me their photos."

"I'll do better than that. I'll show their pictures and ask whether any cops in the precinct recognize them. Then I'll try facial recognition. I'll send you what I learn by tomorrow morning. Wish me luck."

"Good luck." I disconnected.

We returned to the motel and Clint and Gunner hit the sack. The only sleep they'd had the night before was in my minivan, alternating shifts driving to Houston from Port City.

I played *The Fugitive* on pay-per-view before falling asleep. I dreamed the Department of Homeland Security was searching for me. When I woke, I hoped the real feds were not as smart as Tommy Lee Jones's character.

NINETEEN

My phone woke me from a sound sleep. The room was dark, but the screen blazed with light. It showed *4:32*. 4-3-2, like a countdown launching my day way too early. I didn't recognize the number.

"Hello."

"Chuck, it's Gabby Dillon. Did I wake you?"

"No. I had to get up to answer the phone anyway."

"What? Oh, yeah, that's a joke. Sorry, I didn't realize how early it is. My shift starts at 7:00 a.m. so I was awake to do my exercises. You said I should call you twenty-four/seven."

"Gabby, it's okay. I'm sure there's a good reason you called."

"Something weird happened to our evidence from Flathead Pipe Supply. It's gone."

"What do you mean, *gone*?"

"One of my CSIs called me. He's on the 11:00 p.m. to 7:00 a.m. shift. He arrived downtown at our lab at 11:00 o'clock last night to work on the case. The evidence was gone—every scrap. The idiot waited until 4:30 to call me. Said he didn't want to wake me."

"What happened to the evidence? Where is it?"

"That's the weird thing. My guy called the technician on yesterday's

7:00 a.m. to 3:00 p.m. shift and she said several feds came in with trucks and trailers and a judicial order transferring the evidence to DHS custody."

This was as bad and brazen as the DHS walking into the Harris County jail and stealing our suspect. Maybe worse.

"Did your people get a name or a badge number from the agents?"

"Let me phone my guys and call you back."

"Can I call you back instead? I need to shower and dress. I have your number on my phone screen."

"Sure. I forgot and called you from my home phone, but I guess it's okay for you to have the number."

"Would you rather I called your cell?"

"No, no. My home phone is okay."

"Thanks, Gabby. I would rather not call your cell. My contact at the FBI tells me the DHS can access NSA surveillance equipment. Since you are working this case, it's possible they're tapping your phone."

"Without a warrant and probable cause? Don't be silly. Or are you making another joke?"

"No joke. Let me feed you some food for thought: How did the DHS learn that the Houston cops were interested in the Flathead site? How did the DHS discover y'all knew Flathead was a crime scene? More food for thought: Friday night I uncovered a GPS tracker underneath my rented Chevy Tahoe. There is a serious leak somewhere. And your OCU detectives Wilson and Devlin were told by their own captain to back off the case. Something is not right with this investigation."

"Chuck, you're being melodramatic, but, okay, call my home phone."

"Thanks, Gabby. The agents' names would be helpful." I disconnected. Maybe... *maybe* I would uncover who was pulling the strings at the DHS.

I started the coffee. It was ready by the time I finished showering. I poured a cup and called Gabby back.

"Chuck, you're right. Something is off kilter. My guys at the lab were there when the feds came to steal our evidence. The feds showed them the judicial order requiring all evidence be transferred to them. They said the case was a national security matter and wouldn't give us the time of day, because our CSIs didn't have a 'need to know.'"

"Gabby, could you go to the lab and search your security footage? You might find a picture of the agents who stole your evidence."

"Sure, but why would I do that?"

"If you emailed me a video of the agents, I might uncover who they are. I intend to discover why they are letting Tommy Valley get away with kidnapping my sister."

Gabby paused a moment. "Whether or not the DHS is working a national security investigation, there may be a reasonable explanation for why they released your suspect."

"Did you ever come across a confidential informant allowed to kidnap someone and also commit murder? What possible explanation could there be for that?"

"Perhaps some terrorist organization plans another 9-11 style attack. Perhaps the DHS is trying to save hundreds or thousands of lives."

"What does your gut tell you?"

Gabby sighed. "My gut tells me this thing stinks worse than two-week-old garbage."

"You know what to do. Protect and serve, right?"

"Chuck, what you are planning is dangerous. I realize you have a dog in this fight, but technically you're a civilian. I'm not supposed to involve you in our investigation."

"But the DHS said this is no longer your investigation. They stole it from you, from the whole Houston Police Department."

"We'll keep this unofficial."

"That's okay. Everything I've done since I arrived in Texas is unofficial. Can you get me the video?"

"Yes. I hope I don't regret this."

———

Gunner and Clint and I ordered breakfast. I checked the two bikers' travel history on the tracker app. "The bikers returned to the Spoke and Sprocket last night and stayed there three hours." I showed Gunner their timeline on my phone. "They spent the night at a new address."

"Read me the address," Gunner said.

He tapped the address into his phone. "It's another apartment complex. Shady Pines. Maybe they met a couple of girls at the Spoke and Sprocket and got lucky."

"Could be. I didn't spot those two at Lola Salazar's party, and I didn't photograph their license plates in her parking lot. They could be what they seem—blue collar bikers who are barroom buddies with Tommy Valley. They're regulars at the Spoke and Sprocket. Stake out the new address and watch where they go."

Rule Two: *When in doubt, follow somebody.*

Following breakfast, I left Clint at the airport and staked out Tommy Valley. Probably the two bikers weren't undercover DHS agents. The best way to identify the real agents was to keep tailing Tommy Valley until he met them.

Either way, Gunner or I might uncover the DHS contacts. Or not. This case had damnable complications and hidden agendas.

Gunner texted me.

Bikes are parked in a visitor spot at Shady Pines Apartments. If they got lucky, they are sleeping in. I'll surveil as long as you need me. Good hunting to you.

Parking in the spot I used the day before, I settled in for a wait.

Mid-morning Bettina Simpson video-called. "Good news, Chuck. I copied the jail camera footage of the two feds when they collected Tommy Valley. I'll text you their pictures and email you the one-minute clip. I asked whether anybody recognized them at 1200 Baker and at my station. Nobody did."

"Nice work, Bettina. There's been a new development. Gabby Dillon called this morning. Several unidentified agents came to the CSI lab yesterday and hauled away the evidence from the Flathead fire. They gave the CSIs the same national security BS."

"This is serious, Chuck. I'm glad to help. Call me when you need anything else."

"Okay. I copied two new motorcycle license plates yesterday. Two guys who met Tommy Valley at the Spoke and Sprocket Pub. Can you find the names of the registered owners?"

"Sure. I'll run by the station and research them."

Bettina sent me the images of the DHS agents. Something dinged a faint bell in the rear cavern of my mind.

I called Gunner. "How you doing over there, Gunner?"

"At least one target is awake. He walked out to his bike to get something from a saddle bag. I spotted the apartment he was in. It was number 164. We can investigate the occupants later."

"Could you tell what he took?"

"No. It was in a brown paper bag."

"Bettina is researching the two bikes' owners, and she sent me pictures of the two agents who sprang Tommy Valley from the Harris County jail. I'll send them to you in case you eyeball the bastards before I do."

"Are they the two subjects I'm staking out?"

"No, they're not. It's likely your targets are guys who ride Harleys and happen to be barroom acquaintances of Tommy Valley. Hang in there, Gunner."

"Roger that, boss. You always say that ninety percent of the data we investigate is irrelevant. We keep panning the rocks and dirt to extract the flecks of gold."

"That's the spirit, Gunner. Keep panning for gold."

Twenty minutes later, a dark blue Chevy Suburban stopped at the curb fronting Valley's apartment complex. The street's six traffic lanes were not wide enough for a parking lane. That made sense; apartments and businesses lined the street, all of them with off-street parking. The Suburban was the lone vehicle stopped on the street.

Perhaps they came to pick up Valley and didn't want to be seen in his parking lot. The windows were tinted. I couldn't see who was inside.

Grabbing my telephoto camera, I zoomed in.

The front passenger door opened and a man in a gray suit and paisley tie exited and sat in the back seat. Okay, there were at least two people in the vehicle.

The paisley tie was familiar, and not because I own a few paisley ties. I snapped his picture to examine later. I photographed the license plate and texted it to Bettina with a request to ID the owner.

Tommy Valley hurried down the stairs, trotted across the lot, and slid into the front passenger seat. The SUV sped away.

Bingo. The game was afoot. I followed at a discreet distance.

I called Gunner. "Tommy Valley rode off in a dark blue Suburban. I'm tailing them." I gave him our location and direction. "Catch up with us and we'll leapfrog them."

A mile later, they rolled into a Denny's. Several families in their Sunday best dallied on the sidewalk waiting for tables.

I tailed them into the parking lot and stopped in the alley, pretending I was waiting for a spot. I called Gunner. "They stopped at a Denny's." I gave him the address. "If I tag their vehicle, I won't need you to help tail them. Keep heading this way, but I may send you back to the two bikers at the Shady Pines."

"Roger that, boss. Entering the address now… GPS says my ETA is seventeen minutes."

The SUV coasted to the back before parking in an empty spot. Valley and the two suits reappeared, walking to the front. They passed me less than ten yards away and walked inside. I couldn't snap a picture; they might notice me stopped in the alley. A minute later, they exited and stood near the scattered people waiting for a table. I grabbed a good picture before I rolled further along the alley. The second man wore a blue suit and a red tie. Dressy for Houston, especially on a non-workday. It was Sunday, but I'd bet they hadn't attended church that morning.

I continued to the back, stopped behind the Suburban, and stuck a GPS tracker under their bumper. I intended to photograph the Suburban's VIN number, but another Denny's patron walked to her car. I didn't want her to see me snap the photo. There was an AutoZone next door. I parked there where I could observe the Suburban.

"Gunner, I tagged their vehicle. Return to the Shady Pines."

"Roger that, boss."

I retrieved my pictures of the Suburban driver and the man in the paisley tie and compared them to the photos Bettina sent me.

He shoots; he scores. Paisley Tie and Red Tie were the two agents who had snatched Tommy Valley from the Harris County jail. In her photo, one man wore the same paisley tie. In his defense, it was a nice tie.

I waited for the three men to finish lunch. Bettina texted me the owner-ship info on the two bikes and the driver license pictures of the owners. I sent the info to Gunner, then sent a thank-you text to Bettina giving her a gold star for attaching the men's pictures.

An hour later, Valley and the two suits exited. From my post in the AutoZone, I snapped a telephoto picture of the trio returning to the SUV.

Ten minutes later the Suburban dropped Valley at the curb in front of his apartment. I tailed the two feds downtown. The SUV entered the parking garage at Trylen Tower, a forty-story office building.

I parked at a public garage a block away, hotfooted it to the Trylen parking garage, and climbed the ramps until I located the SUV.

If push came to shove, the garage cameras would record me, but they wouldn't have a license plate to trace. My Texans hat and jacket collar would hide my face.

The Suburban was on the near-empty sixth floor, parked by the entrance to the office section of the structure. A Chevy Bolt and a Toyota Corolla electric hybrid were parked nearby. The rest of the floor was empty. I stuck tracking devices under the Bolt and the Corolla in case they were the crooked agents' personal vehicles. I photographed the three VINs.

I sent the photos to Bettina with a request for their registrations. Then I sent a dozen roses to her at the police station to be delivered on Monday. Couldn't hurt.

The door to the offices had an electronic key-card entry. I tried the door handle. Locked. Dead end. I could walk to the main entrance lobby and ride the elevator to the sixth floor except this was Sunday. Trylen is a big building; it has a security guard, maybe several. I would be as obvious as a porcupine in a bathtub.

I trekked down the ramps to the main entrance. It was locked. A guard sat at a desk inside, and I didn't want Trylen Tower's security system to record my visit.

I could return during the work week. The building would be open to the public so I could hide among the crowd.

As I walked back to my parked Honda Pilot, Gunner called.

"I received the info on the two targets and their bikes. They both returned to their own apartment. Should I go back and investigate the Shady Pines apartment where they spent the night?"

"Yes. Knock on the door to unit 164. Tell whoever answers that you're searching for a woman named Naomi Forrester."

"Who is Naomi Forrester?"

"Some name I made up. Use whatever name you like. The trick is to start a friendly conversation with whoever opens the door and learn who lives there and how many. I suspect it's two women whom the bikers met at the Spoke and Sprocket."

"And if they are? Will that mean the bikers aren't undercover cops?"

"No. It will mean they are typical, horny men out for a good time. Tomorrow, the bikers may go to their jobs in the real world. Tail the first one who comes out to figure out where he works. If he works."

"Roger that, boss. I'll go to the Shady Pines, Unit 164. This will be fun."

He disconnected and I called Bettina, intending to brief her on the day's developments. She liked video calls, so that's what I used.

"Hello, Chuck." The background showed her lounging outside: palm trees and swimming pool umbrellas. She held the phone farther away. "I'm at the pool."

She wore a teal bikini and floppy teal hat. She looked good, really good.

"I'm envious."

"Yes. I'm sunbathing with my neighbor, Madison Washington." She pointed the phone at an attractive woman in a yellow bikini that contrasted nicely with her mocha skin. "Say hello to Chuck McCrary, Madison."

"Hello, Chuck. I'm Madison. I've seen you around the last few days. Nice to meet you. Why don't you join us at the pool? It's a lovely day."

"Thanks, Madison. I wish I could, but I'm otherwise committed. Nice to meet you."

Bettina pointed the phone to her face. "As you see, I'm off duty. Should I walk inside so we can talk?"

"Can you take the phone off speaker?"

"Sure." She did. "Okay. What is it?"

"Did you receive the Chevy Bolt and the Corolla Hybrid photos I sent you?"

"I haven't checked. It's possible they arrived, and I didn't hear my phone signal. Let me check... Yeah, I have them. How soon you need them?"

"They can wait until tomorrow morning."

"Good. I start my shift tomorrow in the station. I'll look into it."

"Thanks. Enjoy the pool. You've been working hard and deserve at least part of your weekend off. I'll text your burner with any further developments. You and Madison enjoy yourselves. Remember to use sunblock."

The Watcher

"McCrary moved to a motel Friday night. He's not staying with Bettina Simpson anymore."

"Did you intercept his phone calls?"

"He switches his phone on to use it. All inbound calls go to voicemail. The messages all concern his PI business in Port City or else they're from friends in Florida. His outgoing calls go to people in Port City. He talks to Raymond Snopolski who handles his Port City clients while McCrary is in Houston. No calls to or from Simpson. He and Simpson must be using burners. That's not good. They figured out we're surveilling them."

"Of course, they know we're surveilling them, you idiot. That's why McCrary rented the old Tahoe. That's why they use burner phones. That's why he moved to the motel. What is McCrary doing now?"

"He spent Saturday at a hotel construction site on Loop 8. He is taking Sunday off. His car hasn't budged all day."

"Is there a restaurant at his motel?"

"It's a middle-priced motel. Continental breakfast in the lobby in the morning. No other food service."

"What is he doing for lunch and dinner?"

"Maybe he's ordering takeout delivered to his room."

"I don't believe it. I want eyes on McCrary. D-Day is next week, and I damn sure won't let him jeopardize the mission. We've invested too much in this project."

TWENTY

Carlos McCrary

Monday morning early, I returned to the motel where the Louisiana workers were staying. The bug detector told me the tracker remained attached to the box truck. At 6:45 a.m. I shadowed the Louisiana workers to the job site. My business calls made from there would show I was at the site of the tracker. It was a big new hotel under construction on Loop 8. I parked and waited until 8:00 a.m. local time, 9:00 a.m. Port City time. Switching to my official cellphone, I checked my voicemail and returned my calls.

Ensured that no one was watching me, I reached under the box truck and retrieved the tracker. Time to stir the pot. There was a risk in challenging the bear in his own den, and, in hindsight, it could have been the wrong move, but there you are: Carlos McCrary, a bull in a China shop.

Rule Sixteen: *Sometimes you have to do something, even if it's wrong. At least you'll know you tried.*

Leaving my regular phone on, I drove downtown to provoke Paisley Tie and Red Tie.

By the time I fought the traffic downtown, it was 10:30. I parked in the

Trylen Tower parking garage and called Gunner. "What did you uncover on our two bikers?"

"The first target, Daryl Massey, is a mechanic with a Chrysler-Jeep-Ram truck dealer. The manager told me Massey has worked there for three years. Then I monitored the GPS tracker on the other target, Dalton Hatcher. He works at an auto parts store. I did a quick internet reconnaissance on the two men. If they're undercover cops, they created a solid fake internet footprint. My nose tells me they are what they appear. I recommend we abandon them."

"Good work, Gunner. I concur. Retrieve the trackers from their bikes."

"Suppose they're where they can see the bikes?"

"It doesn't matter whether they see you retrieve the trackers. Pop them off and walk away. Those suckers cost over a hundred bucks each, and I don't just throw them away. If the bikers question you, tell them you're an undercover cop and you just cleared them as suspects in a hit-and-run case. Anything else they ask, tell them you can't discuss an active case."

"*Hmm.* I can do that, boss. You taught me a lot about how to be devious."

"Good. Being devious is one of my better attributes. That and drinking draft beer. Now go register the Caravan's title in my great aunt Catherine Baylor's name. Then install her new Texas license plates, front and back."

"Wilco, boss."

"I'm gonna challenge Red Tie and Paisley Tie in their office. I'll text you the address so you'll know who killed me if I disappear. After you put the Texas plates on the Caravan, come to the parking garage. Telephone me from there."

"Roger, boss. Uh, boss, you were joking about you disappearing, right?"

"I hope so, Gunner. I sure as hell hope so."

I called Gene Lopez in Port City.

"Gene, the federal agents who snatched Tommy Valley from the Harris County jail are operating off the books. They are running a rogue operation, probably involving drug money."

"Okay, so assuming that's true, what do you expect me to do from Port City?"

"You can't do it from Port City; you should come to Houston."

"You believe the Houston FBI office is compromised?"

"You tell me: The bad guys have contacts in the DHS, the FBI, and the Houston police. There's no telling how many bent cops and feds there are. I can't trust any law enforcement officer in Houston except my friend from high school. Can you help me from Port City and keep it unofficial?"

"The FBI takes crooked cops seriously, Chuck. Especially feds. You sure they're plugged into the Houston FBI?"

"You told me your Houston agent removed the DHS contact from the official records. Does that sound legal?"

Lopez was silent for a beat. "For anyone else trying this, Chuck, I'd say they wouldn't have a prayer going against both the DHS and the FBI. On the other hand, you challenged the Chinese Peoples' Liberation Army and won, so I'll try it your way first. Tell me: What do you know?"

I briefed Lopez on the unlisted office at 666 Trylen Tower and the license plates of the personal cars I spotted and tagged in the garage. I omitted the fact I tagged the cars. No point pushing Lopez's buttons needlessly.

"I obtained security cam photos of the agents who released Tommy Valley. I learned two names, one male and one female for the personal cars, which means there might be three agents, not two. I'll text you the pictures and the two names and addresses."

"I'll get on them. And Chuck, they could come at you from a direction you least expect. Watch your six."

I texted Bettina.

Do you have the registration info on the blue Suburban?

She replied in seconds.

Owned by Buffalo Springs LLP in Suite 666 of the Trylen Tower. That's in downtown Houston in the high-rise and high-rent district. The Bolt belongs to Christian Amadeus Bartok, also at 666 Trylen Tower. The Corolla is registered to Luisa Alvarez Tavares. I know… you want background checks on Bartok and Tavares. I'll do those next.

She signed with a smiley-face emoji.

Who was Tavares? Was she a third DHS agent lurking in the background?

I texted Bettina my thanks and walked to the entrance lobby.

Breezing past the two guards sitting at the marble counter in the lobby, I rode an elevator to the sixth floor.

The elevator opened to a high-ceilinged lobby with discreet cameras aimed at each of the three hallways. The floors were polished granite, and the walls were covered with textured vinyl. Nothing but the best for our loyal hard-working federal employees. I tried both restroom doors. Locked. The building management didn't want vagrants wandering off the street to use their restrooms.

A sign pointed the way to the parking garage. I passed four doors marked with modest letters A through D until I reached the door marked *Parking Garage. Must have key to reenter.*

Opening the door, I leaned into the garage. Most parking spaces were occupied. The blue Suburban was where it had been yesterday, but the Bolt and the Corolla had been replaced by other vehicles. Could belong to the personnel at the other sixth-floor tenants. The Bolt and Corolla were personal cars and could be parked elsewhere in the garage. I decided not to locate them and tag them. No, it was time to poke the bear in his den.

Starting with the north hallway, I passed the door to Hightower Financial Management in 616. The other office entrance on the hall was Karpinski, Childers, Maldonado & Klein, attorneys, in 636. The south hall had All Perils Insurance Agency in 656. Next to it was a door with no name, only the number 666.

The number 666 has some biblical significance, but I couldn't recall what it was. The door to 666 was locked. I knocked. No response.

But I figured someone was watching.

The Watcher

The screen showed McCrary knocking on the door. At the same time, the sound carried faintly through the heavy door. Her pulse jumped into overdrive.

That could not be McCrary. He couldn't know who they were. Or could he?

She tapped the intercom. "McCrary is standing outside our freaking door, knocking. What should I do?"

"Chill out, Luisa. That can't be McCrary. He's at the construction site on Loop 8."

So, the boss was hoodwinked. Not a comforting idea that the high and mighty and oh-so-brainy Chris Bartok was out of the loop.

"I recognize McCrary when I see him, boss. His car may be at the construction site, but McCrary, his own freaking self, is standing in the hall knocking on our freaking door. I don't know how he located us, but the SOB did. We need to stop him before he unravels the entire op."

Unconsciously, she reached into her desk drawer and touched a Sig Sauer 9mm Luger. Then she realized what she had done, and horror filled her mind. Her stomach lurched like a bumper car. No, no, that was out of the question, no matter how important the mission was. "Our operation is too important to let him crash it, boss. How far do we go to keep him from interfering?"

"D-Day is Thursday. Killing McCrary now would cause waves we don't need until the op is over. I'll try to force him to stand down until after D-Day. After that, McCrary won't matter. But if he ever discovers our involvement with Angelina Garza, even though it was inadvertent, we may need to sanction him for our own protection. McCrary is the type who makes his own rules, so he might carry out personal retribution against us."

What was this talk about killing McCrary after the operation was over? Surely the boss wasn't serious. Or was he? If he was serious, then he had gone completely off the reservation. She would watch herself to avoid getting sucked into something she had not signed up for.

"Wait a minute, boss. McCrary's walking away. No, he's walking to the insurance agency next door. Why did he do that?"

"Why not? Call me if anything else happens."

––––––––––––

Carlos McCrary

The All Perils Insurance Agency was next door. Their door was not locked.

A middle-aged woman with the face of a cherub and curly salt-and-pepper hair sat at a desk in the tasteful reception area "May I help you, sir?"

I gave her a flustered façade. "I don't know quite how to say this, ma'am. I, uh, I made an appointment with Christian Bartok next door? Do you know him?"

"I have never met the people who work next door, and I don't know what business they're in. Sorry."

I showed her the pictures of Red Tie and Paisley Tie. "Do you recognize either of these men?"

She glanced at the pictures. "I see them on the elevator and in the parking garage, but I don't know the people next door. Sorry. Will there be anything else?" Ms. Salt-and-pepper seemed eager for me to leave.

"Like I said, I have an appointment and… to tell you the truth, their door is locked. Not what you expect from a business, ya know?"

Ms. Salt-and-Pepper gave me impatient signals. "I'm sorry. I know *nothing* concerning the people who work next door, and that includes their office hours. Now, if you will excuse me…"

"Sorry to bother you. Have a nice day."

———

Standing in the hall, I was aware of the cameras. Who was monitoring me? Did I dare pick the lock on door 666?

Yes, I did.

I knocked again using a cop knock with the side of my fist. *Bam, bam, bam.*

I waved at the nearest camera and spoke to it. "I'll pick the lock now. If you're in there, I will find you."

I no sooner fished the lock picks from my jacket pocket, than a smallish brunette woman opened the door, and gestured me inside.

She appeared too young to have finished high school, but there she

227

was, in an office with sophisticated surveillance equipment, a half-dozen monitors arranged at eye-level above her desk. Three telephones on the desk that were not from AT&T. They were for scrambled communications direct to the Kremlin, the Pentagon, and Scotland Yard. Or not.

"Come in, Mr. McCrary. I'm Luisa Tavares." She offered her hand.

I ignored her hand and walked past her to the center of the small seating area in the corner but did not sit. "Who else works in this office?"

Tavares examined her hand like she didn't know what to do with it. She was cute enough she might never have faced rejection in her life.

Her authoritative gray pantsuit, yellow silk scarf with understated white polka dots, and shortish hair tucked behind her ears was the perfect picture of the upwardly mobile federal agent. From what I could see from this angle, she wasn't carrying a weapon.

"I asked who else works in this office," I repeated.

There were two closed doors on the left wall. "Are these their offices?"

I showed my phone with the images of Red Tie and Paisley Tie. "Who are these men and where can I find them?"

The first door on the left opened and Red Tie came out. "I'm Chris Bartok." This time his tie was blue with gold stripes. "Come in. Let's talk." He held the door and motioned me to enter.

Bartok wore a dark blue, three-piece suit, going for the Tom Selleck look in *Blue Bloods*, including the mustache. His hair was grayer and thinner than Police Commissioner Frank Reagan, and he was light on gravitas. His suit was tailored to minimize the shoulder holster he wore.

The office was the size of a three-car garage. A mahogany partner desk sat in the middle with matching accessories and large leather desk chairs on either side. Paisley Tie stood on the far side. One shoulder holster hung on a clothes tree in the corner.

I gave Bartok a nod and gestured at Paisley Tie. "Who is he?"

Bartok waved at his partner. "Meet Gerald Hawley. Gerry, you recognize Carlos McCrary, of course."

Hawley bobbed his head. He wore the familiar paisley tie. Perhaps it was the only tie he owned, or it was his Tie-of-the-Month. Hawley's navy-blue sport coat with brass buttons was hung on the clothes tree next to his weapon. His gray slacks were big on him, held up by a black belt cinched in the last hole, as if he recently lost a lot of weight. His hair was mostly gray, and he was bald on top.

Bartok gestured to a round table and four leather side chairs in one corner. "Let's sit. Would you care for something to drink, Mr. McCrary?"

Bartok hung his jacket on the clothes tree with Hawley's sport coat. He still wore his shoulder holster and weapon.

I remembered the advice of an instructor in Special Forces. "Always be polite and respectful, but make a plan to kill everyone in the room if necessary." If push came to shove, I would first double tap Bartok in the center of his chest. After that, Hawley would be no trouble. I still didn't know if Tavares might be armed in a way I couldn't see.

"Coffee. A little cream or half-and-half. No sugar." I sat with my back to the wall, the window to my left.

Tavares trailed us in.

Bartok waved at her. "You heard the man, Luisa. Gerry and I will have the usual."

Tavares colored and turned to walk out.

When she turned, I took a good look at the back of her suit. She carried no weapon, which meant her handgun was probably in a desk drawer.

She slammed the door behind her. She didn't appreciate being dismissed. The Old Boys Club was alive and well, at least in Suite 666.

Bartok sat across from me. Hawley to my right.

Bartok's smile was all teeth and no eyes. I've seen Florida crocodiles with more sincere smiles. "How can we help you?"

"May I see your credentials, please?"

His eyes widened and he jerked his head back before he recovered. "Sure. Why not?"

Both men showed me their creds. I aimed my phone and photographed each license and shield.

As I returned the phone to my jacket pocket, I pressed the audio record app. Couldn't hurt. "Why did you spring Tomás Valenzuela aka Tommy Valley following his arrest for kidnapping my sister?"

"Who says he kidnapped your sister?" Hawley asked.

Bartok gave him a glare that would freeze a small pond. Bartok was the boss, and Hawley had spoken out of turn.

"Tell Hawley to cut the crap. This ain't my first rodeo. I have security footage from the truckstop where Valley and his accomplices kidnapped Angelina McCrary Garza. I have the video someone made of her Mazda automobile and Teodoro's Jeep and the Flathead Pipe Supply truck in the building before it was torched. And I photographed Valley wearing an earring my sister wore when she was kidnapped. The evidence will stand up in court. With Angelina's body missing, I can't prove he murdered her. But I can damned well prove he kidnapped her."

The door opened and Tavares entered with a tray with three coffees and three spoons and napkins. The tray held a pitcher of half-and-half and a box of no-calorie sweetener. Little Miss Efficiency. She moved like a robot and positioned the tray in the precise center of the table. "Here you are, your majesty. Do you wish me to serve, *sir*?"

Bartok glared at the woman but held his tongue. "Thank you, Luisa. That will be all."

Muttering under her breath, she slammed the door on the way out.

Bartok cleared his throat. "Carlos—may I call you Carlos?"

"I don't care what you call me; just tell me the truth."

He blinked. "Carlos, I researched your background and your military service in the Green Berets, your heroism at Ghar Mesar, and your medals. You are a patriot and loyal citizen of the United States of America."

Blah, blah, blah. I heard but I didn't respond. Let the SOB make his speech. Meanwhile, I added a touch of half-and-half to my coffee.

Bartok was on a soapbox. "The United States deals with many enemies the Department of Homeland Security is tasked to defend against. Among the enemies are terrorists seeking to enter the United States illegally from Mexico and kill innocent civilians in our own country."

It was a speech for Career Day in his kid's high school, if he had a kid.

"Ever since 9-11, we have prevented another attack like the World Trade Center towers. We believe another major attack is planned for the near future, July 4th."

Bartok paused.

He expected me to reply. I didn't. Instead, I sipped my coffee.

"This operation is on a need-to-know basis," Bartok continued. "Even Agent Tavares is not privy to all the details. That's why we can't share information with your friends in the Houston PD. Nor can we allow our own FBI to hear about it. We don't know whom we can trust."

"You suspect these terrorists have a mole in the FBI and the Houston PD?"

Bartok hesitated a couple of heartbeats. "The fact is, we don't know. That's why this is a need-to-know project. Believe me: This mission is bigger than you can imagine."

My BS meter was flashing red lights, ringing alarm bells, and its needle swung clear off the dial. This cockamamie story couldn't be true, or Bartok would have told his superiors I was investigating the case the minute I appeared on their radar. His bosses would send someone I *could* trust, say, a superior officer in the Green Berets. If my Green Beret commanding officer, Captain Hidalgo Ramirez, asked me to stand down, I would consider it. But these guys? No way.

But Bartok had not kicked my appearance upstairs. That meant his own superiors were ignorant of this off-the-books operation. His own words confirmed his guilt.

I had entered a closed room with two armed DHS agents—well, one anyway—and I was separated from the hallway by a third agent. Gunner Knutson was the one person who knew I was here, and maybe Bettina Simpson. Bartok and Hawley had to be aware of the killing and body-disposal business in the former Building 4, so they were accomplices to murder, if not actual murderers themselves.

I had to play my cards right, or Bartok, Hawley, and Tavares could attempt to murder me and make my body disappear as easily as Angelina's and Teodoro's. The woodchipper at Flathead wouldn't be their sole method to dispose of inconvenient corpses.

As usual, I had already made my kill plan.

"That might be true, Bartok," I replied, "but my experience with CIs says that part of the deal is they don't commit serious crimes, for example, kidnapping and murder. You're asking me to stop investigating my sister's kidnapping and disappearance? For me to stand down, I need more information."

"Can I rely on your patriotism and discretion to keep this confidential, Carlos? Nothing I say can leave this room. Do I have your word?"

If I replied immediately, Bartok would figure I had automatically agreed and wouldn't treat the secrecy obligation seriously. Which was true.

I paused long enough for the crooked DHS agent to assume I was considering his request. "You intend to read me in on something important enough for you and your fellow agents to let Tommy Valley walk on a kidnapping charge?"

"Yes. This project is supremely important to the security of the United States. But you must keep anything we tell you in absolute confidence. Can I count on you to do that?"

I leaned back and interlaced my fingers over my stomach. "Very well. You have my word." Now perhaps they wouldn't try to kill me. At least, not yet.

Bartok hadn't touched his coffee.

"Agents Hawley, Tavares, and I are members of a large DHS task force working to stop an infiltration of terrorists across the Mexican border. The *Tres Equis* drug cartel has contracted with Al Qaeda to bring in dozens of *mujahideen* fighters across the Rio Grande. Tommy Valley is a confidential informant working with us to intercept the infiltration and capture the *mujahideen* and the *Tres Equis* drug smugglers."

He leaned back in his chair. "That's why we sprung Valley from the Harris County jail. He is waiting for his contact in the cartel to reveal where and when the *mujahideen* will be smuggled across."

"What happens to Valley at the conclusion to this operation?"

Hawley answered. "He goes into witness protection."

"So, the U.S. government gives a kidnapper and murderer a new name and a new life in a new city."

"That's the deal." Bartok spread his hands. "Carlos, I don't like it either, but we agreed to this months ago, after our listening posts heard rumors of Al Qaeda's plans. Valley is our channel into the *Tres Equis*."

"When did your listening posts uncover this planned attack?"

"Sorry. Can't answer that. It might compromise our sources or methods."

"Okay. What is Escondido Sendero LLC?"

Bartok motioned to Hawley. Hawley said, "That's a *Tres Equis* holding company. All their U.S. assets are owned by companies like Escondido

Sendero LLC. And—before you ask—after the operation concludes, we swoop in, confiscate their assets, and arrest all their gang members in the U.S."

"As you see, Carlos," Bartok said, "this operation will put a large Mexican drug cartel out of business and capture at least two dozen Al Qaeda *mujahideen*." He spread his hands. "This is the biggest, most important counter-terrorist op since we invaded Afghanistan. We must intercept these men to prevent hundreds of innocent casualties. Perhaps thousands."

"What's their target?" I asked.

"That's not clear. Could be anything from the July 4th concert on the Capitol Mall to big regional fireworks shows in New York City or Philadelphia. There are dozens of parks in the country with thousands of civilians every Independence Day. Anywhere from Portland, Oregon, to Portland, Maine. The terrorists can choose from an endless list of targets. And, I might add, they plan to infiltrate enough fighters to attack several events simultaneously. Imagine the effect of an attack on New York City, Boston, Philadelphia and other cities in the Eastern Time Zone at 9:45 p.m. on July 4."

I spread my hands. "The Eastern Seaboard will have millions of people in the same places to enjoy the fireworks. The attacks would paralyze the entire country."

"That's right. You understand why our interdiction operation must succeed."

"When does this border incursion happen?"

"Probably this Thursday night."

I considered what to say next. "That's three days. I can wait until Friday to move on Tommy Valley."

"Carlos, you can't move on Valley *ever*. After the op, he goes into witness protection."

I lowered my coffee cup. "Did you make Valley's witness protection deal before or after he kidnapped my sister?"

"Before. We've been working with Valley on drug deals for months. This terrorist incursion was a surprise to us. We learned of the kidnapping after it happened. Otherwise, we would have stopped it."

"That's your loophole, Bartok."

"What do you mean?"

"Valley broke the terms of the witness protection program. An agreement to not commit future major crimes is part of the deal. Once Valley delivers the terrorists and the drug smugglers to you, you can throw him to the wolves." I leaned back in my chair. "I can wait for you to finish with Valley."

Bartok stood and leaned across the table toward me. "McCrary, you've been warned. Do not interfere with our DHS witness protection agreement, or we will respond rigorously."

"I told you I would wait until you arrest your *mujahideen* and your drug smugglers." I stood and leaned toward Bartok, our noses inches apart. "I won't compromise your operation. I keep my word. Not a whisper leaves this room. But following Thursday night, Valley is mine."

Hawley jumped to his feet. The three of us made a tripod. "You don't appreciate what you're dealing with, McCrary. Don't provoke Tommy Valley."

"Or else what?"

"You will suffer the power and might of the federal government."

Bartok's voice was harsh, and his words conveyed both menace and malice. His tone intended his message to fill the charged air in the room and lurk there, sparking and dangerous—a tray filled with shards of broken glass he was daring me to walk across.

It was difficult not to laugh.

Oh, geez. This guy was so full of himself, he believed I cared about his threats. Fat chance.

Only later did I learn his threats were not idle. And I would not be their only target.

———

Luisa Tavares

Luisa Tavares joined Bartok and Hawley in their office. "What did McCrary say, boss?"

"He said he would give us until Monday."

"And you believe him?" Hawley didn't sound convinced. "Luisa, didn't you tell us Carlos McCrary has a relationship with Bettina Simpson?"

"Yeah. They attended Theodore Roosevelt High School together. Don't know if they were high school sweethearts or not, but that was almost twenty years ago. He did spend a few nights in her condo until he determined we were surveilling him. Perhaps they have a romantic relationship."

"Chris, we could put Simpson on ice. That would guarantee McCrary will stay off the case until after D-Day."

"What do you have in mind?"

"You recall the training thing we did on hacking a vehicle's electronics and disabling it?"

"I need to review it, but, yeah, I remember it."

Hawley explained his plan.

Tavares's throat tightened. She refused to believe what she was hearing.

"Guys, Detective Simpson is a U.S. citizen, and she's a freaking *cop*. You cannot be suggesting this. It violates so many laws we would spend the rest of our lives in federal prison."

Bartok made patting motions with his hands. "Luisa, I don't like this either, but Gerry has a point. Suppose you could have prevented the 9-11 attack by holding a citizen *incommunicado* for a few days and releasing her unharmed. Wouldn't you agree the greater good of saving the lives of hundreds of people outweighs the rights of one person?"

Hawley put a hand on Tavares's forearm. "We can do it and not get caught. No harm, no foul."

Tavares jerked her arm away and jumped to her feet. "This is BS."

Bartok puffed a sigh at the ceiling. "Special Agent Tavares, you're new to the DHS. This is your first significant mission since you finished training."

She was suspicious of where this was going. "So?"

"Agent Hawley and I will evaluate your performance for your personnel file at the end of this operation. That evaluation will affect your career for the rest of your professional life—thirty or even forty years. Your willingness to do whatever is necessary to accomplish the mission benefits you for the rest of your career. And *vice versa*."

"What do you mean?"

"Gerry and I have been in law enforcement for over thirty years. First with the FBI, then in the first class of agents after the Department of Homeland Security was founded in response to the 9-11 attack. We swore to do whatever it takes to ensure another 9-11 never happens." He glanced at Hawley and back to Tavares.

"In thirty-plus years of law enforcement, we have tried to do the right thing. And sometimes the right thing means you balance the greater good—in this case National Security—against a minor bending of the law."

Hawley spoke in capital letters as he invoked national security. But this was no 'minor bending of the law.' Kidnapping was a capital crime. Tavares felt trapped, powerless to counter. She remained silent.

Hawley's voice softened. "Luisa, our task is to prevent another attack on America that could be worse than 9-11. Will you do whatever is necessary to protect America?"

Tavares felt the trap closing, suffocating her. She fought back the tears and left the room.

What the hell was she going to do now?

TWENTY-ONE

Bettina Simpson

Bettina Simpson had a lead on the burglary in River Oaks. Some of the fingerprints the CSIs had collected were from a drug addict named Terence Tilly. Tilly was on probation for his last burglary three years before. It was shoe-leather time. Locate the perp, collar him, search his apartment for stolen goods, etc.

Strictly routine. Bettina and her partner Roger Peters collared Tilly at a large housing project where he lived with his mother. A search of Tilly's closet produced several articles stolen from the River Oaks home. Bettina finished processing the arrest at the Harris County jail downtown, and she and Peters stopped at a cop bar and ate a celebratory dinner. Afterwards, Peters dropped Bettina at the station where her Honda Accord was parked.

Driving home at 9:00 p.m., Bettina rolled along a residential street. There were streetlights on the block, but the thick tree canopy beneath the lights shrouded the street in darkness.

Her car died. Headlights, dashboard lights, engine—everything quit, even the power steering. She muscled her Honda to the curb. It coasted to a stop. Must have been a major malfunction to blow more than one fuse.

No problem. Call Triple A. Her cellphone was paired with the radio's

Bluetooth so she wouldn't fumble in the dark to open her purse. She fingered the dark screen on the dashboard. No luck. Was the entire vehicle's electrical system on the fritz?

Her car interior lit from flashing red and blue lights. A Houston police cruiser stopped behind her. Good. They could call a wrecker.

The cruiser's headlights and flashing lights reflected in her mirrors, blinding her.

Behind her, the doors to the cruiser opened and two uniformed cops exited, one on each side. Standard procedures she'd learned as a new patrol cop years before.

Bettina knew not to open the car door. This was the most dangerous time in making a traffic stop, both for the cops and the driver. She waited with both hands on the steering wheel. The two officers advanced on each side of her car.

The lead cop stopped near the driver's window and shined a flashlight inside. "Lower the window please, ma'am."

The flashlight in Bettina's eyes blinded her, but she could tell from the cop's voice that she was a woman. Good for you, girl. When Bettina was a patrol cop, the department wouldn't let a woman drive unless both cops were female. It was good to see a female cop in charge, even on a traffic stop.

Bettina raised her voice to carry through the glass. "My car's electrical system died, officer. The electric windows are dead too. I'm a cop. Sergeant Bettina Simpson, Robbery-Homicide West Freeway station. Shall I hold my badge to the window? It's in my purse along with my pistol."

The cop's flashlight moved to Bettina's purse resting on the passenger's seat. "Please bring the badge out slowly, using your left hand."

"Can I move my purse to my lap?"

"Yes, ma'am. Just do it slowly."

Bettina complied, pulling her badge wallet out with her left hand, and holding it against window.

The cop's flashlight moved to the badge. "Thank you, Sergeant Simpson. You may get out."

The cop stepped back to give her room. "You know the drill. Please keep your hands in sight."

Bettina set her purse back on the passenger seat. "Unfastening the seat belt. Opening the door." She started to reach back for her purse but changed her mind. It was a dark street, spooky with the trees blocking the streetlights. These cops didn't know her from Adam.

She opened the door and stepped away from the car.

She felt a sting on her neck before everything went black.

Luisa Tavares

"We have her, boss."

Tavares's heart beat a mile a minute and adrenaline flooded her veins. She had never captured or arrested anyone before. She was surprised to be thrilled and, yes, a little turned-on, even though she realized she had crossed a red line she could never uncross.

"Gerry hacked her car's computer system. We monitored her GPS until she drove down a dark street. Then *zap!* Gerry shut off her electrical system with his laptop. We stashed her at the factory."

"Good work, Luisa. And she's unharmed?"

Tavares recalled catching Simpson's unconscious body as it fell. That was a touchy thing; she nearly dropped the detective on the street. Reflecting on it made her cringe inwardly at the risks involved. And the risks were ongoing and even accelerating.

"Yes. The injection knocked her out instantly and Gerry and I caught her before she fell. Not a bruise or a bump. We dumped her in the back seat of the patrol car and left her on the mattress in the factory. We hid her car in the factory loading dock. We left her purse, and car keys in it. She'll be fine until we give McCrary the location."

"And no chance she could identify either of you?"

"None. It's 'no harm, no foul.' I guarantee it." She hoped she was speaking the truth.

Carlos McCrary

Tuesday morning I returned to the construction site on Loop 8 and parked a few yards from the box truck I was using as a decoy with the tracker. I inserted the battery in my official cellphone and booted it. One downloaded text was from an unknown number.

We have Bettina Simpson in a safe place. Stand down until Monday, May 25. If you do, we shall release her unharmed. After May 25, you can chase anyone you fancy. Stand down until then and Simpson will be safe. Do not involve the Houston cops or the FBI, or else... You know the alternative.

My breath caught in my throat. The one thing I had struggled to avoid—putting Bettina in danger—had happened. It was pointless to kick myself. What was done was done.

I was virtually certain this was the work of Bartok and his DHS crew. Almost, but not 100 percent.

The bastards knew I would draw the inevitable conclusions from the damned ellipsis.

I scanned my surroundings for anything amiss. I didn't expect to spot anything notable, but I had to try. The unfinished parking lot at the hotel construction site was half-filled with assorted workers' trucks and cars. Nothing out of the ordinary, but the scene was so random, something could be off and I might not notice. Somewhere among the dozens of vehicles someone might be watching me. Or they were parked across the street or observing from a window in the office building next door.

Too many variables.

I called Bettina's burner phone using my official cellphone. Straight to voicemail. The rogue DHS crew had kidnapped her. They had her official phone and her burner. The call history on her burner gave them my burner's number, so it was time to buy another.

I replied to the text:

Send proof of life.

While I waited for a reply, the real world of McCrary Investigations, LLC continued in Port City. With a distracted mind, I had to review my other texts and voicemails and tend to my business calls, which included a call to Snoop.

I brought him up to date. "The kidnappers sent me a text that they have Bettina. They warned me not to bring in the cops or FBI."

"Of course, they'd demand that, wouldn't they, bud? It's a cliché from an old movie, but will you bring in the cops?"

"I haven't decided. They asked me to stand down until next Monday and they'll release her unharmed."

"Which raises two questions," Snoop said. "First, what's supposed to happen before next Monday?"

My first consideration was that, if Bartok and the DHS were the kidnappers, they were allowing for a delay in the border incursion. If the *mujahideen* didn't cross the border Thursday night, they might delay the incursion a few days. Monday matched with that contingency.

"Whatever it is, it's big when they kidnap a cop to stop my investigation."

"And secondly, do you believe they'll release her?"

"Not in real life. The kidnappers could be federal agents, possibly former FBI. They realize kidnapping is a capital crime. They won't leave witnesses."

"Will you bring in the FBI?"

"The problem is that the kidnappers have contacts in the Houston FBI and the Houston cops. There's no telling whom I can trust, and I don't want to force their hand. For now, Gunner and I will try to locate her."

"How can I help?"

"They have Bettina's burner phone, and the call history includes my burner number, so I'll keep that phone in case they communicate that way, but you shouldn't call it anymore. I'll buy another and text your burner with my new phone number. Other than that, if you keep running my business, I won't worry about my Port City clients. Gunner and I will find Bettina."

"Good luck, bud."

"It's too late for luck, Snoop. So far, all my luck on this case has been bad anyway."

"Then you're overdue for some good luck."

"All luck is distributed randomly."

As I disconnected, my burner phone received a text from Bettina's burner. A fifteen-second video of her lying on a mattress on a concrete floor. Her eyes were closed, but her chest rose and fell. She was alive. So far.

I sent the kidnappers another text:

I won't go to the cops or the FBI, but Simpson is a Detective Sergeant with the Houston PD. When she doesn't show up for work, they will start a search. Nothing I can do about that. Also, she telephones her parents often. When they don't hear from her, they will file a missing person report. Again, not my doing. If you harm Bettina Simpson in any way, the Houston cops and the FBI won't be the only ones looking for you. You should hope the cops or the feds find you before I do, because I will find you and put you down like a rabid dog.

There was nothing more to do.

At the nearest discount store I bought two more burners. It wouldn't hurt to keep a spare. Heck, the way this investigation kept ricocheting like a billiard ball, I should buy burners by the case.

———

The last time I talked to Gene Lopez, I sent him the photos of Paisley Tie and Red Tie and two names. While I was in the discount store parking lot, I called from my new burner.

He answered on the first ring. "Gene Lopez."

"Gene, it's Chuck McCrary. I'm calling from my new burner."

"I figured it was you when I saw the new Houston number. Here's the news: I identified the two men. The guy in the red tie is Christian Amadeus Bartok. The man in the paisley tie is Gerald Taylor Hawley. Both are former FBI. They joined DHS when the department was first staffed. They were partners at the FBI, and they've been partners ever since. Both agents know all the tricks, traps, and shortcuts. The woman is Luisa Alvarez Tavares, age twenty-five, first in her class in the DHS school of dirty tricks. She's worked under Bartok and Hawley for three months, ever since she finished the academy. She would be tasked with surveilling you and your friend electronically. I can email you a full report, but your email may be compromised."

"I created a new email address, Gene. I'll text it to you."

———

Bettina Simpson

She opened her eyes. Twenty-five feet above her was a steel roof supported by dusty steel girders. She blinked and tried to focus her vision. Everything appeared dim and blurry.

Managing to slide her hands back and forth, she sensed she was lying on coarse fabric. She tried to roll over, but her muscles didn't respond enough. They had drugged her, that was for sure. She tried to sit up. Her abdominal muscles strained but produced the same result—no movement. Okay, she'd wait. The drugs would pass through her system. She just didn't know how long that would take.

She stopped struggling to move and let herself drift off to sleep.

The ceiling eased into focus in the gloom. Had she been asleep? No way to tell. The sole illumination came from windows high on two walls. Big industrial lights hung from the girders, but they were dark. In the dim light she spotted lacy cobwebs like miniature hammocks strung between the lights and the girders. What did the spiders find to eat?

She clenched her fists. Did they clench? She couldn't tell, but she felt muscular feedback as though they had clenched. She rubbed her fingers over coarse cloth. Oh yeah, she had felt that fabric before she fell asleep. At least some muscles were responding. Her deep breath filled her nose with the odors of dust, old petroleum products of some kind, and pine-scented cleaning fluid. She sneezed—her breath exploding loudly in the silence.

Gradually, faint sounds came from outside. Nothing she could identify. Could be traffic or maybe the wind. Thunder boomed and rain pummeled the building, drowning out all other sounds.

She rubbed her wrist. Her watch was gone. She didn't bother to search for her purse.

Muscle control returned. She rolled over and raised up on one elbow. She lay on a bare mattress on a concrete floor. The fabric she touched was mattress ticking. Rising to a seated position, she surveyed the room.

The bare concrete floor was roughened by years of use before the factory, or whatever it was, had been mothballed. Small craters marked where machinery was once anchored to the floor.

When she staggered to her feet, the cold concrete floor startled her. She had not noticed she was barefooted. She scanned the area for her shoes. Zilch. The kidnappers had removed them along with her watch and purse. She tottered a few steps. The rough concrete irritated her feet. A few minutes walking the large room would damage her soles.

Okay, she would survey the area and be alert for something to use to protect her feet. Until then, she would walk gingerly and sidestep the pockmarks.

The thunderstorm ended quickly. The clouds rolled away, and natural light flooded through the high windows. Bettina's sole view of the outside was the blue sky. She had been unconscious at least one night.

Below the windows, three small one-story rooms were built against the wall. Each room could have been an office before the factory closed, maybe for a foreman or a clerk. Each had a door and large windows overlooking the larger room. A steel railing atop the rooms framed a deck above. Yes, there was a staircase to the top deck. Boxes were stored there. Later she would search them for tools to aid her escape.

Outside windows punctured two walls. The third and fourth walls might join to a larger building. This room could be one corner of a larger building.

She was viewing this place for the first time, yet it seemed familiar. A suspicion tickled her recall, but she couldn't complete the thought.

Bettina's bladder warned her it was time to pee.

Three doors marked one windowless wall. Two doors showed a men's and a women's symbols. Dodging the damaged areas, she crossed over to the women's restroom. Her walking improved with each step as the drugs lost their effects. The floor was not as jagged as she had feared. She could navigate her improvised prison by avoiding the spots where the machinery was once mounted.

She flipped the switch in the restroom. The lights flicked on. Good. She would be able to see after the sun set, unless she escaped before then.

Someone had left a fresh toilet paper roll and a spare. Optimistically, her kidnappers intended to keep her alive for a few days. She must be a bargaining chip. They would return with a phone to provide proof of life to whomever they were negotiating with—most likely Chuck, but possibly the Houston PD.

She peered into the bathroom mirror. She seemed unharmed. As she fingered the tender spot on her neck, conjecturing what drug they used on her, she realized that she was okay—other than her growling stomach. It reminded her that she had not eaten in at least twelve hours.

The men's bathroom was empty. No paper supplies. They had supplied the women's restroom. Why were they so considerate? One cop who stopped her was a woman. Perhaps she was responsible for the preparations.

The third door opened to a supply closet. Cleaning supplies, a mop, and two brooms. A janitor's cart, a stepladder, metal shelving with assorted odds and ends. Okay, all good. She could break off the broom head and use the handle for a weapon. It would make a club like a cop's baton. She didn't bother to inventory the cans and miscellaneous items on the shelves. She could do it later if needed.

A battered truck door with an electric door opener was on the left. She tried the door. Locked, of course. She punched the green *open* button. Nothing happened, of course. An alarm panel was mounted on the wall between the truck door and a personnel door beside it. The red light glowed in the gloom.

The burglar alarm presented a problem. She glanced at the windows high on the walls. Wireless sensors were glued to the glass in a corner of each window. Unless she disarmed it, the alarm system would signal her captors in less than a minute. The personnel door was locked. Butcher paper covered the inside of the small window at the top.

She tore off the butcher paper. A wireless sensor was cemented to the corner of the wire-reinforced glass. Damn. Four iron bars three inches apart blocked the outside. Steel mounts at the top and bottom held rusted nuts threaded onto the mounting brackets for the bars on the other side. Even with a wrench or pliers, there was no way she could unscrew the nuts. And the second the glass broke, the wireless sensor would signal the burglar alarm.

She would consider the alarm system later. Better to survey the building first. Ascertain what assets she had.

She walked to the panel of light switches beside the personnel door. She flipped each switch and groups of overhead lights triggered. Good. Her unseen captors had not condemned her to live in a cave-like environment.

She left the lights on. Perhaps a passerby would notice the lights on in the abandoned building and investigate.

A firehose cabinet was mounted on the other side of the truck door. She scanned for a fire alarm but found none. Bettina unrolled the hose and stretched it across the floor. She paced fifty feet along it and realized it would not reach the opposite wall. Nevertheless, she reeled the hose back in; she might find a use for it yet.

She inspected the three bump-out rooms. Two contained relics of the offices they had once been. The third had been a workshop with a grimy metal workbench, a lathe, and grinders, drills, and other tools.

The center room had a small new refrigerator and a microwave oven. The boxes they were shipped in were discarded nearby. If the kidnapper had bought the appliances, the serial numbers might allow detectives to trace who had bought them. Fingerprints left on the boxes when her captors opened them would be good, unless they had worn gloves.

The refrigerator held a case of bottled water, sandwich fixings, and a dozen frozen dinners. She microwaved a frozen turkey and dressing dinner and downed it with a bottle of water. She ate at an old wooden desk. Still hungry, she peered into the plastic bags on the desk that contained non-refrigerated food items and made herself a peanut-butter-and-jelly sandwich. Too bad it was white bread; she preferred multi-grain, but you know what they say about beggars…

The food meant the kidnappers intended to keep her a while. That and the fact that the fake cops kept her from seeing their faces told Bettina she was not in immediate danger of being murdered. In fact, she had not witnessed any usable evidence regarding her captors. If she testified, what valuable information did she have? None, except that one kidnapper was probably a woman. Big deal.

Being worthless as a witness meant it wasn't necessary to kill her. With kidnappers, they might not care whether she lived or died after her usefulness was over. Killing her would be less risky. They were keeping her alive for a reason. Safer to assume the kidnappers' generosity was temporary. She needed to escape ASAP.

Finishing her meal, she returned to the mattress. At the time she had regained consciousness, the sun was over there on her left. Now it had moved to her right. That way must be south, and it was approximately 3:00 p.m.

Returning to the microwave, she set its clock to 3:00 p.m. Might be useful to know the approximate time if something happened after dark.

Unless she escaped before dark.

Now that Bettina had tended to her bodily needs, she inventoried her enormous lockup and its nooks and crannies. Her captors had tried to make it escape proof, but in such a large and chaotic environment, they had probably overlooked something.

The treads on the metal stairs to the deck over the three rooms were made of metal lath. They supplied good traction for boot-clad feet, but the lath on the stairs would slash her bare feet the moment she put her weight on them.

Returning to the workshop, she searched the workbench drawers and found a carton cutter. Good, she cut the appliance boxes to make cardboard treads for the stairs.

A few minutes' work with the cutter and she mounted the stairs to stand under the wire-reinforced windows. The bottom of the windows was seven feet above the deck. Too high to see out.

Easy to fix. In the first bump-out office she found a stack of eight folding chairs. She lugged one upstairs and positioned it under the center window.

Steadying herself with a hand on the wall, she climbed on the chair. Standing on tiptoes, she could barely see out but recognized where she was. She was in Building 2 at Flathead Pipe Supply. She and Chuck had cruised the property a few days before. Beyond the gravel, the grass ran another fifty yards to a drainage ditch. Across the ditch was a double set of railroad tracks.

A pine tree farm grew beyond the tracks.

If she reached the trees undetected, she could hide. The problem was the fifty yards of gravel she must cross barefooted. Yes, she could ignore the pain and gut it out, but her feet would be worthless to walk on the paved road to seek help. She would consider the gravel problem further.

The upper windows would break, but even if she disarmed the burglar alarm, the fall on the other side would break an ankle, unless she could drop the firehose through a window and slide down it. There was still the problem of crossing fifty yards of gravel in her bare feet, if she could disable the alarm.

Like the old rabbit stew recipe: First catch a rabbit. She had to escape first before her bare feet became relevant.

Her waking nightmare was that the kidnappers were surveilling her. There were cameras on the outside of the building, and the owners might have installed them inside also. She scanned the corners underneath the roof but didn't notice any. Of course, above the lights the corners were in shadow. If the cameras were there, maybe when they mothballed Building 2, they decommissioned them.

There was nothing to do but ensure that, once she completed her breakout plan, she executed it fast. Too fast for an observer to send someone to spoil her escape.

She did a complete survey of the big room, its equipment, its possibilities... there were lots of possibilities.

TWENTY-TWO

Carlos McCrary

The files Lopez sent were a godsend. A cursory review showed front and profile pictures of Christian Bartok, Luisa Tavares, and Gerald Hawley; extensive biographies; vehicles they owned, with pictures and license plates; and properties they controlled, both home and investment. Bartok and Hawley owned millions of dollars of real estate in their own and their respective wives' names.

Luisa Tavares didn't own real estate, but she had teamed with Bartok and Hawley only three months ago.

My Special Forces instructor often quoted the ancient adage: "No battle plan survives contact with the enemy." Since the enemy had kidnapped Bettina, we had the first contact, and I made a new battle plan.

The tracker planted on the box truck was useless, so I abandoned it. The things cost over $100 each, but I couldn't spare the time to send Gunner to retrieve it. The battery lasted a week. Good trick if it worked.

It was possible the rogue DHS agents had discovered our motel, and prudence dictated that we relocate.

My Honda Pilot might have been compromised when I was last at the Loop 8 construction site. I scanned it with the bug detector. Damn. Sure enough, the bad guys had tagged it. I removed my jacket, crawled under the vehicle, and detached it. I would need to dry clean the pants, but I couldn't go back to the old motel to change into work clothes.

The rogue agents were not aware of Gunner, and they didn't know I had my Dodge Grand Caravan, now registered to my great-aunt Catherine Baylor.

I called Gunner from my new burner and updated him. I told him to not return to the old motel and to locate a new one and wait there.

I drove the Honda to our current motel without being tailed. I packed my belongings and Gunner's and checked out, again making sure I wasn't followed. I met Gunner at the new motel he had selected and rented adjoining rooms.

I copied the files to a flash drive and sent Gunner to an all-night truck-stop that had a copier to print two copies of everything Lopez sent.

I bought two large pizzas from a local shop and took them to the motel. I parked the Honda in the back where it couldn't be seen from the street.

Gunner and I reviewed the files while we ate.

The Lopez files indicated the DHS Internal Affairs department was not aware of their agents' property holdings. Lopez had sent his own sleuths online from the FBI office in Port City, Florida. Funny how Lopez unearthed this info without difficulty, but the Department of Homeland Stupidity was clueless. More likely, they hadn't bothered to investigate Bartok and Hawley since the day they joined the DHS over twenty years ago.

"Gunner, if Lopez and his people discovered this information that easily, why didn't the DHS find this on their own? Were they too trusting of their agents?"

"Or somebody higher in the DHS is protecting them."

"Let's hope it's incompetence rather than more crooked agents." I finished my first slice of sausage, mushroom, and jalapeño pizza. "Judging by the dates Bartok and Hawley bought the properties, these assholes started skimming from drug busts and laundering the money back in the 1990s when they were still with the FBI."

Gunner ran a finger down the property list. "The safest place to stash

Bettina is at one of their own buildings. Do any of these properties seem like a candidate?"

I scanned the list. The first pages listed the details and descriptions of properties Gerald Hawley or his wife currently owned. After that was a list of properties they had sold. "These are the single-family houses and small apartments. Must be a couple dozen houses and... I count seven different apartment buildings with..." I did the math in my mind, "one hundred twenty-seven apartment units. At any given time, the Hawleys must have a few houses or apartments vacant where they could stash Bettina."

Gunner studied the list. "They own too many suspect properties. It would require days to check which units are rented and which are vacant. You're the world's greatest PI. How can we narrow the list?"

"I'm not finished reading the list." I kept reading. The sixth page started with the list of properties Christian Bartok or his wife owned. The Bartoks owned three apartment buildings but were partial to commercial property and vacant land. The address of one parcel flashed a yellow caution light in my memory. I punched the address on Google Street View.

Bingo.

"Gunner, look at this." I pointed to the address on the property list and told Gunner that Tommy Valley's drug lab was there. "This is *Your Grandparents' Attic*. Bartok sold the vacant land to Roberto and Geraldine Hernandez seven years ago to build their storage business. Could they be connected?"

"Bartok may have been doing business with Tommy Valley for years," he said. "You think the crooked agents locked Bettina in a Hernandez storage unit?"

"Rule Seven: *There is no such thing as a coincidence.*"

"It's worth checking out," Gunner said.

"Okay, but let's not go all-in on this one property. I'll finish reading the list; there could be other, more likely sites."

A property on Old Powerline Road was listed on a later page. Bartok used Amadeus Oil Support Trust to buy it four years before. Two years later the trust sold it to Escondido Sendero LLC. Amadeus was Christian Bartok's middle name and Escondido Sendero LLC was the holding company for the *Tres Equis* drug cartel.

The property on Old Powerline Road was Flathead Pipe Supply. Building 2 was empty.

I jabbed the property description with my finger. "We have a winner, Gunner."

"Chuck, how far do you trust Gene Lopez?"

"Why do you ask?"

"You don't want to involve the FBI because the kidnappers might have a mole there. The mole might notify the DHS agents and the DHS bad guys might kill Bettina to cut off a loose end. I follow your logic. However, unless the kidnappers burned or crushed or dumped Bettina's car in the Houston Ship Channel, the GPS is still broadcasting. You and I don't have the equipment to access it, but the FBI does. So, how far do you trust Gene Lopez?"

I considered the question. Suppose I asked Lopez to help with the kidnapping. Would he feel obligated to make his involvement official? Or would he work with me on the downlow? Bettina's life could hang in the balance. I recalled our unofficial cooperation on the train bombing. Gene initially refused to cooperate with a mere civilian. Eventually he changed his mind. We brought the bad guys to justice from a 100% illegal operation, although neither of us ever spoke of it.

I called Lopez's personal cellphone. It rang three times before he responded. "McCrary, do you know what time it is?"

Lopez calls me "McCrary" when he's pissed at me. In this case, it was understandable; it was 8:00 p.m. in the Eastern Time Zone.

"Sorry, Gene. Did I interrupt your dinner?"

"Would it make a difference if you did?"

"No, but it seemed polite to ask. I have an emergency situation."

Lopez sighed loud enough for me to hear it. "Okay. What do you want?"

"Gene, your FBI skills could help this situation, but your help has to be off the books. If the FBI involvement became known, someone could be murdered to keep them quiet. Could you trace a car's location on its GPS if I gave you the plate number?"

Lopez paused before he spoke. "You know I can, but I want a damned good reason to do this on the DL."

Mentally, I held my breath before diving off the metaphorical high board. I hoped the water was deep enough I wouldn't break my neck. Or Bettina's.

I related my conversation with Bartok in their office in the Trylen Tower. "I agreed to stand aside until this so-called incursion across our border happens. I told them I would pursue Tommy Valley after that. Last night someone kidnapped Detective Sergeant Bettina Simpson, who is a personal friend. She is a Houston police detective working on my sister's disappearance with me. I have no proof, but I believe Bartok and Hawley and Tavares kidnapped her." I read him the texts I'd exchanged with the kidnappers.

"They didn't believe you would back off until after the incursion," Lopez said. "You are aware the odds are they will kill her anyway."

My stomach churned. "Yeah. That's why I need your help. Tell us what happened to Bettina's car and Gunner and I might find her nearby."

"Regardless of who the kidnappers are, you should let me refer this to the Houston FBI."

"If the crooked DHS agents are the kidnappers, they won't hesitate to kill Bettina. They are involved in the murders of my sister and her husband. Give me 48 hours to rescue her before you notify your Houston office."

A long pause over the phoneline. "Don't make me regret this, okay?"

"Thanks, Gene. I'll send you her license plate."

"Once you locate Sergeant Simpson, call me no matter what time it is. You read me, hotshot?"

———

Ten minutes later the track of Bettina's car arrived. It listed the latitude and longitude coordinates and times. I posted the first spot on a digital map on my laptop. It was on a residential street in River Oaks. "That's where they captured her, Gunner. She was working a burglary in River Oaks."

"Don't stop. Skip to the end. Where is the car now?"

Skipping to the last entry, I posted it on the map. The GPS signal ceased broadcasting at that spot. "Her car is in Building 2 at Flathead Pipe Supply. The metal building blocks the GPS signal."

Gunner stood. "Let's roll, boss. We shouldn't keep the lady waiting."

———

Bettina Simpson

The sun rolled across the sky. It would be dark in an hour. That was when she would escape.

Bettina had not unearthed anything to protect her feet. She would walk across the gravel as best she could.

Returning to the refrigerator, she fixed another meal. There was no way to predict how long it would take to hike on injured feet from the pine forest to a place where she could find or borrow a phone and call 9-1-1.

In the utility closet, she examined the mop and brooms and selected the one with the thickest handle. She carried it to the room that had been a workshop. Plugging in a dusty circular saw, she cut the head off the broom and hefted the handle. Taking a few swings and thrusts, it felt awkward, and she trimmed off another six inches. She tried two more swings. Good.

Another thunderstorm passed over. This time hail hammered the building. The windows rattled and the roof rumbled like a drumhead.

She scoured the drawers in the workbench and uncovered a long screwdriver. Carrying the screwdriver to an electric grinder in the corner, she flicked the on-off switch. Nothing. She traced the power cord to the outlet. It was plugged in. The grinder should be working. Unless... she inspected the other outlets on the wall and bench. One was a GFI outlet. She punched the reset button and the grinder roared to life.

She ground the screwdriver blade into a chisel edge. She couldn't slash with it, but she could stab. She wrapped the handle with electrical tape to improve her grip.

Electrical tape! She could cut cardboard to cover the soles of her feet, and tape them on like sandals with electrical tape. They wouldn't last forever, but maybe long enough to cross fifty yards of gravel.

Switching off the workshop light, the factory floor plunged into near darkness. The sun had slumped to the horizon while she worked. She switched on the overhead lights and studied the alarm system. The red light taunted her, daring her to disarm it.

Bettina habitually set the alarm in her condo when she left or went to sleep. She had 45 seconds to disarm it after returning home.

If this system were similar, breaking a window or forcing a door would start a countdown to disarm it. She could expect maybe a one-minute head start before the monitoring company called the building owners—presumably the kidnappers. Worst case, the kidnappers were in a different Flathead building and could respond in a few minutes. Best case, they would respond from an offsite location like the shooters in the SUV that attacked her and Chuck when they first visited the site.

She assumed the worst case. Sixty seconds to complete her escape without breaking a window or forcing a door.

Suppose she cut a hole in the wall? That shouldn't set off the alarm. How could she cut the wall of a metal building? She recalled the circular saw she cut the broom handle with. There were electrical outlets spaced along the exterior walls.

Returning to what she thought of as the *dining room*, she fished two half-liter bottles of water from the refrigerator and stuck one in each pocket. She might not be hiding long, but she should prepare for all eventualities.

She returned to the workshop. The saw had a six-foot power cord. Plenty long enough to cut a Bettina-sized hole in the wall.

She pressed the saw blade to the inside wall. It screeched like a siren. Sparks flew and she sniffed burning metal.

She started a horizontal cut four feet above the floor where two metal sheets overlapped. A few inches in, the blade's whine deepened. The cutting slowed as the blade attacked the raised ridge. She stopped the saw to let the blade cool. If it overheated, the blade could lose its temper and the teeth would wear out before she finished. She tested the blade with her hand. Yes, it was cool. She extended the cut until it stretched two feet wide. Dropping two feet, Bettina made a second horizontal cut and a vertical one completing three sides of a square two feet wide. She peeled back the sheet metal until she exposed the insulation.

Digging out the fiberglass insulation with the screwdriver, she uncovered the outside wall. Her freedom was so close Bettina could almost smell the pine tree farm with its promise of shelter.

She attacked the outside wall, but after cutting two sides of the final hole, the blade gave out. The teeth were so dull they would no longer cut the metal.

Returning to the workshop, she located a hammer and cold chisel. She ground the chisel to a sharper edge. Yes, it would cut the remaining side of her escape hatch.

This would be the final cut, and she taped her homemade sandals to her feet in preparation for her run to freedom. Bettina positioned the cold chisel at the spot where the over-heated saw blade had worn out. She swung the hammer at the chisel and the entire wall vibrated with the blow. She pounded the chisel again and began a jagged incision.

In the background, the burglar alarm began its ominous warning beep. Glancing at the alarm panel, she noticed the red light flashing. How the hell did she set off the alarm? Did the blows to the wall with the hammer and chisel disturb an alarm sensor? That was pointless speculation. It didn't matter *how* it had happened; it *did* happen, and she had to deal with it.

Racing the clock, she pounded the cold chisel like a frenzied pile driver, over and over, enlarging the final cut. She extended the opening and prayed to make it through before the alarm went off.

Nearly finished. The beeping stopped. A siren howled outside the building.

Time to run! The kidnappers would be on their way in seconds.

Striking a final blow with the hammer and chisel, she finished cutting the flap in the outside wall. The siren howled louder. She peeled back the final sheet metal.

She tossed the screwdriver and the broom handle through the opening and snatched the extra cardboard strips she had prepared. Draping the cardboard over the jagged bottom of the escape hole, she crawled through and stepped onto the gravel. The siren was mounted under the eave above her head, deafening her.

She retrieved the screwdriver and broom handle and slogged across the gravel toward the pine tree farm. If her homemade sandals survived long enough...

TWENTY-THREE

Luisa Tavares

S he had not had sex for seven weeks, but Luisa Tavares expected her romantic slump was about to end.

She had dated Kendall Franklin twice. The first was drinks after work three weeks ago. Tavares ran a deep background check on Franklin the next day. Her illegal use of federal resources uncovered no red flags, so she accepted the second date. She told herself that Franklin was an Assistant District Attorney and thus a State of Texas employee. That made the background check, if not strictly *legal*, at least *legal adjacent*. No harm, no foul, right?

The second date Kendall took her to dinner at the Cattle Country Steakhouse. She wasn't fond of steak, but she was quite fond of Kendall Franklin. The attraction overruled her indifference to red meat. Every steakhouse served chicken or seafood for people like her.

Things went well between her and the young ADA, and she considered inviting him to spend the night but decided that would appear too eager. Better to proceed at a deliberate pace.

Franklin's confidential employee evaluations, which Tavares also hacked, said his career was on the rise. Again, she told herself *no harm, no foul*.

Looked like green lights and smooth sailing to elevate the relationship. After dinner at a French bistro, she invited him to her apartment for an after-dinner drink. Kendall probably guessed she would invite him to spend the night. As he drove them back to her apartment, she began to run her fingers up and down his thigh, imaging him naked beside her in bed.

She handed Franklin her front door key. As the young ADA held the apartment door open, her cellphone rang.

She locked the door behind them and led him into the living area before she examined her phone. *Oh, crap.* The name on the screen shattered her sexy mood like a ripe melon hit by a sniper's bullet.

"The bar's over there, Kendall. Why don't you pour me a Calvados and whatever you want? Make yourself comfortable. I gotta take this call."

She crossed the room and unlocked her phone. "Luisa Tavares."

"This is Titanium Security. We detected an alarm at Flathead Pipe Supply, Building 2. What is your code word?"

"Code word?" In the months this operation had been running, the alarms on the various buildings had never gone off. Tavares raked her memory. "Code word?"

"To identify you as an authorized person on the alarm. We need the code word."

"Oh yes. It's *national security*."

"Thank you. You are confirmed. It was a break-in alarm and not a fire alarm. Should we call the police?"

Her heart jumped. Did Bettina Simpson manage to escape? How exposed was she to discovery?

Her thoughts shifted into DHS work mode. "No. We will handle this ourselves. Thanks for calling."

Disconnecting, she pivoted to Kendall, who was at the bar. She kept cool although her heart was pounding so fast that she felt light-headed. Was the shit about to hit the fan? How badly would she be spattered?

"Kendall, that was my office on the phone. I need to leave for a few hours."

Kendall brought a glass across the room and handed it to her. "Can you finish your Calvados first?"

Wanting something to calm her nerves, she drained the glass. "I'm sorry, Kendall. I had planned to ask you to spend the night. Next time?"

Franklin grinned. "I could wait here until you come back."

She stroked his arm. "Don't tempt me. No, there's no telling how long this will be, and tomorrow is a workday." She stepped into his arms, kissed him, then rubbed her hand on the bulge in his pants. "Keep that warm until this weekend, okay? I'll cook dinner for you… also breakfast."

She walked him to the door and gave him a long kiss with lots of tongue before closing the door behind him. *Give him something to look forward to.*

Assuming she had a future.

————

Bettina Simpson

The outside lights from Building 3 leaked onto the railroad right-of-way, faintly illuminating Bettina's path. She stumbled as she descended into the drainage ditch and rolled to a stop in a puddle at the bottom. One makeshift sandal was soaked and dissolved into wet paper shreds.

It was just as well; the gravel had cut slits and punched holes in the thick cardboard. Bettina peeled the remaining electrical tape from her bruised and bloody feet and slogged barefoot across the tracks. Before she disappeared into the pine trees, she spun a 360, alert for any movement. So far, so good. No sign of pursuit.

She collapsed to the ground and leaned back against a tree.

The siren ceased its endless wail. It probably reset after five minutes. The sky held a vestige of twilight, but the pine tree farm held nothing but trees. Correction: trees, pine needles, and tiny pinecones that felt like sitting on a field of thumbtacks.

Trying to make her way through the tangled underbrush would shred her feet. No, she must find another route to safety. But what?

She could travel west across grass growing between the railroad and the pine tree farm until she came across a path through the trees that would lead her to Old Powerline Road. Old Powerline Road dead-ended at the Trinity River a few miles east. The road wandered through the prairie, petered out near the river, and didn't approach within a mile of Highway 90.

But if she traveled west on the road instead of on the grass, it was over a mile to reach Highway 13. The pavement would butcher her feet, not to mention there was nowhere to hide from the kidnappers responding to the alarm. No, she needed a smooth surface to walk on.

The railroad tracks! The rails were four inches wide. She used to dance on curbs as a girl and pretend she was a circus high-wire artist. Walking a smooth steel rail was as simple as walking a curb. And the railroad ran behind more businesses on either side all the way to Highway 13. Perhaps she could trigger a burglar or fire alarm at one of the businesses. Worst case, she could hide near Highway 13 until dawn.

She jacked herself upright, stepped gingerly toward the grass strip, and picked the pinecones from the soles of her feet before stepping onto the rail. Lights from downtown Houston reflected off the scattered clouds and provided enough light to walk on the rail. She spread her arms, balancing on a tightrope, and took a few steps. Yes. She was a high-wire artist again. She checked back over her shoulder. Still no pursuit. This might work out.

———

Luisa Tavares

Tavares called Christian Bartok while her computer booted. "Boss, Titanium Security called. They detected an alarm at Building 2. Said it was a break-in, not a fire alarm. They offered to call the police, but I told them we would handle it."

Did she keep her voice calm? Could Bartok tell she was freaking out inside?

"Right. Cops are the last thing we need out there. Where are you?"

"In my apartment. I'm booting my computer to check on the cameras.

Wait a sec... It's booted. I'm loading the app to monitor the security footage."

"Did Simpson escape?"

"That's what I assume. I'm checking the Building 2 cameras... There's no outside light on the building, but there is something new on the wall. Hard to tell from this angle, but it could be a hole. Let me backtrack five minutes... Holy crap, there she is, crawling out of the hole. Simpson cut a hole in the exterior wall. There goes the *no harm, no foul* thing."

Bartok's voice held a sharp edge. "You and Gerry were supposed to check the building for anything she could use to break out."

"That was Gerry's job."

Whatever the cause and no matter whose fault it was, it was done; no use crying over spilt milk, though her career—even her life—was crumbling into smoking ash.

"The video shows Simpson holding something in each hand, maybe tools? I'll zoom... she's out from the shadow and there's some light from the exterior of Building 3. That's a long screwdriver and a bat. Could be a sawed-off broom handle. Let me switch cameras. She walked toward the pine tree farm to the south ten minutes ago. What should we do?"

"We recapture her," Bartok said. "If she makes contact with McCrary, the operation is toast."

This was getting worse and worse. Why did she ever agree to this?

"How do we recapture her without her identifying us? So far, Simpson can't prove who we are or that DHS is involved. We should just let her go."

"No. The Houston cops will tie Flathead Pipe Supply's ownership back to Hawley and me."

That was new information. Did Bartok and Hawley own Flathead?

Bartok continued. "We'll wear ski masks and Covid masks with our black outfits. We'll show nothing visible to identify. We need to reach the pine tree farm before she exits the other side and flags down a car."

"Boss, it's 8:00 p.m. on a Tuesday night. No one lives in the area. There won't be any cars to flag down. Simpson is immovable unless she hikes over a mile in the dark back to Highway 13. And she's barefooted."

"So how did she walk across the gravel?"

"The video showed her walking with a limp. She ignored the pain. You watched her demonstrate her courage in the video of the shootout she and McCrary had."

"We have no choice but to recapture her. I'll have Gerry meet us on Old Powerline Road at the corner of Highway 13. From there we'll search Powerline Road and move east. Let's say we'll meet at 8:45."

"Are you sure, boss?"

"Goddamn it, Tavares, we're committed. We have no choice now but to follow through."

You and Hawley may follow through, she thought, *but not me. Maybe...*

Carlos McCrary

My GPS estimated our arrival time at the Flathead site at 8:40 p.m. I handed my tablet to Gunner. "Use the tracker app and check the location of the vehicles I tagged for the three DHS agents."

"Bad news," Gunner said a few minutes later. "One tracker is in Lafayette, Louisiana, one is in Fort Worth, and one is in Brownwood, Texas."

"I admire the scumbags' sense of humor," I said. "They pulled the same trick on me that I pulled on them. Okay, we don't know where the rogue agents are. Tough luck, but we'll survive. At least we know where Bettina is."

"Where she *probably* is," Gunner corrected.

"Picky, picky."

We rolled a few more miles.

"The good news is that this time of night," Gunner said, "we'll waltz through the front gate."

"Bettina and I tried on a Sunday when the site was deserted. An SUV full of gunmen arrived in a few minutes, and we had to shoot our way out. This time you and I will infiltrate on foot through the pine tree farm. That puts us out near Building 2 and minimizes the chance they'll spot us on the cameras until we make a break for the building."

We reached the barbwire fence on the north side of Old Powerline Road. Fifty yards later I rolled to a stop at the steel gate.

I switched off the dome light. "Gunner, the chain wrapped around the gate and the fence post is fastened by one link. The padlock is for show. Open the gate and refasten it the same way after I drive through."

Soon we made a K-turn and stopped where I parked before. "That's the remains of Building 4. Building 2 is a hundred yards east."

Gunner and I trekked through the trees until we were opposite Building 2. "Last time Bettina and I were here, the building was no longer in use. And now the lights are on."

"There's light in the small window."

"There was no window there a few days ago."

We scrambled over the rails, and across the other side to the perimeter of the graveled area. "Don't go closer, Gunner. They mounted cameras on every building. Somebody cut a jagged hole in the wall. Bettina must have escaped."

"If she escaped through the hole, she was on foot," Gunner said. "This forest is the nearest shelter, but the cameras might spot her running away."

"She either ran straight west, keeping Building 2 between her and the cameras on Building 3, or she ran straight here. If she escaped right after dark, there's no telling how far she's gone on foot." I rotated a slow 360, looking and listening.

Something by the rails attracted my attention. Easing my way down the slope, I lifted a tattered piece of corrugated cardboard with electric tape trailing from it. I held it in the light from Building 3. "Is that blood smeared across the cardboard?"

Gunner lifted the shredded paper. "These tape strips could mean Bettina made sandals to cross the gravel. Smart girl but that means the kidnappers stole her shoes."

"Bettina and I know the neighborhood. Her closest help is at the intersection of Old Powerline and Highway 13," I said. "The businesses on Highway 13 are closed this time of night."

"Then she hikes on Highway 13 until she reaches U.S. 90. Even in the middle of the night there's traffic on Highway 90."

"I don't believe she hiked on Powerline, Gunner. Her bare feet wouldn't last long on rough pavement or on Highway 13. Also, the Flathead buildings have alarm systems. For her to escape the way she did, they locked her up but left her unguarded. The alarm told them when she escaped."

"Not necessarily, boss. Cutting a hole in the wall might not trigger an alarm like breaking a window or opening a door would. Let's hope she escaped without them knowing it."

"Possible but unlikely. Bettina and I were here, and we didn't set off any alarms. But the SUV arrived with guns blazing. Someone monitors the cameras. Bettina squeezed through the hole and the cameras recorded her. You can bet a team of bad guys is on their way here to recapture her. Powerline is the only entrance. No, she'll use the railroad tracks. It's the only way to walk out in bare feet."

"Shall we run down the tracks after her?"

"No. When she looks back—and she will—and spots strange men running her direction, there's no telling what she'll do. The kidnappers are pursuing, but she doesn't know we're here. We gotta pick someplace she'll recognize us. We'll return to the railroad crossing at Highway 13 and wait there. When she sees us standing beside our Caravan, she'll recognize us."

"Suppose she reached Highway 13 and hid someplace to wait for daylight?"

"Hopefully she'll recognize us standing beside the Caravan. Hey, I don't have the answers, Gunner. I'm playing this by ear."

TWENTY-FOUR

Luisa Tavares

Tavares's phone rang and her Toyota Corolla answered on its Bluetooth. "Yeah, boss."

"How far out are you?"

"Ten minutes. Is there a change of plans?" Mentally, she crossed her fingers, hoping Bartok had reconsidered and would abandon this fool's errand before she was sucked in further.

"Yes. Meet us at the railroad crossing on Highway 13."

She hoped Bartok had come to his senses. Enough was enough. Perhaps if they explained to Sergeant Simpson how important their mission was and the effort they made to keep her safe and unharmed, she would understand. She might even cooperate. At the same time, Tavares realized her own future was desperate. She could not be half pregnant. She had committed a capital crime. An undeniable fact. The sole way to survive this was to see it through. To the end.

"Why the railroad crossing?"

"We'll wait for Simpson there."

"I don't follow you, boss."

"You don't need to follow my reasoning. Just follow my orders. Meet us at the crossing." He disconnected.

Ten minutes later, Tavares's headlights picked out Bartok's Chevy Bolt backed up to the closed gate of a storage yard at the corner of the railroad spur and Highway 13. The blue Suburban was parked beside it, also backed in. Bartok and Hawley waited in front of their vehicles. They turned her way as she arrived.

She felt like she was being sucked to her death by quicksand. No matter how she struggled, she kept sinking deeper and deeper. She could scarcely breathe.

Shivering, Tavares turned her Corolla and backed parallel to the other vehicles.

She paused a moment to force back her fears before she opened the door.

Both men were holding masks in their hands. She turned back to grab her ski mask and Covid mask and joined the other two.

"Why are we here, boss?"

"Simpson is barefooted. The only way she finds help is to follow the track to this highway and wait until one of these businesses opens in the morning. We three will wait over there—" Bartok gestured over his shoulder with a thumb, "—in the shrubbery until Simpson shows."

———

Bettina Simpson

She sat on the rail and rested her feet on a crosstie. Her arms were weary from extending them at shoulder level—a highwire artist's balancing pole. She rested her arms awhile before opening a water bottle. She dribbled enough into her palm to wash the soles of her feet and drank the rest.

The clouds thinned, but Houston's reflected lights were bright enough for her to keep her bearings. To the east, it was too dark to know whether anyone was pursuing her, but the siren was loud enough for anyone working late at Building 3 to hear. Ergo, no one had worked late, and no one was back there.

Rising to her feet, she turned west. She could make out the rails for a few steps before darkness swallowed them. Good thing the tracks ran straight as a gunshot across the table-flat land. Too dark to make out anyone who was ahead either. She must be close to Highway 13.

As she trudged west, the clouds cleared and Houston's reflected lights vanished with them, plunging the railroad right-of-way into darkness. In a few seconds her eyes dilated, and she managed to peer a few feet ahead of her as she felt her way along the rail with her bare feet. The tracks were dimly discernable by the new moon.

The bushes rustled beside the right-of-way. Strong hands seized her extended arms, and something bit her in the neck.

As her muscles gave way, her last thought was *Oh, no. Not again.*

———

Carlos McCrary

We spent twenty minutes returning to the Caravan, drove back to the road, and hurried to the Highway 13 intersection. I worried that Gunner was right: Bettina could have reached the crossing and hidden somewhere. And the crooked DHS agents had at least three people searching for her. Perhaps even a crooked Houston cop or two.

As I braked at the Highway 13 stop sign, a lumber truck towing a trailer laden with cut pine timber struggled up the slight upgrade, approaching from the south. We waited for the truck to pass. I glanced down the highway toward the railroad crossing a quarter-mile to the north.

At that distance I couldn't establish the makes or models, but several vehicles were parked at the entrance to a storage yard that adjoined the railroad. One was a large dark SUV, possibly the DHS blue Suburban. The notable thing was the vehicles had backed into the entrance facing Highway 13. When I was a cop, we backed into every parking space so that, when an emergency arose, we could roll out fast without having to back up.

My scalp felt like my hair was standing on end. I knew why those vehicles were in an industrial neighborhood this late at night. The kidnappers had figured out Bettina's escape route the same way we did and had waited for her to come to them.

The SUV steered onto Highway 13 and accelerated across the railroad crossing. The other vehicles parked beside the pavement trailed the SUV. One was a Chevy Bolt; the other, a Toyota Corolla.

Did they find her?

The lumber truck was upon us. I waited for it to struggle past, then punched the accelerator and fishtailed around the corner. Dashing into the left lane to overtake the lumber truck, I was startled by a southbound pickup truck ascending the railroad crossing, surging straight for us.

I leaned on my brakes and jerked back into the northbound lane to avoid a head-on collision. The Caravan was buffeted by the pickup truck's wake as it rocketed past, missing us by inches. The driver honked his frustration and his horn dopplered lower in pitch while he passed, waving his raised middle finger.

"Holy crap," Gunner said, "that was so close I'm lucky I don't need to change my pants."

"I have the reflexes of a cheetah."

"And the intelligence of a doorknob. You couldn't see over the railroad crossing. Didn't you look before jumping into the passing lane?"

I let the question pass without comment. Gunner was right: I had acted recklessly.

I white-knuckled the steering wheel in frustration until the pickup passed, then I slipped carefully into the left lane and overtook the lumber truck.

As I sailed over the railroad, the three vehicles were long gone.

"What do we do, Chuck?"

"Plan B."

"And that is…?"

"We squeeze Tommy Valley like a toothpaste tube."

———

I prodded the Caravan along Highway 13 toward U.S. 90. No point in hurrying. "Gunner, punch up Tommy Valley's tracker."

We mounted the on-ramp. Gunner worked the tablet. "Valley's motorcycle is at the Spoke and Sprocket Pub."

"Excellent. Let's pay him a call. Maybe he'll buy us a beer."

Gunner snorted. "Or not."

The parking lot was half full on a weeknight. I backed the Caravan into a spot by the fence. Valley's Harley was slotted between several other bikes on the front row, which was reserved for bikes. Two other bikes were familiar. They were in the parking area the night of Lola Salazar's party.

"Gunner, I don't want Tommy Valley to learn you and I are together. Swap out the tracker on Valley's bike with a fresh one and plug the old one into the charging port in the Caravan. You see the bikes beside Valley's?"

"Affirmative."

"They belong to Al Fajardo and Ronald Trojanik. Stick trackers on them. Then come inside and sit at another table."

"Roger that, boss."

I paused inside the door to scan the room.

A beefy man sporting a red bandana do-rag and a sleeveless leather vest revealing enormous tattoo-covered arms stood across the room behind the far end of the bar. His posture and attitude announced that he brooked no nonsense. His eyes passed across me then backtracked. I acknowledged him. His eyes locked on me like two laser beams. I was new, and he was the bouncer or the owner. Perhaps both.

Behind him on the wall was a homemade wooden sign that said *Buck's Rules* above a list of numbered items that filled the board.

The scents of leather, machine oil, beer and French fries fought to dominate the atmosphere. The beer was winning.

Tommy Valley slouched at the bar with Fajardo and Trojanik. Valley had at least one and perhaps two other kidnappers with him at the truckstop when he kidnapped Angie. I wondered if Fajardo and Trojanik were his other two musketeers. If they were, they were now dead men walking. The list of people I would exterminate got longer.

Tonight, Valley wore a single earring of a stainless-steel mace. I had hoped he would wear Angie's garnet earring. I intended to take it back and return the pair to my mother.

That would wait until later.

Trojanik's left arm was in a sling—a souvenir of the first time we met. Fajardo's cheek was scraped and bruised where I'd kicked him.

The Three Stooges were engaged in their own conversation and didn't notice me. I picked an empty table out of their sightlines to wait for Gunner. Rule Eighteen: *Always have a backup*. Was that one of Buck's Rules?

A woman with butterflies tattooed on her arms danced across the floor in time to the jukebox. She carried a tablet computer.

"What can I get ya, hon?" Her tee-shirt was two sizes too tight, and her blue jeans were cut short enough to be illegal in some foreign countries. Nice legs too. She danced in place and waited for me to order. Energetic.

"A draft, please."

Butterfly consulted her tablet. "We serve seventeen different drafts, hon."

"Surprise me."

Butterfly laughed. "Hon, you know I'm gonna sell you the most expensive draft, don't ya?"

I grinned at her. "Go ahead; have your way with me."

She giggled. "Don't tempt me, big boy. I might call your bluff if you're here when we close." She deposited a coaster on the table and pranced off, shaking her booty and skipping rhythmically to the music. Miss Congeniality.

By the time she returned with my draft, Gunner had entered and sat at another table.

I tasted my beer. Nutty, hoppy, lightly carbonated, chilled, but not too cold. Butterfly had made an excellent choice. I laid a ballpoint and a small notepad on the table beside my beer to indicate I would return.

The bouncer's eye tracked me while I strolled toward Tommy Valley. He reached behind the bar and hefted an old-fashioned billy club. Smart guy.

I stopped three feet behind Valley and his buddies. "Tommy, we should talk."

Valley glanced at me in the mirror behind the bar. His eyes narrowed to twin slits. He sipped beer with his left hand. He dipped his right hand into a pocket.

Some people never learn.

As Valley spun the barstool, his hand emerged waving a switchblade. The blade snicked open, and he lunged at me.

Grabbing his wrist, I yanked him past me and caught his other wrist when he tried to punch me. I kneed him in the stomach and pushed him back on his stool. Fajardo and Trojanik froze like statues. I collected the knife from the floor.

As the bouncer stepped nearer, I closed the blade, pocketed it, and stepped back from Valley, lowering my hands to my sides.

The bouncer shoved the billy club into Valley's gut. "You know the rules, asshole. Never show a weapon inside. You and your buddies take this outside. Don't come back tonight. You follow the rules, and you can come back tomorrow. *Capisce?*"

Fajardo raised his hand. "This has nothing to do with me, Buck. I got no beef with this guy." He glanced at Trojanik. "Neither does Troy."

Buck kept the billy club jammed in Valley's belly. He queried me. "Well?"

"I want a friendly conversation with Tommy. Inside or outside—doesn't matter to me."

Buck eased the club back and leaned his nose inches from Valley's. "Outside, asshole." He waved toward the door and walked away.

"Hey, Buck," Valley said, "what about my knife?"

Buck paused and half-turned. He pointed to *Buck's Rules* behind the bar. He read from it. "*Any weapon you show will be confiscated.* This dude confiscated your switchblade, so I don't have to. You want it back, deal with him—but do it outside. And don't come back in tonight." Buck returned to his post at the end of the bar.

"Shall we?" I stepped back and motioned Valley towards the exit.

As Valley limped toward the door clutching his ribs, he glanced over his shoulder at Fajardo and Trojanik. His eyes seemed to plead for them to follow us.

Fajardo grinned and waved. "Have a nice chat, Tommy."

I clapped Valley on the shoulder and urged him toward the door. "Don't worry, Tommy. I only want to talk."

When we reached the outside, I led him ten yards from the entrance.

Silently as a fog, Gunner trailed us out the door.

Valley spotted the giant Viking gliding toward us and jumped reflexively.

"Don't worry, Tommy. Gunner won't bother you. Unless you piss him off. Then you should worry a lot."

Valley knotted his fists on his hips. "I'm out here, buddy. What do you want?"

"I'm not your buddy. In case you forgot my name, Tommy, it's Carlos McCrary."

"Okay. McCrary. What do you and your friend want?"

"Let's talk about the man in this picture." I showed him my phone with a picture of Saco made from the video Angie recorded at the party. "What is happening this Thursday night?"

Valley peered at the screen. "Never saw him before."

Gunner snorted.

"Careful, Tommy. Gunner is getting pissed."

Valley cut his eyes to Gunner and back to me.

"Best not to lie when Gunner is around. He hates liars. You recognized this photo of Santiago Ruiz Iglesias aka Saco. He's a big deal in the *Tres Equis* drug cartel—the guys who supply you with drugs. Your DHS buddies Bartok and Hawley told me Saco plans something big for Thursday." I jabbed Valley's chest with my finger. "And you're in it up to your fancy earrings."

"I don't know what you're talking about."

I glanced at Gunner and shrugged. I put my phone away and stepped a few feet back from Valley.

Gunner's expression never changed as he stiffened his fingers and jabbed Valley in the solar plexus. Valley doubled over and vomited. He stumbled backward and fell on his butt.

Grabbing him by the hair, I dragged him away from the barroom door and the vomit puddle. "What do you suppose Saco will do if he learns you lost your iPhone?"

Valley struggled to catch his breath. "I didn't lose my iPhone." Valley patted his vest pocket. "It's right here."

"That iPhone has your Mexican drug connections detailed in its address book. But it's not the one you had when you and I first met. You lost that one. Ask me how I know."

Valley's eyes widened. "I lost my phones that night. That's all—I lost them."

"I stole your phones the way I stole Troy Trojanik's and Al Fajardo's phones—while you were unconscious."

"My phones was locked. You can't do squat without the passwords."

"Wrong, Tommy. I pressed your thumb on the iPhone screen and unlocked it. And your Samsung was already unlocked. If I keep both phones charged and turned on, they will stay unlocked forever."

Valley wilted like the air had escaped from his balloon. He visibly shrunk and the tautness left his muscles.

"What do you want me to say, McCrary?"

"What do you imagine Saco will do if he finds out what happened to your phones?"

Valley swallowed and chewed on his lip. He would balance the possibility of future retribution from Saco against the certainly of immediate vengeance from Gunner and me.

"Okay. What do you want to know?"

"What is supposed to happen Thursday night?"

Valley glanced over his shoulder and lurched toward the far side of the pavement, waiting for me and Gunner to move with him. He stopped near my van, his eyes jumping back and forth. No one to overhear us.

"*Tres Equis* is bringing a duffle bag full of cocaine from Mexico. Fifty kilos. But not regular cocaine—this is the pure snow, uncut."

"That could be worth millions of dollars," I said.

Valley scoffed. "Try four million. That's what *Tres Equis* paid the Venezuelans to buy it."

"What's your role in this?"

Valley's eyes drifted toward Gunner then back to me. "Bodyguard. *Tres Equis* plans to resell the coke to a Cuban gang from New Jersey for $5,000,000. We're meeting them Thursday night."

"What are Fajardo and Trojanik's roles in this?"

"Bodyguards, same as me."

"Who else will be there from the *Tres Equis* side?"

"Ray Santos, Val Dias, and a couple other guys I haven't met."

"If you toss fifty kilos of cocaine and $5,000,000 in cash in the same place at the same time, there are a dozen ways that deal can go sideways."

Valley scoffed. "No shit, Sherlock. The problem is no one from the New Jersey gang trusts *Tres Equis* and the Mexicans don't trust the Cubans. But Saco, he gets the bright idea to make a low-key exchange involving three people on each side. He says that top secrecy is the way to go. One *Tres Equis* guy carries the bag of coke. The Cubans have one guy wheeling in a trunk full of Benjamins."

I stopped to do a mental calculation. "Five million in hundreds weighs fifty kilos also. So, each side will bring two guards plus their carrier?"

Valley scoffed. "That's Saco's big plan. Personally, I think it's bogus. Once we collect the coke, we should keep Al and Troy and Ray and Val with us, along with several other guns. The Cubans are bound to bring extra guns to the meeting, if only to escort the coke back to New Jersey. We'll lose the coke *and* the money. And our lives too."

"What do Bartok and the other DHS agents plan to do?"

"After I learn where the exchange will happen, I text Bartok. Bartok will bring a dozen DHS agents there. Bartok will wire me up and give me a bulletproof vest. We'll record the two sides confirming they intend to sell dope for the cash, and the DHS sweeps in and arrests everyone. Once the perps are in jail and the plea deals made, I disappear into witness protection in East Buffalo Fart, Idaho, or some other exciting place to live the rest of my life."

Valley shifted his weight from one foot to the other. "Okay. I been cooperating with you. You should cooperate with me. How about you give me my knife back?"

"Tommy, the only way I give this knife to you is to spike it in your chest. Be thankful I don't cut you for trying to pull that crap on me."

I grasped something new concerning Tommy Valley's motives. First, he had no idea that I knew he had kidnapped and murdered Angelina. Second, the poor shlub believed Bartok's sleazy venture was legit. I figured Bartok and his crew planned to kill everyone on both sides, the *Tres Equis* and the New Jersey Cubans, and steal both the cocaine and the cash.

Valley and his buddies were patsies. Bartok and his crooked agents would kill the Three Stooges for me.

But if Valley assumed Bartok was on the level, then the DHS agents did not tell him they kidnapped a Houston cop. There was no point in asking Valley where they were holding Bettina.

I would need to ask Bartok or Hawley or Tavares.

———

Bettina Simpson

Bettina opened her eyes. She lay slumped on the concrete floor. An industrial fluorescent fixture buzzed overhead. The bulbs were hidden behind the plastic diffuser. The ballast sounded ready to burn out. She prayed it didn't fail before she escaped; it was the only light in the storeroom.

She rose and stretched her cramped muscles. *Déjà vu* all over again.

The plain steel door was locked with a keyed deadbolt and a straight barndoor handle. She tugged on the handle; the deadbolt held firm. She rapped on the door. Heavy-gauge steel door and heavy-gauge steel frame. No way she could kick that door open.

There's more than one way to get to the post office, she thought.

———

Carlos McCrary

Gunner brought two beers from the motel refrigerator, handed one to me, and sprawled at the other end of the couch. "What now, boss?"

"I believe the other shlubs, Fajardo and Trojanik, were the other men in the van who kidnapped Angie." I lifted the bottle and drained an inch. "What do we do with the Three Stooges? Leave them for Bartok and his crew to massacre?"

"It's more satisfying to squeeze the trigger yourself, boss, but Bartok and his crew can do the job with no blowback on us. So, yeah. Leave them to Bartok. But what about Bettina? How we gonna find her?"

"The list of properties Bartok and Hurley own is too long for us to search. Thursday night is forty-eight hours away."

Gunner referred to his phone. "It's past midnight. It's already Wednesday morning."

"Following Thursday night, Bartok won't need Bettina. We'll go straight to the source. Luisa Tavares is the low person on the totem pole. I met the three of them in their office, and her body language told me she resents the hell out of Bartok and Hurley's Good Ole Boys' Club. Or maybe she's antsy over the off-the-book aspect. She's a generation younger than them. Could be she's uneasy with Bartok and Hurley's plans."

"Or she doesn't know their real plan."

"Good point, Gunner, and she hasn't been with Bartok and Hurley long enough to steal enough drug money to guarantee a secure financial future. She might crack if we apply pressure."

Gunner finished his beer. "We're not getting any younger, boss. At this hour of the morning, Tavares should be at her apartment."

———

The windows in Tavares's apartment were dark, and her Toyota Corolla sat in her assigned spot. That made sense: It was 1:30 in the morning.

Pausing the Caravan at the entrance to the parking area, I studied her front door. "That's a video doorbell. The view covers her parking spot." I activated another GPS tracker and handed it to Gunner. "Stay out of camera range. Hide this under her rear bumper. Just in case."

Gunner opened his door. "You buy these things by the dozen, boss?"

I grinned. "I earn a better discount buying by the gross."

Turning, I idled out of camera range and waited for Gunner to return. He got back in the car, and I rolled to an empty visitor's spot.

As we walked up to her apartment door, a motion-sensitive porch light switched on. I rang the doorbell and stepped back where Tavares could observe us both in the picture on her cellphone.

———

Luisa Tavares

"Someone is at the door."

The video doorbell announcement roused Tavares from a deep sleep. She swung her half-closed eyes to the clock on her nightstand. *01:43.* Whoever was at her door at this ungodly hour, it couldn't be good news.

Sometimes the pesky video doorbell was super sensitive. A strong wind gust could set it off. She had been awakened before by a large pickup truck passing her apartment.

She rolled over and tugged the sheet over her head.

The doorbell rang. *Damn, why couldn't it be a false alarm?*

She opened her phone's doorbell app and tapped the front door image to see a live view. It was Carlos McCrary and another man. A big blond gorgeous Viking. Handsome as a movie star.

She sat up in bed and activated the speaker. "What are you doing here, McCrary?"

"We need to talk."

Oh geez. Now what?

She swung her legs over the side and rose to her feet. She was half asleep and nearly lost her balance. "You and I have nothing to discuss. Agent Bartok warned you. Interfering with our operation is a federal crime. Go away."

McCrary leaned so close to the camera that his nose bulged like a clown's. He spoke in a soft voice. "Luisa, if your doorbell is like mine, the monitoring company records our entire conversation and saves it in the Cloud. It's there forever, and anybody with a search warrant can access it for evidence. We should talk... inside."

OMG, McCrary's right. The doorbell company saves everything online. She wasn't sure whether she could delete it. Was anything ever deleted on the internet? Not likely.

Too late to ignore him. Why had he come? "Who's the guy with you?"

"Gunner Knutson."

Gunner raised his hand and smiled. Tavares's heart fluttered.

"He works with me. Can we come in?" McCrary smiled. "I promise to bring Gunner in with me. You can feel his biceps if you like."

Her mind was sluggish, operating with glacial slowness. Should she let them in?

"How did you know where I live?"

"I'm the world's greatest private eye."

She was glad he couldn't see her smile.

"What do you want?"

McCrary leaned toward the camera and lowered his voice. "Bartok and Hawley plan to cut you out of the Thursday night prize and split the, uh, proceeds two ways instead of three."

"What the hell does *cut me out* mean? I don't follow."

"Luisa, do you really want to discuss this through your doorbell? Your doorbell is recording both sides of our entire conversation."

She was waking up now. McCrary was right; she shouldn't allow their conversation to be recorded.

"Give me a minute to get dressed."

"Fine. We'll wait here."

She turned the door speaker off and walked to her closet. She hung her sleeping shorts and tee-shirt on the hook. She studied her clothes selection. She slipped on a University of Houston tee-shirt with a scoop neck and matching shorts.

Turning to the bathroom, she combed her hair and debated whether to apply makeup. That Gunner fellow looked like the cover model for one of her romance novels. Wouldn't hurt to spruce up in case things didn't work out with Kendall Franklin. Always good to have a backup, especially one who looks like a freaking Norse god.

With a last inspection at the full-length mirror, she was satisfied. Gunner the Viking was fair game.

She opened the front door. "Okay, gentlemen."

Tavares led her visitors to the living room and gestured to chairs. "What's this about my colleagues cutting me out of a prize?" She made air quotes around "prize."

"Bartok and Hawley will kill you tomorrow night and keep your share of the loot."

"Loot? What loot? We're arresting a bunch of Muslim terrorists."

"No, you're not. Your bosses have been lying to you."

She had suspected the senior agents were not following DHS procedure, but they had thirty years of experience, and she was a rookie. Why would they lie to her?

"I don't believe you. What makes you say that?"

"Bartok and Hawley have become rich by stealing dope and cash from criminals over the last thirty years."

"No. I don't believe you."

"It's true," McCrary said. "They are far richer than honest federal agents should be on their salaries. Didn't you suspect they were into something fishy?"

Yes, she thought. They had ordered her to kidnap a U.S. citizen. That was definitely illegal. Now that McCrary mentioned it, they did live in expensive houses and drive flashy cars. And their wives dressed in clothes Tavares could never afford.

"Bartok is 64 years old, and Hawley is 63. Retirement age." McCrary handed her a sheaf of paper. "This is a tally of real estate they each own."

Tavares scanned the list. It was several pages long. "Where did you get this?"

"Tell you in a minute. You asked how I know they plan to kill you. Consider this: Their properties are owned free and clear. No mortgages. Add the appraised values and you'll discover Bartok and his wife are worth over $28,000,000. Hawley and his wife are worth over $19,000,000."

Tavares thumbed through the list as she read property descriptions at random. She returned her focus to McCrary. "Okay. That's a lot of property. What does it all mean?"

"It means they are both rich enough to retire in style. If you check those property lists, you'll see that they each bought a waterfront condo in Naples, Florida, right after you began working for them. Both bought their condos with cash. This deal on Thursday night is their last hurrah before they ride into the sunset. It's not worth the risk for them to keep robbing drug dealers. But you already know too much; they will get rid of you. Permanently."

That can't be true, she thought. "Tomorrow night we're arresting a couple of dozen *mujahedin* terrorists who plan a July 4 attack."

McCrary sighed. "That's what they told me too when we met privately in your office. But that's not what's happening. There are no *mujahedin*. Thursday night is a giant drug deal. After you help your bosses kill the drug dealers, you will be expendable. You will be of no further value to them. Hell, even I might be tempted to kill you for $3,000,000."

"$3,000,000? What's that?"

"That is one-third of Thursday night's loot."

"They never mentioned splitting any criminal assets with me."

McCrary locked eyes with her. "Your so-called partners lied to you about this entire operation."

As McCrary told her details of the fifty kilos of cocaine and the $5,000,000, her stomach began to churn. Her once-promising career at the FBI was teetering like a house of cards.

"They plan to kill you and Tommy Valley and the *Tres Equis* and the Cubans. They'll net $9,000,000 from this takedown. They will machine gun a dozen or more people—one of the victims will be you. The whole massacre will be passed off as a shoot-out between rival drug dealers. They'll say you were killed by the cartel members. They might even get you a posthumous medal for valor."

Her stomach protested. The world became a giant Tilt-A-Whirl. She stood and grabbed the top of her chair to steady herself. "I'll be back." She hurried from the room and reeled into the master bathroom.

Her stomach rebelled and she gagged and retched repeatedly.

Her stomach finally emptied itself, but her body didn't get the message; it kept heaving. This had not happened to her since her twenty-first birthday party. Her body felt wrung out like a threadbare washcloth. She pushed upright and clung to the lavatory with both hands, waiting for the world to stop bucking.

The walls of the tile room felt like they were closing in on her. It seemed like the whole world was shrinking around her, about to crush her.

She ran water into the lavatory and bathed her face. She blew her nose and consulted the mirror.

She repaired her hair and makeup. *Keep up appearances. Never let them see you sweat.*

She glanced at her reflection in the mirror. Okay. She was good enough to rejoin civilization.

She went to the kitchen and started the coffeemaker.

She returned to the living room and smiled at the Viking. "How do you take your coffee, big guy?"

Her visitors told her, and she returned to the kitchen, where she prepared coffee. She considered her options while she waited for the coffee to brew. She found herself shivering as she stared at her reflection in the microwave door.

She had worked for Bartok and Hawley for three months. She knew practically no one else in the Department except the agent who recruited her. Tavares had no reputation, good or bad. No one in the Department would take her word over the words of two thirty-year-plus veterans.

How much did McCrary know and how much could he prove? She could deny everything and brazen it out. She could claim her superiors duped her. She deliberated for a few heartbeats. That wouldn't fly. An innocent dupe with a 150-point IQ and a master's degree in computer science? Ha! She imagined how ridiculous she would appear claiming she was only following orders.

No closer to a solution, she set the coffee pot on the tray and carried it to the living room. "Here. Help yourselves, gentlemen."

She leaned back on the couch and gazed at the Viking while they poured their coffee. The Viking drank his black. She expected that. Surprisingly, McCrary drank his with a little creamer. Not very macho.

McCrary held the cup on his knee. "Two days ago, I told the SAC of the Port City office of the FBI about the three of you. He's closing in on your bogus mission as we speak."

"The SAC is investigating our operation?"

"SAC Eugenio Lopez sent me the list of your bosses' properties. He also sent me copies of the personnel files for all three of you."

That was a big surprise. McCrary was connected even higher than she was.

McCrary sipped his coffee. "I told Lopez that you three kidnapped Bettina Simpson. Twice."

Tavares's eyebrows raised. "Who is Bettina Simpson and what makes you suspect we kidnapped her?"

"Luisa, Bettina Simpson is the main reason Gunner and I are here. It's no skin off our nose whether Bartok and Hawley kill you or not. You're not my monkey and this isn't my circus. We're here to locate Bettina Simpson. Period. Keeping you alive is a side job to encourage you to cooperate."

McCrary brought the Viking into the conversation. "Gunner, tell Luisa what we've done the last few hours, starting with what we observed on Highway 13 at the railroad tracks."

Gunner leaned back in his chair. "Luisa, Chuck and I witnessed you and Bartok and Hawley recapture Bettina Simpson near Highway 13 at the railroad tracks after she escaped from Building 2 at Flathead Pipe Supply. Yes, we know you used Flathead Pipe Supply to hold Bettina. We were close enough to recognize the three of you, but too far away to stop you. We came to ask where you stashed Bettina the second time."

McCrary said, "We don't care about your escapades stealing dope and money from criminals—"

"I'm not involved in that. I swear."

"Okay, let's assume you didn't realize this operation was off the books. We uncovered this scam as a side effect of my search for my sister's killers and to rescue Bettina."

"What does SAC Lopez plan to do with us?"

"I asked Lopez to hold off for a couple of days to give Gunner and me time to locate Bettina. Once we do that..." McCrary spread his palms in a *who-knows* gesture.

"One thing you can count on: Your oh-so-patriotic superiors have sucked you into a criminal conspiracy. You can argue with a federal prosecutor as to whether you knew it was illegal. Regardless, all three of you are living on borrowed time. Gunner and I *will* locate Bettina Simpson. Then Gene Lopez and the FBI will sweep y'all up like a tray of broken glass on the kitchen floor."

Tavares processed this new information. She was out of time and out of options.

Leaning back, McCrary sipped coffee. "I know one possible way you might avoid a prison sentence."

He waited for Tavares to meet his gaze.

"Okay, I'll bite: What do you suggest I do?"

"Your best chance to survive this without a life sentence is to cooperate on Bettina's kidnapping and help Lopez build a case against Bartok and Hawley."

McCrary leaned back. "Luisa, you are out of time. Prove you're innocent. Tell us where you stashed Bettina."

She looked at Gunnar Knutson. "You'll tell SAC Lopez that I cooperated?"

———

Carlos McCrary

Before leaving Luisa Tavares's apartment I gave her a burner phone with my contact info labeled with a question mark.

"In case your phone falls into the wrong hands. The phone number is linked to this burner. Pack a bag and walk to one of the motels we passed a few blocks away. Don't move your car. Bartok and Hawley can locate your car the same way you tracked my first rental car. At the hotel, pay cash and check in under an assumed name. If the hotel clerk insists on seeing your ID, show them your badge and tell them you're under cover." I gave her five hundred dollars.

"Why should I run?"

"Bartok and Hawley will soon learn Bettina has escaped again. They will figure that you told us where she was. They may come after you. You will be a loose end they need to cut."

I noticed her expression. "What, you didn't think that far ahead? Don't worry. Gunner and I will drive straight to the apartment complex to free her. If you don't know a safe place to stay, at least don't stay in this apartment. But I urge you to leave your car and your phone here. They can monitor your car's GPS and also track your phone. I'll call you on the burner once Bettina is safe, and we'll figure out where you will be safe too. But it's better we don't know where you are."

No point in letting Tavares learn where Gunner and Bettina and I were staying. She may have flipped for us, but there was no guarantee she would stay with the good guys. Three million reasons could make her switch sides again. I would connect her with Gene Lopez when he arrived in Houston. After Gene took custody of Tavares, I could focus on Tommy Valley and his best buddies, Fajardo and Trojanik.

First, we had to rescue Bettina.

TWENTY-FIVE

Bettina Simpson

The storage closet held no food and no toilet. The kidnappers must have intended to return before she starved to death. They didn't want her dead yet because they could have killed her while she was unconscious.

Cleaning supplies and a mop, bucket, and broom were stored beside a utility sink. She cupped her hand under the faucet and slaked her thirst.

Six-foot and eight-foot folding aluminum ladders leaned on one wall. Three sets of gray metal shelves held assorted spare lightbulbs, A/C filters, various replacement parts, and a leather tool belt complete with tools.

Those idiots had ignored the most basic steps to escape-proof the room. They must have been in a frenzied rush. It would be simple to remove the metal door from its hinges.

Surveying the tool assortment, Bettina selected a flat-head screwdriver with a six-inch blade. She wedged the screwdriver blade between the bottom door hinge and the flange of the hinge pin. She tapped a hammer on the screwdriver handle, forcing the hinge pin out a fraction of an inch. Wiggling the screwdriver back and forth, she eased the hinge pin out enough to grasp the pin with slip joint pliers. She hammered upwards on the bottom of the pliers and forced the pin out of the hinge.

One hinge done, two to go.

Three minutes later, the door was held in place solely by friction and gravity. She wedged a twenty-four-inch crowbar between the door and the jamb above the center hinge. Pushing the handle to the right, the door slid toward her with a screech of distressed metal.

She leaned the crowbar farther toward the wall.

The hinged side of the door slid free from the jamb. She grabbed the barndoor handle with one hand and the hinged side of the door with the other and slid the deadbolt from its slot. Sliding the door to one side exposed a carpeted hallway outside the doorway.

Thank God for the carpet. With her feet cut, bruised and bloody, she didn't believe she could survive walking across another graveled field.

Taking the crowbar, she stepped through the doorway. The hallway was lined with numbered doors. To her right the hallway stretched more than fifty feet and then turned. A sign on the wall said *Apts. 118-132* with an arrow pointing to the left. Sixty feet to the left the hallway ended at another metal door with a crash bar labeled *PUSH TO EXIT*.

A sign at eye level said *Door can be opened in 15 seconds. Push until alarm sounds*. A fire alarm and a fire extinguisher hung on the wall beside the door.

Bettina grinned. She jerked the fire alarm. It rang and she leaned on the crash bar until it opened. Beyond the door was a parking lot. At least she wouldn't need to stumble across a field of gravel.

The occupants of the apartments began to stream out the doors, most clad in pajamas or robes.

Bettina walked gingerly across the sidewalk to the parking lot. She scanned both directions, considering her options. She didn't know where she was, but she was in deep trouble if the kidnappers returned before the fire department arrived. Her only defensive weapon was the crowbar.

On the other hand, the people living in the building were milling around in the parking lot or driving away. If the kidnappers returned, they would be unlikely to attempt to recapture her in the midst of the crowd.

She considered hiding in the bushes until the fire department responded. If she must walk on the pavement, she would, but it would be great if the fire department arrived in time to save her feet from further trauma.

A pair of headlights bounced up the entrance ramp and turned toward her, easing its way through the pedestrians. Her heart jumped and she jerked to a stop. She squeezed the crowbar instinctively. If these were the kidnappers, she could never outrun them. The headlights flashed high beams on and off. The driver's side window of a white Dodge Grand Caravan rolled down and the driver waved at her.

The minivan rolled to a stop. The driver's door and the second door opened, and Carlos McCrary hopped out. "Thank God you're safe."

———

Carlos McCrary

Was that Bettina? Yes! I had no idea how she escaped but she could tell me later. The important thing was that Gunner and I need not search the whole apartment complex to locate the specific maintenance closet Tavares had described.

I flashed my headlights. In the high-beam glare, her feet were streaked with red marks and splotches. I turned to Gunner. "You drive and take us to the closest hospital. I'll sit in the back with Bettina."

I popped both the left doors and jumped out. "Thank God you're safe." I rushed toward her and opened my arms.

Bettina started to throw her arms around my neck, then noticed she was holding a crowbar. She tossed it onto the sidewalk. It clanged on the concrete. "I won't need this after all."

She stepped into my embrace and squeezed me tight for a moment before looking up at me.

"How did you get here?"

"Long story. First, your feet are bloody enough that we should carry you to a hospital." Scooping her up in my arms, I carried her to the van. "Slip into this seat. I'll ride on the other side."

"My feet look worse than they feel, but the hospital is a good idea.

Once I escaped, I pulled the first fire alarm I saw. The fire department and the cops should arrive any second. Maybe I should wait and tell them it's a false alarm and why I set it off."

"I'd rather you didn't. If you talk to them in person, they'll want you to wait for an ambulance and their questions will delay you too long. We can drive you to the hospital quicker."

"Okay, let's roll," she said. "Who's your friend?"

"I don't believe you've met Gunner Knutson. He works with me."

"Thank you, Gunner. Chuck has mentioned you, and it's nice to meet you in person."

"My pleasure."

I scurried around to sit on the other side.

Gunner slipped into the driver's seat and told the GPS to navigate us to the nearest hospital.

The first police car and a firetruck arrived as we exited.

It was 4:30 in the morning in this part of Texas and 5:30 in Port City, but I called Gene Lopez anyway.

Four rings later he answered. "Since it's 5:30 in the morning, Chuck, I assume you located Sergeant Simpson."

"You said to call you once we located her, no matter what time it was. I am with Sergeant Bettina Simpson right now. We are driving her to the ER with non-life-threatening injuries. They will treat her and turn her loose. I doubt they'll admit her."

"That's great news, Chuck, but how bad are her injuries?"

"It's no big deal. The kidnappers took her shoes. She escaped in her bare feet and did some minor damage to her feet running across a graveled field."

"Does this mean I can refer the case to the Houston FBI?"

"Someone at the FBI may have been protecting Tommy Valley. The Houston FBI agent may have been duped by the rogue agents, or he or she is in on the scam. It's your call, but you don't know whom to trust. It might be safer to task this mission out of Port City."

In the silence I imagined Lopez's eyes as he considered the alternatives. He responded, "I'll fly to Houston with some agents this afternoon. May I speak to Sergeant Simpson? I need to take her statement so I can start things rolling from this end."

"Sure." I held the phone toward Bettina. "This is SAC Gene Lopez. He wants you to give a statement."

Bettina gave me a *stop* motion with her hand. "I should call my parents first. They're bound to be worried sick."

"Of course." I retrieved the phone. "Gene, Bettina wants to call her parents. I'll ask her to call you ASAP."

I disconnected and handed her the phone.

From listening to Bettina's side of the conversation with her parents, I learned they had not known she was missing. She gave them a toned-down version of the events, apologized for waking them, and called Gene Lopez.

"Good morning again, Special Agent Lopez. This is Detective Sergeant Bettina Simpson. Can you record this phone call? Good. I will dictate a preliminary statement."

Bettina related the events from the time of her abduction. She was thorough and unemotional—a true professional. She had progressed to describing her escape from Building 2 by the time Gunner rolled into the ER driveway. "Special Agent Lopez, we have arrived at the ER, and I should let them attend to my feet. I will call you back once the ER people finish. Yes, sir, thank you."

Gunner slipped the gearshift to *Park* and jogged into the ER. He reappeared pushing an empty wheelchair.

I wheeled Bettina into the ER lobby. We had to wait, so I briefed her on everything that had happened since she disappeared.

———

When the doctors and nurses finished with Bettina, Gunner pulled the Caravan around to the hospital entrance and an orderly rolled her out to the curb in a wheelchair. The orderly handed her into the back seat and Gunner put the minivan in gear. "Where to, boss?"

I leaned toward Bettina. "I recommend you don't return home until this is over. When Bartok doesn't find you where he stashed you, he could make another run at you to keep you from testifying. I'll rent you a room at the motel where Gunner and I are staying. Is that okay?"

"You believe Bartok will try to kill me?"

"He may know you couldn't testify to anything damaging, because they covered their tracks so well. However, I don't base battle plans on what the enemy will *probably* do. I plan based on what the enemy is *capable* of. And these guys are capable of murder."

I explained my theory that Bartok and Hawley planned to massacre everyone at the drug buy, including their own subordinate. "I could be wrong, but it's better to be cautious."

"I'll stay at your motel, Chuck. Stop at an all-night Walmart and let me buy some clothes and other necessities."

"Sure. On the way I'll stop at a 24-hour drive-thru and order us something to eat. At Walmart, you stay in the van and save your feet. I'll be your personal shopper."

That early in the morning Walmart was not crowded, and we were soon on the way to our motel.

Bettina said, "What's next for you?"

"Gene Lopez is flying to Houston this afternoon with a team of Port City agents. They're driving to our motel, and I'll give him everything I've collected. That and your statement should convince the FBI to arrest Bartok and Hawley."

"I hate to bring this up again, but what about Angie? Have you found out who killed her?"

A pulse of tension pounded behind my forehead. "Valley and two other men who kidnapped her. They killed her."

"Were the other two men Fajardo and Trojanik?"

"I'm certain Tommy Valley was one of Angie's kidnappers. I'll give my evidence to Lopez, and he'll charge Valley with kidnapping. I'm not a hundred percent certain that Fajardo and Trojanik were the other two. I'll confirm that with Valley before I give him to Lopez. And I'd bet Saco ordered the hit on Angie, so he is equally responsible—more actually."

"You figure Valley will rat on his accomplices? We know that Saco is a bad dude. No way Valley would do that."

In the front seat, Gunner overheard us. He glanced at me in the rearview mirror and winked. "Bettina," he said, "excuse me for interrupt-ing, but whatever Tommy Valley knows, he'll tell Chuck. I've worked with Chuck a long time and I've learned that, for important questions, it's all in the way Chuck asks."

Bettina's eyes widened. "What— what will you do to him?"

I gave her a smile that had no trace of humor. "I'll say *pretty please*."

We rode the rest of the way to the motel in silence.

TWENTY-SIX

Christian Amadeus Bartok

Bartok nosed the blue Suburban into the apartment parking lot. He tracked the driveway around the building, intending to park in a loading zone by the emergency exit.

As he made the final turn, he jerked the Suburban to a stop. "What the hell?"

A Houston firetruck and a Houston police black-and-white with their red and blue lights flashing blocked the driveway. Orange traffic cones marked the space between both emergency vehicles and the emergency exit door, which was propped open with another cone.

Bartok's heart began to race as he snicked the transmission into *Park*, tugged his ski mask off, and shoved it in his pants pocket. He peeled off his nitrile gloves and pocketed them. "Gerry, hide your mask and gloves."

Hawley removed his mask and gloves. "What's with the cruiser and firetruck?"

Bartok triggered the emergency flashers. "Maybe Detective Simpson escaped."

Exiting the SUV, he walked over to a firefighter who was stowing gear.

He showed his DHS credentials to the woman. "What's going on? Was there a fire?"

The firefighter continued stowing the gear. "*Nah*. False alarm. We're packing our gear to return to the station. The cops are inside trying to figure out who set off the alarm. Apparently there was something weird about it."

"What was it?"

"Huh?"

"What was weird about the alarm? You said a false alarm."

"You should ask the detective inside." The firefighter returned to stowing her gear.

Bartok stepped through the emergency door without touching anything. Halfway up the hall a uniformed police officer and a woman in business attire stood talking.

As he walked closer, Bartok noticed the storage closet door was missing from the frame. *Holy crap! Simpson did escape.*

The woman's phone rang. "Detective Rhodes," she answered. She listened for a moment. "Is Bettina okay? What hospital? Where is she now? Okay. Thanks, Royce."

Detective Rhodes turned to the cop. "You knew Detective Sergeant Bettina Simpson went missing?"

"Yeah, sure. Every cop in Houston is searching for her."

"That was Royce Wilson with Organized Crime. Turns out Simpson was kidnapped. She was held in this maintenance closet."

"You mean this one? She was in there?"

"Yeah, she escaped a couple hours ago. She's the one who pulled the fire alarm. She didn't recognize where she was, and she was injured. She summoned the fire department. Mystery solved. Royce said Simpson is safe. I'll call the CSIs. The kidnappers might have left fingerprints or something."

Bartok felt certain that he had left no fingerprints in or around the closet. He and Hawley had worn Covid masks also. Nevertheless, he or Hawley might have been seen. They had to get away from the apartments.

He stopped in the center of the hallway and patted his pockets as if he had forgotten something. He did an about-face and returned to his vehicle, cranked the engine, and slipped it in gear.

Hawley peered over his shoulder at the emergency door fading away behind them. "Where are we going? Where's Simpson?"

"The bitch escaped."

"Escaped?"

"Yes, you idiot. Don't you speak English? The bitch escaped. She slipped the closet door off its hinges and pulled the fire alarm."

Hawley's shoulders sagged. "We're screwed."

Bartok spoke through gritted teeth. "Not yet, we're not. There's no way Simpson knows who kidnapped her. Call Luisa. We can control the damage."

Hawley called Tavares. The call went straight to voicemail. "No good, Chris. Luisa's phone is turned off."

"I told her to catch up on her sleep. She could have turned her phone off or put it on *do not disturb*." Bartok pulled a U-turn. "We'll go to her apartment. Simpson's escape changes things. Now we have no hold on McCrary. Luisa can sleep once we decide what to do with that damned McCrary."

By the time they reached Tavares's apartment, the sky was bright enough for the Suburban's automatic headlights to turn off. Bartok parked in a visitor's spot. "Her car's here. Let's wake her."

The two men stepped on Tavares's porch and Hawley rang the doorbell. No answer.

"Ring it again, Gerry."

They waited another minute. Gerry spread his hands. "She's not home, but her car's here."

"This is a video doorbell," Bartok said. "If she's not home, she can access it from her cellphone."

"Yeah, but her phone is either off or silenced." Hawley banged on the door. "What now?"

"She has a personal phone in addition to her work phone. Let's check inside."

Bartok extracted a set of lockpicks from his jacket pocket. "The neighbors are asleep. She may carry a second phone to answer the doorbell. She could be viewing us now. Luisa," he said to the video doorbell, "we are concerned for your welfare. In case you were burglarized or assaulted. I'll pick your lock and make sure you are not injured inside."

Bartok opened the door. "Let's go." He led Hawley into the living room. "First, see if there are video cameras inside. You check the rooms to the right of the hall." In a few seconds, they met in the hallway. "No surveillance cameras inside on the left. How about the kitchen and guest room?"

"None. She's not here so she's not injured. What now, boss?"

"Go to the rooms you cleared and search for anything that might tell us where she went. I'll search the master suite."

Bartok started with the bathroom. A toothbrush holder with four slots sat beside the lavatory, empty. There was a smudge of white where one brush usually sat. Opening the cabinet drawers, he searched for a cosmetic kit. There wasn't one. Three pieces of a four-piece luggage set lined up at one end in the walk-in closet. One middle-sized case was missing, but Bartok noticed the indentation on the carpet where the case sat between trips. It was impossible to tell whether she packed shoes, underwear, and clothes, but Bartok saw enough: Luisa Tavares had packed a bag and left.

Bartok found the other agent in the kitchen rummaging through the drawers. "Anything useful?"

Hawley closed the drawer. "A calendar, but nothing to say where she went. There are clean dishes in the dishwasher. She washed dishes before she left but left before the wash cycle finished. Notice the *clean* sign lit on the panel."

"Yeah, one suitcase is missing, also her toothbrush. But we need her for D-Day tomorrow night."

Hawley scanned the kitchen, walked across and closed a cabinet door he had not quite shut. "Luisa could have figured out we aren't expecting terrorists. Who told her? Did Tommy Valley let something slip?"

"Valley has never met Luisa. But Valley had a run-in with McCrary when he first arrived in Houston. And McCrary clued the Houston cops concerning Valley's storage units. McCrary knows Valley and he's met Luisa. McCrary must be connected to her disappearance."

"You think Luisa flipped?"

Bartok waffled a hand. "Luisa has become a loose end. She could land us in federal prison for life. We should cut off that loose end."

"Boss, we knew from the get-go this couldn't last forever. I say it's time to pull our golden parachutes and bail out before this thing crashes and burns."

"We've invested months in this project, Gerry. We're tired and not thinking as clearly as we should. Let's knock off and grab some sleep. We can meet tomorrow for dinner. We'll think of something."

"What about McCrary, Chris?"

"McCrary may have blown our $9,000,000 payoff."

TWENTY-SEVEN

Carlos McCrary

I t was 8:00 a.m. by the time I checked Bettina into her hotel room and dropped Gunner at his room.

We had about 36 hours until the drug bust and—I assumed—Bartok and Hawley's machine-gun massacre.

"Bettina, Gunner and I have been awake over 24 hours. We all need sleep. Can you wait that long to eat?"

"Sure. Call me once you're awake. My feet are healing faster than I expected. I want to kiss you, but I have Dragon Mouth, and I'm too exhausted to clean up enough to give you a proper kiss." She kissed her fingertip and touched it to my lips.

I held her hand in mine and kissed her fingertip on the same spot. "My breath isn't the greatest either. I must have Dragon Mouth too."

"And a bonus—I stink worse than a locker room. The second you walk out the door, I hit the shower and brush my teeth. I plan to sleep forty days and forty nights—or until you wake me."

She pressed me toward the door. "Soon you can spend the night in my room. Or I can spend the night in yours. I recommend we celebrate my escape by making love until we both cry for mercy."

"I look forward to it once the dust settles." I pressed a few hundred-dollar bills into her hand. "In case something unforeseen happens, it's good to carry emergency cash until you can replace your credit cards. I'll call in a few hours."

I made it to my room and set an alarm for 4:00 p.m. Gene Lopez and his Port City crew were due to land at three o'clock. I stayed awake long enough to shower and brush my teeth. Dragon Mouth. That Bettina—so colorful.

The alarm woke me at 4:00, and I didn't recall going to bed.

I made coffee with the in-room coffee service. Following two cups and a fresh shave, I felt 80 percent recovered.

I checked my text messages. Gene Lopez had landed and was on his way to my motel.

I called Bettina. "Wake up, buttercup. How are you this morning—I mean 'this afternoon'?"

"I could eat a whole cow without cooking it. What room are you in?"

"You sure your feet are ready to walk?"

"I changed the bandages," she said. "My feet are better than you'd imagine. What room are you in?"

"Suite 149. I'll make coffee and send Gunner out for food."

I called Gunner. "Time for work, Gunner. Gene Lopez and his crew are on their way from the airport. Can you pick up food for us? I'll call Lopez and ask if he and his agents are hungry. Can you come to my suite at your early convenience?"

"Let me shave, shower, and such. Give me twenty minutes."

———

Gunner returned with our lunch orders as Lopez and two other federal agents arrived. The older one was a middle-aged woman named Alicia Fernandez. The second one was a younger man named Varticus King. Good thing I rented a suite. After introductions, we gathered at the table and Gunner passed out sandwiches and drinks.

I handed Lopez my burner phone labeled *Ball Hawk*.

"What's this?"

"It's a burner phone paired with another phone I gave to Luisa Tavares. For security reasons, I don't know where she is. Use that phone to call her. One of your agents can pick her up and take her statement. Find her an attorney and work out an immunity agreement first."

"Is she ready to cooperate?"

"Seems like it. She says Bartok duped her. She believed their operation was covert because of national security. She's a rookie, new to the DHS, started working undercover for Bartok and Hawley as a raw newbie. She's the one who told us where Detective Simpson was being held."

Lopez left the room with the phone, returning a few minutes later. "Agent Fernandez, I have Luisa Tavares on the phone. Find her location and remove her to our safe house and have her call her attorney. Do not question her until she has an attorney." He handed the phone to Fernandez. "Carry your sandwich with you. Here are my keys. I'll ride with Varticus."

Fernandez grabbed her sandwich and the phone. "Ms. Tavares, I am FBI Agent Alicia Fernandez." As she walked out the door, she said, "We will keep you safe and secure…"

Luisa Tavares was one less ball to juggle.

As we ate, Lopez interviewed Bettina to squeeze every relevant fact from her memory. He signaled he was through with Bettina. Gunner cleared the food remnants and trash from lunch.

"Gene," I said, "since this is an FBI case, Gunner and I will bow out. Your colleagues have our burner phone numbers. Ask Gunner or me about anything you need from us for your case."

"Are you driving back to Port City?"

"Gunner is. My Aunt Catharine lives twenty minutes away in Spring. I haven't seen her since Christmas. I'll have a meal with her and spend a couple days visiting family in Adams Creek. Shame to be a two-hour drive from my hometown and not visit them." I grinned. "I'd never hear the end of it."

Lopez chuckled. "My family is the same way." He pivoted to Bettina. "What about you?"

"My boss told me to take a few days' sick leave until I'm physically fit for duty. I intend to hide out until Bartok and Hawley are in custody. Now that Chuck mentions it, I might catch a ride with him to Adams Creek. I was born there too. You can call me anytime."

"All right." Lopez eased back from the table. "Agent King and I will adjourn to our own hotel. I'll text you both once we arrest Bartok and Howley."

"Before you go, Gene, did you discover who in the Houston FBI office deleted the file of Bartok and Hawley after they grabbed Tommy Valley from the Houston jail?"

"Yeah. She was a new agent Bartok snowed and hoodwinked into breaking the rules. She will have time to contemplate the consequences of breaking the rules in her new posting in Fairbanks, Alaska. Now, Agent King and I have things to do."

Bettina waited until the FBI contingent left the suite.

"What do you *really* plan to do, Chuck?"

"Ask Tommy Valley who kidnapped and killed my sister."

"After he confirms what you already suspect, then what?"

"I slash and burn them and piss on their graves, unless the FBI beats me to it."

"Of course, they'll beat you to Tommy Valley. Agent Fernandez is on her way to collect Tavares. Tavares will brief her regarding the phony mission."

"I doubt it. They'll provide her an attorney first, and the attorney will negotiate an immunity agreement. They won't have the agreement before the drug deal tomorrow night. No, I'll get to Valley first."

I handed Bettina an extra keycard to my suite. "Why don't you move to my room? I have no idea when Gunner and I will finish, but this suite is more comfortable than your room."

Bettina winked. "You read my mind."

TWENTY-EIGHT

Christian Amadeus Bartok

Bartok powered his Chevy Bolt up the ramp and slotted the car into a space beside the blue Suburban at the edge of the Denny's parking lot. Hawley waited in the Suburban with the engine running.

Bartok locked his Bolt and got into the Suburban's passenger seat. "You're worried how to stop Carlos McCrary, aren't you, Gerry?"

"Yeah. We don't know where he is since Bettina Simpson and Luisa Tavares disappeared."

"Here's the thing, Gerry: McCrary doesn't know where we are either. Neither Simpson nor Tavares knows where the drug deal is going down. Tommy Valley called me a few minutes ago. We ignore McCrary, Simpson, Tavares—all of them."

"We can't carry two H&K MP7 machine guns and expect to get the drop on a dozen gunmen. We expected Luisa, Valley, Fajardo, and Trojanik to be with us. She would be a third machine-gunner and the three bikers would carry pistols. Tavares is no longer on the team."

"Suppose we hijack the cocaine before it reaches the parking lot?"

"You mean steal fifty kilos of cocaine and forget the $5,000,000?"

"No. We intercept Saco and his guy with the duffle bag before they reach the Astros parking lot. Valley, Fajardo, and Trojanik are with *us*, not Saco. They plan to meet Saco and the Mexican courier in a grocery store parking lot in Richmond to escort the cocaine. That's over 30 miles from the Astros stadium. Saco believes Valley, Fajardo, and Trojanik will accompany him and the drugs to the Astros parking lot. We tell Valley to delay Saco in Richmond until the Mexican escorts leave, then we kill Saco. I'll loop Tommy in on the plan ahead of time. Once we control the coke, we complete the sale to the Cubans as planned. With Tommy, Al, and Troy, we have five guns and the element of surprise against the Cubans."

"You're out of your freakin' mind, Chris. If we get the drop on the gangsters—which I doubt—I wouldn't mind wiping out a bunch of scumbags, but not near innocent civilians. Even if there were no civilians there, the drug dealers have automatics. We're not twenty-year-old punks looking for a big score. We're senior citizens who scored millions of dollars over the last three decades. I say we abandon the project. Hell, we have plenty of money and too much to lose. Let's take the win and quit while we're ahead."

Bartok stared at his partner of many years. Gerry Hawley had grown old and timid before his time. If Hawley chose to quit, screw him. Bartok would use Valley and his two henchmen, and they would do this without his old partner.

"You may be right, Gerry. We've been through a lot together. Could be time to hang up our cleats. Let's have dinner with the wives Saturday night and tell them we're retiring."

Bartok shook hands. "Why don't you make the reservations and text me where to meet you?"

"What time Saturday night?"

"Mona and I are flexible. Pick a nice restaurant. Take whatever time you can." They shook hands. "It's been nice. Until Saturday... good luck."

He returned to his Bolt, where he called Tommy Valley.

———

Carlos McCrary

The GPS tracker stuck to Valley's Harley was at the apartment he shared with Lola Salazar. The sun was low in the west and the pavement lay in shadow when Gunner and I arrived.

The Harley was parked alone. I didn't see Fajardo's or Trojanik's bikes anywhere. That was no surprise. I would find the other two kidnappers later. First things first.

"Gunner, lurk between those two vehicles over there in case Valley is not in Lola's apartment. If he shows up from someplace else, hold him for me. You have plastic ties? Good. If he's home, come over and join us. We'll double-team him like we did at the Spoke and Sprocket."

A few apartment resident commuters filtered into the lot. I reached the bottom of the stairs simultaneously with a thirty-something woman in a pants suit. I made an "after you" gesture. She studied my face, smiled, and climbed the stairs. I let her move far enough ahead so she would know I wasn't stalking her. On the other hand, did she realize I was admiring her backside? It was a very nice backside, and I'm only human.

She turned left and paused when I reached the top. "You look familiar. Didn't I see you a couple of weeks ago at Lola Salazar's party?"

She stepped closer. "Yes, I remember your face, but I can't recall your name." She extended her hand, "I'm Marla Johansen."

What could I do? Only a jerk would ignore her, so I shook hands. "Carlos McCrary." Maybe this wouldn't take long. If Marla drove all the way from downtown, she might need to visit the bathroom.

She didn't let go of my hand. "I remember now. People call you Chuck, right?" She threw me a big smile. "How did you meet Lola, Chuck?"

Oh geez, she wanted to schmooze me. Probably angling for me to ask her out. I had no time for that, but I didn't want to be rude either.

"To tell the truth, Marla, I have business with Tommy and I'm late for our meeting." I shook her hand one more time and pulled loose. I turned slightly away. "Nice to see you again, Marla. Have a nice day."

Marla handed me a business card. "And you, Chuck. I hope to see you again sometime. That's my personal cell number on the card."

"One can never predict the future, Marla." I stepped firmly away. One less distraction to concern me.

I had paid the rent on Angie's apartment through the end of the month. I toured every room. Valley told me Angie gave keys to a lot of people, and I was gratified that nothing obvious had gone missing since my last visit. HPD's CSI team had left the apartment untidy when they processed Angie's flat.

Returning to Lola's and Valley's door, I knocked politely. No cop knock required. At least not yet.

The door bumped against the security chain, and Valley's eye peeked through the crack. "What do you want, McCrary?"

"We should talk, Tommy."

"So talk."

"Not through a slit in a doorway. You come out or I'll come in." I stepped back to encourage him to come out.

"I'm okay to talk through the crack."

"Tommy, within five seconds that door will open. Either you open it, or I kick it in. Your choice."

Valley rolled his eyes. "Okay, okay."

I signaled Gunner to join us.

Valley rattled the chain off and opened the door. I shouldered in, shoving him ahead of me. I left the door open for Gunner.

I pressed Valley toward the hall. "Let's go to your room."

Valley stumbled and regained his balance. "Not so fast, McCrary. I'm going, I'm going. Let me catch my breath."

As he rose upright, he turned to throw the sucker punch.

I grabbed his fist with my left hand. I crushed it hard and bent his wrist backward, forcing him to his knees. I didn't bother to punch him. Some people don't learn from their mistakes. Tommy Valley was one of them.

Clutching his fist, I hauled him back toward the front door. Gunner stepped in the doorway. "That's all I'm going to take, Valley. We're going next door."

I handed Angie's door key to Gunner. "Open Angie's door, will you, Gunner?"

Dragging Valley behind me, I shadowed Gunner into Angie's apartment. I flung Valley onto the living room floor and twisted the deadbolt.

Stepping to the dining room, I snatched a chair and set it in the middle of the kitchen.

"Gunner, please set Valley in this chair and fasten him with plastic ties."

"With pleasure, boss." He dragged Valley to the kitchen and pushed him into the chair. He reached into his pocket for plastic ties.

Valley tried to stand.

I gripped his right shoulder, squeezed it until he cried out, and tossed him into the chair. Holding him there with my hand, I waited for Gunner to fasten his ankles and wrists. "Valley, I have been gentle with you, but you keep trying to make things difficult. Try to stand up again and I will stop being polite."

I leaned close to his face. "*Capisce*?"

I could tell he intended to spit at me. I kicked his shin. "Don't try to cross me, Valley."

I lifted Angie's garnet earring from my pocket and held it inches from his nose.

His eyes grew wide. "Where did you get that? Did you steal it from my closet?"

Valley believed I searched his closet and uncovered the earring there. He didn't grasp that I knew it was Angie's.

I sighed for his benefit. "Gunner, please remove Valley's keys from his pocket."

Gunner did that, held them beside the key to Angie's apartment. "This one is the same brand as Angie's key."

"Valley," I said, "this is your best chance to keep your fingers in one piece. If I send Gunner into your closet to search the wooden box on the shelf, and he finds the mate to this earring, I'll break one of your fingers."

I stepped back to give him space. "Where is the mate to this earring?"

His shoulders drooped. "Where you said. It's in the box in my closet."

"Gunner, go to Valley's bedroom. It's the second one. There's a wooden box on the closet shelf. Bring me the mate to this earring."

"Roger that, boss." He left the door unlocked when he left.

I swung back to Valley.

"Next question—who else besides Fajardo and Trojanik were involved in kidnapping my sister?"

"Huh? Was Angie kidnapped?"

I grabbed the little finger of his left hand and bent it slowly backwards. It bent close to ninety degrees, and he screamed. "It was just the three of us. Nobody else. Nobody else, I swear."

"You three carried her to the building at the rear of Flathead Pipe Supply. Oh, that reminds me—the other buildings at Flathead have numbers painted on them. Why doesn't the building at the back have a number?"

"I never asked, man."

"What does Saco call that building when he tells you to take someone there? I mean, he wouldn't say 'Take this guy to the small building at the back with no number.' He has a nickname for the building. What does Saco call it?"

Valley shrugged. "Saco calls it 'the chipper.'"

A crash of nausea squeezed my gut. Valley had confirmed my worst fears regarding Angelina's fate. Saco sent someone to the chipper, and they disappeared forever. The images and odors from the building tumbled through my mind like an elephant stampede. My vision blurred and my gorge rose. I dashed toward the kitchen sink.

I nearly made it.

I remembered the mop and bucket were in the pantry. I finished cleaning my mess before Gunner returned.

Gunner handed me the garnet earring. "Right where you said."

I got my emotions under control while I closed the pantry door, then dropped the earring in the evidence bag with the other one. "Thanks, Gunner. I'll return these to Mother and Dad next time I visit Adams Creek."

"Regarding Saco," I said, "why did he order Angelina killed?"

Valley gazed toward the ceiling like he expected the heavens to open and a host of angels to descend to rescue him, or his Fairy Godmother would whisper in his ear and tell him what to say. Sadly for him, neither happened.

This time I seized his right thumb and twisted it toward his wrist. "As I keep twisting, the first thing to happen is your thumb will dislocate. Next, the bones will break, and the joint will rip. After that, the ligaments will tear loose. By then, your thumb can never be repaired by surgery. It might be amputated. It would be tough to play your guitar with no thumb, don't you think?"

Valley sobbed. "Okay, okay, okay. At first Saco didn't say to kill Angie. I don't think he even knew who she was. Lola showed me the party video the next day, and I spotted Saco and his crew sitting around the fire pit. I told him about it, and he sent me to bring Angie and the video back. He didn't say nothing about killing her."

"But when you and Fajardo and Trojanik captured her at the truckstop, she didn't have the video, did she?"

"No, so I called Saco and told him she didn't have it. He asked me where it was and did I search her apartment."

"Why was Saco so obsessed with the party video? Hell, there must be lots of photos of him floating around. Everywhere anyone goes nowadays, a security camera takes their picture. Lots of people have Saco's picture."

"Yeah, but they don't know they have it. Security cameras capture pictures of hundreds of people. Maybe thousands. Anybody looking at a security camera recording doesn't know that one of those hundreds of anonymous faces is Saco's. At the party, she videoed him with other gang members. The cops could use those other guys' faces to identify Saco as a cartel member."

"So the guy is paranoid? Is that it? He kills an innocent woman just because she took his picture? Surely he had some other reason."

Valley shrugged. "What else can I say, man? Everybody knows that Saco is nuts. Just plain crazy."

I couldn't believe Saco had ordered my sister's killing over something this inconsequential, this… trivial. Angie probably didn't even know who Saco was when she made the party video. Then Valley told her, and she bolted. To Saco, Angie was a mosquito buzzing around his kitchen that he tells his maid to swat. Rage welled up within me that Saco had so little regard for human life. Angie was not an insect!

Valley continued to talk, and I wrenched my attention back to what he was saying.

"Then Saco said he was tired of messing with her. Said we should take her to the chipper."

The last link in the evidence chain snapped into place. The proof that Angie was dead. My rage condensed, compressed, and solidified into a glowing coal of intensity, of fervor, of *lust* for revenge. A lust I might not be able to satisfy. With difficulty, I suppressed my emotions, walling them up for a future time when I hoped to give them full expression.

If the cops or the FBI didn't get to Saco first.

I kept my face impassive. Acted like the revelation was of minor importance.

Saco gave the order to murder my sister. Saco was the man who jerked the puppet strings. Valley and his two thugs were the puppets. The Three Stooges pulled the trigger, but Saco aimed the pistol. I could live with letting the FBI catch and punish the Three Stooges, but Saco was *mine*.

"Valley, where and when is the drug buy supposed to happen?"

He explained, and I asked clarifying questions. Who else would be there? How likely were other members of either *Tres Equis* or the Cuban gang to show? When? Was the time flexible? What could make the time shift either earlier or later? Where would the exchange occur?

I grilled him for half an hour. He didn't resist. I didn't twist any fingers or threaten him further. Like he said: He was cooperating. Why?

The interview was over, so I turned him lose.

Gunner locked Angie's door behind Valley. "That was too easy, Chuck. Something's fishy."

"I agree, Gunner. There is other related information he didn't give us. But I have no conflicting evidence to prove he was lying. Let's go with his info until we learn better."

I called Gene Lopez. "Gene, I have more information on the project your suspects have planned. Can Gunner and I meet you somewhere?"

Lopez gave me his hotel name. "I'll be there in a half hour. Park your Caravan in the west parking lot and I'll come to you."

"We'll see you there."

I briefed Lopez on everything I knew concerning the planned drug buy. Let me rephrase that: I briefed him on everything I *thought* I knew.

The FBI agent scratched notes in a small spiral notebook.

"They make the exchange in the parking lot while the Houston Astros baseball game is going on," Lopez confirmed, "and it's gonna be a night game?"

"Yeah. According to Tommy, the *Tres Equis* guys and the Cuban gangsters from New Jersey have not done business together before. They figure a parking lot in a public place is the safest way to keep anybody from surprising anybody else."

Lopez studied his computer screen. "We would have nowhere to hide our agents to watch for the drug exchange. There are hundreds of parking spaces. That one block measures 500 feet on a side and has nine or ten driving aisles, depending on how you count them. No reserved spaces. It's first-come, first-served. We can't predict where the buyers and sellers will meet. If the suspects arrive at the same time, they blend with the other traffic and park at random. But their vehicles will be adjacent, and we'll be on the outside looking in."

He turned the screen where I could see it.

"What do you plan to do?"

Lopez studied the monitor, switched it to Street View, and moused the image around the entire block. "There's one gate in the middle of each side. Four ways to enter and exit. We could control four gates easily."

"But there's no fence. Anyone on foot could run through dozens of pedestrian passes between the hedges. Hell, they could run a car or truck through them. The curb is low enough to bounce over. The gates are designed to collect parking fees, not to keep anyone in or out, and certainly not anyone in a motor vehicle."

We studied the monitor.

"Okay, Gene, let's say you station four vehicles crammed with agents in the lot ahead of time, one in each quadrant. You tail the gangsters to the lot with one unmarked vehicle with agents wearing Houston Astros baseball caps. Your tail vehicle shadows the bad guys to the vicinity where they park. Your tail notifies the waiting agents where the drug dealers park. There will be enough confusion with baseball fans arriving that your agents could approach on foot. No one will notice them if they dress like fans. You spread your guys within two or three parking spots of where the drug dealers park."

Lopez swung his gaze to the ceiling then to me. "Not a bad plan."

"Glad you like it. On a related matter, Gene, Bartok and Hawley plan to hijack the drug buy. If they're there, you'll have three competing teams. Bartok and Hawley may assume your agents are bad guys. They might hose everyone there.

"How are you progressing with Luisa Tavares's plea deal and cooperation? Do you have enough to nail Bartok and Hawley for kidnapping Sergeant Simpson before they arrive at the drug deal?"

"We sequestered Tavares in a safe house this morning. Her lawyer arrived a couple of hours ago. The lawyer and our DOJ guys will negotiate the details tonight. We can interview her in the morning."

"Does that give you time to apprehend Bartok and Hawley?"

"Depends on whether they're in the vehicles we know about. All of them have GPS, but they might change vehicles..." Gene shrugged. "We do the best we can."

"If Bartok and Hawley arrive at the parking area with machine guns, you risk civilian casualties."

"That risk makes me want to let them make the exchange and tail them and arrest them on a street somewhere. But, if they make the exchange during the game, and the fans have left the parking area, we go in hot and hard," he said.

"And if there are innocents in the vicinity when the exchange happens...?" I asked.

"I signal everybody to stay hidden."

———

I called Bettina from Lopez's hotel parking lot.

"Gunner and I are finished for the night. Shall I bring takeout back to the suite?"

"Yeah. Bring me a Korean pork Bento Box. Make sure the Bento Box includes kimchi. And I need chopsticks."

"I haven't eaten Korean food in months."

"And Chuck…" she added, "if they have it, bring me a bottle of Soju. It helps me sleep. My body clock is off schedule from the last few days."

Thirty-five minutes later, Gunner and I picked up the food and arrived at the motel. Gunner opened the Caravan door and grabbed his sack of food. "I'll leave you and Bettina to eat alone. I'll climb in bed soon as I finish eating. Call me in the morning." He walked down the sidewalk to his room.

I called Bettina's burner so I wouldn't surprise her by opening the door.

As I held my keycard to the door, Bettina opened it. "Come in. I'll carry the sacks." She peered over my shoulder. "Where's Gunner?"

"He went to bed early. Carried his food to his room. Should you be on your feet? Your soles were cut pretty bad."

"*Nah.* The blood on my feet when you found me looked worse than it was. I changed the bandages. I'll be better with a good night's sleep."

She positioned the sacks on the table and unpacked the food. "As long I don't do jumping jacks barefooted, I'll be okay."

As she set our plates, I started to brief her on recent developments. "On second thought, I have to email my parents the same news. You can read it over my shoulder."

"Read it out loud as you type."

I sent the email and Dad called in a few seconds.

"Dad, can I put the phone on speaker? Bettina should listen to our conversation. She helped with the case from the get-go. Hell, without her, we couldn't have solved it."

"Sure, son. Hello, Bettina. Andrea and I appreciate you helping us with Angie's disappearance."

"Glad to do it, sir. Here's Chuck."

"I assume you have questions," I said.

"First one is to confirm that you're certain Angie is dead, and there is no doubt that Tommy Valley was responsible."

"That's correct."

"I presume you recorded Valley's confession. Can you give it to the police so they can arrest him for murder?"

"I didn't record the conversation with Valley. He was under duress. His confession would never be admissible in a courtroom. But I am now certain of the identities of all four people who are responsible for Angie's death."

We talked a few minutes more, then wished each other good night.

Bettina dished out the food on her own plate and set the table with her own silverware. She preferred chopsticks.

I forked a piece of bulgogi.

Bettina smiled. "You don't use chopsticks, do you?"

"Too much work. I promise to use chopsticks if I ever travel to Korea, China, or Japan. Until then…" I forked the bulgogi into my mouth.

She gave me a smug smile. "What are your plans tomorrow?"

Bettina rolled a bit of rice in a kimchi leaf using her chopsticks and stuck it in her mouth.

"Now you're just showing off."

She smiled and sipped her Soju. "Regarding your plans for tomorrow…"

"I'll scout the Astros parking lot."

"Is Lopez letting you join his crew for the takedown?"

"Of course not. Lopez won't realize I'm there."

"*Ah*. You'll be in stealth mode observing the drug deal from afar?"

"Don't know. I'm playing this by ear. A case is a living thing. It evolves and matures. Evidence I considered last week can look different, or mean something else, or reveal a new significance when I reexamine it from a new viewpoint in time or space."

I waffled my hand. "I don't tell you everything, so I won't ask you to lie to the cops. Thus far, you can tell them anything I have done in your presence or told you. *No problema*."

Bettina's eyes gleamed. "Listen, buster, Bartok and Hawley engineered this kidnapping nightmare. And I do mean nightmare. When they captured me a second time, I figured I wouldn't survive. If you think I'll consent to hang out at the hotel while you chase the bad guys, you are kidding yourself. I've been on this case since the beginning, and I *deserve* to be there at the takedown."

"Bettina, you do deserve to be at the finale. And if you were physically fit, I'd say yes, but you're not 100% and I can't protect you with just myself and Gunner."

She flourished her chopsticks like a conductor's baton, punctuating her words. "My feet should be good tomorrow morning. If I can't keep up, I'll stay in the car. You know I can take care of myself, so don't blow any smoke up my skirt about protecting me. I've been a cop longer than you were, smart guy."

I raised my hands in surrender. "I admit when I'm beaten. Besides, you're correct about my reluctance to place a woman at risk. Part of me lives in the twentieth century."

"*Humph*. Twentieth? Try the nineteenth," she said.

But she smiled.

"On another matter, Royce Wilson is obtaining a search warrant for all of Flathead Pipe Supply's buildings. Luisa told me they left your car and your purse and other belongings in another part of Building 2. Call Royce and he'll bring your phone and personal effects."

"Why the hell didn't you tell me earlier? I've been dreading the phone calls I need to make to straighten out the mess from my purse disappearing."

"With the excitement today, I forgot. I'm sorry." I handed her my phone. "Royce's number is in the directory. It's not too late to call him. I'm sorry I forgot to tell you."

She patted my hand. "I forgive you, hot stuff. This day has been filled with chaos for all of us."

Bettina telephoned Royce. He had her purse and her car. He asked where to bring her property.

"Could you bring my car and belongings to Chuck's motel tonight? I'm going to bed soon, but you can lock my car and leave the key at the front desk. You could ask a black-and-white to drive you home… That's great, Royce. I owe you one. I'll text you the address."

She disconnected and handed my phone back. "I prefer to use my own equipment and my own car. Royce said he'll bring it here ASAP."

Bettina finished her Soju and chunked the bottle in the trash. "Too bad they don't provide a recycle bin for guests." She borrowed my fork to fish the last tidbits of vegetables from the compartments in the Bento Box.

"Now you use a fork?"

"I'm no fanatic about chopsticks. For some tasks, a fork is better."

She dumped her to-go box in the trash. "We both have kimchi breath. I intend to brush my teeth and give you a serious good-night kiss. I will sleep in the same bed with you, but I am too tired to make love to my usual high standards." She winked. "But, FYI, when I wake tomorrow, I'll be rested and randy."

She closed the bathroom door behind her.

I decided to let her fall asleep before I went to bed. I caught up on my other emails.

Tomorrow was another day…

TWENTY-NINE

Thursday morning Bettina and I lolled in bed until 8:30. She was right; if she didn't do jumping jacks, she was good to go.

My week-old beard itched something awful, but Bettina loved the way it tickled. I shaved my neck which made me look like a man with a short, fashionable beard instead of a homeless drifter.

I needed to contact Felicia Moreno aka Desiree, but I didn't know her work schedule. Instead of waking her with a ringing phone, I composed a text for her, then proofread it.

You said to call anytime if you could help with Angie or anything else. I need your help with something else. Please call me at your earliest convenience.

I debated whether the reference to "anything else" might give her the wrong idea. I edited the message down to:

You said to call anytime if I needed your help. Please call me at your earliest convenience.

Yeah, that would be okay. I tapped the *send* button.

Bettina didn't join Gunner and me for breakfast. She went to buy comfortable shoes. She claimed her feet were okay, but they would bother her if she walked far. The comfortable shoes were more important than breakfast.

Gunner and I used my GPS to locate an IHOP. Our food arrived as Felicia Moreno called.

"Good morning, Carlos. This is Felicia. You called?"

"Do you know Saco's new phone number?" Royce Wilson had tried to ping Saco's phone and the old number was no longer working. Most gang leaders change numbers often. But if Saco was keeping in touch with Felicia…

"Sure thing. I'll send it to you soon as we finish. Anything else I can do? I make a *fabuloso* French fish soup."

"I love fish soup, but Bettina and I are still tight."

"Keep me on the list, Chuck. I'm okay with being a backup girlfriend."

"Thanks for the offer, Felicia, but I still pass. Anyway, you deserve to be someone's only girlfriend, not merely a backup."

Felicia's text arrived with Saco's new number. I laid the phone on the table in front of Gunner. I sopped my pancake in strawberry syrup.

Gunner eyed my phone. "You gonna send Saco's number to Gene Lopez?"

I waggled my hand. "I haven't decided."

"And I suppose sending it to Royce Wilson is not being considered."

"Right."

"You want your shot at Saco first."

"You okay with that?"

Gunner swabbed his French toast in maple syrup to finish the last of his breakfast.

"Considering the times you saved my butt, I'm okay with almost anything you suggest. That doesn't mean I agree with the vigilante justice, but I'll go along. But suppose Bettina joins us today. She's a sworn Law Enforcement Officer. How will she feel about you targeting Saco for your own justice?"

"I'll ask her. If she objects to me dealing with Saco my way, I'll send Lopez and Royce the number. They can fight over whose case he is." I chased the last of the strawberry syrup with my last fork of pancakes.

"As long as I've known you, you haven't cared very much about other people's opinions. Why Bettina? Are you getting serious about her?"

That question caught me by surprise. Perhaps I'd been too close to the trees to see the forest.

"Good question, Gunner. I'll cogitate on that."

Gunner finished his coffee. "If we go after Saco and don't handle him, that means you and I will be dead. Maybe Bettina too, if she goes with us."

"Yeah, well, a vanishingly small possibility does exist. That's why I'll ask her."

"We could leave without her, boss…"

"Not gonna happen. I said she could be there for the takedown—at least Bartok's and Hawley's takedowns. It's personal for her. More personal than it is for me."

"Could be that's for the best. Like I said, I understand you even though I don't agree with you."

I texted Saco's number to Captain Jorge Castellano of the Port City PD.

Jorge, where is this number now, and where has it been for the last 24 hours? It involves Angelina's case.

"Okay, Gunner, Bettina should be back at the motel with her comfy shoes. Let's roll."

The drug deal was scheduled for 8:30 that night. I didn't expect the drug dealers to be prompt, but that was the schedule. That should allow time for us to deal with Saco assuming I could find him, but we didn't have time to waste either.

Jorge's email arrived by the time we were back at the motel to gear up. He gave me the coordinates and times of every stop Saco's phone had logged in the last twenty-four hours.

I loaded an online map of Harris County and input Saco's current coordinates. "Hmm. He's in Richmond. Why would Saco go to Richmond?"

Bettina studied the screen. "Switch to satellite view."

I did. "Is that a vacant field?"

"Not today, it isn't," she said. "This week the field is a pop-up flea market. I read it in my news feed."

"Why would Saco visit a flea market?"

"Perhaps he's shopping for a set of antique China."

Gunner snapped to attention and threw me a textbook salute. "Let's find out, boss."

Bettina geared up with her weapons, her detective shield, and two pairs of handcuffs.

"What are those for?" I asked.

"To arrest Bartok and Hawley if we find them. This is personal."

Gunner grinned at her. "You go, girl."

———————

We merged onto I-69.

Gunner half-turned in the passenger seat. "Chuck, say we locate Saco, what is our mission?"

The ember of vengeance in my gut flared a little, then died down. I didn't need it yet. "If you asked me that question five years ago, I would say the mission was to kill Saco, Valley, Fajardo, and Trojanik and piss on their ancestors' graves." I glanced at him before returning my gaze to the highway. "That and to get away with it."

Gunner nodded once. "They murdered people. Death-penalty crimes in Texas."

"Also in Florida, but just because a bad guy deserves to die doesn't give me a legal right to execute him without a judge and jury. Yes, they killed Angelina and her husband Teodoro. And God knows how many other victims of either the woodchipper or selling them the drugs to overdose."

"An eye for an eye," Gunner said.

"Right. But now…"

"What's changed?"

I noticed Bettina leaning forward from the second-row seat. So far, she had remained silent but attentive.

"I've learned to contemplate my actions in a wider circle. Everyone's actions cause ripples that spread a long way, especially mine because my actions are often risky. If I go vigilante and dispense frontier justice to Saco or any other bad guys—even if the DA says it's a righteous shoot—the big stink on the local news would spatter mud on Bettina because of her association with me. I don't want to hurt her career."

What I was thinking, but didn't say, was those bad effects would only happen if I were caught. But I had never killed anyone unless I had no other option.

"Don't worry, Chuck," Bettina said. "I'm with you a hundred percent."

"That's the point, Bettina. I am no longer one hundred percent certain that, in this case, my direct action—our direct action—is justified."

Gunner said, "No one knows Bettina is helping us, Chuck."

"Several Houston cops know, including Royce Wilson and Art Devlin, and Devlin dislikes Bettina for some reason. He will go out of his way to discredit her. Rule Ninety-nine, Gunner. *Eventually, everything becomes known.* Never count on anything staying secret forever."

"I remember now: That's why you wouldn't let us kill the Chinese soldiers that murdered Phil Franks and kidnapped me."

"Yep, that's when I formulated Rule Ninety-nine. *No one keeps a secret forever.* If the media criticize me, it stains Bettina even though she wasn't involved. She doesn't deserve that. It would also disturb my family if I risked my own life and reputation. And it would be big news in Port City, where some people consider me a cowboy with a loose-cannon reputation. The shade people throw at me impacts anyone who works with me: you, Snoop, Jorge, even the attorneys who represented me in the past."

"I don't care that people think I'm guilty by association, Chuck."

"You may not care, Gunner, but I do. If you or Snoop or Jorge—hell, even Tank Tyler—if any of you are mauled in the media, it shouldn't come from me committing some half-baked act that I could have avoided."

Gunner shrugged. "Whatever."

He lifted his coffee from the drink holder, tipped it for the last sip, and tossed the empty in the litter bag. "You didn't answer my question. What is the mission?"

"In an ideal world, we capture Saco and call Gene Lopez to take him off our hands."

Gunner grunted. "However, in the real world, Saco won't be alone. What then?"

I kept my gaze firmly ahead. "Gunner, until now I haven't planned that far ahead. As usual, I've been improvising as events unfold until you asked me to define the mission. You know me: I'd fight a forest fire with a water pistol. I always assume that, in the heat of the moment, I will make the right decision."

I cut my eyes to him, then to the road. "But that's not fair to you or Bettina. Now that you asked the question, I've decided to confer with Gene Lopez."

"Chuck, I would follow you to the gates of hell, but I'm glad you're bringing in the FBI. This thing is way bigger than when we started."

I checked my mirrors, tapped the turn indicator, and curved into the exit lane. "Let's stop for coffee, and I'll call Lopez."

We stopped at a Starbucks in the next block. Sometimes it seems like there's a Starbucks on every block. And that's a good thing.

Bettina opened the side door. "I crave a breakfast sandwich. I'll buy the coffee. I'll use some of the $300 you gave me last night."

Gunner lifted his tablet from a pocket in his camo pants. "I'll track us on a satellite view of the area."

Bettina went into Starbucks, and I called Gene Lopez.

"I'm kinda busy, Chuck. Can this wait?"

"From those phone coordinates you sent me, I know where Saco is right now."

"Hold on a sec." Lopez spoke to someone else in the room. "It's Chuck McCrary. He has Saco's location. Can you go with a handful of agents? Try to intercept him before the drug trade?"

The other person said, "Can I talk to him?"

"Chuck, Agent King wants to speak to you."

There was a short pause. "Chuck, this is V.K. King. Thanks again for the sandwich yesterday."

"You're welcome, V.K. An army travels on its stomach. I figured y'all might not have eaten. How can I help?"

"Where is Saco?"

"First, let me give you his current cellphone number so you can track his phone." I read Saco's number to the agent. "Right now, his phone is in Richmond, Texas, 30 miles from Houston. The location shows as vacant land, but Bettina Simpson says it's a pop-up flea market this week."

"There are bound to be innocent people at a flea market. If we try to arrest him there, there could be casualties."

"Right, but it takes an hour, best case, to reach there with Houston traffic. My friends Gunner and Bettina, whom you met yesterday, are with me, and we are halfway there. The location I have is one hour old. You'll want to ping his phone while you and your team are on the way. Assuming I can locate him, we'll tail him until you arrive with the cavalry."

"Sounds good, Chuck. I'll send you my phone number, in case your plans change. We'll see you when we see you."

Bettina pushed through the Starbucks door with a paper bag in her hand. She walked to the Caravan and handed two coffee cups to Gunner and buckled her seatbelt. "Let's roll."

"Lopez is sending V.K. and a team of agents to meet us in Richmond." Gunner wedged my coffee in the drink holder, and I drove away.

———

The flea market covered ten acres. A mile before the entrance, roadside yard signs advertised *The Famous Floating Flea Market: Knick-knacks, Antiques, Collectibles and Junque.* One side of the tract was filled with a dozen grassy aisles lined on either side with a hundred or more vendors' tents. The rest of the land was a grassy parking area already half full.

We spent the better part of an hour searching the parking lot for Saco's vehicle. I counted twelve black SUVs in the giant parking area. I started sending their license plate pictures to Jorge. The seventh one was registered to Escondido Sendero LLC. If Saco had driven anything other than the black Lincoln Navigator, we might never have located the correct vehicle since he and his phone were no longer with the car.

"Bettina, Gunner and I will do a lot of walking. You should stay in the Caravan, and we'll search for Saco. I'm pretty sure we won't arrest him in a flea market. Too many innocent bystanders."

"Sure. Leave the keys in the ignition. Hell, leave the A/C on. Call me when you spot him."

A heavy cloud bank was pushing in from the east, and shadows scudded across the flea market. I scented moisture in the wind.

Gunner stuck a GPS tracker under the Navigator, and we scoured the rows of booths for a familiar face.

Eventually we hit paydirt. I rang Bettina.

"We located Saco. He's with Valley, Fajardo, and Trojanik. Gunner, you see him? He's wearing an Astros hat and sunglasses, but it's him."

"What's he doing at a flea market?"

"He's shopping for a set of antique dishes."

Bettina laughed.

Gunner grinned. "Or not, boss."

"The more interesting question is why didn't Valley tell me about this side trip to Richmond on the day of the drug deal?"

"Makes you question what else he left out, doesn't it," Bettina said.

"Saco came here to meet someone, and since the drug deal is less than nine hours away, it could be related. He could be here to collect the drugs from the *Tres Equis* courier. I'll leave the phone on and stick it in my pocket. You can eavesdrop on what's happening, and my hands will be free."

"Thanks, Chuck. I'll use my phone to record the call. Just in case..."

"Good idea."

Gunner and I walked past row after row from fifty yards away, lost in the crowd of shoppers and sellers.

"Bingo. Don't make any sign, Gunner. Saco's body language says he spotted the man he's here to meet. We don't know which one he is."

Saco beckoned Valley to his side and talked in his ear. He made gestures with his hand, directing Valley to where the other man was.

"Stay on Saco, Gunner. I'll shadow Valley."

Valley nodded to Saco and walked purposefully to the end of the aisle. He skipped two aisles over. I skipped one aisle and advanced parallel to Valley. He disappeared and reappeared as he snaked through the crowd.

Valley stopped near two men I recognized and spoke softly.

"Bettina, Valley met Ramon Santos and Val Torres. They're the men Saco huddled with when Angie videoed the party at the porn house."

Valley's lips moved but he was too far away for me to hear him. Santos and Torres stared at him like a cat eyes a canary. They listened for a moment. Then Valley wheeled and retraced his steps. "Bettina, Santos and Torres are trailing Valley from ten yards behind."

I spotted Gunner and Saco in the next aisle. Saco stepped toward the parking lot. He must not have seen an antique tea service he fancied.

Valley led the new men to the edge of the lot and exchanged a few words. "Bettina, the three men are at the parking area. Valley is following them. I believe he'll ride in their vehicle. Yes, it's a dirty crew-cab pickup truck with Oklahoma plates coated with red dirt. I can't read the plates. I'm disconnecting now. Gunner and I will be there in a few minutes."

The clouds darkened and the breeze freshened. I checked my weather app. Thirty percent chance of rain within the next two hours. Forty percent chance of thunderstorms later this afternoon.

I zoomed in on the Oklahoma plates and snapped three photos. I sent the pictures to V.K. and Lopez. One of them might enhance the pictures and read the letters and numbers. Santos and Torres sat in front and Valley in back.

Saco and Fajardo and Trojanik walked toward the Navigator. Fajardo drove and both vehicles joined the line queueing at the exit.

Gunner appeared at my elbow. "You noticed?"

"Yeah. Let's play follow-the-leader, but from a half mile behind."

Gunner tapped my arm. "You ain't gonna believe this, boss, but take a gander over there."

DHS Agent Bartok, wearing old blue jeans and a denim jacket topped by an Astros baseball hat, was unlocking his Chevy Bolt.

"Where's Hawley?" Gunner asked. "Bartok doesn't go anywhere without Hawley. Do you see the blue Suburban?"

"No. He must be in another vehicle. We'll keep our eyes open. See if you can find his Suburban with the tracker I put on it. The battery should still be good."

Gunner and I returned to our minivan.

The Oklahoma pickup bounced across the rutted field toward the road. The Navigator fell in behind it. Bartok's Bolt stayed put.

Gunner booted his tablet. A few seconds later, he shook his head. "The blue Suburban ain't showing. He must have found the tracker and dumped it." He set the tablet aside.

"Bartok stuck a GPS tracker on one or both of the Oklahoma pickup or Saco's Navigator, or he's monitoring the Navigator's internal GPS."

"He could hang back out of sight, and he might spot us," Gunner said.

"Nah. We're in a white van with Texas license plates," Bettina said, "and Chuck has a beard and a Houston Texans ballcap and sunglasses. Bartok has never seen you, Gunner. I will sit in the back row of seats. With the window tinting, he won't see me."

I tapped the phone emblem on my Caravan's screen and told the Bluetooth to dial V.K.'s number.

The FBI agent's voice carried from the radio. "Hey, Chuck. I received the picture of the pickup. What's the story on the truck?"

"We followed Saco to a giant flea market. He's in a black Lincoln Navigator. There are three bikers with him, Tommy Valley, Al Fajardo, and Troy Trojanik. In the flea market, Saco met Ramon Santos and Val Torres. They are driving the pickup. They might have driven to Mexico to buy the fifty kilos of coke. We tailed them to the flea market, and we spotted Chris Bartok in his Chevy Bolt. You have his plate number."

"What's Bartok doing there?"

"Probably tracking them like we are. We're staying behind Bartok."

"Is Hawley with him?" V.K. asked. "We're still 15 minutes out."

"No clue. We assume Hawley is driving another vehicle we haven't spotted. Bartok hired the three bikers to double-cross Saco. The five of them might ambush Saco and the guys in the pickup and steal the cocaine. I predict Bartok and Hawley will then try to kill the three bikers. I planted a GPS tracker on Saco's Navigator and we're monitoring him from a half mile back. Soon as we figure out where they're going, we'll call you."

"My people will tap the GPS in the Navigator and the one in the Bolt. We can track them as well as you."

I laughed. "Better. I'll call you when they reach their destination."

———

The pickup truck slowed in the right lane. The Navigator hung back half a block. Bartok narrowed the gap between himself and the SUV.

Bettina leaned over my shoulder. "Whatever we do today, Chuck. I *personally* plan to slap the cuffs on Bartok and Hawley."

"Bartok and Hawley are important, yes. But the cartel members are more deadly to the public. They must be our top target. You may need to abandon Bartok and Hawley to the tender mercies of the FBI."

Bettina gave me a hard look. "I intend to *personally* slap handcuffs on Bartok, and Hawley too. You and Gunner can cover the cartel members, but the kidnappers are personal with me. *Capisce?*"

I saluted. "Yes, *ma'am!*"

I closed the space on the pickup. It turned into a parking lot at a shopping mall. The Navigator followed and turned right, no longer trailing the pickup.

I accelerated and entered the lot, searching for the Navigator.

The shopping mall was ancient, waiting for a developer to raze it and build something fashionable. A six-bay tire store bracketed the parking lot from the corner opposite the mall.

Customer cars occupied the spots closest to the mall entrance and filled less than half the lot.

Where the hell was the Navigator? "Gunner, look for the Navigator on your tablet."

I called V.K. and gave him the address of the shopping mall. "Watch for a sign saying *Bluebonnet Plaza*. How far out are you, V.K.?"

"Seven minutes."

Gunner consulted the GPS tracker monitor on his tablet. "The Navigator should be a hundred yards ahead and to our right."

I idled in that direction and spotted the dirty pickup roaming the rows of parking. I rolled across the end of the rows and glimpsed the Navigator. The pickup slipped into a spot next to it.

Scattered raindrops streaked the windshield.

"V.K., the pickup parked beside the Navigator. Oh, crap. Bartok just arrived. He's parking his Bolt between two bigger vehicles. He picked that spot so the drug dealers wouldn't see him approach. No sign of Hawley."

"Chuck, we can't allow a gunfight in a crowded parking lot. Can you delay them until we get there?"

The lot was not crowded, but I appreciated V.K.'s intent.

"What do you expect me to do? Wave a white flag and arrange a truce until you arrive with the cavalry?"

"Chuck, we're six minutes out. Improvise."

Okay." I twisted partway toward Bettina. "V.K. asked me to delay. Can you reach the rifle behind your seat?"

"Sure." She clicked off her seat belt and leaned over the seat back. "I have it."

"Hand it to Gunner."

I slid the Grand Caravan along the driving lane behind the pickup and Navigator and buzzed down the passenger window. "Shoot out a tire on the Navigator and one on the pickup. That's delay whatever they have planned."

Gunner unfastened his seat belt. "I could shoot a hole in Bartok's tire too. We show Bartok that we're here, and he might reconsider starting a shootout."

"Good idea. Go for it."

"Delay the gunfight," V.K. had asked. It was still four minutes until the FBI arrived.

Gunner swung to his right, extending the barrel of the Varmint rifle through the window. "Slow... slower... walking speed."

Even with the suppressor, the shots were loud enough for a middle-aged couple parking their car in the next row to turn and gape.

The rear of the Navigator settled on one side.

Three of the Navigator's doors flew open. Saco jumped from the SUV with a Heckler & Koch MP7 machine gun. Fajardo and Trojanik tumbled out holding handguns beside their legs.

Gunner fired again and the pickup's right rear tire emitted a puff of dust. The truck tire settled onto the rim. I slammed the accelerator.

In my side mirror, I watched the pickup's doors on the right side open and three more gunmen rolled out. They each carried H & K MP7s and crouched between the pickup and the Navigator. That made four machine guns and two handguns that I could see.

The middle-aged man who heard the shots studied the situation and began tapping his phone.

I trusted he was calling 9-1-1.

I spun left at the end of the driving lane and raced toward Bartok's car. Delay, delay, delay. The FBI was drawing closer every second.

After Gunner shot a hole in the Bolt's tire, I turned and jammed to a stop seventy yards away where we watched the men from the three disabled vehicles stare back at us.

The six gunmen we'd lured from their vehicles loitered nearby, weapons at the ready.

Seventy yards was far enough for them to see we weren't planning to advance. At the same time, they couldn't shoot accurately at that distance... unless they sprayed the area where I was standing with machine guns. Hopefully they were trying to avoid attracting more attention than they already had.

If they vacillated a few more minutes, the FBI would arrive.

"Bettina, call 9-1-1. Tell them shots were fired at the Bluebonnet Plaza parking lot in Richmond."

Bettina tapped her phone, identified herself as an off-duty cop and gave her badge number. She identified the three vehicles Gunner had shot and recited the license plates of the Navigator and Bolt from memory.

"I believe there's gonna be a shoot-out between a half dozen gunmen in the parking lot of Bluebonnet Plaza mall. Send several black-and-whites, code three, and a SWAT unit. I am accompanied by two private investigators with handguns, but we three are no match for six machine guns. We can keep them in sight and try to protect civilians until you arrive. We are in a white Dodge Grand Caravan." She recited our license number from memory.

She ended the call and grinned. "I exaggerated about the six machine guns."

"Rule Nine: *You can never carry too much firepower.*" I said. "Better the Richmond cops bring more muscle than they need."

I called Saco's cellphone. He wouldn't recognize my number, so he might not answer.

He reached in his pocket and studied his phone. He rejected the call.

I left him a voicemail. "We are the guys who shot out your tires. We don't plan to start a gunfight; we want to make a deal. A deal that makes us all a lot more money."

Stall them three more minutes and the FBI should be there. Or the Richmond cops might arrive first. I opened the driver's door and stood beside my vehicle where the six gunmen saw me. I called Tommy Valley. He glanced in my direction, and I waved.

He raised the phone to his ear. "McCrary, what the hell are you doing?"

"We came to do a little business, Tommy. Ask Saco to play his voicemail."

"Why should I?"

"You have nothing to lose, and Saco might like my deal. There's something in it for you also."

"What deal?"

"That's above your pay grade, Tommy. I talk only to Saco. Tell him to listen to the voicemail and call me." I disconnected.

Two minutes until the FBI arrived.

Seventy yards away, Valley leaned in and talked to Saco. He pointed my way. I waved. It helps to be friendly and approachable. *Suuure* it does. Saco held the machine gun pointed at the ground.

Keep talking, boys. Tick, tick, tick. Be sure to debate whether to return my phone call.

The FBI was speeding closer. A minute passed. Saco tapped the screen. My phone rang.

I took my time to answer. Where was the FBI? They should have arrived. I lifted the phone from my pocket and studied the screen. I drew a blank on what to say but I needed to answer. Beathing a small prayer to the gods of improvisation, I accepted the call.

"Carlos McCrary speaking."

Three black SUVs glided into the lot. V.K. sat in the front passenger's seat of the lead vehicle, which aimed straight toward the Navigator. The second SUV turned left, the third veered right.

Saco did a double-take at the arriving SUVs, cursed me in Spanish, and heaved his cellphone at the first FBI vehicle. Wheeling toward the disabled pickup, he leaned his machine gun against the fender and jerked the back door open.

Saco wrestled the hundred-pound duffel bag from the truck. It had a distinctive design of orange fabric with dark blue trim and a Houston Astros logo. He squirmed the strap over his head. Snatching his weapon, he galumphed toward a GMC pickup truck that was turning into a parking space ten yards away.

Saco shouted at Valley in Spanish, telling him to bring extra ammunition from the Navigator.

Valley opened the Navigator's rear door and hauled out a green canvas bag. He slipped the strap over his shoulder and ran at Saco's heels. The other four gunmen scanned in various directions, confused about what was happening.

Saco and Valley ran to opposite sides of the GMC and shattered the side windows with their gun butts. Pointing his weapon at the terrified couple in the truck, Saco shouted at them to get out. They spilled from both front doors and ran away, leaving their doors open. The GMC continued rolling across the pavement. Saco heaved the duffel bag into the bed of the pickup and chased the truck. He gained the driver's seat and stomped the brakes. Valley tossed the canvas bag behind the passenger's seat and jumped in after it.

The three FBI vehicles erupted with armed agents who leveled automatic weapons at the other four gunmen. They dropped their weapons, hit their knees, and raised their hands.

The wheels of the GMC screeched their protest. Saco jammed the accelerator and aimed the truck at the exit.

Jumping into the driver's seat, I shoved the Caravan into gear. "Buckle up, folks. It's gonna be a bumpy ride."

Bettina popped her door open. "I'm going after Bartok. And Hawley if he shows." She jumped out and slammed the door. "Good hunting."

"You too." I punched the accelerator and flew after the GMC.

———

The Caravan's bumper scraped the pavement as I bounced down the ramp, across the gutter, and onto the street. I spun the steering wheel and scurried after the stolen GMC.

In my rearview mirror, I saw three Richmond PD patrol cars race into the parking lot with lights flashing and sirens wailing.

The GPS on my dashboard showed our location in a bird's-eye view. "Gunner, I'm not familiar with this part of Texas. Where are they going?"

Gunner consulted the tablet in his lap. "They're moving in the opposite direction from Houston. Maybe they're afraid that more FBI agents might be chasing them from Houston."

"They have to drive to the Astros parking lot to sell the cocaine. How will they get there?"

"In downtown Rosenberg, South First Street hits an entrance to I-69 two miles south. That leads straight back to Houston."

"How far to the turnoff?"

"Three miles more or less."

I phoned Bettina. The Caravan's Bluetooth grabbed the call when it connected. I read her the GMC's license plate. "Tell V.K. we're westbound on Highway 90 Alternate toward Rosenberg."

"Tell him yourself. V.K.'s bunch are marooned at the mall with four prisoners to process. Five as soon as I arrest Bartok. Six, if Hawley shows."

"You're chasing Bartok?"

"On the move now. He's forty yards away."

"You have backup?"

"He's sixty years old, and he has no backup either. Hawley never showed."

"Go get 'em, Tiger."

"I'll tail him into the mall. I'm gonna be too busy to talk." She ended the call.

I called V.K. and gave him the GMC's license number.

"It'll be a while before we can follow you, Chuck. The biggest danger is that Saco and Valley carjack a different vehicle and we won't know it. Or they might split up. Can you make sure they don't change vehicles or split up with the cocaine?"

"We'll stay on them, V.K."

———

Bettina Simpson

Chris Bartok loitered beside his Chevy Bolt contemplating the flat tire. He fingered the hole in his tire like he couldn't believe it was real. Bettina wondered whether, in the confusion, he didn't hear the suppressed rifle shot that destroyed his tire. That was possible; his windows were closed, and the Bolt's air conditioning was running in the muggy Texas heat.

Bettina walked purposefully toward the building behind Bartok, glad she was wearing comfortable shoes. If he noticed her, he might assume she was there to shop in the mall. Unless he recognized her...

Her phone rang. It was Chuck.

When she finished talking to Chuck, she left her phone tucked against her ear while she walked. She moved twenty-five yards closer before Bartok scanned his surroundings. Bettina hoped her phone hid her face. No good. Bartok spotted her and ran toward the mall.

He was moving pretty fast for an old guy. She hoped she could keep up with her damaged feet.

Her feet had healed for two days. She was young and fit, and she wore her new, comfortable shoes. She couldn't sprint, but she could jog. What she lost in speed, she made up in endurance. A thirty-something cop versus a sixty-something criminal. No contest. Unless Bartok was one of those old guys who ran every day to keep in shape.

The sixtyish kidnapper ran at a fast jog. She trotted behind Bartok. *Just keep him in sight,* she thought, *until he gets tired.*

Bartok paused at the mall doors and threaded inside with several other shoppers.

She gained ten yards on him.

He rushed down the central aisle, dodging people and drawing curious stares. At the central atrium he jumped onto the *up* escalator. He climbed the escalator steps until he was blocked by a woman holding hands with her daughter.

Bettina gained another ten yards. She mounted the steps next to the escalator two at a time and reached the second level seconds behind Bartok.

He grabbed a middle-aged woman around the neck and jammed his pistol to her temple. "Stop where you are, or the woman dies!"

People heard the shouted threats and backed away. Some grabbed their children and scurried in the other direction. Some held their ground and aimed their cellphones at Bartok and the woman.

Idiots, Bettina thought.

She jolted to a halt about ten yards away, pulled her weapon, and held it at her side. She raised her voice with her left hand holding her badge.

"I am Detective Sergeant Bettina Simpson with the Houston Police. This man is wanted for kidnapping and murder. You folks stand back and walk away. I don't want anybody hurt."

She lowered her voice to a conversational level. "Bartok, it's over. You have nowhere to run. Let her go and place your pistol on the floor before someone gets hurt."

His face and neck were shiny with sweat. His breath came in wheezes.

"No. You drop your weapon. Take the escalator down. When you reach the bottom, I'll let the woman go."

Behind Bartok, a fiftyish woman set her shopping bag on the floor. She reached into a spacious purse hanging on her shoulder and removed a small revolver. With her other hand, she held her finger to her lips. She winked at Bettina and tiptoed toward Bartok from the rear.

That was the last thing Bettina wanted. An untrained civilian could escalate this into a mass shooting, but she was powerless to stop the civilian.

The woman sneaked behind Bartok and jammed her pistol into his ribs. "Mister, the pressure you feel in your side is a Sig Sauer .380 pistol. I am a United States Marine. I will count to three. You will release the woman and drop your weapon by the time I reach three. Otherwise, I squeeze this trigger three times. The odds are certain that one of those bullets will hit an artery, a lung, or your heart. You won't live long enough for an ambulance to get here. One… Two…"

Bartok raised both hands and pointed the pistol at the ceiling with his finger off the trigger. "Don't shoot. Sergeant Simpson, come take the pistol from my hand before this crazy woman kills me."

The woman kept her pistol in Bartok's side until Bettina seized the kidnapper's weapon.

"Hands behind your back."

Bettina snapped handcuffs on Bartok and smiled at the woman. "Thank you for your service, ma'am, and thanks for your help. I'll take it from here."

The woman slipped her pistol back into her purse. "I retired from the Marines three years ago, but you know what they say: Once a Marine..."

"...always a Marine," Bettina finished. "Everybody knows you don't mess with a Marine."

THIRTY

Carlos McCrary

The spotty rain clouds that had loomed for the last hour eventually consolidated into a light but steady rain.

Gunner kept pace with our progress on his tablet, and I kept one eye on my GPS. We shadowed them from a hundred yards behind.

"They should turn on First Street in a half mile," Gunner said. "Switch to the left lane."

I waited for a gap in the afternoon traffic and shifted lanes. "If they plan to turn at the next traffic light, why are they still in the right lane?"

"That doesn't make sense. And they haven't tried to lose us either. I say Saco is leading us into a trap."

"No. He didn't know we would tail him to the flea market. I think he panicked. Either that or he has something else planned."

Saco didn't turn on South First Street. A few blocks later he turned right on State Highway 36. "Where does Highway 36 lead?"

I slowed the windshield wipers to *intermittent*.

Again, Gunner consulted the tablet. "It runs straight as a string to Wallis, Texas, 15 or 20 miles."

"Does that tablet show you anything in Wallis that Saco might be interested in?"

"From the satellite view, it looks like a farming community."

We trailed from two hundred yards back for a few miles. The highway paralleled a railroad track. We outran the rain, and the sun peeked out. The GMC slowed at a side road beside a billboard that advertised *Rancho Mariposa Mud Ranch, coming this Fall. Watch for our Grand Opening.*

The stolen truck turned on the narrow street that ramped across the railroad track and headed straight north. I followed the road on my GPS. The rearview mirror showed no one behind me. I slowed and zoomed out on the GPS screen. "This is a dead-end road. Saco and Valley are trapped. He doesn't have a plan; he just panicked and ran."

"My tablet shows the road ends a couple miles north of the railroad."

"Where is the Rancho Mariposa Mud Ranch? At the end of the road?"

Accelerating, I reached the turn-off and bumped over the poorly patched railroad crossing. In the distance where the pavement ended, the GMC kicked up a dust cloud. A hundred yards past the tracks we rolled past a *DEAD-END* sign and the pavement turned from questionable to problematic.

Another sign said the Rancho Mariposa Mud Ranch was 1.5 miles ahead. *Coming this Fall. Watch for our Grand Opening! Fun for the whole family!*

I stopped at the sign. The flanking farmland was pool-table flat. The field crops were punctuated by scattered farmhouses nestled among groves of trees. I checked my phone for signal strength. Only three bars. "What's your signal strength?"

"Two bars. No, now it's three. Now it's two."

"What is Saco trying to do?"

"Beats me, boss. He must have lost his cool, and he's freaking out."

"Saco and Valley's sole escape is to cut cross country. Their GMC is better at cross country than our minivan. He can power across the fields till he reaches the next road. Then he turns back toward Houston. Or they hide behind a thicket of trees near a farmhouse. They lie in wait with their machine guns. We have one rifle and four handguns. The bad guys have the advantage in firepower."

"What are we gonna do, boss?"

"Catch up to them and keep them in sight. If they turn cross country, we break off the pursuit and notify the FBI. If they push into the trees, we'll see it and take appropriate action."

"How we gonna notify the feds with no cell signal? The farther we move from the highway, the worse the signal is."

"Roger that. We could knock on a farmhouse door. The farmers must have landlines."

I pressed the accelerator and narrowed the gap with the GMC. The Caravan jounced and juddered on the rough road.

"What's at the end of this road, Gunner?"

"Let me zoom the view. It ends at a cattle guard. Could be the entrance to a ranch instead of a farm. From there, it continues as a private road leading to the Brazos River. The problem is the mud ranch is under construction and the satellite image is four years old. No telling what changes the construction has made to the site."

Another mile and we reached a sign, *End of County Maintenance*. The ancient pavement petered out, replaced by a gravel road. The uneven road forced me to reduce speed. The GMC's dust cloud made it impossible to know how far behind we were.

To the left, twin ranks of Bradford pear trees lined a neat driveway leading to a freshly painted white farmhouse from the last century. On the right, a sturdy steel fence marked the boundary of another farm.

The ancient pavement ended at a steel gate which barred the end of the county road. Ten yards of steel fence on either side of the gate anchored the barbwire that ran off toward the horizon on each side. A few cows with calves grazed behind the fence.

Behind the cattle guard, a sign arched across the road.

Rancho Mariposa Mud Ranch
Opening this Fall!
Fun for the whole family!

The mangled steel gate lay crumpled beside the fence. A broken chain with the padlock attached dangled from the fencepost. "Saco rammed through the gate."

As I rumbled over the cattle guard, the road became a twin track scraped across the ground. The primitive path disappeared in the dust trail. Surveyors' stakes lined the road ahead until it vanished into the forest.

"Boss, we can't see doodley-squat in that dust cloud. We could barrel down this road into an ambush. Let the dust clear. Let's drink a bottle of water, stretch our legs, and take a pit stop."

I killed the engine and focused my binoculars on the area ahead—flat, scrubby pasture with scattered live oaks, prickly-pear cactus, and mesquite trees. A two-story Welcome Center with an observation platform on top was under construction. Between us and the forest, there was nowhere the GMC could hide.

"He's already out of sight."

Gunner handed me his tablet. The satellite image showed a private road meandering through a forest and ending near the Brazos River, approximately three miles to the north. On the way to the river, small dirt trails peeled off and wandered through the forest before they rejoined other roads. There was no bridge across the river.

"This image is too old, Gunner. There's no telling how much change the mud ranch construction made to the site. We have no map."

"But neither does Saco," Gunner said.

I exited the Caravan and joined Gunner to stretch my legs too. We each drank a half liter of water. Gunner reloaded the Rock River rifle and stowed two extra magazines in his jacket pocket. I selected a camo fabric fisher's vest replete with pockets. I shrugged into it over my body armor, transferred the extra Glock magazines to the vest, and added two extra Browning magazines.

"Why the vest, boss? We gonna track them on foot?"

"Like two wild hogs in the forest."

I motioned Gunner to join me in the shade of the Caravan's open rear hatch. "This is a satellite view of *Rancho Mariposa* before the construction started. The ranch is on a peninsula. See where the road curves there? That was virgin forest clear to the Brazos River. The river loops us on three sides and that hasn't changed. Saco will probably travel a few hundred yards into the jungle and post himself on the driver's side of the road and Valley on the other thirty yards further on. Then he tries to shoot me when the van pulls even with him. The van rolls ahead, and Valley finishes the job on the passenger side."

"Or Saco and Valley hide behind trees," Gunner said. "If we come anywhere near them, they strafe the Caravan from bumper to bumper with their fifty-shot magazines and riddle us with bullet holes before we reach the forest."

"Right," I said. "Unless a bullet sets off our gas tank, in which case we'll be toasted marshmallows."

"If we park the van somewhere between here and the forest, when we start to hike, they can surveil us from the trees. If we walk to within, say, twenty yards… *Rat-a-tat-tat!* We're yesterday's news."

"That's why we park the van to block the exit. Divide and conquer. You go over there where the forest curves next to the river. Stay in the trees to make your way back to the road."

"Where will you be?"

"I'll keep to the fence until I reach the forest at this end of the river loop. When you contact the enemy, make sure you have a clear field of fire beyond the target, so you don't shoot me. I'll text you when I reach this point in the forest. We may have enough cell signal to send a text." I pointed to the screen. "Then we close in on them."

Gunner patted his calf. "I'll use the Ka-Bar. No bullets, no noise."

"Good idea but wipe the Ka-Bar clean first. Put on nitrile gloves. Don't leave fingerprints on anything we use."

Gunner tugged on nitrile gloves, drew the lethal knife from its scabbard, and wiped it clean before restowing it.

"Okay, boss, I'm ready to roll."

"I'll park this Caravan crosswise in the gate. If they get past us, that forces them to power through a fence. If we're lucky, the barbwire will puncture their tires."

As I maneuvered the Caravan to block the gate, the rain overtook us again.

"This could be a good thing, Gunner. My weather app forecasts thunderstorms this afternoon. The noise from the rain masks any sound we make sneaking through the forest. And heavy rain reduces visibility so they won't see us when we cross the pasture."

Gunner went his way; I went mine.

Were we walking into a trap?

———

Thunder rumbled in the distance. I was halfway along the fence and 150 yards from the trees. The steady rain reduced visibility, but the breeze was gentle. So far.

When I reached the forest, I pressed forward into the trees. Two bars of signal. Should be enough bandwidth to text Gunner.

In position.

Gunner responded in seconds.

Headed your way. Meet you at the bad guys.

I paused a thousand feet west of where the road turned. The satellite view showed the lane meandered northwest and ended at the river. By now, the construction had added roads, mud bogs, obstacle courses, and other amenities.

Creeping and pausing every ten yards, I stopped, looked, and listened. I collected golf-ball-sized stones whenever I found one and pocketed them until I had a half dozen.

I progressed east for a half hour, dodging the mud bogs and stacks of tree trunks used to make obstacles. I made one wide detour to avoid a nasty briar patch.

The sharp scent of marijuana smoke irritated my nose.

Adrenaline coursed through my veins. Every sense stretched to its limit.

I checked my phone. One signal bar. Nothing ventured…

Stifling the urge to sneeze, I texted Gunner.

Marijuana smoke. Do you smell it?

Thirty seconds later he replied.

No. But the storm already hit here. Can't smell anything but rain. It's hard for me to advance. Lots of fallen trees and briars to detour. Also mud bogs and rutted roads.

I replied with an *OK* icon.

I tracked toward the scent. Step, step, step, stop, turn, sniff, listen, repeat. The spoor grew stronger, and I advanced more cautiously.

Between thunderclaps, I heard a Zippo cigarette lighter click open and closed, open and closed.

The storm front reached me, and the rain swelled into a soaker. Trees waved in the wind and flung raindrops in random directions. The underbrush had been wet; now the harder rain soaked in, and it turned slippery.

The rain cleaned out the marijuana smoke. Trees rustled in the wind so loud they would drown out the Zippo if the smoker were still clicking it.

I waited for the rain to slacken. I wouldn't proceed until I could see more than ten yards.

The rain finally lessened. I detoured to bypass another briar patch. Visibility improved and I glimpsed the duffle bag's orange and blue pattern beside an ancient native pecan tree.

Saco stood on the far side of the same tree, guarding the cocaine. His shoulder and arm stuck out from behind the tree trunk. He held his H&K gun upside down to keep the rain out of the barrel. Saco fixed his attention on the dirt road, oblivious to my presence.

There he was—the predator responsible for murdering my sister and probably my brother-in-law and God knows how many other victims.

Saco had sentenced Angie and his other victims to death-by-woodchipper. Tommy Valley, Troy Trojanik, and Alejandro Fajardo may have stuffed Angie's body into that bloody hopper, but Saco was the butcher who ordered it.

And he was at my mercy. Practically had a target painted on his back. Each time it thundered, I inched closer.

I could have shot him in the shoulder blade and finished him off as he fell to one side. But I didn't do that. Not because shooting was too good for him; any form of death would be too good for Saco except boiling in oil. I was not too honorable to shoot someone in the back if the circumstances called for it. No, Saco or Valley would kill Gunner and me any way they could without qualm or hesitation. The first rule always was to survive.

But I couldn't shoot Saco in the back and then tell the FBI or the local cops that I had fired in self-defense. They would scrutinize the crime scene and his body and find the entry wounds from my weapon in Saco's back.

Lightning flashed so bright that the thunder crashed instantly. I used the noise to cover my steps, stepping behind an elm tree for cover. The dirt road was five yards beyond Saco. I scanned both directions, but I couldn't see, hear, or scent Valley. The rain transformed the dirt road into a bog.

I tossed a rock toward the road ten yards to Saco's left. It struck the underbrush with a crunch.

In an instant, Saco stepped to one side and swung the H&K to the ready position. *Bra-a-ap!* He fired a short burst at the sound of the stone. The wet jungle absorbed the echoes.

He crouched, exposed. He rotated halfway to his left.

Valley's voice carried through the forest. "Did you see something?" he asked in Spanish.

"No," Saco shouted back, "but I heard something."

"McCrary is coming for us *now*." Valley's voice rose an octave.

"Easy, Tommy. Probably a deer. Or a raccoon. These woods are full of animals."

I texted Gunner.

Valley is on your side of the old main road. Saco is in range in front of me. Twelve or fifteen yards.

The uncertain cell signal meant that my text might not reach Gunner.

I waited one minute; he didn't answer. Okay, time to play the hand I was dealt.

I fished two more stones from my pocket and hefted them. I pitched them hard toward Valley's voice. The stones crackled through the forest on their fall to earth.

Bra-a-ap! Bra-a-a-ap! Bra-a-a-a-p! Bra—.

Sounded like Valley panicked and shot his entire magazine.

I listened for the sound of Valley changing magazines but didn't hear it. Either Valley was so far away the metallic snaps and clunks didn't carry through the woods, or he left his extra ammo in the GMC. I wondered where they parked the GMC. It had four-wheel drive, but maybe it was stuck in the mud anyway.

From the direction of Valley's shots, I estimated where he was and, thus, where Gunner should be, but wasn't.

I texted again.

Where are you?

Again, Gunner didn't reply.

Saco stood straighter, as if he could see better from a few inches higher. "Did you see something, Tommy?"

Gunner or no Gunner, Saco was in range. Now to inveigle him to turn toward me...

"Tommy, I asked if you saw something..." Saco's voice climbed higher too. "Tommy, what did you see? Tommy, where the hell are you?"

Good, Saco was panicking like Valley did.

Valley shouted in Spanish. "My gun is empty. Do you have an extra magazine?"

Raising the Glock, I braced my forearm on the tree. I aligned the sights where I predicted Saco's center mass would be if he turned toward me.

I drew a soft breath and recalled my sniper mantra. *Easy squeezy, nice and easy.*

"Tommy saw the Angel of Death, Saco," I said in Spanish.

Saco whirled and leapt sideways, raising the MP7. *Bra-a-ap, bra-a-ap.* Short bursts to conserve his ammo. Splinters flew from the pecan tree.

Damn. I had not figured he would jump sideways. I squeezed the trigger, but Saco jumped far enough to the left that my shot missed.

He dodged through the forest and sprinted in a northerly direction.

Did Saco carry an extra magazine, or did he too leave his spares in the truck?

I jogged the more direct route, dodging mud puddles. I tracked the curvy road, keeping Saco in sight and staying between him and the cocaine. No way I would let him retrieve that poison. Fifteen seconds later, I was close enough to spot the GMC. Both front doors were open.

Somewhere behind me I heard Valley stumbling through the underbrush. Gunner never made so much noise, even on a dead run. Was Valley returning to the cocaine stash?

For a few seconds I debated sneaking back to guard the cocaine. Before I could turn back, Saco stepped into the road and spun toward me, raising the machine gun. I leapt into the underbrush and rolled further from the road, landing in a briar patch.

Saco sprayed the forest with wild bullets until the magazine was empty. Two of them slammed my Kevlar jacket, but it didn't feel like they broke any ribs. I might survive with only a few bruises plus the bloody scrapes the thorny vines sliced through my shirt on my forearms.

I started untangling the briars. My nitrile gloves gave no protection against the thorns. In seconds the gloves were shredded, and my hands were cut with stinking, prickly nicks, punctures, and slices.

The GMC's engine roared to life. I heard the turbine whine of tires spinning in the mud. The GMC's four-wheel drive kicked in and the sound changed.

I stepped into the road with my Glock extended.

The GMC had disappeared.

In its place were twin ditches dug by the tires when they spun their way free from a muddy bog. The ditches pointed toward the river.

In the distance the GMC's engine noise faded as the truck sped away on the dirt road.

To my right, I heard Valley stumbling through the jungle.

Saco could run, but he couldn't hide. The road dead-ended at the Brazos River and the new side roads built for the future mud ranch all curved back to the main road.

Most importantly, there was no way Saco would abandon five million dollars' worth of cocaine.

Fifty kilos of pure uncut cocaine made the backpack a ticking time-bomb. It was enough to kill more people than 9/11. You couldn't flush it down the toilet; it contaminates the ground water. Perhaps it could be burned, but would the fumes or smoke be toxic?

One thing I decided: I would not leave the cocaine where it might be discovered and distributed to poison hundreds or even thousands of people.

I edged my way along the road on the right side next to the trees.

By the time I reached the pecan tree with the backpack beside it, the rain had petered out. At least for now.

I rotated a slow 360, listening and sniffing the moist air. Nothing.

I hoisted the sodden backpack over my shoulder and retraced my original route into the jungle.

Two hundred fifty yards back, I recalled passing a live oak that had been toppled by a storm. Yes, it was perfect. I edged down into the cavity left by the fallen tree's root ball. Unzipping the backpack, I dumped the cocaine packages into the hollow, and buried them with loose dirt.

The moist dirt made the cuts on my hands feel better.

Scrambling out of the hole, I examined the hiding place. No. Not good enough. I climbed back down and pushed more dirt over the drugs.

Regardless of what happened to me, Saco would not feed that poison into the marketplace.

I tried another text to Gunner.

I captured and hid the cocaine. Saco and Valley won't leave without it. Saco is loose in the jungle with the truck, but he will abandon it to pursue me on foot. Valley is wandering around on foot. If I don't make it, make sure the drugs are safely destroyed.

I included the GPS latitude and longitude coordinates my phone gave me. In case Saco or Valley killed me, the cocaine would not be lost. No telling who would unearth it in the unknown future, especially with more construction scheduled at Rancho Mariposa. If the Venezuelans had sealed the packages well, the drugs would be lethal for many years.

Saco would grab extra magazines for his MP7 from the GMC and pursue me on foot.

A game of cat and mouse. I intended to be the cat. But so did Saco, and he had me outgunned. And Tommy Valley was out there somewhere.

While I was mucking around in the hole beneath the tree, I smeared my face, neck, and the back of my hands with a film of mud.

First, I would bait the trap. I crammed the orange and blue pack full of leaves until it bulged like it still held the cocaine. Lugging it to the pecan tree where I first found it, I propped the fake prize against the trunk.

I faded into the forest where I crouched—a cat waiting for the mouse.

―――

Thirty minutes later, a faint rustle came from the woods. Either Valley or Saco was returning for the cocaine. But was it one of them or both?

My phone vibrated in my pocket. It was a text from Gunner.

I am tailing Valley. Don't shoot him. I am in the line of fire.

Good. Gunner had enough signal for his texts to work. I sent him a thumbs-up icon and deleted both his text and my reply.

The noise from the woods grew closer, then stopped. Twenty seconds passed. A muffled cry followed by the grunts and groans of a struggle. A crash of something falling. Then silence broken only by the buzzing of an insect.

My phone vibrated again.

Valley is in Valhalla.

I sent Gunner another thumbs-up and added...

Any sign of Saco?

Gunner replied.

No. He's smarter than Valley. But then, he would have to be.

He inserted a smiley-face and continued...

I'm twenty meters NE of you, across the road. I'll back you up from here.

I scanned to the northeast and saw what I expected to see—nothing.

I sent him another thumbs-up and continued...

Now we wait.

The clouds parted and the late afternoon sun baked down on the woods until the heat and humidity made it feel like a jungle. Sweat dripped off my nose, but I didn't wipe it off.

A few minutes later I heard the click of a Zippo lighter in the distance behind me, trailed seconds later by the acrid smell of marijuana smoke.

Saco was not as smart as I figured. In the stillness of the forest, his Zippo lighter could be heard for fifty yards.

I received another text.

Yes, I smell the marijuana. I will infiltrate behind him and herd him in your direction. I will stay out of your line of fire.

No matter how I focused my gaze and my hearing to the north and northeast, I could not detect Gunner when he shifted into position.

A few minutes later, I heard a rock Gunner threw behind Saco. That was followed by a long burst from the MP7. Someone rustled in the underbrush.

The mouse was advancing.

Or was Saco still the cat?

The noise in the underbrush stopped.

Either Saco had paused or he was moving stealthily.

Had he spotted the new trails that curved and rejoined the main road somewhere south? Did Saco plan to bypass me?

Staying in a squat, I pivoted from the Astros backpack toward where I estimated Saco was hiding.

A twig cracked in the wilderness. Seconds later another unknown noise sounded 30 degrees to the left.

Saco was detouring around me. How did he know where I was? Or perhaps he didn't. Maybe he decided to approach the cocaine stash from the south, which was the opposite direction from the way he'd fled.

I rose to a crouch and eased through the woods toward the south.

Saco jumped into a small clearing twenty yards away. He raised the MP7. I leapt sideways.

Bra-a-ap! Bra-a-a-ap! Bra-a-a-a-a-p! Bra—.

He emptied his magazine at me as I rolled into the brush.

I rolled twice more and rose to a standing position in the midst of a copse of seedling pines.

Saco was fumbling to change magazines.

I raised my Glock.

"Drop the gun, and I'll let you live."

Saco's eyes widened. He heaved the empty magazine at me. It missed wide.

"There's nowhere to run, Saco. Drop the weapon."

Saco threw the empty H&K at me.

I dodged the gun. "Give it up, man. Valley is dead. Your men have been arrested by the FBI. You're alone. It's over. Enough people have died today. Don't be another one."

Saco hauled a knife from a scabbard strapped to his right calf and charged.

I rapid-fired four bullets. Saco jerked to a halt as the third bullet hit him in the left shoulder.

He opened his mouth but only blood bubbled out. He fumbled for his jacket pocket and collapsed like a bag of old clothes, his knife still gripped loosely in his hand.

The H&K lay in the grass between us.

Stepping past the empty gun, I kicked the knife from his hand and felt for a pulse. There was none. I frisked him and discovered a Smith & Wesson .38 Special in a pocket. I tossed it beyond reach. I had seen "dead" men rise before in Iraq.

It was over.

THIRTY-ONE

G unner emerged from the forest cleaning his Ka-Bar knife on a handful of fallen leaves. He stared at Saco's body. "Good, he faced you before firing." He pointed over his shoulder with a thumb. "What do we do with Valley's body? I can't claim self-defense."

"Let me see the Ka-Bar."

I pulled on a fresh set of nitrile gloves.

Gunner reversed the knife and handed it to me butt first.

I leaned over Saco's knife. "That resembles your Ka-Bar." I took up the knife. "We need Valley's blood on Saco's blade. Show me his body."

We walked a hundred yards back down the road. Gunner stopped at the bushes by the trail. He drew the underbrush back and gestured at Tommy Valley sprawled in death like a discarded doll.

"Did you search his pockets?"

Gunner removed a few bills from his pocket. "He had nine hundred bucks and I pocketed six hundred. I left three hundred for the FBI to inventory." He peeled off three bills and handed them to me. "Here's your half."

"Thanks."

I rubbed Saco's blade in a blood smear on Valley's jacket. I wiped it with a tissue from my pocket. "This indicates Saco made an unsuccessful effort to wipe the blood off."

We returned to Saco's body where I replaced the knife in his hand.

Gunner grinned. "Saco surprised Valley and killed him so he wouldn't need to split the stolen cocaine with him."

Saco had twenty-five hundred dollars on him. I left five hundred and split two thousand with Gunner. "Spoils of war."

Gunner grinned. "A centuries-old tradition. To the victor belong the spoils."

"Time to call the FBI."

Gunner glanced at his phone. "Two bars. I can hike to the gate and call from there."

"And reposition the Caravan so they can drive past."

———

V.K. arrived with an SUV full of agents a half hour later. He eyeballed my face. "What happened to you? You take up mud wrestling for a new hobby?"

"I used the mud for combat face paint."

"And your hands?"

"The first time Saco fired at me, I jumped into a bunch of briars."

"*Humph.*"

V.K. walked around Saco's body. "He has a knife."

"I told him to drop his gun. Instead, he charged me with the knife."

The FBI agent lifted the cuff of the gangster's pants leg revealing the empty scabbard. "That's where he stashed the dagger?"

"Yeah, and I found the Smith & Wesson in his jacket pocket. And no, I didn't touch anything but the fabric of the pants and the jacket and I wore nitrile gloves, so no evidence was tampered with."

"Why did you search for the pistol?"

"I learned in the Army to make sure the enemy is disarmed before you check his pulse. Sometimes a person you assume is dead, isn't."

V.K. regarded Gunner. "Where were you when this was happening?"

"I stumbled across Valley's body around the time I heard Saco's H&K go off. Valley's throat was slit. I followed the gunshots to here. There were only the four of us in this forest, so Saco must have killed his own man."

V.K. considered that, then turned to me. "What happened?"

I told V.K. a slightly altered version of the truth.

"How many rounds did you fire?" V.K. asked.

"I was busy not being killed. Everything happened so fast that I don't recall. Check my weapon. I had a full nineteen-round magazine before we started." I presented my Glock butt first to V.K.

He handed the pistol to another agent. "Count how many rounds are missing."

He turned back to me. "Where's the other body?"

"This way," Gunner said.

V.K. and I trailed Gunner to Valley's corpse.

V.K. leaned closer and examined Valley's slit throat without moving the body.

"Someone surprised Valley. I don't see any other obvious wounds. At least none I could find without moving the body." He stood and surveyed the small clearing. "How do you suppose he caught Valley by surprise?"

Gunner shrugged. "Who cares?"

"He was Valley's boss," V.K. continued. "Hell, he might have said, Squirrel! and slit the poor bastard's throat when he looked away. But why kill his own man?"

"Didn't you see the Astros backpack?" I asked. "It's supposed to be full of cocaine. I guess Saco didn't want to share."

"I assumed the cocaine was in the back of the truck," V.K. said. "Did we pass it on the way in?"

"The bag is a few yards off the road behind a pecan tree. I'll show you."

We hiked back down the road, and I led him to the duffel bag and told him what I did with the cocaine.

"Quick thinking," V.K. said. He motioned to another FBI agent. "Go with McCrary and bring back the cocaine. Here. Empty this bag and put the drugs back in it.

A half hour later, we brought the cocaine back.

V.K. unzipped the bag and whistled. "That's the most cocaine I've seen in one place this year."

"Tommy Valley told me it was fifty kilos," I said.

351

V.K. closed the bag. "That's enough motive to kill your own man."

Gunner was standing behind V.K. He winked at me.

"Works for me," I said.

———

V.K. questioned us for over an hour before he was satisfied with our statements. The CSIs arrived and methodically processed everything from the stolen GMC to the battered gate that Saco smashed through.

V.K. shook hands with Gunner and me.

"My office will transcribe your statements and email drafts to you both to approve before you sign them."

V.K. glanced at his phone. "Wow, time sure flies when you're having fun. It's six p.m. My guys missed lunch. How about you and Gunner?"

"Can't you hear my stomach growl? Gunner and I ate our protein bars before you arrived. We'll pick up Bettina and eat dinner as soon as you turn us loose."

V.K. touched us both on the shoulder and gave us a light shove. "Go, go. You've both done more than enough."

As we drove back toward the highway, I called Bettina. "Have you eaten?"

"No, I waited for you and Gunner."

"Where are you?"

"On a bench in the mall, praying Saco and Valley don't kill you."

"They tried, but we prevailed. I'll tell you at dinner. We finished giving statements to the FBI and we're on our way to you. My GPS says we'll be there in 17 minutes."

"Pick me up at the south mall entrance."

———

We stopped at the Bluebonnet Plaza. Gunner transferred to the second row of seats and Bettina slid in front.

She clicked her seat belt, then wrinkled her nose.

"It smells like a locker room in here, fellas."

"We've been sneaking through the jungle in a rainstorm and crawling in mud. You want me to lower the windows a little?"

"Naw, I'm no bouquet of flowers either. And what happened to your face and hands?"

"You should have seen them before I stopped at a gas station and washed up in the men's room." I told her what happened.

"Briar patch, huh?"

"Let's find a dinner place with outdoor tables."

"That probably means barbecue."

"You're always telling me Texas barbecue is the best," said Gunner.

Bettina asked her phone to direct us to a neighborhood barbecue joint.

I lowered the windows anyway. "How did it go with your hunt for Bartok?"

"I chased him into the mall and the funniest thing happened." Bettina related the events in the mall.

"What happened to the Marine?" I asked.

"She faded into the crowd. I never learned her name."

At the restaurant, we collected our food and sat at an outdoor table. We were alone; the heat and humidity had kept the other customers in the air-conditioning. We briefed Bettina on our pursuit of Saco and Valley. By previous agreement, Gunner and I stuck to the version of events we told the FBI.

Gunner told Bettina he found Valley with his throat slit.

Bettina gave me a skeptical wince. "His throat was cut with Saco's knife?"

"Yeah," I said.

Bettina was between me and Gunner. She leaned to her right and frisked Gunner's left leg from his knee to his ankle. "That's your Ka-Bar I feel?"

Gunner squirmed under her gaze.

"And you didn't use it today?" she asked.

Gunner shook his head.

"*Ri-i-i-ght,* and I'm your Fairy Godmother."

She gave him a saccharine smile. "That's okay. I can swear under oath that's what you told me."

We finished our meals. Bettina piled our paper plates and plastic utensils onto her tray. "You bought, so I'll bus the table."

As she shoved our refuse into the trash can, I marveled at this remarkable woman. Twelve days earlier, Bettina had not seen or spoken to me in five years. Yet she had volunteered without hesitation to help me find my sister. We both thought it was a routine missing person case. No biggie. Unexpectedly, her contributions grew more crucial as events developed. Her personal risk intensified as she became entangled in the spiderweb of my sister's case. Bettina was even kidnapped herself. My sister's case morphed into a bet-your-life gamble. Yet Bettina never complained and never wavered.

How many other people would do that? I knew I could never repay her. She knew it too, but never hinted at how much of an emotional debt I owed her.

It was twilight by the time we headed toward Houston.

"How do you suppose the Feds are doing in the Astros parking lot with the New Jersey gangsters?" she asked.

"No longer our concern. Trojanik and Fajardo are in federal custody and Gerald Hawley soon will be, unless he blows his brains out. Gunner and I finished our mission. Everyone involved in Angelina's murder has been brought to justice, one way or another."

"Then it's safe to take me back to my apartment."

'Yeah. I'll swing by our motel and drop off Gunner first. Collect your belongings while we're there and I'll take you home."

———

An hour later I parked the Caravan in front of Gunner's room. "Would you mind taking an Uber to the airport tomorrow?"

"I figured we would share the driving back to Port City."

"Thanks for the offer, but I'm not coming back to Port City just yet. My great-aunt Catherine lives about twenty miles from here and she needs to sign over the title to my Caravan so I can transfer it back to my name. I haven't seen her since Easter. If I don't visit, she'll be hurt. We'll cry a little and reminisce about Angie. I'll spend tomorrow night with her and give her a ride to Adams Creek for Angie and Teodoro's memorial service on Monday."

I would return Angie's garnet earrings to my mother. She and Dad would cherish those for the rest of their lives.

"What about my gear, Chuck? I can't check it as baggage; it would never get past the X-ray."

"Good point. Stow it in the back and tomorrow I'll FedEx it to my office. You can pick it up there." I popped the rear hatch.

As Gunner stowed his gear in the minivan, Bettina joined us in the back. She hugged Gunner. "I can never thank you enough for rescuing me, Gunner."

Gunner blushed. "All I did was drive you to the hospital. You had rescued yourself by the time we found you in the parking lot. But I accept the sentiment you offer. You're one tough cookie, Bettina. I enjoyed working with you."

She raised on tiptoes and kissed his cheek. Her eyes were red when she turned away.

I decided not to pry. I pretended I hadn't noticed.

Gunner walked to his motel room door, paused, and waved goodbye.

Bettina and I returned to the Caravan, and we drove to her room on the other side of the motel.

She laid her hand on my forearm. "Why don't you retrieve your stuff too? Spend one last night with me."

"*One last night*? That sounds like we'll never see each other again."

Her eyes were red again. "Last time, five years passed before another case brought you to Houston. When will I see you again, if ever? What are the odds?"

I placed my hand on hers and gave it a squeeze. "Pretty good actually. I visit Adams Creek every Easter and Thanksgiving, and it's only a two-hour drive from your condo. I'll visit during Thanksgiving week, and I would love to spend a couple of days with you."

Even as I said it, I wondered if there might be a way I could spend more than a couple of days with Bettina. A lot more.

"Did your boss tell you to take a few days off while you recuperated?"

"Yeah, so?"

"Have you ever taken a cruise?"

"Nope. I've thought about it from time to time but have never taken the plunge. Why do you ask?"

"I never got to finish my cruise with Ruby because of Angie's disappearance. So I've never finished a cruise. I would like to take you on a cruise as a 'thank you' for all you've done for Angie and me the last couple of weeks. It would also let us get to know each other better without the outside pressure we've been under."

"Sounds great. When would we do this?"

"How about right after the memorial services for Angie and Teodoro? We could just drive to Galveston and select a cruise from there. Or we could drive back to Port City where there are more choices available. Whichever you like. What do you say?"

Her eyes sparkled like crystals.

"Fantastic."

THIRTY-TWO

W e rolled into Bettina's parking lot at 11:00 o'clock on a Thursday night. The lot was crowded with vehicles and devoid of people. Finding an open visitor's space, I slotted my minivan into it and grabbed her suitcase.

"You get the door. I'll bring our bags."

Bettina picked up her overnight bag, and I trundled both her suitcase and mine inside.

"You want this in your bedroom closet?"

"Thanks, Chuck. I'll unpack it tomorrow."

I followed her into the closet where she left her bag, then threw her arms around my neck. "Right now, I feel like celebrating with some champagne."

"You have champagne?"

"Follow me, lover."

She grabbed my hand and led me to the kitchen. She removed a bottle of champagne from the back of the fridge. "I keep this here for emergencies." She opened a cabinet door. "Take that ice bucket and fill it with ice from the freezer."

I did and she wedged the champagne into the ice before turning to me.

"I think we both need showers while the champagne cools."

She ran her fingertips lightly down my arm.

"Would you care to join me?"

I took her hand. "You don't need to ask twice."

A few minutes later we emerged dripping from the shower. I reached for a towel and Bettina wrapped her arms around me and steered me toward the bed.

I pulled back slightly. "We're still wet. And what about the champagne?"

Bettina pushed me onto the bed.

"The champagne isn't going anywhere. It's been two weeks since you found that tracking device on your car and moved into a hotel. That night was the last time we made love in my bed. Let's not wait any longer."

"Good idea."

———

Bettina rolled off me, moisture clinging to her body. I couldn't tell if it was water from our shower or sweat from our lovemaking.

"After a workout like that, we both need another shower," she said. "You want to join me again?"

"If I do that, we might wind up wet on your bed again."

She gave me flirty eyes. "So?"

I took the hint.

Yes, the bed got a little more damp, but I fell right to sleep afterward.

It had been a busy day. Hell, it had been a busy two weeks.

———

Bettina Simpson

Bettina woke up and rolled over toward Chuck.

The other side of her bed was empty. She rubbed her palm across the sheet. Dry now, of course. Maybe he was in the bathroom. No, the bathroom door was open, and the light was off.

As she threw back the sheet, the fragrance of ground coffee beans wafted into the bedroom. Chuck must be in the kitchen.

She strolled toward the bathroom and smelled bacon too. She smiled to herself.

Fifteen minutes later, Bettina emerged from the bathroom, teeth brushed, bedhead repaired, and makeup refreshed. She studied her image in the full-length mirror as she turned one way, then the other. Not bad for a woman in her late thirties. She considered prancing into the kitchen naked. No, she corrected herself, she would be s*tark naked.*

She smiled as she reached for her robe. *No, the bacon would burn for sure.* She tied the sash of her robe and adjusted the bow just right. If the opportunity presented itself, one quick pull and the robe would fall open. She tested the bow with a quick pull. The robe fell open. A quick shrug of her shoulders and it dropped to the floor around her feet.

She smiled at her image in the mirror, retied the robe, then glided into the kitchen.

"I smelled breakfast cooking all the way in the bedroom."

Chuck turned from the stove far enough to grin at her.

"I woke up early, so I slid out of bed without waking you and used the guest bathroom."

She stepped closer and stroked his cheek with the back of her fingers.

"You shaved off your beard."

"The case is over, so I don't need it anymore."

Chuck tapped the start button on the coffee maker and turned the bacon. "I made omelets; the bacon is almost ready."

The champagne bottle was still waiting in the ice bucket, only now the ice had melted. Bettina pulled the bottle, dried it, and stuck it back in the fridge. She dumped the ice bucket, dried the condensation, and placed it back in the cabinet.

Bettina plugged in the toaster. "How many pieces of toast you want?"

"Two please, with peanut butter."

Thirty minutes later, they dawdled over a second cup of coffee.

Bettina finished her coffee and stood. She stacked the breakfast dishes and carried them to the sink.

Chuck followed Bettina to the sink and began rinsing their dishes.

Bettina loaded the dishes into the dishwasher. "Run the water until it gets hot."

Chuck left the sink faucet running as he stepped to the towel rack and dried his hands.

Bettina tested the faucet water with her hand and shut it off. She started the dishwasher, then faced Chuck.

"When should we leave for Galveston?"

"I suggest Monday afternoon after Angie and Teodoro's memorial service if that works for you.

Why don't you spend Monday night here before we drive to Galveston?" She grinned. "That champagne still needs drinking."

"That's the best idea I've heard today."

"Here's another good idea." She pulled the sash. The robe dropped to the floor. She shrugged out of it and did a pirouette. "Ta-da."

As Chuck stopped into her embrace, she thought, *And on the cruise you and I can talk about the future.*

ACKNOWLEDGMENTS

My thanks to my editor Marsha Butler. Ms. Butler has edited all my fiction works. I keep hiring her because she makes me a better writer. Her email is swmpwriter@gmail.com.

My thanks also to Royce D. Wilson, former Assistant Professor of Criminal Justice at the University of North Georgia for his helpful comments on my manuscript. Professor Wilson (now retired) is a former Director of Forensic Services with the Hillsborough County Sheriff's Office in Tampa, Florida, and a former Crime Scene Investigator with the Tampa Police Department. He was also a licensed private investigator in Florida. Professor Wilson spent more than 35 years in law enforcement forensics. He is an expert in forensics, fingerprints, and crime scene investigations. Any mistakes in the story are solely my responsibility.

ABOUT THE AUTHOR

Dallas Gorham's books combine murder, mystery, and general mayhem with a touch of humor—all done with a PG-13 rating. His Carlos McCrary, Private Investigator, Mystery Thriller Series can be read and enjoyed in any order.

Dallas writes in the mystery, thriller, and suspense genres. (Take your pick: His novels have all three elements) His stories will get your heart pounding and leave you wanting more. He writes to hit hard, have a good time, and leave as few grammar errors as possible (or is it "grammatical errors"? Hmm.)

In his previous life, Dallas worked as a shoe salesman, grocery store sacker, florist deliverer, auditor, management consultant, association executive, accountant, radio announcer, and a paid assassin for the Florida Board of Cosmetology. (He is lying about one of those jobs.) If you ask him about it, he will deny ever having worked as an auditor.

Dallas is a sixth-generation Texan and a proud Texas Longhorn, having earned a Bachelor of Business Administration at the University of Texas at Austin. He graduated in the top three-quarters of his class, maybe. He has also been known to lie about his class ranking.

Dallas and his wife have homes in both Texas and Florida. Like his fictional hero, Chuck McCrary, he lives in Florida in a waterfront home where he and his wife watch the sunset over the lake most days. He is a member of Mystery Writers of America and the Florida Writers Association.

Dallas is married to his one-and-only wife, who treats him far better than he deserves. They have two grown sons, of whom they are inordinately proud. They also have seven grandchildren who are the smartest, most handsome, and most beautiful grandchildren in the known universe. He and his wife spend waaaay too much money on their love of travel. They have visited all 50 states and over 100 foreign countries.

Dallas writes an occasional blog post at http://dallasgorham.com/blog that is sometimes funny, but not nearly as funny as he thinks. The website also has more information about his books. To get an email whenever the author releases a new title (and sometimes a free book), sign up for the VIP newsletter at http://dallasgorham.com/

If you have too much time on your hands, you can follow him at the following social media links:

www.DallasGorham.com

f facebook.com/DallasGorham

X x.com/DallasGorham

a amazon.com/author/B00J4LISCS